THE BOOK
1303 South Monroe Street
Tallahassee, Florida. 32301
Phone (904) 224-2694

"I Am a Wanted Man.
Three Hundred and Fifty Guineas.
Alive or Dead."

"A lot of money for a man to carry on his head, Captain. And there are some who have tried to claim it."

Cambronne's voice, when he replied, was scarcely above a whisper. "You are better informed than I gave you credit for, sir."

"In particular—there was a woman. To give her the benefit of the doubt—a lady. And she betrayed you, Cambronne. When the armed Revenue men came to fetch you from the Kentish tavern that was your favorite hideout, you were in your bed and that lady in your arms. Like Samson with his Delilah. Only they did not take you, for you escaped by diving headlong through the window. But before doing that—what?"

Silence. Mr. Harkness from New York sniffed loudly and cleared his throat. His companions glared at the intolerable intrusion.

"Before I left that room," said Cambronne, "I killed her whom you call Delilah. And now you know, gentlemen all, why I am here offering my services. I am a man who has nothing left to lose but his life."

THE BOOK SHELF
1304 South Monroe Street
Tallahassee, Florida 32301
Phone (904) 224-2904

ROBERT CHALLONER
JAMAICA PASSAGE

PUBLISHED BY POCKET BOOKS NEW YORK

This novel is a work of historical fiction. Names, characters, places and incidents relating to non-historical figures are either the product of the author's imagination or are used fictitiously. Any resemblance of such non-historical figures, places or incidents to actual events or locales or persons, living or dead, is entirely coincidental.

Another *Original* publication of POCKET BOOKS

POCKET BOOKS, a Simon & Schuster division of
GULF & WESTERN CORPORATION
1230 Avenue of the Americas, New York, N.Y. 10020

Copyright © 1982 by Robert Challoner

All rights reserved, including the right to reproduce
this book or portions thereof in any form whatsoever.
For information address Pocket Books, 1230 Avenue
of the Americas, New York, N.Y. 10020

ISBN: 0-671-44308-9

First Pocket Books printing May, 1982

10 9 8 7 6 5 4 3 2 1

POCKET and colophon are trademarks of Simon & Schuster.

Printed in the U.S.A.

To G.P. with Love

PROLOGUE:
The Slaver

In the general way in which all sailors are romantics, Makepiece, captain of His Britannic Majesty's sloop-of-war *Circe*, was romantic; just as, like most sailors, he was not excessively fond of his calling, regarding the sea as a hard taskmaster and a poor payer. The romanticism and aversion often had Makepiece dreaming of resigning his commission and setting up as a tavern-keeper in Dorset, which was his home county.

"Six bells, sir!" A cry from the quartermaster.

"Lay her over on the larboard tack."

"Aye, aye, sir!"

The two men on the wheel bore down. The watch on deck saw to their lines. Like a flutter of dry washing, H.M.S. *Circe*'s sails spilled the wind and took it up again. A general creak of rigging, the rattle of blocks, a hiss of water at the stem, and the sloop-of-war settled to her new course, which was almost due south, pointed to Falmouth, Jamaica, fifty nautical miles over the wavetops.

A westerly wind would have been a blessing, thought Makepiece, so as to reach Falmouth before dark. He glanced up at the ensign snapping from the mizzen, and sighed.

> O western wind, when wilt thou blow,
> That the small rain down shall rain?
> Christ that my love were in my arms
> And I in my bed again!

His bed was in Dorchester, the love his wife, his Mary. Come another five years, thought Makepiece, and if he did not get a command of a ship-of-the-line, or even of a modern frigate, then he would carry out his plan. Meanwhile, it was the old *Circe*, who was fit only for the breaker's yard—or for anti-slavery patrol in the Caribbean. Not that he would have wished himself elsewhere in the circumstances, for though the sea was large, the slavers few and fast (he had not set eyes on one of the scoundrels in the twelvemonth he had been out on the station), the prize-moneys were unbelievable. As a captain of eight years' seniority commanding a crew of 130 officers and men, his share of a captured slaver could be . . .

"Sail-ho! Fine on the larboard quarter!"

Makepiece climbed to the mizzen chains. Rawlins, his first lieutenant, was well up the ratlines before the older man had made himself secure and was awkwardly fumbling to bring his telescope to bear.

"What course?" demanded Makepiece. He seldom openly admitted that, at fifty-three, his eyesight was failing; but this was an exceptional occasion, perhaps the opportunity of his lifetime. God, if we had gone about ten minutes earlier, the slaver—if slaver she was—could have slipped past our counter unseen. . . .

"Nor'-west, sir. Cuba bound."

Cuba! The slave trade might have been abolished sixteen years since, but in this Year of Grace 1824 the poor black devils were still being shipped in large numbers to Cuba and Brazil. Might this be one such? Had his luck changed at last? The apogee of nearly forty years of largely undistinguished service, with nothing but a sixth-rate command and the Trafalgar medal to show for it.

Makepiece snapped his telescope shut with an air of finality.

"Beat to quarters and stand by to go about!" he ordered, and forty years of service had schooled him to keep even the suspicion of excitement from his voice.

Bosuns' pipes joined with the tinny kettle drums to summon all hands. They came running, barefoot and naked to the waist. No sooner had *Circe* gone about and was pointing downwind towards the distant sails than the gun ports were opened, the eighteen long pieces loaded and primed.

Rawlins had gone below to the gun-deck, and Makepiece had been joined by the master and his mate. He was aware that they were both watching him closely, weighing his every gesture and expression. His orders, when delivered, would be obeyed with the force of King's Regulations to back them up, not to mention the tarnished gold lace on their captain's coat; but in two years since the ship's present commissioning they had never fired a shot in anger. Makepiece was known to them only as a good man in a gale of wind and a not too harsh disciplinarian. He might well wear the Trafalgar medal, but the smoke of that illustrious victory had cleared eighteen years since, bringing the *Pax Britannica* which turned fighting sail into watchdogs of that peace. The slaver—if a slaver— might well carry up to fifty-odd cannon and the men to serve them.

What then, Captain?

"Do we signal them to heave to, sir?" Rawlins was back on deck again, and eager as a puppy to get to a bone.

"It would be a waste of bunting, Mr. Rawlins," replied Makepiece. "Our ensign and our course will make our intention plain. We will close with him, and if his conscience is clean, he'll heave to without our having to order him."

In the event, the other ship, which proved on closer acquaintance to be an old East Indianman, maintained its course till *Circe* was within gun range and then turned broadside-on to the approaching warship.

"By God! I do believe he's going to open fire!" exclaimed Rawlins.

Almost immediately after, the East Indianman fired a ragged volley that started from the bow and revealed a battery of ten guns a side. Makepiece counted three misfires out of the ten, and watched seven spouts of white water erupt a cable's length short of where he stood.

"There's no quality aboard there," was his comment. "Mr. Rawlins, how are you loaded?"

"Chain-shot, sir," was the response.

"We will close with him, and I'll have a broadside to his rigging, please."

"Aye, aye, sir."

Five minutes later, *Circe*'s starboard guns fired a salvo at close range: nine sixteen-pounders discharging together at the other's sails and rigging; nine pairs of cast-iron spheres joined together by heavy links of chain tearing into wood, canvas and cordage; bending upon themselves, colliding and redoubling, pulverizing, ripping, tangling, irremediably. When the blossoms of white gunsmoke cleared, the Indianman's main topmast was careering down to the deck in a parcel of torn canvas and a cat's cradle of rigging, while the entire foremast was a bare pole hung with strips of rag.

"Reload, but don't prick and prime," ordered Makepiece. "They won't have stomach for any more."

It seemed that he was right. From the other's deck came

cries of pain and panic. As *Circe,* the wind spilled from her sails, wallowed slowly closer, they saw two men leap from the taffrail, strike water, and almost immediately disappear. As they drew closer still, there was borne towards them an indescribable miasma: the stench of humanity packed like animals. If Makepiece and his crew had any further doubts about their adversary's business, they died with that appalling reek. The East Indianman was a slaver.

The sharp snap of a single twelve-pounder drowned the noise of shouting. Flying lead hummed like angry bees over the sloop's bulwarks, scoring wood, cordage, cloth, flesh and bone. The slaver had made its last, defiant answer: a round of faggot, an iron cylinder sliced into sections, made to destroy men.

Makepiece was struck by a giant's fist and slammed back against the mizzen, where he lay and watched with a curiously detached interest as a gush of bright blood seeped out of him and formed a pool on the holystoned deck. A few paces from him, a boy midshipman lay on his face, feet feebly drumming.

"Captain, sir, are you in great pain?" Rawlins was on his knees beside him.

"Fire—and continue to fire till he strikes his colors," he whispered in reply.

"Done, sir," responded the first lieutenant. "He's already struck and I'm sending a prize crew aboard. Lie still, sir, while I call for the surgeon's mate."

Makepiece closed his eyes. Odd that he felt no pain. So the old *Circe* had brought him luck after all. A slaver captured intact. There would be prize-money in plenty. Rawlins had not mentioned it, but Rawlins had a private fortune and was not dependent upon pay and prize-money.

He smiled with contentment. The apogee of an undistinguished career. The opportunity, now, to retire with honor to that tavern in Dorset, in the west country that he loved so well. And his Mary.

A Lieutenant Jamieson, it was, who led the boarding party of twelve men that rowed over to the wounded slaver. On the way, he held a handkerchief to his nose—for the stench grew stronger with every stroke of oar—and reckoned on the ship's chances of reaching Falmouth in good time, with a jury sail rigged for'ard.

"Toss your oars!" The coxswain bellowed the order as the

cutter came under the slaver's companionway, rising and falling in the waves that slapped against the high side. Jamieson jammed his hat hard down upon his head, checked the priming of the pistol at his belt, and swung himself up.

Gaining the deck, he saw a group of unshaven rogues by the mainmast. They had clearly been trying—and with no discernible success—to clear away the topmast, yards and mess of sails and cordage in order to free the unfortunates who were pinned underneath, one of whom was moaning loudly. They treated Jamieson to a sullen glance and went back to their task.

The cutter's coxswain joined Jamieson on deck. He nodded towards the defeated enemy. "Nasty-looking bunch!" he said. "Foreigners by the cut o' their jibs. Portugueses or Spaniols, I shouldn't wonder, sir."

"Follow me," ordered Jamieson. He led his men to the end of the quarterdeck and under the screen of the poop, past the abandoned wheel. The passageway was decently paneled in exotic woods, but there was filth, and the stench of filth, everywhere. A door at the far end indicated one of the main stern cabins. Jamieson cocked his pistol and nodded to the sailor at his elbow, who kicked open the door.

Tropical sunlight flooded in through a raking line of stern windows, reflecting the shifting waters of the Caribbean on the deckhead above. A man with a thick thatch of tangled hair was slumped in a high-backed chair, his head and arms sprawled across a table that bore the detritus of a meal. A half-empty decanter of spirit and an upturned goblet lay by his hand. Jamieson gingerly took hold of a greasy tuft of hair and lifted the head, revealing a heavily bearded face; he let it fall back again.

"Dead drunk," he said in disgust.

"Mr. Jamieson, sir," called the coxswain. "Look 'ere at what I've found."

There was a bunk built into the paneled bulkhead, and in it was huddled a black girl: no more than her wide and frightened eyes and the top of her frizzed head emerged from the blanket that covered her. With a coarse laugh, the coxswain ripped away the blanket, revealing the girl's nude, black form in all its pathetic vulnerability of slender limbs, dimpled belly, nascent breasts.

"The cap'n o' this ship doesn't do himself amiss," declared the coxswain. His fellow sailors guffawed, and one stretched out a hand to paw the girl, who made no effort to prevent him. "Better'n Cap'n Makepiece, I fancy."

"Damn you, keep a civil tongue in your head!" snapped Jamieson. "Leave her be and follow me."

The men on the upper deck were still struggling ineffectually with the wreckage when the Britishers emerged into the sunlight; they paid no attention as Jamieson pointed to a grating forward of the mainmast.

"Open it up," he ordered. "We'll get the blacks on deck, drop each and every one of them over the side on the end of a line. When they're bathed and decent they can clean out their quarters. Open up! Smartly now!"

The men lifted the heavy grating, revealing a companionway that led down into Stygian darkness from which issued the source of the stench that had made hardened sailors retch at half a mile's distance. When, presently, their eyes grew accustomed to the gloom, the Britishers gradually discerned what seemed to be six concentric bands of blackness that entirely filled the vessel's hold, and were then revealed to be six broad rings of Africans, men, women and children, packed so closely that each was touching his or her neighbor, side by side and head to foot. And as the ship swung in the wind, causing a shaft of light to descend into that unholy pit, the innumerable eyes, row upon row, were to be seen staring up at them. And white teeth, also, bared in the sullen frenzy of despair.

"My God!" breathed Jamieson. "There must be a thousand of them packed down there. I never knew, never guessed . . ."

"One thing's certain, sir," said the coxswain. "There'll be no goin' down there to unchain the brutes and bring 'em up on deck. Why, they'd tear us to pieces alive, so they would!"

The slaver's captain, still dead drunk, was brought aboard the British sloop-of-war for swift transport to Jamaica for trial, inevitable condemnation, and hanging. Lieutenant Jamieson was left behind to make what shift he could of bringing the slaver and its living cargo to port under jury sail.

First Lieutenant Rawlins had a last, shouted exchange with Jamieson before the two vessels parted company:

"Good luck! As soon as I've landed the wounded, I'll put out again and escort you into Falmouth."

"For that, much thanks!" responded Jamieson. "As to the wounded, how is the captain?"

"What?"

"The captain—how is he faring?"

"Great heavens, man, he lived only a matter of moments! A slice of faggot cut him clean in half!"

CHAPTER 1

The secret watcher saw the arrival of the carriages—barouches and landaus, old-style coaches and phaetons after the English manner—and some horsemen, all traipsing up the long, curved driveway to Mr. Cyrus J. Holt's colonial-built mansion on Copp's Hill, to be greeted by wigged Negro footmen bearing flambeaux, their pampered passengers and riders being ushered forth, handed down, bowed into the august portals of what was arguably Boston's finest townhouse.

It was uncomfortable in the lower limbs of the chestnut tree, and the watcher had been there since nightfall, when he had scaled the high wall surrounding the property; but he stayed for a little longer, in case the hourly patrol broke custom and retraced their steps. Two big blacks they were, both armed, and handling red-eyed mastiffs that would tear a man's throat out on the word of command.

At eleven o'clock (Christ Church chimes came to him quite clearly), he decided that most of the guests must have arrived. A solitary horseman, only, and then a smart town phaeton. Nothing after. The watcher counted slowly up to a hundred and then checked the priming of the under-and-over pocket pistol that he carried, opening and closing the frizzens, setting the hammers at half-cock. He then lowered himself to the ground and felt the rich mulch of undergrowth yield like a Persian rug beneath his feet.

He cocked an ear. Distant, tinny laughter and the hum of voices was counterpointed by a string ensemble playing a lively gallop. The party was well under way. Time for him to make ready.

He had been carefully instructed in his task, had studied a ground plan of Mr. Holt's mansion, which had been built by a prominent British nabob in the days of George the Third of

1

tarnished fame, in the Palladian style, with fine, fluted Ionic columns, a pediment carved in the representation of Julius Caesar receiving the acclamation of the Legions, and a nobly proportioned cupola over all. It was towards the rear of the mansion that the watcher bent his steps.

He passed unobserved, for rhododendron bushes grew thickly to the edge of the lawns surrounding the building. Wide French windows along the eastern terrace were opened wide to allow the guests freedom of access to a handsome water garden, strung out with Chinese lanterns, where Negro lackeys moved silently with trays of champagne and tidbits, and an enormous fountain gushed roof-high from the open mouth of a bronze dolphin ridden by a naked naiad. The secret watcher passed within feet of the richly dressed, mouthing throng till he came, at last, to the rear of the mansion, where the severe symmetry of the design was broken by a rounded apse with three tall windows and four grave-faced caryatids supporting its cornice. There was no one to see him emerge from the undergrowth and press himself into the shadow of a deeply recessed window.

It chimed the quarter hour. A reassuring touch of the pistol's butt and he peered through the window, which was unshuttered and revealed the interior to be a semi-circular chamber whose walls were lined with bookcases. A single chandelier dimly picked out a large, round leather-topped table about which were set a dozen chairs. There was no one in the room.

He composed himself to wait in patience—that quality which is the prime stock in trade of the successful spy.

"Miss Virginia, you stop a-prancin' mother-nekked in front o' that pier-glass and gimme chance to put on yo' gown!" The plump and comfortable Eloise regarded her young mistress with the detached affection that comes with having been most intimately concerned in rearing a girl-child from infancy to new womanhood.

"Am I better shaped than Suzanne Duveen, Eloise? Tell me straight. And I need no corset to flatten me in front and push up my bosom like a pouter pigeon's. Oh, why do you fuss me so?" Virginia Holt, blonde, pretty as a Dresden shepherdess, eighteen and thoroughly spoilt, sullenly submitted to having her new party gown put on.

"Miss Virginia, you is late for yo' own birthday party, and there's no excuse for a lady to keep her guests awaitin'."

"Let them wait," said Virginia. "I intend to make a spectacular entrance down the staircase, and I'll not have any late-comer missing it. You never answered me about Suzanne Duveen."

The black woman met her own gaze in the pier-glass and rolled her eyes. "Miss Suzanne, she's a mighty nice shape too," she declared.

"Roly-poly."

"Carries herself well."

"But fat. Tell me she's fat, Eloise."

"Comfortable."

"Fat!"

"Hold your breath while I fasten you up. Miss Virginia, I do declare you've growed round the middle since Mrs. Hackforth did the last fittin' o' this gown."

"I hate you, Eloise!"

"Yes, Miss Virginia. Now will you stand still? And here's yo' momma come to see what's keeping her missin' chile. Any minute now, Mrs. Holt, ma'am. You wouldn't believe the trouble I've had."

Virginia's mother closed the door behind her and leaned against it, regarding her daughter. She was her only child brought to full bloom, with traces of silver among the gold, a suspicion of shadows in the same blue-gray eyes, figure a mite too full, showing just a little too much of an admirably structured bosom. She doted on Virginia, seeing in her the reincarnation of her own youth and a promise of a better fulfillment. Augusta Holt, married at seventeen to a man fifteen years her senior whose only concern was for making money and yet more money, was reputed not to have shared a pillow with her husband since Virginia's birth eighteen years before.

"You are beautiful, my darling—beautiful!" she breathed.

Eloise sniffed.

"A fig for your opinion, Eloise!" snapped Virginia. "I'd die and bone and skeleton before you'd hand out any compliments."

"But you must hurry on down, my sweet," said her mother. "The guests are waiting to see the birthday girl." She looked coy. "And a certain gentleman in particular is chafing at the bit."

Virginia made a *moue*. "Henry Davenport," she said. "If I thought he'd improve with keep, like a good wine, I'd keep him waiting all night."

"Hope, like apples, grows stale from being stored too long," replied her mother. "You can't keep poor Henry dangling on the end of a string forever. One of these days you'll wake and find him gone, and then you'll repine your lost chance."

"Henry Davenport," said Virginia, "is a booby!"

"Henry Davenport," retorted her mother, "belongs to one of the best families in New England, as well as the richest." She looked earnest. "Henry won't ever have to burn midnight oil to make himself a millionaire, for his father can make him one with a stroke of the pen. Imagine it, Virginia, you'd be able to travel the world together: Venice, London, Paris—all the places your father was going to take me to, but never quite did."

"Venice with Henry would be like taking mustard with caviar," said Virginia. "Henry's presence—the way he looks and talks, the long and painful silences—would mask the delicate flavor of an earthly paradise. I wouldn't go to Timbuctoo with Henry, let alone Venice!"

Her mother shook her head, but took consolation from another brief inventory of Virginia's physical attributes, and thought again of her own lost opportunities.

"Well, hurry on down, darling," she said. "The dancing has begun. Father is holding a meeting of the Anti-Slavery Society during the recess. They're all here: Josh Winterburn, Amos Trubb, the Onslow brothers, Mr. Harkness from New York, and all the rest. They're all dying to greet the birthday girl."

"Silly old bores, all of them!" declared Virginia. "All right, Mama, I'll be down just as soon as Eloise has fixed my hair."

With the departure of her mother, Virginia submitted herself to the ministrations of her lady's maid, formerly her nurse. Eloise bestowed a hundred strokes of the brush on the mane of shimmering gold, and afterward gathered it into a simple chignon, adding a spray of artificial violets. It was all the attention that Virginia's hair ever needed; below the chignon it fell in natural ringlets about her ears and cheeks, and was the despair of every girl in Boston society.

Her toilette finished, Virginia appraised herself in the pier-glass and liked what she saw. Turning, her glance strayed past the unshuttered window and returned.

"Eloise!"

"Yes, Miss Virginia?"

"Who is that man down there?"

The maid joined her at the window and looked down. Virginia's bedroom suite commanded a view of the west side of the mansion, which the fancy of the English nabob's expensive landscape gardener had turned into the semblance of a miniature Versailles, with formal hedges of box and yew set in geometrical shapes. A solitary figure was slowly pacing up and down one of the graveled paths, hands clasped behind back, head slightly bowed, a long cheroot clamped in his mouth. Broad back and shoulders announced by well-cut tail-coat of midnight hue, and a plain white neckcloth. Powerful legs showing to advantage in formal knee breeches, after the almost defunct style of the previous century.

"I sure ain't seen him afore, Miss Virginia, I don't reckon."

"Hush! He's going to turn around."

Reaching the far end of the path, the man paused, exhaled a cloud of tobacco smoke, and turned, revealing himself as someone in his mid-thirties, with a thatch of black hair cut *en brosse* and a complexion like an Indian, from out of which stared a pair of eyes which—even at that distance, and in moonlight only vestigially augmented by Chinese lanterns—Virginia perceived to be gray and stormy like the sea off Cape Cod.

His was a face to remember. The sculptor who had fashioned it had rounded off his task by drawing two lines, with the tips of both thumbs, from the cheekbones to the corners of the mouth, deeply scoring the malleable clay and imparting to his handiwork an expression of harsh austerity. And then, as if in compensation, the same two thumbs had stabbed dimples of good humor in each bronzed cheek and sliced a deep cleft in the firm chin.

"I sure ain't seen that gentleman afore," repeated Eloise. "Lordy, I sure would have remembered if I had've!"

"Shut up!" hissed her mistress.

He could not possibly have heard; it was almost certainly the brusque, small gesture of her hand with which she had accented her command to silence that caught his eye. He looked up, saw the blonde with the chignon and a complexion of wild roses and buttermilk, and the handsome, middle-aged negress next to her.

He grinned: a wide, warm, male grin that would have sent men into the cannon's mouth, or put into hazard the virginity of maidens—most maidens.

"What damned insolence!" snapped Virginia. And she slammed close the window shutter. "Who is that creature, to be pulling monkey faces at me as if I were some dockyard strumpet?"

The appearance of Miss Virginia Holt, when she finally condescended to show herself to the guests at her eighteenth birthday ball, created a palpable stir that was immediately translated to the sensibility of the young woman concerned, causing her a most agreeable *frisson* of self-satisfaction. Nor did the wistful looks of her friend and confidante from infancy, Miss Suzanne Duveen, in any way detract from her pleasure, for it is truly said that mere success is not enough; it is also necessary that one's friend should fail. And fail poor Suzanne most certainly did on that occasion: a near-scandalous *décolletage* revealed that, tight-lacing or no, she had been translated from puppy-fat to overblown rose without any pause for reflection. Virginia greeted her best friend with a grateful kiss, accepted her compliments at their face value, and moved on.

Her father stood among his cronies and business associates, the small coterie of intimates whom that humane pillar of the Episcopal Church was manfully attempting to weld together into a movement for the abolition of slavery in the American continent. Mr. Cyrus J. Holt was a self-made man, was proud of being a self-made man, and spoke of it often. Shipping was his line. Beginning with an ex-British brigantine impounded in Boston during the war of 1812, which he had purchased at knock-down price from the Navy Board and put to running military supplies along the eastern seaboard, Holt had, by judicious loans and a readiness to switch from one commodity to another, one routing to another, built the Augusta Line (the title was a delicate compliment to his lady wife, who, together with her beauty, had brought a modest, useful dowry to the marriage) into the largest and most prosperous shipping concern in Boston, specializing in the lucrative transatlantic conveyance of grain and dry goods. In his mid-fifties, with no son to succeed him in the business, it was said that Holt had turned to philanthropy as an outlet for his energies. Hence the embryo Anti-Slavery Society, which had so far done little but publish denunciations of the slave states and call for stronger measures against slave-running to Cuba, Brazil and elsewhere, which, despite the patroling cruisers of the Royal and United States Navies, was still bringing fresh human cargo from the West African littoral to the tune of an estimated 50,000 a year.

A bearded face was bowed over Virginia's hand. This was Amos Trubb. He had been Papa's partner from the first, her godfather to boot. Why, then, did he so unashamedly peer down her corsage and slobber his too-moist lips all over her white glove? Then there were the Onslow brothers, and the austere Mr. Harkness from New York, who never said anything.

And there was Josh Winterburn . . .

Winterburn—another original partner of her father's, her other godfather—Virginia could scarcely bring herself to think of, much less look upon, without flinching. He was, had always been, the living epitome of all the villains of her fairy stories, the true manifestation of the arch-bogeyman who had lent a particular horror to Hallowe'en. His face—perfectly formed, yet pitted all over with the blemishes of some past disease—was of a peculiar gray hue, and out of it glanced the eyes of a reptile: quick, flower-bright, questing, utterly cold. They said he led his stupid, puddinglike wife a hellish life, that he was a swine as far as women were concerned; that he drank, imbibed Asiatic drugs, molested children, mistreated animals, robbed the poor, mocked religion. They—that is to say Virginia's contemporaries and former schoolmates— stated these things plainly of Josh Winterburn and believed them like Holy Writ—as did Virginia.

"You look so beautiful tonight, my dear," whispered Winterburn, bending his ageless, demonic profile over her reluctantly proffered hand.

"Thank you, sir," she faltered in reply, and saw with revulsion that the scalp of his bowed head, across which the gray hairs had been combed with the perfection of wavelets approaching a shore, was encrusted with ancient filth. She shuddered and looked away.

A familiar face swam into view. In contrast to Winterburn's it was like the face of an archangel. The sensation did not persist; a couple of moments and Virginia felt unaccountably cheated.

"Happy birthday, Virginia."

"Oh, hello, Henry."

He pecked her cheek. His lips were dry and cool—and that described Henry Davenport to perfection. Harvard had forged him, Christ Church, Oxford, had turned and polished him. But where was the man within? His hair was sandy-colored and crinkly. Crinkly, also, was his smile. Beautiful teeth. The unwavering blue eyes told her nothing, for there was nothing to tell.

"Did you receive my present?"

"Yes. Thank you. It was very fine."

"You'll save me plenty of dances?"

"My dear Henry, you are not the only beau at the ball," Virginia retorted. "One has one's obligations to the other gentlemen guests." She opened the dance program that hung by a golden ribbon from her slender wrist. "Where are we now?"

"They have just finished the second gallop," he said. "Next is a schottische and then a trio of valses."

"I will put you down for the first valse," she said, marking her program with the silver pencil attached. "And another one after the recess. Don't pout. You don't own me, Henry Davenport. And now, will you please go and fetch me a glass of champagne, or must I die of thirst at my own birthday ball?"

He went uncomplainingly, and Virginia took the opportunity to move away. Nodding to left and right, acknowledging smiles and good wishes, she left the hallway and passed into the salon, where a six-piece string ensemble was tuning up for the schottische. Her lips, her gestures, were for those who greeted her; but her eyes were elsewhere. Searching.

"Happy birthday, Virginia." It was a boy named Joe something. They had attended Miss Winn's kindergarten together, and he had once tried to kiss her.

"Thank you, Joe."

"May I put myself down for a dance, Virginia?"

"Mmmm?" She was scanning the throng at the far end of the salon.

"A dance, Virginia."

"Oh, I'm so sorry, Joe. Do you know? I don't have a single empty space on my dance program. Not one. So sorry."

He bowed and left her; and Virginia walked the length of the salon, still searching for a face that she had seen but once and then only briefly. But to no avail.

A recess was declared at one o'clock. The ladies retired to the bedrooms that had been apportioned for them, where their maids divested them of their outer clothing, loosened their stays, took off their slippers, and assisted them to lie down on chaise lounges to recover from the exertions of the dance. Virginia went to her own room, and with her went Suzanne Duveen.

In the dead hour of the night, while the ladies were resting and the strings were silent, Cyrus J. Holt called an extraordinary meeting of his so-called Anti-Slavery Society in the semi-circular library at the rear of his mansion. They sat twelve at the leather-topped table, and they sat in silence while a Negro footman closed the shutters and snuffed all but one of the candles, afterward departing.

"Do we have to sit in the confounded dark?" growled someone. "Goddamn it, what've we got to hide from each other?"

"Tonight is different," replied their host.

"How so?"

"Tonight, we have a thirteenth member of our society— The Man!"

"The Man—*here?*"

They exclaimed loudly and eyed each other in awe, those hard-bitten men of politics and commerce, even the taciturn Mr. Harkness from New York; till presently their ringleader called them to attention:

"Order, order, gentlemen! Before The Man shows himself to us again, I call upon our secretary, Mr. Harkness, to read the minutes of the last meeting. Mr. Harkness."

Harkness, tall and gangling in his seat, adjusted a pair of thick-lensed spectacles on the tip of his tapirlike nose, cracked bony knuckles, and began, peering short-sightedly in the dim light at the sheaf of papers before him.

"Ah, Mr. Chairman, Gentlemen. I will—um—in the interest of brevity and with your permission give only a précis of our last deliberations, commencing with the treasurer's report. Hem!

"Treasurer's report: 'Half-yearly profits commencing August first, 1822, were five million dollars, sixty-eight cents.

Merchandise transported in August, three hundred shipments. In September, one thousand and eighty. In October . . .'"

"Mr. Chairman, if i may interject?" said Josh Winterburn, who sat slightly apart from the rest and had been regarding the proceedings with flickering, reptilian eyes. "Can Mr. Secretary not account in terms of units rather than in shipments? Every ship has a different carrying capacity. The term shipments leads to confusion. Units, on the other hand, spell out their own message. Or am I being difficult as usual?"

The chairman assured him he was not, and the secretary resumed his report accordingly:

"Due to the maximum frequency of the hurricane season in August of last year, only one ship, the *Gorgon,* made the passage to the Caribbean, and the *Gorgon* possesses a very low carrying capacity, in addition to which an outbreak of yellow fever aboard the vessel necessitated the disposal of some fifty units."

"Alive—or dead?" demanded Winterburn. "Pardon me for asking, but I don't recall the details."

Harkness peered more closely at his notes. "More than half were already dead," he said. "The remainder were thrown overboard as a precaution against further spread of the disease, to the number of fifteen men, five women and two infants—both of them suckers and of no immediate commercial value."

"Pardon my asking"—it was Winterburn again, and all other thought died in the air, and men looked away, as his questing eyes flickered from one to the other and then back to Harkness—"but at what stage does an infant become of commercial value? I merely ask."

The secretary looked baffled, and turned to the chairman for assistance. Holt sucked his teeth, fussed a little, avoided Winterburn's gaze, and addressed the man on his left:

"Amos, the merchandising is your department," he said. "When does an infant become of commercial value, is the question asked."

Amos Trubb had done business in Charleston and knew the trade. "Potentially upon successful passage and arrival in one hundred per cent fitness," he said. "That is, if the mother is also in good shape and giving adequate suck. A motherless sucker is a liability and you might as well forget it. As to price, a healthy one will add, say, ten per cent to the price of the mother. But there is no immediate commercial value till it's a three-year-old and can be put to simple, repetitive work. Like on a treadmill, for instance.''

"Does that satisfy your query—er—Josh?" asked Holt with a distinct note of anxiety.

Winterburn smiled—a rictus grin that sent his companions' eyes scurrying back to their notes. "I am answered," he said. "We are in this business, Mr. Chairman, up to our necks, and it is well, from time to time, that we acquaint ourselves with the less salubrious minutiae of that business. Would you not agree?"

"Quite so," responded Holt hastily. He felt a twinge of unease. Josh Winterburn, an odd fellow at the best of times, had been curiously more so of late. His wife, Lucy, had recently confided to Augusta that she believed her husband had sold his soul to the devil—but then Lucy's open secret was her addiction to the bottle, and who was to blame her, married to a fellow like Josh?

Holt's unease must have communicated itself to the other members of the organization, for there was silence for at least a minute before the proceedings were resumed, which caused a slight puzzlement to the eavesdropper outside the library window, who had been crouching with an ear pressed to the shuttered glass, catching at least two words out of three. And the complete sense of what that pillar of the church, Mr. Cyrus T. Holt, and his colleagues were up to—which was nothing to do with the abolition of slavery!

The business proceeded quite briskly after that, mainly because Josh Winterburn, after his initial interpolations, had withdrawn into a watchful silence. The minutes having been read, and sundry small items of business disposed of by voting with a show of hands, Holt looked at his watch.

"Gentlemen, we will now be addressed by the Patron," he said. "The usual rules apply: you will remain seated; no one will address a remark to The Man save through me as chairman; and no one will leave the room during the time that he is here. Is that understood by you all?"

A mumble of acquiescence answered him. Holt rose and crossed the room to a curtained alcove at the far end, almost beyond the loom of the single candle's exiguous glimmer. Reaching there, he drew back the curtain. There was a door at the rear of the alcove, performing the function of an entrance to a theater box. Seated at a small console table and facing the occupants of the room was a figure attired all in black: black was the color of the robe and hood like that of a monk, black the gloves. And the head was entirely concealed under a mask such as medieval executioners wore, with two narrow slits for the eyes. The effect, from the distance of the table at which the watchers were sitting, was that of total anonymity. Nor did the masked man's voice, when he addressed them, give any indication of the quality of personage he might have been; muffled by the mask, it possessed a strangely inhuman timbre, and no clear characteristic save that of a certain—menace.

"I have been listening to some of your deliberations. I think you are pleased with the return upon your investments. Correct?"

"Why, yes, Patron. Yes indeed!" Holt, who had resumed his place at table, answered up hastily for them all.

"You should be," came the answer. "Seven hundred per cent profit per annum on a capital outlay, at no personal risk to yourselves, is by no means picayune." The muffled voice took on a perceptible edge of contempt. "Particularly when it provides you with the illusion of being in control of the business."

"Patron, I assure you—we assure you . . ."

The gloved hand silenced Holt with a gesture.

"Enough! It amuses me that you play your grown-ups' games of Board and Committee meetings, your passing of resolutions and amendments, your minutes and your memoranda. Such activities will serve to console you for sundry disappointments and additional demands upon the community purse."

Holt gazed at his companions for inspiration; finally, receiving none, he framed the words himself:

"Patron, I—I'm afraid I don't understand. You speak of disappointments? Additional demands? . . ."

"I have just received news," said the masked man, "that one of our largest ships, the *Jeremy T. Fawcett* of Brooklyn, has been intercepted while on passage from the Gold Coast to Santiago, with a full load of eleven hundred blacks."

"Good God!" exclaimed Holt.

"That would be ill news in itself," continued the speaker, "but I have worse to tell. The *Jeremy T. Fawcett* was boarded, her captain and crew taken prisoner, and the blacks set free. I am given to understand that the British navy is transporting the latter back to the Gold Coast from whence they came. But I have yet worse news to impart."

"What could be worse?" The challenging voice of Josh Winterburn.

"Josh—for God's sake . . ." A weak protest from Holt.

A moment's silence, and then the speaker resumed: "There was an exchange of cannon fire, in which the captain of the British sloop-of-war was killed."

"They killed a Limey skipper!" Josh Winterburn rose to his feet, reptile eyes flickering from the masked figure to the horrified faces of his peers and back again. "Then I tell you, Mr. Patron, there'll be no end to it. They'll hound us to our graves, every one. They'll scour the seven seas for our ships and track them down, one by one. I tell you, sir, that this enterprise is finished! Finished! You had as lief transport corpses from Africa to the Caribbean for all the profit that lies in front!"

Winterburn's companions, the other eleven in the conspiracy, were staring at him with the look of mingled horror and pity that people will throw at the victim of a particularly unpleasant accident, or at someone who is being led up the steps of a scaffold, there to be half-hanged and flayed alive.

There was no word of recrimination; no need for Holt, as chairman, to call the offender to order; nor, by sign or utterance, did the masked figure in the alcove betray any displeasure, but the silent wall of instant menace could have been cut with a knife.

If Winterburn felt the menace, he gave no sign. The man's fortitude, his iron self-containment that set him apart from all the rest, his air of inviolable devilry, served him well in his encounter with the sinister masked figure in the alcove.

A nerve-paring silence, and then: "You may retire, Mr. Winterburn," whispered The Man.

A rictus grin from Winterburn flashed to those about him. He gave a mocking bow.

"As you please, Mr. Patron," he said. "Mr. Chairman—gentlemen."

He crossed to the door. It closed behind him. Someone sighed.

When he spoke again, The Man did so in a voice that was brisk and matter-of-fact, immediately dispelling the atmosphere of intolerable menace that had pervaded the room.

"No one regrets the *Jeremy T. Fawcett* incident more than I," he declared. "Her captain should not have opened fire upon the Britisher—and I am reliably informed that it was she who fired first—without the certainty of victory. Fortunately, my representative in Jamaica has secured the escape of the captain, but the crew will hang in Kingston dockyard. And there the matter will end. No more of our ships will be intercepted with any success, and our operation will continue as before."

Silence. Holt cleared his throat.

"You are about to comment, Mr. Chairman?" came the mocking inquiry. "You are perhaps about to ask how it is that we shall continue to make a seven hundred percent per annum return upon your capital outlay when both the British and United Staties navies, all professional rivalries and past rancors forgotten in what they will regard as the dastardly murder of one of their own kind, will quadruple their united efforts to crush our trade? I will answer your question, Mr. Chairman. We will continue in business because of—*a very special ship.* I will explain . . ."

No sound but the ticking of the long-case clock at the opposite end of the library from the alcove interrupted The Man's discourse. His twelve listeners sat spellbound, breathless upon every word.

"As men engaged upon the shipping trade," said The Man, "you will perhaps have heard of Vincenzo Alfieri, perhaps not. Alfieri was a Venetian. He died last year in New York, where he had come after the downfall of his master the Emperor Napoleon. You will recall that that ill-starred dictator, when aged only twenty-nine, made a fair bid to conquer Egypt and march on to India, and was only thwarted by Nelson's victory of annihilation at the Nile. His plans in ruins, Napoleon Bonaparte abandoned his army and returned to France by sea in a frigate named *Le Muiron;* and it is here, gentlemen, that the story touches us very nearly. *Le Muiron* was arguably the fastest sailer in the French fleet. As chance had it, she evaded Nelson's patroling cruisers and passed unseen; but her distinguished passenger was repeatedly assured by her captain that, even if she were sighted, there was not a ship in the entire British fleet to which she could not show a clean pair of heels. Bonaparte was impressed, and inquiring as to the vessel's antecedents, was informed that she had been built in Venice. He inquired, also, about her designer and was given a name: Vincenzo Alfieri. There the matter might have rested but for the mentality of the dictator: Napoleon Bonaparte never forgot a name, or a face, that might conceivably be of use to the furtherance of his own interests.

"A very few years later, as we know, the young man who might have conquered the East was bestriding Europe as Emperor of the French. It was then he remembered the Venetian naval architect and, sending for him, commanded Alfieri to build such a ship as had never been seen before. Napoleon's brief was disarmingly simple: the Venetian was to design a vessel for the Emperor's own personal use—*and it was to be the fastest sailer afloat in all the Seven Seas.*"

A pause, as the long-case clock struck the half-hour. The Man resumed: "We do not know, we can only speculate, the reason that prompted Napoleon to command such a vessel. Perhaps it was his intent to sail in her up the Thames to London, when, England having been conquered, he went there to be crowned king of yet another vassal state in Westminster Abbey. It may be that, remembering his successful escape back to France after his Egyptian debacle, he saw in her the means to fly to the ends of the earth in the event of an even greater debacle—such as finally befell him. We only know that Alfieri did indeed design such a vessel; that her keel was laid in a Brest shipyard, and she was worked on by the finest Breton craftsmen, and was part-finished when the news of the Emperor's downfall brought an end to the work.

"Alfieri saw his brain-child burned in an anti-Bonapartist riot in Brest, narrowly escaping with his own life. To New York. And that, gentlemen, is nearly the end of my story. Questions?"

Holt found his voice. "The ship, Mr. Patron," he said. "The vessel of which you speak? . . ."

"The vessel now exists!"

"You say it—*exists?*"

"By a series of circumstances with whose irrelevance I will not burden you," said The Man, "one of my agents ran Alfieri to earth in the Greenwich Village attic that had become his last refuge. Half-starved, more than half-crazed, he nevertheless convinced my agent that he was who he was and what he was. Furthermore, he produced from a locked chest the designs and plans of the super-vessel that he devised for Napoleon. And those he was pleased to sell for the

magnificent sum of twenty-five dollars." He laughed, and it
was like the croak of a carrion crow in a graveyard. "No
better bargain was struck in that vicinity since Peter Minuit
purchased Manhattan Island from the Indians, I fancy!"

"But the vessel is built, you say—*built?*"

"She is already launched," came the answer. "Built in
conditions of extreme secrecy in a quiet backwater in Boston,
the super-vessel has a figure that will effectively swallow up
our organization's profits for the current year and much of
next. That, gentlemen, is the additional demand upon the
community purse of which I spoke earlier. Not only did the
technical problems involved in building such a revolutionary
craft call for the finest naval architects and craftsmen of this
country and Europe, but we have had to buy secrecy and
silence. And those two commodities, gentlemen, are dearer
than love and virtue combined, I promise you."

Silence, while the men around the table made a mental
computing of the fortunes they would have to forgo in the
months ahead. And then Holt said: "Er—could you, perhaps,
describe this vessel, Mr. Patron? In layman's terms, I beg
you. Some of us are not thoroughly conversant with matters
nautical."

"In appearance," came the answer, "she looks like a
smallish schooner of about a hundred and fifty tons burden,
with two masts rigged with fore-and-aft sails. But there any
resemblance to, and any comparison with, the ordinary ruck
of schooners ends. The secret lies in Alfieri's genius: the
supremely painstaking mind that calculated the underwater
shape of the hull, the balance of the sails, the stresses that the
extremely light construction would have to withstand at
speeds of up to fifteen knots or more. . . ."

"Did you say—*fifteen knots?*" interrupted Holt. "I beg
your pardon, Mr. Patron, but I am sure that you are . . ."

"I am not mistaken," came the instant response. "The
chief architect of the project was so convinced that the design
was the work of a madman that he insisted on first building a
quarter-sized working model. From calculations of that model's performance in high winds off Long Island, that same
astounded man declares that the finished vessel is, indeed,
what Napoleon demanded: the fastest sailer afloat in all the
Seven Seas!"

By now, Cyrus J. Holt's associates—for all their shortcomings accountants all, and well aware of how many beans make

five—were whispering among each other and passing hastily scribbled notes to their chairman. Holt spoke for the lot of them:

"Mr. Patron," he said, "without a doubt, we have here a very fine vessel, but a hundred and fifty tons burden does not commend itself for the merchandise that we are in the habit of carrying."

"The vessel will not carry merchandise," came the answer. "Only a crew of about seventy-five. Together with eight cannon of the latest pattern, plus half a dozen swivel guns."

"But—where shall we put the slaves?" cried Holt. It was the first time that the 'merchandise' had been given its true name in that gathering.

"The super-vessel will not carry slaves," was the reply. "She will escort our regular slavers, two or three of them in convoy. Like a sheepdog protecting its flock, she will engage any who threaten the flock's survival. With her unmatchable speed and uncanny maneuverability, she will confound and bedazzle even her most powerful opponents, feinting and riposting, striking with snakish quickness and deadly power. To alter the metaphor, she will be like a peregrine falcon among a flock of fattened turkeys."

"And who, sir, will command this vessel?" It was Mr. Secretary Harkness who spoke up, against the stern protocol of that strange gathering.

The Man replied: "He is with us here tonight. Be so good as to admit Captain Cambronne, Mr. Chairman."

He had been waiting in the corridor outside the library since one o'clock, and the tang of his cheroot smoke hung heavily in the air out there. He turned on his heel as Holt emerged from the library door and beckoned to him; his dark, hawkish face was quite impassive, a glitter in the stormy, blue-gray eyes.

"Will you please come in now, Captain?"

The blue-gray eyes narrowed in the gloom of the dimly lit chamber. He took in the figures seated around the table, picked out the black-clad form in the dark alcove, and let his gaze rest there.

"You are Captain Jason Cambronne, born in Saint Helier, Jersey, sometime a post captain in the Navy of His Britannic Majesty?" The question came from behind the black mask.

"I am." The newcomer's voice was deep and with a biting edge.

"Be seated."

Cambronne did as he was bidden, yet with an air of serene independence, as if the notion had sprung from his own mind; nor did he hurry himself, but settled down carefully, flicking a speck of imaginary dust from his immaculate breeches, crossing his powerful, long legs and folding his arms. One of the brothers Onslow, who sat nearest to the chair that had been set apart for the newcomer, and who was of a fanciful turn of mind, afterward observed to his sibling that Cambronne in repose put him in mind of a leopard or a panther: totally relaxed, yet with every nerve, muscle and sinew on instant call.

"For the benefit of the assembled company generally, you will now wish to give a brief account of your career to date, Captain," said The Man.

The captain's severe face, like the sun coming from behind a cloud, was instantly warmed by a good-humored grin.

"Of course," he said. "Where to begin?"

"I will direct you."

"Please go ahead."

"Origin, as we have already said: the Channel Island of Jersey. Origin of parents?"

"My father was English, my mother of French descent. Both dead. On quitting the navy, I adopted my mother's maiden name of Cambronne."

"A man of mixed allegiances, one would have thought. Considering that the early part of your naval career coincided with the end of the Napoleonic wars. Yes?"

Cambronne shrugged. "We are—were—Channel Islanders. That is to say, Jerseymen first, English second, Jerseymen third. Does that answer your question?"

"Succinctly, Captain. Let us pass briefly over your early naval career. Joined as midshipman at age fourteen; promoted lieutenant at nineteen; commander at twenty-two; captain at twenty-five. A notably rapid record of advancement. Took part in none of the major battles of the Napoleonic wars, but sailed your first command to a successful engagement with an American frigate during the war of 1812, for which the Patriotic Fund presented you with a sword of honor." The masked head, which had been inclined over an *aide-mémoire*, flicked upward. "Correct?"

"Quite correct," responded Cambronne.

"So far, a highly creditable achievement professionally," said the interrogator. "Clearly you must have been an officer marked for admiralcy, would you say?"

"Yes." The reply was prompt, flat, unconcerned. An admission of fact.

"Which brings us to the year 1816, and the attack upon, and burning of, the city of Algiers by a combined British and Dutch fleet under Admiral Pellow, in which you, a young captain, commanded the frigate *Persephone,* twenty-eight guns. Would you be so kind as to apprise the assembled company of your part in the assault?"

Cambronne re-crossed his legs and settled himself in a position that, to the observant Onslow brother, seemed if anything even more relaxed.

"I intercepted one of the *xebecs,* the fast assault craft of the Barbary pirates operating from Algiers," he said. "They were making a dash for Egypt with a cargo of their white captives."

"In fact, you boarded the *xebec* and captured it by a *coup de main,*" said his interrogator. "And what did you find there?"

"There were about fifty captives," said Cambronne. "Mostly Spaniards and Portuguese, men and women both. Upon the approach of the *Persephone,* the Algerians had cut their throats, every one."

"European men and women, you say?" The interruption came from Amos T. Hart. "Slain in cold blood by those black devils?"

"The slavers killed their slaves rather than let them be recaptured—yes," responded Cambronne without a trace of irony.

"We are not concerned, here, with the morality involved," said The Man, "but with what followed. What *did* follow, Cambronne?"

"As you say, I boarded the *xebec,*" replied the other.

"Discovering, upon doing so, that the pirates had murdered their victims?"

"That is so."

"And?"

"And then I hanged them, captain and crew, from their own spars and masts."

"Bully for you!" cried Hart. "Bully for you, Captain!"

Cambronne had eyes for no one but the dark figure in the

alcove, who said: "One is informed that you hanged these people, these Barbary pirates, without semblance of a trial. Was that not a high-handed procedure, even for a captain of one of His Britannic Majesty's ships-of-war?"

"It was so deemed to be," replied Cambronne.

"At your court-martial."

"At my court-martial."

"Brought by their Lordships of the Admiralty."

"Brought by their Lordships of the Admiralty," repeated Cambronne. "Upon pressure by those same tender-hearted folk whose concern for the wretched European slaves of Algiers led to the attack by the combined fleet in the first place."

"You were found guilty, Captain Cambronne. But you were not dismissed from the service in disgrace, nor were you reduced in rank."

A shrug of those broad shoulders that was almost imperceptible. "There was scarcely any need for that. I was relieved of my command. A captain without a ship, and that at the end of a great European war, with officers who had commanded ships-of-the-line vying with each other for the captaincy of a bum-boat. With paid-off frigates lying like strings of washing from Spithead to Devonport." The blue-gray eyes narrowed in good humor and the Jerseyman dismissed his ill fortunes with a shrug. "Not one for spending the rest of my life on the beach, I took to another trade."

"You took to one of the traditional trades of the disgraced naval officer, Captain Cambronne. You became a smuggler—and a highly successful smuggler at that. Correct?"

"Correct. Brandy and tobacco. Finest French wines. Silks. Lace."

"So successful, in fact," said The Man, "that in five years, the price on your head has been raised from fifty guineas to two hundred and fifty guineas. Correct?"

"Your information is not up to date, sir. In February of last year, I ran foul of a Revenue cutter off Dover. The cutter gave chase, which was unfortunate for him, since I know the shoals of the Kent coast like the body of a loved one. My little sloop drew only four feet of water. I led him over a sandbar and left him stuck there, to be pounded to pieces in a gale that followed. After that, I became worth three hundred and fifty guineas. Alive or dead."

"A lot of money for a man to carry on his head, Captain.

And there are some, as I understand, who have tried to claim it?"

It was a question, and it hung in the air for a few moments, unanswered. Cambronne's voice, when he replied, was scarcely above a whisper.

"You are better informed than I gave you credit for, sir."

"In particular—there was a woman. To give her the benefit of the doubt—a lady. And she betrayed you, Cambronne. When the armed Revenue men came to fetch you from the Kentish tavern that was your favorite hideout, you were in your bed and that lady in your arms. Like Samson with his Delilah. Only you were Samson unshorn, Cambronne. They did not take you, for you escaped by diving headlong through the window. But before doing that—what?"

Silence. Mr. Harkness from New York sniffed loudly and cleared his throat. His companions glared at the intolerable intrusion.

"Before I left that room," said Cambronne, "I killed her whom you call Delilah. And now you know, gentlemen all, why I am here offering my services. I am a man who has nothing left to lose but his life."

There was never any doubt, after that, but that they would take Cambronne as commander of Vincenzo Alfieri's super-vessel. The Jerseyman's manner and responses throughout the interrogation had been so frank and open-handed, so free of apology or excuse, and even his last, shocking admission uttered without rancor or regret, that to the group of middle-aged businessmen he appeared as a creature from another planet, driven on by strengths and passions that were totally beyond their comprehension. Some among the assembly (the more perceptive Onslow brother in particular) might have wished to have questioned Cambronne more closely about the woman whose life he had taken. His cryptic confession admitted several interpretations: had the woman been his lover in the true sense, or had she merely been his strumpet for the night? If the former, here were the makings of real tragedy. If the latter, then this man they saw before them possessed a brutal directness that those sheltered businessmen—for all that they dealt at considerable remove with the brutal traffic in human flesh—could only contemplate with mingled horror and respect.

None of them demanded further and better information

from Captain Jason Cambronne. He whom they knew as
"The Man" seemed already to have satisfied himself; and,
surely, he must have done that before admitting the Jerseyman into their secret circle.

Now he was telling Cambronne the tale of the super-vessel,
and the disgraced naval officer turned smuggler and murderer
was leaning forward in his chair, eyes narrowed in concentra-
tion, hawk face set, expressive hands sketching staccato
gestures as he interrupted his informant with brief and
pointed questions of detail concerning the vessel. And when
The Man was done, his listener sat back and nodded.

"With such a ship as you describe, sir," he said, "a skilled
captain and a trained crew could take on a pack of navy
frigates to the number of three or four, run rings round them,
rip the masts and sails off any who were fool enough to be
caught aback or in irons, and bring your convoy safe to
port."

"You imply that you would aim at sails and rigging only,"
replied The Man.

"To lay such a vessel alongside a navy ship and engage in a
killing match would be to throw aside the advantage,"
declared Cambronne. "I would load only with chain and bar,
for cutting sails and cordage, aiming always to slice past my
opponent's unprotected stern—what we called in the navy
'crossing the T'—and rake his masts in passing."

"And where shall you raise a trained crew to man such a
ship, Captain?"

The directness of the question, the change from the
speculative to the concrete, was not lost upon Cambronne.
He smiled.

"I shall hand pick them, sir," he replied. "One by one, the
most important first. Trailing my cloak in places where such
men are to be found. When shall I begin?"

"You will sail for the West Indies within the month,"
replied The Man. "Immediately upon arrival in Kingston,
Jamaica, you will receive further instructions. Holt will pose
as your employer and you will so regard him. We shall meet
again—perhaps in Jamaica. In the meantime, I will wish you
good luck and fair winds." He made a gesture, in response to
which Cyrus J. Holt padded swiftly over and drew the curtain
of the alcove, shutting the masked figure from their view.

Moments later, they heard a door quietly close.

Holt cleared his throat and looked at his watch. "I reckon

as I hear the orchestra tuning up again, gentlemen," he said. "Shall we rejoin the ladies?"

Outside the window, the eavesdropper relaxed and took out his watch also. Give it another quarter of an hour, he thought, and the patrol would be around. Let them go past and he would make himself scarce. Meanwhile, he must bide himself in patience.

One thing: he certainly had plenty to think about.

Virginia, rested after her none too strenuous efforts of the night, and with only one valse penciled in upon her dance program after the recess, made her second and equally spectacular descent of the great, curved staircase lined on each side with wigged Negro footmen bearing many-branched candelabra, to the vast appreciation of the concourse below.

She descended slowly, lingering with every step, her blue eyes scanning the upturned faces below, seeking, but not finding. Suzanne Duveen, who had spent most of the recess in prattling on about her amours, real and imaginary, was speaking to Henry Davenport: much fluttering of eyelashes, bending forward to offer the advantage of her tight-lacing. A fig for Suzanne; come to think of it, she and Henry were made for each other.

Three steps from the bottom of the staircase, Virginia gave an involuntary intake of breath as, over the heads of the assembled guests, she saw the library doors open at the far end of the ballroom, and her father emerge with his fellow members of the boring Anti-Slavery Society. And among the bald heads and the paunches, the round backs and the baggy eyes, was someone who walked straight and tall. He was listening to something that her father was saying, head slightly inclined, eyes questing the other man's face. Even as Virginia paused in her descent, those blue-gray eyes flickered up to meet hers, and he smiled: that maddening smile was more of a grin—masculine, dominant, unnerving to an un-tried maiden.

Hideously conscious of the flame mounting to her cheeks, Virginia ran down the last three steps and was hidden from him. During her progress across the ballroom, she took several deep breaths and contrived to achieve a decent composure, less like—the simile that came to her mind was indelicate, but, untried or no, Virginia was country-bred—a mare being brought to a stallion.

When she reached the group, her father was introducing the stranger around. To her mother; and did Mama really have to show quite so much bosom at her age? She was positively *simpering* up at that man. Shades of Suzanne Duveen!

"Ah, it's the birthday girl herself." Father's eyes lit on her at last. "Virginia, my dear, I should like to present Captain Cambronne, who has just joined the Augusta Line and is taking command of a new trading schooner that's just completed here in Boston. Cap'n, this is my daughter, my only child, who is eighteen this very day. Now, what do you think of that, hey?"

Cambronne bowed low over her proffered hand, kissed the air an inch above her gloved fingers. She had a mind to snatch the hand away, feeling unaccountably slighted by the gesture, which seemed too European and effete for the sort of man she had imagined him to be.

"Birthday greetings, Miss Virginia," he murmured in a voice like a double bass violoncello with a gravelly edge. And before she could reply, Father was introducing him to someone else. Virginia turned away, craving for a cool drink, meeting her mother's flushed face that seemed curiously young-looking and vulnerable in the flattering candlelight. Really, Mama was still not half-bad looking . . .

"Enjoying yourself, darling?" asked her mother. "Dance program filled to overflowing, I shouldn't wonder."

"Quite overflowing," lied Virginia.

She moved on, nodding and smiling acknowledgment to those who greeted her, but with only a small part of her mind attending to the civilities.

Cambronne. Cambronne. An odd sort of name. And he spoke with a slight accent. French, perhaps . . .

"Virginia! My dear, who is that heavenly man who was presented to you just now?" It was Suzanne, fresh from charming the birds down from Henry Davenport's tree.

"Oh, him?" Virginia wrinkled her nose. "One of Father's new captains. I didn't quite catch his name."

"Mmmm, well I think he's marvelous-looking," opined Suzanne. "So—well—male. And dangerous, wouldn't you say?"

"He doesn't impress me as being dangerous," lied Virginia.

The orchestra struck up the first dance of the second half of the program: a gallop. "Henry will be looking for me," said

Suzanne. "Do you know? He's taken every dance with me for the rest of the night—all except the next valse, which he's having with you." Her rather stupid eyes grew cunning. "I say, you two haven't fallen out, have you?"

"No, said Virginia. "It's just that—well, Henry's not the only beau at the ball, is he?"

"Well, let's wait here together," said Suzanne. "Our beaux will find us. "Who's your partner for this one, Virginia?"

Who, indeed? Think quickly, Virginia. Take a few deep breaths. Does one go around and drum up some business from such as Joe Something? I think not; at such a late stage of the evening, even the Joe Somethings of this world have managed, by shy blandishments and puppy-dog appeal, to make a piecemeal filling of their programs from the sort of girls who, the long and patient hours devoted to their coiffures, their maquillages and their ensembles having proved as fruitless as ever, were prepared to settle even for the Joe Somethings. No—anything but that!

Virginia felt her breath quicken, as a tall figure came in sight from behind a pillar and started to walk obliquely away from where she and Suzanne were standing. He had not seen her.

"There is my partner!" she said. "Looking for me now."

"Oh, Virginia—not *him!*" breathed Suzanne, awed. The tone of her voice was music to Virginia's ears. It stiffened her resolve, carried her the half dozen steps to overtake Cambronne, steeled her nerve to reach out and lay a hand on his arm, which felt like supple steel beneath her fingers.

"Captain Cambronne, dance with me!" she hissed. "Don't look surprised. Don't argue. Just dance with me. Now!"

He smiled: the smile that was more of a grin and carried an edge of amused mockery, so that the spoiled, high-stomached girl could have smacked that dark and severely sculptured face.

"Of course, Miss Virginia," he replied. "Your hand, ma'am."

Christ Church chimes struck a quarter hour. The distant strains of the orchestra also came to the spy's ears as he crouched in the shadowed window recess. And then— something else. He stiffened, and his hand sought for the reassurance of the pistol in his pocket.

They came from around the eastern side of the mansion:

two dark figures, one of them with two mastiffs leashed in hand. They skirted the trim, scissor-cut lawn, shaping a course which would take them close by the edge of the undergrowth, whose dark recesses could most easily hide an intruder. The very audacity of the present intruder had saved him thus far: the guardians of Holt's secrets could not envisage that anyone would dare venture out into the open so close to the mansion.

They were soon out of sight. The spy relaxed; speculated on how it was that the regular habits of such dull creatures who took on the protection of other people's property made one's task so easy, and how the hourly patrol had not deviated by a minute or by a yard throughout the time he had been inside the high walls surrounding the mansion.

Looking to left and right, he bounded swiftly across the lawn and plunged into the rhododendron bushes. The best place for scaling the wall, he knew, lay some fifty yards further to the east, where chestnut trees lay conveniently close to the tall stone surround. Fifty paces would do it. Over the wall. A short walk down the hill, to where he would maybe still be able to pick up a late-night cab and be back at his lodgings for a few hours' sleep before rising to write out his report on the Anti-Slavery Society.

And there was the wall, with a low branch of chestnut all but touching the top of it. Mark you, there was a long drop on the other side. Was he not perhaps getting a mite too old for this game?

Arriving by the wall, he reached up and, taking a handhold upon the lowest branch of the chestnut, levered himself up. As he did so, the sound of a twig cracking underfoot brought his other hand to his pistol pocket.

He never had a chance to draw the weapon before a dark forearm was wrapped about his chest. He had just time to realize that, for once, the patrol had varied their perambulations, before the keenly honed edge of a fish-gutting knife was dragged deeply across his exposed throat. There was no pain; just the shocked awareness that the hot torrent which cascaded down and drenched his nether clothing was his own life's blood.

CHAPTER 2

They were dancing a minuet, whose elegantly artificial figures had made it much in vogue with the Boston younger set: overtones of eighteenth-century decadence, pre–French Revolution, Lafayette and all that. Virginia knew every step and gesture of every figure, for she practiced it weekly at Miss Hornbuckle's dancing academy in Charles Street, and was reckoned to be the best pupil in the class.

Cambronne also knew his minuet, which surprised her. The hornpipe or the jig would have been more his style, one would have thought. But no—his lean and muscled tallness was well suited to the markedly epicene posturings demanded of the male partner, and provided a revelation of what the minuet must have looked like in its heyday, with the menfolk vying with their ladies in splendor of silks and lace, powdered wigs, faces painted and patched, bodies scented and pomaded —a facade for the reality of the swordsman's wrist, high-tempered honor quick to insult, a love of killing, a disdain for death. So had they danced in Versailles, with the barefoot mob already marching upon them to make an end of the aristocratic reality with the dream of revolution.

Virginia cocked a glance whenever they passed a pier-glass, and was gratified with what she saw. She was incomparably the prettiest girl in the room, her coiffure the most becoming, her silks the best chosen. And her partner—well, silly Suzanne was perfectly right: Cambronne was all male, and looked dangerous with it. The touch of his hand, when next they advanced to bow and curtsy, made her skin prickle. His eyes met hers and he smiled in that maddening way of his. She had betrayed herself and hated him for it. A half-turn, a changing of hands, a short promenade, and they were face-to-face with the next couple: Suzanne and Henry. The wistful envy in the face of the former, the sulky pout with which the

27

latter regarded her, made a bird sing in Virginia's heart. She forgave Cambronne on the instant.

"Captain, while you are in Boston, you must invite me aboard your ship," she said, loudly enough for Suzanne and Henry to hear.

"I am yours to command," replied her partner. And who could have wished for a better response? Suzanne's trussed-up bosom fairly heaved with a gasp of resentment.

The next figure promenaded them past the row of old biddies who sat against the longest wall: dowagers and duennas, Virginia's own mother, other mothers. Mama was next to poor, drunken Mrs. Josh Winterburn. Everyone—the whole row of them—had eyes for no one but the tall dark stranger and the blond girl in the springtime of her maiden-hood. Virginia supposed—hoped, indeed—that everyone was talking about them and commenting on the fact that they had danced every dance since the recess.

A pause, a bow. The harpsichord announced the final figure with a protracted chord that faded in an exquisite vibrato. There was a moment of silence, and the dancers stood poised like Dresden figurines.

"Henry, will you take me to the ball at the State House Saturday?"

"I guess so, Suzanne."

Virginia stiffened, scarcely believing the evidence of her own ears. She flashed a glance over her shoulder. Suzanne had been watching for the movement: her eyes were sidelong and sly, her too-moist lips parted like some cheap wanton. And Henry was blushing like a boy caught kissing himself in a looking-glass.

Flute and violins tumbled headlong into the final figure. Caught unawares, Virginia missed her step and all but tripped over her skirts in the attempt to reach her partner's out-stretched fingertips. Cambronne caught her and supported her.

"Damn you, are you laughing at me?" she demanded, face to face, almost mouth to mouth.

He released her. "No, ma'am," he said, his dark face full of merriment. He had heard the exchange between Henry and that bitch, of course—and guessed the implications.

The rest of the minuet was a misery. Every time she scanned her reflection in a pier-glass, she seemed oddly diminished, with skinny shoulders, no breasts and a childish face. Cambronne looked old enough to be her father—as, indeed, he probably was. She was glad when it was all over.

"Fetch me a cold drink," she said, as they left the floor.

"Certainly, Miss Virginia," He bowed and left her.

He was gone an interminable while. Time for the orchestra to start tuning up again.

"My dance, I believe, Virginia." It was Henry. And, by the look of him a very contrite Henry, with the Oxford veneer hastily assembled to cover his indiscretion.

"I think not," she said.

"But . . ."

"I have erased you from my program sir," she said. "The valse I have now given to Captain Cambronne."

"Oh, I see." The Oxford veneer slipped off him again, and he was the little boy caught in the act. Go dance with your new friend, boy. She turned her back on him.

Cambronne approached her across the empty dance floor, a tall glass in his hand.

"I brought fruit cup," he said. "Will that suffice?"

"I'm not thirsty any longer," she said.

He shrugged, laid the glass down upon a side table.

"Miss Virginia," he said. "The time has come when I . . ."

"Tell me later," she said, gathering up her skirts with devastating elegance and offering him her other hand. "The valse is beginning."

He took her proffered hand; did the irritating trick of placing a phantom kiss an inch above her fingertips.

"Goodnight, Miss Virginia," he said. "It has been a very great pleasure."

"You are not leaving me!" she cried.

"Indeed I am, Miss Virginia."

She glanced sidelong. No one appeared to have noticed the exchange. Not yet. The matter could swiftly be rectified. She re-addressed herself to the man before her.

"You will dance with me!"

He shook his head. "I regret not, ma'am. Late though the hour, I have business to do."

She stamped her foot, made a brusque gesture with her gloved hand, caught her finger in the gold chain that suspended a garnet droplet from her slendor neck. The chain broke, fell to the floor. Cambronne stooped to pick it up.

"Leave it be!" she hissed. "You'll have every eye in the room upon us next. Just take hold of me and dance!"

"No, Miss Virginia." The blue-gray eyes were steady and quite implacable.

She stamped her small, slippered foot.

"Do as I say!"

"With a million regrets—no."

The floor was now fairly filled with dancers, all awaiting the opening chord. From the corner of her eye, she saw Henry Davenport leading Suzanne to the center. They were watching her.

"Captain Cambronne," she whispered, "I command you to stay and dance with me. You are in my father's employment." She took a deep breath. "One word from me, and you will be dismissed!"

That hateful, male, mocking grin filled all her world.

"My contract with the Augusta Line," he said, "has a fair number of clauses and conditions. But so far as I recall, Miss Virginia, there's nothing in it that requires me to pander to the whims of spoiled little girls fresh out of school. Goodnight, Miss Virginia."

She smacked him full across the mouth.

In the shocked silence that followed, while he still smiled at her, she turned on her heel, and, with a sob, ran for the stairs. The throng parted to let her pass. On and up she went, tripping over her hem, losing one of her slippers; intent upon nothing but to hide her shame.

The orchestra had struck up the valse by the time she reached the upper floor. No one had followed her. She paused, breathless, in the long gallery that ran the entire length of the mansion and contained Cyrus J. Holt's famous collection of Italian and Dutch Old Masters, bought by the yard from a smooth art dealer in New York.

"Why, Virginia, m'dear. Why aren't you dancing?"

Recumbent upon a brocaded sofa was an elegant figure in black tail-coat and dove-gray pantaloons. Lazy eyes, heavy with sleep, gazed up at her from under hooded lids arched with gray. Gray, also, was his thick thatch of leonine mane. His face, unlined by years, was as firm and tautly muscled as that of a man half his age.

"Oh, Uncle Jeff—you gave me a scare!"

"Not crying, Virginia, not on you birthday?"

"Oh, Uncle Jeff, I've been so stupid. Made a complete fool of myself."

He reached out and took her hands in his. His were dry and cool, smooth as well-kept leather. "Sit down and tell Uncle," he said.

She obeyed and let her head fall upon his shoulder, soothed by the hand that smoothed her hair. He had always possessed the power to calm her; the little girl in short frocks sobbing over a broken doll, the gawky twelve-year-old bewailing a lost puppy, and as now. Uncle Jeff Carradine, man-about-town and lifelong bachelor, despair of three generations of beautiful women, was Virginia's godfather, but uncle only by title. Somewhere around the time of her parents' marriage, Carradine had strolled into their lives and stayed on the periphery, an observer, seemingly as detached from the Holt family as from the outside world that he blandly looked out upon from the window of his exclusive club in Copley Square.

"I had a fight with Henry Davenport for a start," she said.

"Henry Davenport should be fought frequently," declared Carradine. "I opine that he picked up some uncommonly slovenly manners in England. The trouble with Oxford, as I have always said, is that there are too damn many clergymen. But you are not crying on account of mere Henry Davenport, I think?"

"I was rude to someone else."

"But by design, child? Tell me swiftly, I beg you. To have been unknowingly rude would have been contrary to all the precepts I have tried to teach you."

He smiled at her waggishly; she smiled back, blinking away her tears.

"Whichever way, I was really rude," she said.

"Is that a disaster—for you?"

"I don't know."

"Sounds bad. Do I know the gentleman concerned? I am presuming that he is of the male persuasion."

She shook her head. "No. I don't think so. I didn't see you downstairs when he was being introduced around."

"I have been here all evening," confessed Carradine, "for, as you know, I am of a sedentary disposition. Even to watch others dance taxes my energies to an unbearable degree. To tell the truth, I have been fast asleep since the music began."

"They told me," said Virginia, "Mama has said so many

times, that you dance like an angel. She said that the girls
used to have the vapors over the way you valsed."

"Your mother," said Carradine, "as I have frequently
observed, is a lady whose extreme physical beauty is exceeded
only by her quite indiscriminate generosity. What are they
playing now, child?"

"A valse, Uncle Jeff," said Virginia. "As you well know."

"Shall we dance?"

He took her hand; she rose up with him. One hand at the
small of her unbelievably slender waist.

He smiled jauntily down at her.

"Now we begin," he said. "One, two, three . . ."

Turning, turning, they glided up the long gallery, past the
fashionably dark pictures in their gilded frames: the simpering Madonnas of dubious provenance; sylvan landscapes that
suggested Hoboken, New Jersey, rather than Hobbema; High
Renaissance nudes painted on good New England hickory;
one quite genuine Rembrandt that had slipped through the
smooth New York dealer's fingers unregarded. An elderly but
upright *flâneur* leading a beautiful blonde whose tears he had
charmed right away; his button boots a-twinkling at the turns
and counterturns, and never a pause for breath. And she
thinking: tomorrow is another day, and a fig for Cambronne.
As for Henry, I've only to snap my fingers and he'll come
running back. Not that I want or need him. And what can
Cambronne be doing in the line of business at such an hour as
this?

All seaports (and Boston, for all its pretensions, for all that
it had become a city and had its streets first lit by gas two
years previously, was a seaport or it was nothing) have a
flavor of their own, though they are all related.

It was Cambronne's first night in Boston. He was a total
stranger. Some seaports he knew well. Falmouth was one. As
first lieutenant of a corvette, he had sailed in and out of
Falmouth a thousand times, and knew every shoal, every
treacherous fang of rock; could have steered a safe course
through deep water, past Black Rock on the larboard hand
and St. Mawes opening up to starboard—and all with his eyes
shut. In his very first ship he had been navigating midshipman
under a master's mate whose brilliance, undimmed by excess
of drink, had rubbed off onto the impressionable young

Jerseyman. From his mentor he had learned the intricacies of approaching the Hook of Holland—as different a landfall from Falmouth as could be found anywhere on earth. Cambronne had only to close his eyes, twenty years later, to see the flats of Voorne and Goeree coming up on the lee shore, with the leadsmen calling four fathoms deep and a north-easter bearing down; with Master's Mate Nickless taking a nip from the flask he carried always and nodding that all would be well, that they'd weather the sand bars and make safe anchorage on the flood tide. They always did.

Falmouth and the Hook, Dover and Ramsgate, Gibraltar, Algiers, Cadiz and Corunna—seaports all, familiar and be-loved as the tools of any journeyman's trade. Boston was unknown to him, but, by reason of its nature, was bound to resemble all the others in many particulars.

Cambronne had arrived at the Holt mansion in a hired cab. He left it by the same means; there was a string of hirelings waiting patiently outside the guarded gates in hope of picking up a fare when the birthday party broke up. He gave succinct instructions to the driver, who took his English sixpence, bit upon it and, finding it to be silver, cheerfully drove him down to the waterfront.

The city at night, a jewel box of lights descending from Beacon Hill to the waterfront, with the tiny fireflies out in the Roads toward Long Island that told of ships putting out on the ebb tide. Over the bridge to South Boston, and down into the dockland area, place of ships and seamen. He had given his driver a wide brief: keep moving. Quite soon he found the place that was a replica of a hundred such places in ports all over the world. It was called the Lobster Pot—so announced by one of the said items hanging on a gallows above the entrance, on whose dark lintel the legend was scrawled in misshapen letters by a deck-scrubber dipped in tar. The building itself was of three floors and a pair of attics set in a steeply pitched roof; the whole edifice was only prevented from falling into the black waters of the dock by the rickety support of heavy timbers propped against it. One light burned in a top window, the rest were shuttered. And the sound of tipsy carousing came from the ground floor. It was three o'clock in the morning. Cambronne bore down upon the latch and entered.

It was as he had expected. It was Falmouth and the Hook,

Ramsgate, Algiers, Cadiz and all the rest: a night haunt of men without homes, without wives, children, roots. Some of them, perhaps, were even without a ship to call their home.

The top-room was dimly lit by tallow dips, permitting of considerable anonymity to the clientele. Cambronne, tall and striking in appearance though he was in his dramatic boat cloak, merited scarcely a glance as he closed the door behind him and slipped as unobtrusively as he was able into an empty, high-backed pew in a shadowed corner and beckoned to a passing potman.

"What's your pleasure, mister?"

"Brandy," said Cambronne.

An opened bottle and glass were set before him. He poured himself a good measure and, raising the vessel to his lips, peered out over the rim, scanning the scene before him. Searching, searching.

There were, perhaps, a hundred men in the room, and half as many women. The former, by their rough slopclothes, weather-beaten looks and indefinable air, were all seamen. A certain tawdry finery, overloading of paint and powder, and an indiscriminate geniality announced the latter to be members of the oldest profession in various degrees from postulant to mother superior. The very serving wenches carried themselves with cheerful compliance, suffering their clients to kiss and handle them freely as they passed between the crowded settles and tables with their laden trays of drink, eyes and lips roaming freely, bodices wantonly unlaced for the delectation of seeing and touching. The air was choked with the stench of tobacco smoke, strong spirits, cheap scent and humanity.

At the next pew from Cambronne, four scoundrels in headscarves and leather jerkins were solemnly and silently dicing. There was a pile of coin in front of each and a larger pile in the middle of the table. One of them had a cocked pistol lying at his elbow. . . .

Without warning, a bearded giant with brass earrings leaped to his feet in the center of the room, cried aloud a blasphemy, and crashed to the floor like a felled tree. No one took the slightest notice. A serving wench gathered up the stricken man's empty pot, half-playfully brushing off a hand that insinuated itself beneath her skirts.

A struck chord upon a guitar directed Cambronne's attention. At the far end of the room, seated on a low stool by the open fireplace, was a red-haired young man in seaman's jerkin and pantaloons of dirty white duck. His head, bowed over his instrument, rendered his features a mystery to the observer. The hubbub of conversation was only part-quenched by the sound of his music. The dice players next to Cambronne did not look around, but continued their throwing as the redhead began to sing in a deep and vibrant baritone:

> *"Here, a sheer hulk, lies poor Tom Bowling,*
> *The darling of our crew;*
> *No more he'll hear the tempest howling,*
> *For death has broached him to . . ."*

The singer was English—his accent betrayed as much; the song, by the popular ballad composer Charles Dibden, a firm favorite with sailors and landsmen the world over. Cambronne had heard "Tom Bowling" in places as far apart as Vauxhall Gardens and Madagascar, Alexandria and Quebec, and was always curiously warmed by the unashamed sentimentality of the lyric, the heavy-handed metaphors:

> *"Faithful below, he did his duty,*
> *But now he's gone aloft,*
> *but now he's gone aloft . . ."*

There was a serving wench, a tow-headed chit with a turned-up nose and an elfin grin, who went over and kissed the singer on the forehead, to which he made no response. In the act of turning away, she met Cambronne's eye across the room. When next he replenished his glass, she slid into a vacant place on the settle by his side, put her small hand upon his thigh.

"Goin' to buy a poor gal a drink, sailor?"

Cambronne snapped his fingers to the potman and called for another glass.

"Singer a friend of yours?" he asked of the girl.

"Jack the Cat?" she said. "He's nobody's friend isn't Jack the Cat. What's your name, sailor? Want a warm berth for the night? My place is just at the end of the street. And listen . . ." leaning forward, she whispered into his ear—and surely, considering the company, not for fear of giving offense—the most highly colored details of the encounter that might follow if he took up her offer. Cambronne poured a measure of spirit and put the glass into her hand. She could not have been a day over sixteen.

"Tell me more about Jack the Cat," he said. "Friendless, you say?"

The brazen glance grew cunning. "Why aren't you interested in me?" she demanded. "Why do you want to know bout him? Hey! Are you . . . ?"

Cambronne sighed, took out a sixpence and slipped it into her gaping bodice, between the scarcely budding breasts.

"Why is Jack the Cat nobody's friend, you say?" he demanded.

She took out the coin, looked at both sides of it, sniffed. "You another Limey, eh? From the way you talked, I had you for a Frenchy."

"Jack the Cat," prompted Cambronne.

She shrugged, hid the coin somewhere upon her person, took a deep swallow of her brandy—with the air of someone who knows that payment might soon be withdrawn for non-delivery of goods.

"You'll not need me to tell," she said. "Take a look at his face next time he lifts his head."

> *"Yet shall poor Tom find pleasant weather,*
> *When He, Who all commands,*
> *Shall give, to call life's crew together,*
> *The word to pipe all hands . . ."*

The red thatch was still bowed over the instrument, the hands—curiously long and slender hands—glissaded over the strings, the voice caressed each mellifluous nuance of the ballad. It was an impressive performance; even the dice players at the next pew ceased for a while to rattle the ivories. Cambronne narrowed his eyes, settled back more comfortably in his seat—and waited.

> *"Thus Death, who kings and tars dispatches,*
> *In vain Tom's life has doff'd;*
> *For though his body's under hatches . . ."*

The strumming rose to a crescendo with the ending of the last verse, and the voice rose with it. The better to project the words to the far recesses of the smoke-filled room, or perhaps

in response to the soundless question that was being carried
to him by the force of Cambronne's will, or perhaps merely to
strike horror into the hearts of his listeners, the singer raised
his head at the final line.

> *"His soul has gone aloft!"*

"My God!" whispered Cambronne.

"Now you know, dearie," hissed the girl at his ear. "Now
you know why he's called the Jack the Cat who walks alone!"

Under the thatch of ill-kempt hair was a face that—
considering the well-formed body of which it was a part—
must have been young. The destruction wrought upon that
face put it forever beyond the ravages of time; age would only
soften, a benevolent putrefaction do no more than erase, the
worst of it.

The eyes were the first to command: they searched the
room from behind lidless slits, striking this way and that,
narrow and gleaming in the firelight, the eyes of a cat. In
response to the desultory applause that greeted the end of the
ballad, the mouth parted in a travesty of a grin. It was a
mouth that had by some hideous means been extended all
across each cheek, so that the action of the grimace was to
bare two rows of gleaming teeth from end to end; a cat's grin.

Distance and the poor light mercifully hid the finer details
of that ghastly countenance from Cambronne; but he was
able to see that the skin was crisscrossed, from forehead to
chin, by weals and contusions, some old and healed, some
fresh and livid. It occurred to Cambronne that the man was,
or had been, a prize-fighter, but he dismissed the notion at
once; even the bare-fisted brutes who hammered each other
to pulp for a purse and the delectation of their well-heeled
patrons could not mark flesh with mere flesh to such a degree;
it would have taken a pugilist of ancient Rome, with his
gloves of spiked steel, to turn a man into a semblance of Jack
the Cat.

His song finished, the singer left his place by the fire and
carried his guitar over to a shadowed corner, where he
became another dark shape in a crowded room.

"Drink up, dearie," came the mocking voice at Cambronne's side. "You don't look too good. Gave you quite a
turn, seein' that face staring out at you, eh? Not a nice thing
to come across in some dark alleyway, eh?" She laughed,

choked on her last mouthful of brandy. She was still coughing
when the street door opened to admit a giant of a man in a tall
and gleaming hat. A group of cloaked and muffled figures
came in behind him; but it was the first comer who commanded attention.

Recovering her breath, Cambronne's companion whispered: "you're in luck tonight, dearie. Here's Chelsea Nye
and his bully-boys. There's sport for you tonight, dearie—if
you've got the stomach for it."

"What kind of sport?" asked Cambronne, grinning,
amused at the child's condescension. "And why shall I need a
strong stomach?"

But she would not tell. "Listen to Chelsea Nye," she said.
"He's going to start his cheapjack patter. The dirty dog—as I
should know, who've been used by him!"

The man called Chelsea Nye was no seaman; that could be
determined at a glance. There was something of the fair-
ground about him; Cambronne had come across his like
wherever men—and some kinds of women—congregate for
the purpose of vicarious enjoyment: the vendors of pleasure
—at a price. Mark the way his cravat was over-large and
flowery, the points of his high collar reaching halfway up his
well-barbered cheeks; and the tail-coat, a mite too tight at the
waist and wide at the shoulders; pantaloons into which he
looked to have been poured, so remarkably well did they
define the muscled flanks and calves, the protrusion of the
loins. Chelsea Nye was a big man, and a trifle overweight,
with a self-pampered look about the dove-gray gloves, the
silver-knobbed cane, the auburn hair that was surely not
innocent of the curling iron's touch. Over-florid complexion,
over-moist mouth. And a voice like a rasp wrapped in velvet.

"Gentlemen all!" he said, by way of introduction. "You all
know my profession!"

This was greeted by a ragged chorus of whistles and
catcalls, which were received by the speaker with a moist,
lopsided smirk and a wave of his gloved hand to command
silence; this having been restored, he continued:

"Gentlemen, my assistants will presently pass amongst you
in the usual manner. Upon the receipt of a purse of one
hundred dollars . . ."

He was interrupted by another chorus, this time indicative
of disbelief and derision; all of which he dismissed by closing
his eyes and shaking his head till the racket had ceased.

"Upon the receipt of one hundred dollars in the coinage of this fair Union, being the purse for this evening's bout of no-holds-barred fisticuffs-cum-rassling, I will then produce my champion and await the challenger. You know the rules, gentlemen. Should the challenger survive one half hour of no-holds-barred fisticuffs-cum-rassling with my champion, said challenger will receive four-fifths of said purse, the derisory balance being retained to cover my expenses and help to maintain a roof over the heads of my wife and kids. Any questions?"

"Is it gonna be in the rules," shouted a voice from a far end of the room, "fer to use a bottle or mebbe a chair leg? Answer that straight, mister!"

A roar of approval demonstrated that the mood of the gathering was strongly in favor of the motion, a fact of life to which Chelsea Nye made a graceful acknowledgment.

"Chair legs and bottles will be allowable," he declared. "Likewise any portable instrument, be it sharp or blunt. But no firearms. The purse will now be collected. And let this be said: no hundred dollars, no contest!"

The showman's "assistants" proved to be a quartet of ruffians who could have passed for the worst type of footpad. With them was a dwarf of cheerful appearance. Cambronne wondered which of the former would prove to be Chelsea Nye's champion, and privately resolved to resist all temptation to challenge any one of the brutes. It was the dwarf who came up to him, shaking an over-large hat under his nose and grinning most agreeably. Cambronne, who had a liking for dwarves, found a dollar piece among the mixed coinage in his pocket and dropped it into the hat. The bearer winked at him and moved on.

The girl nudged Cambronne's elbow. "Call for another bottle of the same, dearie," she advised. "You're going to need it, and me likewise."

Scarcely had the second bottle been brought and Cambronne replenished both of their glasses, when, the collection having been completed and the moneys counted, Chelsea Nye announced that the purse met his requirements and called for his champion to step forward and strip for the contest—subject to a challenger being forthcoming.

"Make way, there!"

"Stand aside! Gangway for a naval officer!"

Amid raucous sallies and loud guffaws, Chelsea Nye's

champion came forth from somewhere near the door. Men
and women were all on their feet. Cambronne, for all his
height, had to crane his neck to see, and only caught the back
of a head and a pair of wide shoulders wrapped in a cloak.
Not till Chelsea Nye's assistants had pressed back the throng
in the center of the room and cleared an open space free of
seats and tables did the suddenly astonished Jerseyman see
what he had bought for his dollar.

The champion stood a whisker under six feet, with arms
and shoulders to match. Flaxen hair parted in the middle and
drawn back in two plaits, Indian fashion; pale skin offset by
ruddy cheeks and blue eyes that told of a Teutonic origin. A
face that had once been handsome, now well past its best. A
face marred by a hardness about the mouth and eyes, and by a
broken nose.

Astonishment, followed by disbelief, was confirmed by
certainty as the champion shrugged off the cloak.

The girl jabbed Cambronne with her elbow. "Take a long
swill of your brandy and hang on to your seat, sailor," she
whispered. There's more to Dutch Olga than meets the eye!"

Chelsea Nye's "champion" was a woman!

They were calling to her from all sides, and she responded
with amused contempt, returning insult for compliment,
obscenity for importunity; all that company, the sweepings of
a great seaport, could make no dent upon her towering
self-containment; she stood and outfaced them all, hands on
hips, proud as a Norse goddess.

She had removed most of her upper clothing. The bodice of
her coarse cotton dress hung about her broad hips. Gone
were her stays, leaving her ample breasts to jounce insolently
beneath a thin, sleeveless shift that was none too clean.

"I challenge the wench! It'll not take me half an hour to
down the bitch, and when I do . . ." The speaker was an
oldster, tall as a crane and thin with it. He was so drunk he
could scarcely stand. Comradely hands pulled him back onto
his seat.

"Gennlemen, gennlemen," cried Chelsea Nye. "This will
not suffice, I tell you. I call for a serious challenge from a man
of quality. This is not boys' business, gennlemen. This is not
old men's business. You all know Dutch Olga's reputation on
the waterfront. She has killed her man. Not once, but thrice.
The feller who downs Dutch Olga will have a quality about

him. So who's it to be? And it's no holds barred, mark you. Fisticuffs-cum-rassling"—he looked about him encouragingly —"chair legs allowable, as stated."

The girl dug Cambronne in the ribs with her sharp elbow. "Why don't you take a tumble from Dutch Olga, sailor?" she said.

"Drink your brandy and have peace," growled Cambronne.

"The purse is not returnable," said Chelsea Nye. "You know my rules. The purse only commits me to present my champion for the night. It could be Dutch Olga, it could be Gwen the Thrush, old Meg the Mangler—doughty fighters, all. If there is no challenger, the purse, after sundry deductions for my own expenses and the maintenance of my wife and kids, will go to Dutch Olga and my assistants."

"This is your last chance, sailor," whispered the girl. "Another minute, and Chelsea Nye will be gone and the purse with him. There's not a man here tonight with the spunk to try a tumble with her after what she did to them fellers down at the old harbor last fall. But you, sailor." She kneaded his upper arm between her probing, small fingers. "I'd sure like to see you stripped and facing Dutch Olga. There's spunk in you, all right."

"Have done," said Cambronne. "I never laid a fist upon a woman, and I . . .

He broke off, as a clear voice silenced the hubbub in the room.

"I challenge her!"

A young voice. A young woman's voice.

They parted ranks to let her through, and gaped at what they saw. There must have been a dozen such as she in the Lobster Pot that night. The chit at Cambronne's elbow was cut out of a similar piece of flawed cloth, but a few years younger. This one had on a tawdry cheap dress and wore her blue-black hair in a cascade about her shoulders and across her brow. Her cheeks were painted, her mouth a slash of carmine also. But she was no more than twenty, surely. If a whore, then a whore not far gone. Cambronne noted, with a wayward touch of compassion, that she was barefoot, and her shoulders looked slight and vulnerable.

Chelsea Nye was dismissive. "Now, see here, gal," he said, "you've had your joke and it's been mightily appreciated. I'm sure the gennlemen present here tonight will appreciate my

gesture in giving you this silver dollar to go away and buy
yourself something pretty to wear and . . ."

His voice was drowned in a concerted howl of lustful,
drunken men in full flight after prey. They bayed for the
challenge to be accepted. They would have none of the young
wench being fobbed off with a dollar to buy herself something
pretty. The landlord of the Lobster Pot, roused from his
stupor and hauled to his feet, was directed to inform Chelsea
Nye, furthermore, that if he refused to allow the challenge,
he could look elsewhere to stage any future contests. The
showman, complaisant as ever to *vox populi,* shrugged his
elegantly suited shoulders and hissed to his champion:

"All right, Dutch. What've we got to lose? They want a
show. Give 'em a show. What's a few minutes here or there
with a hundred safe in the purse? Only, don't kill the kid. Just
mark her bad, so's to discourage any other cheap strumpet
who wants to make a name for herself on the waterfront!"

Dutch Olga showed her remarkably fine, white teeth in a
grin of acquiescence, an act that won a whoop of delight from
the assembled company.

The chit of a girl seized hold of Cambronne's arm. "Stop
them!" she whispered. "You've got to stop them, sailor. You
don't know that Olga. The things she's done to grown men.
And that gal . . ."

"Friend of yours?" asked Cambronne.

"I never saw her before in my life."

"Then why do you concern yourself?" he asked. And he
turned his gaze again to the drama that was being enacted.

Anticipation about the promised spectacle had immediately livened business in the Lobster Pot. There was a brisk
ordering of fresh drinks. Seamen down to their last few cents
cadged loans from their more affluent comrades, the drunk
girded up their loins to become more drunk, the very
drunk—stimulated by the sight of the flawed blonde goddess
faced up to by the slip of a girl with the mane of blue-black
hair—found room in their hearts to refill their pots. As always
in times of stress, the great god nicotine was invoked by
billowing new clouds from freshly lit cheroots and clay pipes.

"Go to it, Olga!"

"My money's on the darkie!"

Chelsea Nye said: "Let her have it, Dutch!"

One hand still on hip, Dutch Olga swaggered forward,
breasts swaying with every step, and the sailors whistled in

time to her movements. Her opponent—the challenger— waited and watched, hands twitching nervously, biting the corner of her painted mouth, seemingly irresolute. If she knew of the champion's lurid reputation, of the innumerable rough and tumbles in crowded taverns, prize-fights galore, strong men beaten to the spit and sawdust and three lying in eternal sleep in paupers' graves, she gave no sign and made no retreat.

She flinched when Olga made a feint with one hand as if to strike her in the face. A hoot of laughter went up when the champion reached with the other hand and, taking the neck of the other's dress, ripped it down to the navel. Dutch Olga knew the clientele, knew how to put on a show. Chelsea Nye drew deeply on his cigar and let his pouched eyes twinkle good-humoredly. All unexpectedly, so it seemed to him, a whole new horizon of showmanship and spectacle opened itself out ahead. He had made a modest fortune by pitting she-Goliaths against hard-bitten sweepings of the eastern seaboard. Suddenly this chit of a girl had suggested a fresh and perhaps more lucrative combination. Meanwhile, the presumptuous challenger herself had to be punished; for it must always be the showman, and not the talking horse, who collects the bows and picks up the thrown pennies, or the world is out of kilter.

The dark-haired girl (and she must, surely, have been very new to the trade of whoring around in dockland taverns to have retained such a touching degree of maidenly sensibility) snatched at her rent bodice and made some effort to conceal her breasts. Dutch Olga took the opportunity to loop one muscular arm around the other's neck, put a massive fist about a slender wrist, and drag her victim to the front row of the leering audience, to the face of an unshaven lout in a bandana and an eye-patch.

"Ya wanna give a kiss to the pretty gel, sailor?"

Dutch Olga held her there. One-eye took his kiss, and a fumbled manhandling besides. He essayed another kiss—and screamed like a stuck pig when the girl drove her sharp, white teeth into his nether lip. They all laughed. They laughed again when the girl bit Dutch Olga's wrist and drew a sharp fountain of bright blood.

The blond she-Goliath released her hold and stepped back, sucking at her scored wrist.

"You die for that, little bitch," she hissed.

•

There followed a soundless echo of her threat, loud in the smoke-laden gloom of that crowded, reeking room. The dark-haired girl stood almost listlessly, hands hung by her sides, careless now of the puckered pink nipples bared for all eyes.

"Hell, I don't wanna see this!" whispered the child at Cambronne's elbow, and hid her face. Cambronne took a long suck at his brandy and watched. Unwaveringly.

Of what followed, those who were present on the occasion spoke freely abroad, adding to the folk-history of the waterfront, so that echoes and murmurs of that night persisted in many a garbled version wherever seafarers gathered together. In the many versions, compounded of hearsay, speculation, embellishment, downright lying, there remained one common element: Dutch Olga took up a pewter pot and hit the black-haired girl on the head.

After that, hearsay and the rest parted company; versions differed.

Cambronne, who witnessed it from beginning to end, all but felt the ring of the pewter pot against the side of his own head; flinched when Dutch Olga swung back her muscular arm to deliver another blow. The blow never landed.

One waterfront version had it that Dutch Olga tripped over the feet of the bearded giant with brass earrings who had succumbed some time earlier and been left to lie where he had fallen. Others said—and persisted in the account to their deathbeds—that the champion must have suffered some kind of seizure; otherwise, how could she have . . . ? It was impossible, against the dictates of nature and the proper order of things, for had not Dutch Olga killed three men and injured innumerable others in fair fights? Well, as fair as they come on the waterfront . . .

Cambronne saw it plain. Dutch Olga made a wide swing with her heavy pot. The dark-haired girl, clearly dazed, her tangled mane hanging over her eyes, moreover, must have seen the peril in which she stood, but made no attempt to avoid it; instead, she held her ground till the older female had closed with her, and then, lifting her ragged skirts to her thighs with both hands, she kicked out at her opponent with her bare foot.

The movement was almost too quick for the eye to follow. To have blinked an eyelid was to have missed it, and many there were who did. There were many who were unable to account for the way in which Dutch Olga dropped the pewter pot and fell back a pace, clutching at her generously rounded middle, china-blue eyes starting from their sockets, mouth agape and framing a soundless scream of agony. There was suddenly silence, and the girl struck again, and once more with her right foot, the skirts held high. This time the terrible blow took Dutch Olga in the chest, a little lower than the deep cleft of her breasts, driving the air from her lungs in a gusting sound. She swayed, was about to fall of her own volition, when a blow to the side of the neck from the heel of the girl's hand impelled her to the sawdusted floor like a poleaxed ox, where her blond head connected loudly with the worn timbers.

In the hubbub that followed, the girl drew together the torn edges of her bodice and looked shyly about her, seemingly overcome by the rapturous response with which her astonishing feat was being greeted. Some tried to press glasses of brimming spirit into her hand, others patted her frail shoulders, kisses were rained upon her. Cambronne remained seated, a thin curl of cigar smoke drifting past his impassive eyes.

"She's dead! The slut's killed the best fightin' wench on the waterfront!" That was Chelsea Nye's verdict. He was on his knees beside the stricken champion, chafing her limp hands. Helpful onlookers were assisting him in the merciful act of trying to revive Dutch Olga, to which end one self-appointed physician had deemed it necessary to unbutton her shift, the better to listen against her bare breasts.

"She ain't dead, Chelsea," declared this fellow. "I kin hear her breathin.' Not much, that's fer certain, but enough to show she's livin'."

"Let me have a listen," said another of the medical inclination.

"Get outa the way!" bawled Chelsea Nye, thrusting aside the willing helpers and gesturing to two of his assistants. "Jago—Sam—get a hold of her and take her back to my place. Then fetch Mother Rattigan, that is if she ain't laying-out or delivering. Tell her there's a bottle of gin if she can put Dutch back on her feet."

The two obeyed, bowing at the knees beneath the great weight of the blond fighter.

"Please—I would like my money. Eighty dollars, isn't it?" The girl with the blue-black tresses spoke up shyly.

Chelsea Nye stared at the girl as if she had uttered a blasphemy. The notion that she, having brought his best woman surely to within sight of Abraham's bosom, was now demanding her rightful reward struck him as bizarre in the extreme. He calculated that in round figures Dutch Olga was worth from a thousand to fourteen hundred dollars a week to him; that is to say, she fought two bouts every night, seven nights a week, for purses ranging up to a hundred dollars. She had never before been defeated, for, no matter how big and brutal her opponents, there had never been one who would stoop to the dirty tricks of which Dutch Olga was capable in a tight corner. And now it would be all over the waterfront that she had been bested by a slip of a girl. The purses would go down. He might not even be able to raise another purse on her.

But wait . . .

A great truth suddenly illuminated the dark recesses of Chelsea Nye's uncomely mind, and he looked at the girl with fresh eyes. Was it possible—could it be true—that the slight form, those slender thighs and calves, that tiny foot, held the power to fell the likes of Dutch Olga? True indeed, for had he not seen it with his own eyes. Hell, if Dutch Olga was worth nigh on fifteen hundred a week at her best, what might not this scrawny little bitch . . .?

"Kid, you've got yourself a job," he declared, laying a not unkindly hand on her shoulder. "Starting tomorrow night, you fight for Chelsea Nye."

She shook her head. "No, I just want my money."

"Kid, kid—" he was all honey and unction, eyes crinkling at the corners with good humor. He came closer to the girl, giving her the full benefit of his charm, for he reckoned himself something of a devil with women and prided himself on tumbling all of his fighters. "There's a lot of money in the game, and you'll take a big piece of every purse. A year—two years—and you'll be able to retire from the fight game with a big enough dot to win yourself a college-educated feller for a husband."

"My money, please," she responded, holding out a hand. "My eighty dollars—as promised."

He shook his head. "I'm going to do you a favor, kid," he said. "A favor for which you're going to thank me on bended knees not long hence. I'm going to put that eighty dollars to your account on my books, and pay it to you, together with your share of the purses, at the end of your first month's work. What do you think of that?" He extended the question to embrace the onlookers, who had been listening with breathless interest to the exchange. "Gennlemen all, is that not a fair offer? And remember, you will all be seeing the little lady fight again in this very tavern."

It was the tail end of this peroration that secured him the backing of the Lobster Pot's clientele. Shiftless, drunken and vicious they might have been, but your seaman has an ingrained sense of fair play and the fulfilling of bargains—life in the cramped foc'sle of a ship would be impossible without such a code. All things being equal, they might have forced Chelsea Nye to give the girl her money, but every man present had been curiously aroused by her feat and wanted to see more.

"Take him at his word, lass!" enjoined one of them.

"Aye! We'll see to it that he pays you, kid!" declared another.

Still the girl shook her head. "I don't want to work for you," she said to Chelsea Nye. "Give me my money now, so that I can go."

But Chelsea Nye, now that he had the company behind him, was firmly set upon his course of action. Hefting the carpetbag into which he had deposited the hundred dollars worth of loose change, he brushed past the girl.

"You'll come to your senses, kid," he said. "When you've slept on it, you'll figure out that there's more to be earned in the fight game than in whoring, and when you do, just look me up at the Sign of the Golden Globe in Dock Street. Goodnight, all."

They parted to let him pass, the two remaining ruffians and the dwarf at his heels.

But not all: one figure barred his path to the door. It was he they called Jack the Cat, narrow eyes gleaming, two pinpoints of reflected light, hideous mouth set in a hard line.

"You will give her the money!" His voice was deep and pleasantly inflected. The voice of an educated Englishman.

Chelsea Nye sneered. "I know you," he said. "You're the crazy feller who's forever trying to get himself killed. Out of my way, crazy feller, or I might oblige you this time."

"Go right ahead," was the cool response.

Chelsea Nye suffered a moment of irresolution, then, turning to the brutes at his back, he jerked a thumb toward the hideously disfigured man with the red hair.

"Get him out of my way!" he rasped. "And trample him plenty!"

The two moved forward to obey, an action that brought a grin of fierce pleasure to the face of Jack the Cat, splitting it wide apart, baring the bright teeth. Taking a pace to one side, his eyes never leaving his two assailants, he seized a brandy bottle by the neck and smashed it against the table edge.

"Come, gentlemen," he breathed. "Who's to be first?"

The bright shards of dripping glass stuck out from his proffered fist. His grin was unwavering.

Undeterred for more than a moment, Chelsea Nye's henchmen produced their personal weaponry: one a knife with a cruel ten-inch blade, the other a weighted blackjack. And the dwarf began to circle round the back of the red-headed man, smiling the while and nodding his oversized head.

The knife man made the first assault, slashing diagonally across his opponent's body. Jack the Cat took half a pace back and the razor-sharp edge passed within a hairsbreadth of his seaman's jerkin. He lunged with the broken bottle and the knife man, dropping his weapon, screamed with agony and retired from the fray, one hand fighting to stem a jet of arterial blood that blossomed from his bare forearm.

"One settled for, and one to go," said Jack the Cat, giving his terrible grin.

The brute with the blackjack was more cautious than his comrade; furthermore, he was aware that he had the assistance of the dwarf, who had insinuated himself behind Jack the Cat without the latter noticing and now crouched in readiness to make his small contribution to the outcome.

The narrowed, catlike eyes watched his opponent's approach, their attention fixed upon the weighted head of the blackjack as it circled menacingly at shoulder height. Finally, with a shout of triumph, Chelsea Nye's man made his play, striking for the thatch of red hair. As before, Jack the Cat backed away a pace. And then another.

The second pace back was—literally—his downfall, for the nimble dwarf had darted forward and, falling on hands and knees behind the unsuspecting man, had turned himself into a living stumbling block. The broken bottle flew from Jack the

Cat's hand. He lay helpless before his opponent. The cruel
blackjack was raised on high for a blow that was meant to
brain.

A pistol-shot sounded shatteringly loud in that crowded
room. The blackjack was plucked from the would-be killer's
hand as if by a mighty gust of wind and smashed against the
far wall.

Every eye turned to regard Jason Cambronne, who sat
imperturbably with a half-smoked cigar between his lips, a
small under-and-over pocket pistol in his hand. A thin haze of
white powder-smoke hung in the air about him and was soon
gone.

"Give the girl her money," he said.

"Now see here, mister . . ." blustered Chelsea Nye.

"Give her the money—or I blow your head off on the count
of ten!" The twin muzzles of the pistol shifted aim—slightly
upward.

"Mister, you heard the very fair business offer I made to
this young lady here . . ."

"One—two—three . . ."

"It's great opportunity I'm offering her . . ."

"Four—five—six . . ."

"You wouldn't shoot! Hell, you wouldn't kill a feller for
eighty stinking dollars!"

"Seven-eight . . ." There was the click of the hammer
being thumbed back to full cock.

"Wait . . . !"

"Nine . . ."

"Take it!" screamed Chelsea Nye, hurling the carpetbag
across the room, so that it landed with a jangle of coinage at
the feet of the girl with blue-black hair. "Take the damned
lot!"

With one last, hate-filled glance at the man with the pistol,
Chelsea Nye fled the company, followed by his henchmen,
the wounded knife man nursing his bleeding arm. The street
door closed behind them, and a cacophony of excited chatter
filled the awed silence.

Jack the Cat was on his feet again. He sauntered slowly
over to where Cambronne was sitting. The terrible grin split
his face.

"I think it not unlikely that I owe you my life," he said.

"But I understand that you deliberately seek death,"

replied Cambronne. "Which being the case, my action possibly does not merit your thanks."

The other shrugged. "The tales of my pursuing death are exaggerated. But not greatly exaggerated."

"In that case I am sorry for you."

"You will survive your sorrow, my friend," said Jack the Cat. "It is truly said that we all have enough strength to bear other people's troubles."

"You turn a good phrase," said Cambronne. "It seems to me that you must be a man of learning."

"I have some Latin and mathematics," said the other. "And less Greek."

"You interest me," said Cambronne. "Will you sit down and take a drink?" The seat beside him was empty, Cambronne's female companion having left in a hurry at the approach of Jack the Cat.

"With much pleasure. Ah, there goes the object of all our chivalrous efforts. And without so much as a thank you."

Sure enough, the girl with the blue-black hair, having gathered up the carpetbag, was making her way to the door, and sparing not a passing glance for the two men to whom she owed her good fortune.

"What does it matter?" commented Cambronne. "I've a notion that you, at least, were in no way concerned about the rights and wrongs of her case."

The hideous grin broadened. "Not in the slightest," admitted the other. "The little slut walked into it with her eyes open. If she's spent any time at all on the waterfront she should know that the likes of Chelsea Nye will always bilk on a wager."

"But her method of fighting," said Cambronne. "Now, that was interesting. Did you remark it? That method—the striking of blows with the foot and with the open hand—is oriental in origin. I have seen it only twice before. Once by a Chinee, then by a Burman. Where would a little dockland trollop gain such expertise in such an arcane discipline?"

"From a Chinee," said Jack the Cat. "Or a Burman. There are plenty such on the waterfront." The long and hideous upper lip curled with contempt. "A fifty-cent whore such as she would scarcely take account of a man's color."

With slow deliberation, Cambronne lit a cigar and took a long pull at it before he replied: "But perhaps a fifty-cent whore such as she might shy at tumbling on a mattress with—you?"

The awful grin never wavered. "You have no compunction, have you, about driving home the knife?" said Jack the Cat. "And having driven it home, you turn the knife in the wound. I think that you must be testing me. What did you say your name was?"

"I didn't," said the other. "But the name is Cambronne. Jason Cambronne. Captain."

"Captain?" The grin became quirky. "Are you, perhaps, a captain in the way that so many gentlemen on the waterfront declare themselves to be captain? That is to say they once commanded a bum-boat and are living—and drinking—on the memory. Or have you a ship?"

"I have a ship," said Cambronne. "To be precise, she is not yet commissioned but when she is, she will be a craft to be reckoned with. And I am seeking a crew. A very special sort of crew."

Their gazes locked, each to each. "A crew, perhaps, for whom the pursuit of death does not hold the terrors that strike the common ruck of men so very forcibly?" asked Jack the Cat.

"There will be—certain dangers," said Cambronne.

"Within the law?"

"Outside the law."

"Lucrative?"

"A handsome share of the profits from the merchandise."

"And the nature of the merchandise—if one may ask?"

"One may not ask—not yet."

The appalling grin broadened. "I think we may do business, Captain Cambronne," said Jack the Cat. "As you so sensitively point out, my appearance is such that even fifty-cent whores—like the creature who was sitting here with you—flee into the undergrowth upon my approach, which means that I, who—between carrying on a protracted flirtation with death—have precisely the same desires as whole men, and with just the same urgency, am obliged either to slake my lusts upon the sort of drabs who venture out only on the darkest night and in the foulest of weathers, and are grateful to earn even ten cents in return for giving one a brief illusion, a far-off vision, of Paradise, or to buy the favors of those well-endowed daughters of joy for whom cash, and not aesthetics, is the criterion. Do I make myself plain? I need money, a lot of money. And I am also an extremely competent seaman."

It was a fine night, and there was no hope of a cab at that hour and in that seedy ambience. Cambronne, when he left the Lobster Pot, resolved to walk back to his lodgings, a tavern on the slope of Beacon Hill. He was well-satisfied with his night's endeavors.

Mounting the narrow, steep street that led from the waterfront, he looked back over his shoulder at the vista gradually being displayed behind him: a line of winking lights described the scattered islands and islets that all but enclosed Boston Roads. Out in the central darkness, a single lighthouse burned steadily. To the right of it, the lanterns of an incoming vessel shifted and changed position as it went about. A bell-buoy tolled forlornly and far off.

He had done well, he decided, in finding and securing the services of Jack the Cat. In such a place as the Lobster Pot he could have expected to find hard men of the kind he sought; his crew of around seventy-five would all need to be hard. But a few of them—the key men, and not necessarily the officers, but those who had the closest dealings with the watchmen— would need to be of a very special sort. And in all Boston waterfront there would not—could not—be more than a handful of such.

Walking on, he speculated on the quality he sought. They would be lonely men—like himself. Men who had been bruised by life, and who bruised in return. Men, furthermore, with the will to survive, yet who scorned death.

Men who were—flawed.

As Jack the Cat was flawed, As he, Jason Cambronne, was flawed.

CHAPTER 3

From the first of June to the end of August, weather permitting, the Holts took breakfast *en famille* on the terrace at the rear of the mansion, sheltered by the fine Ionic portico and by the wall of delicately pink-shaded tulip trees that grew beyond.

Breakfast, Virginia had long since decided, was a bore. Her father seldom spoke, but immersed himself in the contents of a dispatch case that his secretary, one Uriah Needham, deposited by his master's chair punctually every morning.

Her mother, on the other hand, seemed to feel it incumbent upon herself to fill the empty air with inconsequential chatter requiring to know what Virginia had done the evening before. And who among her schoolfriends had written to her recently? And what was she going to wear today?

That morning, the morning after the birthday party, they breakfasted late. Father was more than usually preoccupied with the finances of the Augusta Line, seeming scarcely to notice when she dropped a kiss upon his newly barbered cheek. Mama, too, seemed unusually subdued, and sat with her chin resting against her hand, absently stirring her coffee. Mama, as usual, was breakfasting *en pantouffle,* in a too-youthful-looking pink *peignoir* with nothing under it but her drawers and stays, and with her hair of faded gold piled into a chignon. She only looked up when her daughter kissed her.

"Hello, my darling girl," she said. "Did you sleep well after all your efforts? I declare you must have danced every dance last night. And you even inveigled Jeff Carradine onto the floor, which is more than I've been able to do in nigh on twenty years."

Not a word about that dreadful, humiliating scene with that appalling Cambronne man. Nor, when Uncle Jeff had brought her downstairs after their solitary valse in the picture gallery (it was he who had done the inveigling, not she), had her mother alluded to the matter, though everyone in the ballroom must have seen her strike Cambronne. But Mama was like that. Nothing was ever brought out into the open and examined. Awkward topics were simply not discussed. Virginia guessed that already her mother was halfway to persuading herself that her darling daughter had not made a scene at her birthday ball.

"Thanks, I slept quite well, Mama," she replied, and addressed herself to a croissant.

"Well, I was woken early," said Augusta Holt. "Which is inconsiderate when one considers that my head never touched the pillow till nearly four. I was woken by—would you believe?—a message from Lucy Winterburn."

"Mmmm," commented Virginia, and stifled a yawn. Lucky Mama, to have slept by four o'clock; she herself had lain wakeful long after, with the vision of a mocking face before her. But not to think of that . . .

"She sent her maid," said Augusta Holt. "Lucy Winterburn sent her maid, with instructions that I was to be woken, would you believe? Do you hear that, Cyrus? Cyrus, I'm talking to you."

Virginia thought: I suppose it will be inevitable that I shall see him again, since he's now one of Father's captains. Well, at least I shall not make any effort to anticipate the meeting. When next our paths cross will be soon enough for me. I am no Suzanne Duveen, to go flaunting myself to every man who catches my fancy.

Cyrus T. Holt looked up from his balance sheet. "What did you say, Augusta?" he asked uninterestedly.

Virginia smiled to herself. Her mother sighed and said: "Lucy Winterburn sent to say that Josh didn't come home last night. What do you think of that?"

Holt shrugged. Of all his business acquaintances, Virginia guessed that her father liked Winterburn least of all—and with some justification. The man was a walking bogeyman.

"Perhaps he spent the rest of the night at his club," said Holt. "Or with some woman."

"Cyrus!" A bright pink spot appeared on each of his wife's smooth cheeks. She flashed a sidelong glance at her daughter, and, meeting Virginia's ready smile, looked hastily away. "How can you say such things in front of . . . ?"

"Josh Winterburn was a womanizing rakehell in his youth and has turned to God knows what vices since," declared Holt. "This is known to everybody in town, including his wife and yourself. And also the servants—which means that every child with a pair of ears to put to the kitchen door knows it also. And if it isn't common knowledge among the pupils of Miss Hornbuckle's dancing academy they must all be walking around with cotton wool stuffed in their ears. And speaking of Josh Winterburn reminds me that I need to send a message to Captain Cambronne. Ring for Joseph, will you, Virginia honey?"

Virginia obediently tinkled the table bell, conscious as she did so that the mention of *that* name had made her breath quicken and her pulse race. Joseph the footman, being summoned, was told by his master to fetch secretary Needham, who arrived by the time Virginia had managed to bring her involuntary responses under some sort of control by drinking half a cup of hot coffee.

"Sir?" Needham was young, thin, pale, intense and, surprisingly—in spite of his private erotic fantasy, in which he robbed himself of sleep by nightly making love to his employer's daughter—quite efficient.

"Uriah, I want you to take a message to Captain Cambronne right away. You know his lodgings, I guess?"

"Yessir," said the secretary. He cast a sidelong glance in Virginia's direction and was elated—then instantly confused—to see that she was gazing at him with lips half-parted, and with a dewy-eyed intensity the like of which she had never bestowed on him before. "That's—er—the Lincolnshire Arms in South Street."

"Well, get you straight away to the Lincolnshire Arms," said Holt. "My compliments to Captain Cambronne and will he present himself at Nogg's Wharf to make the acquaintance of his ship this afternoon? It had best be pretty late this afternoon"—the shipowner took out his pocket watch—"I've an appointment with the Governor at three. Call it an hour with him. Another hour to the wharf. I'll see Cambronne there at around five o'clock. You bring him along, Uriah, Call for him at the Lincolnshire Arms at four and take him there in a carriage. Right?"

"Very well, sir." The secretary bowed. "Mrs. Holt. Miss Virginia."

Virginia quietly exhaled a lungful of breath that she had been holding throughout her father's instructions to Uriah Needham.

The Lincolnshire Arms . . . !

She knew the place. Had never set foot inside, of course, but it was a familiar landmark on the slope of South Street. Not the sort of place that a respectable woman would enter. But who recognizes a respectable woman under a large bonnet and a veil?

She trembled at the thought. It was madness. Why, she hated the man . . .

"Well, anyhow," said Augusta Holt, "poor Lucy is real het up about Josh. She must be, mustn't she?—to have me woken up in the early hours."

How like Mama, thought Virginia, to break in upon one's dark and secret thoughts with such trivialities.

The Lincolnshire Arms in South Street was, as its name implied, a relic of colonial days. Built in the early years of the Puritan immigration and for a long time a temperance hostelry, after the War of Independence it became a regular posting-house, with rooms for lodging, a decent taproom and a fair reputation as a chop-house.

Cambronne had a room with windows overlooking the coach-yard, and views over the opposite rooftop as far as the sweep of gray ocean beyond Telegraph Hill.

After his efforts of the previous night, he slept in late, rising to take a breakfast of ham and eggs washed down with a small beer at ten. It was during this repast that he received the call from his employer's secretary, and was glad to agree to their assignation that afternoon. The thought of setting eyes on and treading the deck of the super-vessel of such amazing provenance filled him with a strange elation. And to think that such a ship was his to command! He drank deeply of his small beer and rejoiced. Hard upon the heels of the departed secretary came another messenger: this time an urchin from the waterfront, who declared that he had been instructed to demand ten cents from Captain Cambronne in return for his pains, and, on receipt of the coin, promptly produced a note from his ragged pocket.

Cambronne took the note to his room and, upon unfastening the seal, found that it was penned in a sprawling italic hand that spoke of education lightly borne, or a refinement of mind grown mildewed with misuse. The opening phrase revealed that it was from the man they knew as Jack the Cat:

> The Waterfront
> Dawn, or thereabouts
>
> My dear Captain,
>
> Your crewman has not wasted the last hour, but has repaired to a common seamen's lodging where at present abide six good topmen who lately sailed with the present writer in the *Dainty* brig out of Charleston, the captain of some having put a bullet through his brain. You will accept my assurance, of course *(verbum sapienti satis est),* that these men will admirably suit yr. needs. They, on the other hand, have duly accepted by assurances *memine contradicente* regarding your own character.
>
> I am at yr. service. A message to the Lobster Pot will summon me within the hour.
>
> I remain, sir,
> Yr. obdt. servant,
> Jack Smith, known as Jack the Cat

Cambronne was digesting this missive, and congratulating himself that he had, in one stroke, enlarged his crew list from zero to seven, when a knock upon the door announced the proprietor of the establishment, who, with sundry sly looks and buttonholing gestures, gave him to understand that there was a visitor inquiring for Captain Cambronne. And when Cambronne bade the fellow show him up, coyly let slip the detail that the visitor was a lady. Cambronne, intrigued, yielded to the landlord's unspoken importunities to the tune of a silver dollar slipped into his none-too-clean palm, and the fellow departed to direct the visitor upstairs.

In the time before her approaching footsteps halted outside his door, and before, after a brief and pregnant pause, there came a tap upon the panel, the Jerseyman, having examined all the options, had discarded all but two: his visitor must either be the little whore who had shared his pew and drunk with him the previous night, or—a long shot, this—the dark-haired chit whose winnings he had been part-responsible for securing had somehow got hold of the name of his lodgings and was calling to give her belated thanks. In words—or in kind.

He opened the door.

She wore a bonnet with heavy veiling, and was quite clearly neither of the girls of the previous night, for her clothing was of the most expensive imaginable—or so it seemed to his untutored eye. She wore a day-gown of silk, striped in dark blue and dusty gold, whose tight bodice suavely revealed the mysteries of her upper torso. The mittened hand that she extended to his was slightly damp in the palm, and he could have sworn that it trembled.

"Good morning," he said. "Won't you come in and take a seat?"

"Thank you."

There being no other seat in the austerely appointed room but an armchair by the window, Cambronne ushered his visitor to this and stood over her. He saw her give a swift glance of apprehension down into the busy coach-yard, in reponse to which he drew one of the shutters part closed, shielding her from the sight of anyone who might have chanced to look up.

"To whom am I indebted for this kind morning call?" asked Cambronne gently, noting how she started at his voice.

"I—I scarcely know how to begin . . ."

"Do I know you, ma'am?" he asked.

"Yes," she whispered.

"Ah!"

"We have met only once," she said. "But I believe—I sincerely hope—that you will know me instantly."

Whereupon she untied the ribbon of her bonnet and removed the voluminous and concealing headgear, veil and all, shaking out her sleek blond hair that was gathered in ringlets at the nape and about the ears.

"Ah!" exclaimed Cambronne. And again: *"Ah!"*

She smiled. Her lips—and he supposed that it was done in deference to what she no doubt presumed to be the convention for a visit of such a kind—were painted, and her lashes darkened with kohl.

"You *do* know me!" she breathed.

"Of course," replied Cambronne. "What man could forget, even after so short an acquaintance?"

The somewhat clumsy gallantry of his response seemed to unnerve her, and it was as if she became suddenly aware of the paint and the kohl, perhaps of the busy, milling throng in the coach-yard below the shuttered window. In any event, she avoided his eye.

"I—I came about Virginia," she said. "To apologize."

"To apologize?"

"For her quite dreadful behavior last night. I saw it all, you see. And I divined the reason for it. It was to make her beau jealous that she monopolized you all evening. You mustn't blame Virginia, Captain Cambronne, she's very young and . . ."

"Mrs. Holt, I beg you—" She gave a guilty start when he addressed her by her style, so he instantly amended it: "Dear lady, I perfectly understood Miss Virginia's behavior, which I attributed to the cause you mentioned. I took not the slightest offense, either then or later. The young—one must make tremendous allowances, always, for the innocent vagaries of the young. Don't you think, ma'am?"

She looked relieved. "Oh, yes, Captain Cambronne. And Virginia, she is very young, you know. Young, even, for her age. And I was younger than she is now, you know, when I had her. Would you believe that?"

"Difficult though it might be," said Cambronne, "I have to accept the fact. The evidence is before me. You look like her sister."

A post-horn sketched out a fruitlessly ambitious flourish in the yard below. With a clatter of hooves and rattle of iron tires, a stagecoach rolled out of the archway to the loud farewells of the departing and their friends.

"Well, that's that," said Augusta Holt. "I've done what I came for. What my conscience dictated."

She got up. They faced each other. She began to tremble.

"Won't you take coffee while you're here?" he asked.

"Oh, yes," she said. And, after a moment's reflection, "Do you mean that we go down to—the public room?"

"That won't be necessary," said Cambronne. "One of the serving wenches could bring it up to us here."

"A serving wench!" Her china-blue eyes widened with alarm. "Oh, I really don't think I want coffee after all, Captain Cambronne. I think I had better go."

"So soon?" he murmured.

Her eyes avoided his. "Yes. It was very—indiscreet of me to visit you here," she whispered.

He shrugged. Grinned. "Perhaps," he said.

She took a deep breath. "But I had to see you," she said. "To explain and apologize about Virginia. And since I happened to be passing this way . . ."

"What more natural?" said Cambronne.

"I was visiting," she said. "In addition to helping my husband with his splendid work for the Anti-Slavery Society, I also visit the sick and needy. So . . ."

"The sick and needy," said Cambronne. "Very commendable, ma'am."

"So I—I thought to kill two birds with one . . ."

"With one stone?"

"Yes," whispered Augusta Holt. She gave a sharp intake of breath as his hands came up to the neck of her bodice, from which a line of pearl buttons described the proud profile of her upper torso as far as her tightly corseted waist. And watched in mute fascination as he unhurriedly proceeded to undo them.

She woke to the sound of a distant clock chiming the half-hour, and thought nothing of it till the realization of where she was and with whom returned to her sleep-lulled mind. She sat up in bed with a start, covering her bare breasts with both hands and stealing a glance to the figure by her side.

Cambronne was still asleep, one bronze, dark-pelted arm sprawled over the coverlet. His head was turned away from her. He was breathing lightly and steadily.

Half past the hour. But half past *what* hour? She remembered that her fob watch was still pinned by its gold clasp to the front of her bodice, and the striped day-gown lay with her other things, where they had been thrown, at the far corner of the room; and she, who had been taught at her prim boarding school for young ladies always to put away her clothes nicely, would normally, lady's maid or no lady's maid, never have dreamed of undressing without applying the golden rule of her girlhood: outer clothes on hangers and dirty linen in the laundry basket.

She must find out the time. Now. Immediately. It might still be quite early. Early enough to be home for luncheon and invite no comment. But how to cross over to the other side of the room with not a stitch on? Supposing—as was most likely—she disturbed *him?* And no question of, say, wrapping the coverlet around herself, for it was trapped under his hand and arm, and its slightest movement would wake him.

But what if it was not early? What if—the thought sent her mind in dizzy spirals—what if it was half past three, and with Uriah Needham calling here, as she well knew, at four?

She was out of bed on the instant, careless of the creak of the bedspring and the sound of her feet padding on the parquet. She snatched up the candy-striped gown, fumbling for the fob watch.

With a sense of blessed relief she saw the time was half past one. Too late to get back home for luncheon, but not too late to matter . . .

She then became aware that Cambronne was awake and watching her. Hastily she held the gown before her, covering as much of her nakedness as she was able.

"What time is it?" he asked.

"Half past one."

"Still quite early."

"Yes."

"We've two hours, Augusta. Come back to bed."

His manner conquered her: the smile that was compounded of tenderness and admiration; the extended hand. Added to that was her awareness—overlaid since her awakening by her sudden terror about the hour—of a sense of well-being the like of which she had never before experienced in her life. She dropped the gown back onto the floor and went to join him, taking his extended hand and allowing him to draw her close against his male, muscular hardness. They lay eye to eye, mouths almost touching, hearts beating one against the other.

"I'm a wicked woman," she whispered.

"Yes," said Cambronne.

"But I wouldn't have you think that I do—this—all the time."

"It never entered my head," said Cambronne.

"My husband, though not a husband to me in the full sense of the word, is very good to me," she said.

"That I can well imagine."

"You wouldn't believe the depth of Cyrus's kindness. Why, even with all the worry and responsibility of running the shipping line, he still works himself to death for the Anti-Slavery Society."

"Yes, so I've heard. Mr. Holt is a true philanthropist."

"Only—as I said"—she traced a line with her fingertip across his chest—"we don't live together as man and wife. Nor have we since Virginia was born. And you are the first man I have known since then. Does that surprise you, Jason Cambronne? Or did you find me—inexperienced and woefully inadequate?"

His arm tightened about her waist, fingertips probing the deep cleft at the small of her back. She gave a moan against his ear and pressed herself closer to him.

"Experience," said Cambronne, "invariably blunts the keen edge of enthusiasm. Adequacy, one simply has or has not; it is a matter of ardor. Do you feel yourself to be ardent, Augusta?"

"Yes, oh yes!" she whispered. "Don't stop doing what you're doing, I beg of you."

Their dalliance continued, protracted by the knowledge that time was of no consequence. And they talked. She must probe her lover in every way possible. Did he admire her complexion? Her hair? For a woman of thirty-five who had borne a child and given suck, did she not still have a mighty fine bosom? And she was emboldened to sit up in bed so that he could judge for himself; nor was she contented with that, but took his hand and commanded it to touch, to weigh each generous orb, to caress the swollen nipples.

Having satisfied herself that he admired her wholly, she turned her attention to him. He had had, of course, many women. Cambronne admitted as much, saying that he was no more, or less, than any other man in respect of appetites. She was quite satisfied with his reply, grateful even.

"But have you loved, Jason Cambronne?" she asked. "Has there been one woman above all others for you?"

She felt him stiffen in her arms, his whole body becoming alien and withdrawn where formerly it had insinuated itself against her, matching contour for contour as hers had done to his. She drew back, so as to see him more clearly. He was not looking at her: the gray eyes were stormy and fixed upon an inner vision.

"My dear, I have offended you!" she whispered. "I had no right to ask that. Jason, I beg you—look at me. Say that I am forgiven. Please . . ."

And she, who had no practiced wiles, no cunning with men, but only the new awareness of her body's use and an assurance freshly flowered in Jason Cambronne's arms and in the light of his fastidious tenderness, sought to assuage the hurt she had given by the only way she knew. Let him withdraw from her; then she would pursue him. Let his arms slacken about her; then she would hold him more tightly than ever. If his lips avoided hers, she would take his face in her hands and win those lips.

His response, when it came, at first delighted, then appalled her. His taking of her, so at variance with the first time, when he had borne her to the skies in a chariot of fire and brought her back to earth on swansdown, was brutal, short and uttterly selfish. The rutting done, he sprang from the bed and, crossing naked to the window, looked out across the rooftops to where the line of ocean glinted in the afternoon sunlight beyond Telegraph Hill.

She lay where he had abandoned her, weeping quietly to herself.

Shortly before the appointed hour of secretary Needham's arrival, Cambronne, dressed in sea-going broadcloth and a flat cap with a band of tarnished braid, quitted the Lincoln-shire Arms and went in search of a jeweler's shop. He found one two blocks from his lodging.

"What is your pleasure, sir?" asked the jeweler.

"I would like you to mend—this," said Cambronne. And unfolding a bandana upon the counter, revealed a broken gold chain, on the center of which was attached a pendant of dark red stone.

The jeweler took it up, stuck a magnifying glass in his eye and examined the chain closely.

He sucked air through his teeth. "Oh, I don't know, sir. Take some time to fix this. Both links broken, you see, sir. Your lady wife must have given it a mighty powerful wrench."

"How long?" demanded Cambronne.

Another sucking sound. "About a week, sir. This is very fine workmanship, this chain. Twenty-two-carat gold in the bargain. Odd, to see such a fine chain on what's only a semi-precious stone, but then the garnet's her birthstone, eh, sir?"

"Quite so," said Cambronne. "July. Yesterday's date, to be exact."

The man's eye—the one without the magnifying glass—flashed him a suspicious glance.

"Not July," he said. "A garnet, that's the birthstone for January."

"Is it?" said Cambronne blandly. "Then we've been mistaken all this time. How long did you say—about a week? Put the work in hand, will you? Good afternoon to you."

When he arrived back at the Lincolnshire Arms, Uriah Needham was waiting for him outside the coach-yard in a two-horse town phaeton.

Augusta Holt had quitted the place half an hour since.

The drive to Nogg's Wharf took them through Charlestown, skirting the busy commercial docks with the forests of masts and rigging, to the quiet backwater of Chelsea River, which sheltered numerous small ship- and boat-building yards.

They journeyed in silence most of the way, exchanging only the commonplace coinage of casual conversation. Needham handled the two quite spirited horses with some expertise, a fact of which he seemed well aware, for Cambronne detected —or thought he detected—a certain smugness in the young man's manner. It was not till they reached the lane that served as a towpath along the riverbank that their desultory conversation took a disquieting turn.

"Are you comfortable in your lodgings, Captain?" asked Needham.

"It's adequate," replied Cambronne. "More room than on shipboard, but not so homely."

"But it suits all tastes," said the other.

"I don't follow you."

The secretary smiled to himself, still looking ahead. "I mean, the landlord's not too particular about comings and goings," he said. "Broadminded, you might say."

"Just what are you getting at?" demanded Cambronne.

Again the smug, tight-lipped smile. "I was early this afternoon," said Needham. "The traffic wasn't too heavy in the town, you see. With half an hour or so to kill, I decided to drive on past the Lincolnshire Arms and take a turn down to the waterfront."

"And?" Cambronne's voice was flat. Ice-cool.

"The bonnet and veil didn't fool me for an instant," said Needham. "Really, to have completed the disguise, Mrs. H. should have worn something new. That striped gown—she's had it for years and I'd know it anywhere. How was she in bed, Captain? I am presuming that it wasn't a social call. Not from the guilty way she darted out of that place and scurried up South Street."

"Did she see you observing her?" asked Cambronne.

"No, Captain. Put your chivalrous heart at ease. The lady is of the opinion that her little peccadillo went unnoticed."

"What now, then?" demanded Cambronne. "Is this a prelude to blackmail?"

"Blackmail?" The young man's pale and indeterminate eyes turned to regard his passenger. The pale, long face was pinched with an expression of indignation, and Cambronne remembered the tag about hypocrisy being the homage that vice pays to virtue. "That is a perfectly scandalous suggestion, Captain. I am an honest man. A hard-working man, who has—in the phrase—dragged himself up from genteel poverty by his boot straps."

"But . . .?"

The pale gaze wavered. "But, Captain, I am an ambitious man, and though I have come a fair distance in my occupation there is a long way, yet, for me to go. And along the way, I take every opportunity of making as many useful friends as possible."

"Among whom you now wish to number me?" said Cambronne.

"I know a little," said Needham, "a very little, of what you are about—you and my employer. One would not have to be adept at reading a balance sheet to know that there is more to the Augusta Line than shipping grain and dry goods to Plymouth, Brest and Lisbon. I do not ask to know what you are about, Captain—indeed, it seems to me that I could put myself in very grave danger by inquiring too closely as to what you are about. All I ask, Captain, is that you remember that you owe me a favor."

"And what favor is that?"

"The favor of—my silence."

Cambronne did not reply. Nor did they exchange another word till, a mile or so further up the north bank of the Chelsea River, they came upon a towering pinewood fence that was only slightly overtopped by the last few feet of a schooner's twin mastheads.

"Nogg's Wharf," said Needham, and in the tone of voice he might have used if they had had the weather and the price of bread as the principal burden of their conversation. "And yonder lies your ship, Captain Cambronne."

* * *

Entry into Nogg's Wharf (and, surely, thought Cambronne, secretary Needham's name must be known to everyone within, and furthermore their arrival was expected) was not a matter of knock and enter, but of an exchange of passwords, a careful scrutiny by a jaundiced eye through a Judas window, an unlocking, a mighty rattle of securing chains.

The afternoon sunlight behind him cast Jason Cambronne's long shadow before. It shone upon the group of figures regarding him: his employer, Cyrus J. Holt, a bent, and bearded oldster wearing a battered tall hat. And Virginia Holt.

"Right on time, Captain," declared Holt. "We beat you by only five minutes, isn't that right, Virginia?"

"Just so, Daddy," she replied. "Hello, Captain Cambronne. I trust I see you well—and that your late-night business did not prove too strenuous." Her voice carried an edge of mockery.

She was dressed in riding-out habit of rifle green: tightly fitting tunic frogged with black cord, narrow skirts, boots, a rakish hat with a curly brim. Her spun-gold tresses (how like her mother's, he thought, as they had lain across his face) were drawn back into a severe chignon at the nape, with a teasing array of corkscrew curls before each tiny ear.

"This," said Cyrus J. Holt, "is Mr. Walberswick, the naval architect whose acquaintance I have only just had the pleasure of making. The builder of the ship in question"—he pointed, and quite unnecessarily, for, after seeing Virginia Holt, Cambronne's eyes had flashed immediately to it—"*your* ship, Captain Cambronne."

The schooner lay under bare poles by the jetty. Cambronne's first reaction was that of mild disappointment; the legendary brainchild of the Venetian Vincenzo Alfieri looked, to all intents and purposes, just like any other schooner: two-masted, neat and tidy at bow and stern, a shallow-draughter undoubtedly, and useful in shoal waters. But capable of dealing with, and besting, a cloud of navy frigates . . . ?

"Don't be fooled by the externals, Captain." The remark came from the bearded oldster in the tall hat, the naval architect Walberswick. His observation was interrupted by a fit of racking coughs. When he had done, the handkerchief that he had pressed against his whiskered mouth was bedabbled with bright flecks of blood. "She is not what she seems. Observe, Captain, that there is a second, and extensible, jib-boom, permitting of an area of canvas for'ard which is in excess of anything that has been carried by a ship of her tonnage since men first learned the art of sail."

"And is that vast area also balanced aft?"

"Yes," was the response.

"But, sir," said Cambronne. "Such a weight of canvas, surely, would carry any conventional schooner's hull right over when close-hauled in a stiff blow?"

Walberswick smiled, his long and ill-looking countenance appearing to find difficulty in assuming the expression. "She is no conventional schooner, Captain. Which is why, before her keel was laid down and before ever a nail was hammered, I caused yonder high palings to be erected, lest an idle eye chanced to discern our secret. She now lies in the water, her nether secret hidden." He coughed. "What would you reckon to be her draught, Captain?"

Cambronne's practiced eye made a swift calculation of the vessel's length, took into account the height of the raking masts.

"Five feet," he said. "That *should* be my answer. However, bearing in mind what you have told me about the area of canvas she carries, I would say considerably more. Perhaps—twice that much?"

Again that painfully assembled smile. Walberswick shook his head. "Twenty feet," he said.

"*Twenty?*" Cambronne returned his astounded gaze to the schooner. Was it conceivable?

"Think of her as a yacht, Captain," said the other. "For that was how she was conceived—well before her time—by Alfieri. In this respect, she greatly outclasses the sloop *Jefferson* which was built in 1801 for Captain George Crowninshield of Salem, and on which I worked as master shipwright. She is a yacht, with the deep iron keel of a yacht."

"That is a disadvantage," mused Cambronne.

"I concede that," admitted Walberswick. "You have the draught of a first-rater, Captain. A ship-of-the-line. But oh, what advantages you have to outweigh the draught! She carries two suits of sails. One is white, one blue. With the larger, blue suit, which acts upon her hull as on an orange pip squeezed between finger and thumb, you will reach speeds not unadjacent to—what would you say?"

"I have heard fifteen knots spoken of," said Cambronne. "But I find it difficult to believe."

Walberswick nodded. "She will do it, Captain," he said. "She has not done it yet, for I have never bent on the blue suit of sails, let alone tried them before the wind. But even in her white, smaller suit and without her great flying jib and mains'l, she can run away from every schooner on the eastern seaboard. As you will observe this afternoon."

At this, Virginia Holt, who, like her father and secretary Needham, had been listening to the exchange between Cambronne and the shipbuilder, clapped her hands like a child anticipating a treat. "And may I come too, Papa? May I, please?"

"You must ask Captain Cambronne," replied Holt. "I am merely the owner, and Mr. Walberswick the builder. The schooner is now his to command, and all who sail in her."

Virginia pouted prettily and addressed herself to Cambronne.

He grinned. "Of course you may come, Miss Virginia," he said. "The maiden voyage of my new command will be greatly enlivened by your presence."

The compliment seemed to please her, though she had clearly not enjoyed being made to ask a favor of Jason Cambronne.

"I have the men bending on the white suit of sails, sir," said Walberswick, addressing Holt. "It will not take long. Would you and your party like some tea—or maybe something a little stronger?"

"Tea will suit me admirably," said the ship-owner. "With something stronger added as makeweight."

Walberswick smiled thinly. "Very risible, sir. Very risible, I'm sure. Will you please step this way?"

He led the party to a gangplank which brought them to the upper deck of the vessel, where a gang of half a dozen men were attaching a startlingly white mainsail to the long boom of the mainmast. They looked up as their employer and his guests went past them toward the poop, then returned their eyes to the task they were about.

Cambronne and Virginia were at the tail-end of the group, he having assisted her up the gangplank with a hand at her elbow. It seemed to him that she was deliberately tarrying behind in order to speak with him. When they reached the steps of a companionway leading down to the after quarters, she turned to him.

"I have not forgiven you, Captain, for disobeying my wishes last night," she said. "Nor for making me lose my temper."

"The business I was about, Miss Virginia, while not so pleasurable as dancing with the belle of the ball, had a certain importance that justified my conduct," said Cambronne.

"Indeed? A very odd, late hour, wouldn't you say? Was there, perhaps, a lady concerned in this business?"

"Only incidentally, ma'am," said Cambronne.

"Ha. And afterward you returned to your lodgings, since by then it was too late, or surely you would have come back to the ball."

"That is so."

"And slept the clock round, I shouldn't wonder?"

"Some of the time, I slept," said Cambronne, adding gravely: "And some of the time I did not."

The after quarters of the schooner were, considering the beam of the craft, tolerably spacious, and tricked out with no regard to expense in matters of workmanship and materials. Walberswick was swift to point out that the scantlings were of oak and teak, the paneling of bird's eye maple, the deck similarly of teak; nor was there an ounce of iron in her; all the fittings were of copper or brass.

The captain's living cabin occupied the after end of the space, with a handsome bow window looking out from the stern. There were three more windows at the side, each of them admitting light into the living cabin and two smaller compartments one each side of it, one for the captain, the other for the first officer.

The furnishings were spare, plain and excellently well made. There was an oblong table in dark oak that was securely fastened to the deck. Round it were six chairs, and it was upon these that the party took their places, while a Negro steward brought in a silver tray of tea and a tantalus of spirits.

"It is my intentions, with your approval, Captain, to take her out as far as Long Island Head this afternoon. Do you know Boston and its approaches?"

"I do not, Mr. Walberswick," replied Cambronne.

"No matter, we have excellent charts, and you will swiftly

become . . ." He broke off with a start, as there was a reverberating crash upon the deck for'ard, followed by a yell of pain.

"What was that?" cried Virginia Holt. "Did someone fall down from the mast?"

"Stay here, Miss Virginia," said Cambronne, who was already on his feet and following Walberswick to the companionway.

The scene that greeted their eyes when they gained the upper deck did not permit of a rapid comprehension. The foot of the mainsail, which had by then been attached to the boom, was flapping idly in the breeze, unattended by the group of men who stood regarding one of their number—a cadaverous fellow with a lantern jaw and eyes that burned like coals under the jutting promontory of his beetled brows. And he was holding forth in a deep and sepulchral voice that had the ring of a preacher's.

"The abomination of blasphemy!" he boomed. "This servant of the Lord will not abide the tongue of blasphemy. Just as I have smitten Ebenezer Harker, so will I heap mischiefs upon them, I will spend mine arrows upon them— Deuteronomy, Chapter 32, Verse 23." At the conclusion of this declaration he stooped and picked up by the collar of his jerkin a fellow who, from his fearful looks and air of injury, was clearly he who had made heavy contact with the deck.

"O Ebenezer Harker," boomed his tormentor, "nor you, nor others will utter blasphemy in the presence of this servant of the Lord. This servant is aware of such as you, Ebenezer Harker, being lovers of their own selves, covetous, boasters, proud, blasphemers, disobedient to parents, unthankful, unholy. Without natural affection, trucebreakers, false accusers, incontinent—Second Epistle to Timothy, Chapter 3, Verse 2 and part of 4. Do you mark what I say, Ebenezer Harker?"

"Yes, Tobias," wailed the unhappy Harker.

"Then get you to your labors," retorted the other. "For the Psalmist tells us that the Lord rendereth to every man according to his work, and there may yet be health in you, Ebenezer Harker."

So saying, he set the other man back upon his feet, and himself turned to gather up the swag of flapping sail and bring it under control.

Cambronne and Walberswick, who had been spectators of this encounter from the top of the companionway, exchanged glances, and the shipbuilder shrugged.

"Tobias Angel up to his bible-thumping ways again," he said. "Still, he keeps the men at it. Best foreman of the yard I ever had, for all his shortcomings."

"He interests me," said Cambronne. "What is his background? Seaman?"

"Bosun of a deep-water Indianman," said Walberswick. "Out in the China trade. They say he was wrecked and spent three years alone on a bit of an island and went half-crazy in consequence. Anyways, he took up hellfire religion. And drink. The religion I can abide, but I advise everyone to run for cover when Tobias has been at the bottle."

"And he'll be coming out with us today?"

"He'll act as bosun," said Walberswick. "To tell the truth, he regards this schooner as his own, and has done since the keel was laid." He looked closely at Cambronne. "You're not telling me that you want to take him on permanently?"

"I might," said Cambronne. "I might at that—if you can bear to part with him."

The shipbuilder was taken with a racking fit of coughing and did not reply.

"She must be named!" declared Virginia Holt.

The sails were all bent on, and the schooner was edging gently into midstream on her headsails. Tobias Angel was at the wheel.

"A capital idea, Virginia," said her father. "What do you think of that, Cambronne? A naming ceremony, such as she should have had at her launching."

"With champagne!" cried Virginia. "Oh, Daddy, we should have brought a bottle of champagne with us."

"Don't suppose you have such a thing aboard, Mr. Walberswick?" asked the ship-owner.

Walberswick shook his head. "All I can offer is the best part of a bottle of gin, sir," he said.

"Then that will have to suffice," said Holt. "Now—what shall be her name, Virginia?"

"The *Argo*," she replied, with a sidelong glance at Cambronne. "What other name could one possibly give her, considering her captain's given name."

"Jason and the Golden Fleece!" exclaimed the ship-owner. "The voyage of the *Argo*. A spendid idea, Virginia. What do you say, Jason Cambronne?"

"I am deeply honored, sir," said Cambronne, and the two men shook hands. Uriah Needham, who was standing at the taffrail, met Cambronne's eyes as they made the salutation. His lip curled in a smirk.

And so the *Argo* was named in Chelsea River, as she sailed with barely a foot to spare under her deep keel—on the first of the ebb, taking wind in her swan-white wings, gathering speed, so that the water hissed and creamed at her sharp stem. Virginia Holt went up into the bows to perform the ceremony, and one of the men brought the opened bottle of gin with a length of codline tied to it. Swinging it on the end of the line, the girl broke the bottle against the bows at water level.

"Haul taut your sheets, men!" said Walberswick, acting as Master for the occasion of the *Argo's* first sea-trial with her captain. "Steer sou'-sou'-east, Tobias Angel."

"Sou'-sou'-east it is, sir!" responded the religious zealot at his wheel. Tobias Angel had looked with some disapproval upon the naming ceremony, though whether by reason of the waste of good gin or on account of the heathenish name that his beloved vessel had been given he gave no indication.

They were now passing down the main ship-channel, with Charlestown on the starboard and East Boston on the larboard. The *Argo* must certainly have attracted some attention and speculation from the boatyards and wharfs that lined both sides; but, as Cambronne had first discerned, the schooner looked like any other schooner, with no hint of the power that lay below her waterline and in her sail-locker. It was with this thought in mind that he went to join Walberswick, who was standing in the waist. Holt was trying, and with no discernible success, to engage the helmsman in conversation. His daugher and secretary were by the taffrail, where Virginia was pointing out the passing landmarks—to Needham's obvious pleasure.

"The other suit of sails, Mr. Walberswick," said Cambronne. "The blue suit. I presume that you had specific orders not to show them afloat in Boston Harbor and its approaches."

Walberswick jammed his tall hat more firmly down over his

straggling gray locks as a gust of wind took the schooner. His ill-looking eyes were shrewd.

"I think you are on what the legal gentry call a 'fishing expedition,' Captain," he said.

"That's right," said Cambronne.

"To find out how much I know about the reason for this schooner being built in the first place?"

"Something like that."

"Well, this much I'll tell you, Captain, and with pleasure," said Walberswick. "I had my orders to build this vessel in secret, and have been well paid for my pains, as have all my craftsman. And my orders are not from Mr. Holt, who I never saw before this day, and who I am now informed is the owner of this vessel. That's all I know, and it's all I want to know. Wait—I'm an old man, with not much time left"—here he tapped his chest—"being far gone in the consumption. But an old and dying man is surely entitled to a touch of curiosity. Will you answer me one thing, Captain?"

"Ask it, Mr. Walberswick," said Cambronne.

The shipbuilder jerked a thumb to the ship's side, to the stout bulwarks with their capping of varnished pine.

"This thing you're at," he said. "When you'll be wearing the blue suit of sails and showing a clean pair of heels to every other ship afloat—will there be cannon lined up along those bulwarks?"

"Yes."

"And swivel-guns to the number of dozen set fore and aft?"

"That is correct."

The shipbuilder smote a fist into the palm of his other hand. "I knew it!" he declared. I knew there was devilry afoot, God help me! Alfieri's plans, you see, allowed for eight cannon and a dozen swivel-guns as extra top-hamper. When I first conferred with—with those who commissioned me to build the schooner, I pointed out that, by disregarding the guns, I could make a better adjustment betwixt draught and sail area. I was told to stick to Signor Alfieri's original conception."

The *Argo,* taking a southerly wind, was sailing close-hauled and scarcely heeling in a stiff blow. A few white-capped wavelets, smacking against her speeding bows, were reduced to a million flying droplets that hung in the air and made rainbows. Not a drop came aboard.

"The weight of cannon will give her even greater stability," said Cambronne. "Far better that you have stuck to the Venetian's plan."

"'Tis a terrible thing for a dying man to contemplate facing his Maker with blood on his hands," said Walberswick. "Tell me true, Captain. Is it piracy that you're to be at in this schooner?"

"Not piracy."

"What then?"

"You asked to put one question to me, Mr. Walberswick, and that I answered. There's no more."

Walberswick coughed agonizingly, dabbed his lips with the blood-flecked handkerchief. "I have known men in all shapes and persuasions, Captain," he said at length. "And I reckon I can make a good summation of a man's character from the way he talks, the way he bears himself, the observations that he makes about others." The sick eyes scanned the Jersey-man's countenance. "And I wouldn't say, from what I've seen of you in this short time, that you'd be in the killing game. Not for profit of money."

"Then that must be your consolation, must it not, Mr. Walberswick?" returned the other. "With that thought in your mind, you may address yourself to the early prospect of meeting your Maker with a clean conscience and clean hands. Exactly how much were you paid to build this vessel, Mr. Walberswick? And how much extra for your silence?"

Half shifty, half prideful, the sick man's eyes met the Jerseyman's.

"That is no concern of yours, Captain," he whispered.

"Then, as I have said, Mr. Walberswick," retorted Cambronne, "the questioning between us is at an end." He turned on his heel and strode back to the poop.

By now, *Argo* had won free of the river and was sailing, still close-hauled, down the main ship-channel, sweeping past barges and wherries as if they had been standing still, outpacing the busy river traffic like a greyhound in full chase. Nor did the helmsman need to do more than give a light correction from time to time, as, for instance, when a large and heavily laden barge, passing upriver, made a slight swell and caused the schooner's bow to pay off a point. And he was steering with only one hand on the big wheel.

Cambronne nodded to Holt and walked past him to the rail, looking for'ard and aloft. The schooner was handling well with only a crew of five and a helmsman. But this was in relatively sheltered water, and under her normal canvas. Later, things would be different . . .

Later, when she was working out from—say, Jamaica—and under full press of sail from her blue suit, with eight cannon and smaller arms to man, things would be vastly different. Then she would need her full compliment of seventy-odd.

Seventy-odd, of which he had as yet secured seven, plus a thought of taking on the ex-bosun of religious persuasion and alcoholic impulse.

But things were on the move . . .

Walberswick addressed no more than a few words to Cambronne for the remainder of the evening. There was scarcely any need. The crew's handling of the vessel was exemplary. On a chart-table close by the wheel that had a tarpaulin cover against the weather, the shipbuilder indicated his intended course with the tip of a pair of dividers and marched off the distances with the same. Cambronne merely nodded agreement.

The Jerseyman, with nearly two-thirds of his life as a seagoing officer and navigator, could read a chart with the speed, accuracy and attention to detail with which a woman can size up, put a price to and finally demolish a rival's ballgown. He noted that the shipbuilder, having demonstrated the schooner's abilities when close-hauled, was following it with a run on a westerly course to the northernmost tip of an island designated Long Island, where a hundred-foot crag rose steeply above wave-torn rocks: a run of about two sea-miles, with the wind almost on the starboard beam.

And what a triumphant run it was! Halfway to Long Island Head, they came up on, and overtook, a fat-bellied cutter with a man and a dog huddled over the tiller at the taffrail. Neither man nor dog saw, heard or suspected the approach of the white-sailed schooner till she was upon them and slicing past. The dog barked. The man at the tiller could only stand and stare, open-mouthed.

Walberswick busied himself during the run by supervising the measuring of their speed. This was done by the time-honored method of throwing overboard a piece of wood attached to a line on which were a number of equally spaced knots, so that the number of knots that passed over the taffrail gave the vessel's speed.

A dozen times he ordered the maneuver to be repeated. Not till he had done this, added the results together and taken the mean, did he make the brief announcement to Cambronne:

"Over a run of a mile—ten and a half knots!"

Cambronne nodded acknowledgment. Ten and a half on a broad reach, that was something. It beggared the imagination to think what the *Argo* might achieve with that suit of blue sails, close-hauled and in a really stiff breeze!

They came close to Long Island Head, close enough to see the jetty with men fishing from it, the tall wooden lighthouse, the fangs of rock at the base, a small child paddling in a rock pool.

"Ready about!" ordered Walberswick. "Lee Ho!"

Tobias Angel had relinquished the wheel to Ebenezer Harker, that same wretched creature whom he had lately been obliged to chastise for blasphemy. It had been an injudicious move, for Harker, whether by the weight of his sin or as a direct result of his late chastisement, was inattentive to the order. And for a ship sailing at ten and a half knots and heading for a rocky shore, the moment's inattention was a recipe for disaster.

"Put up your helm, man!" screamed Walberswick, choking on a mouthful of sudden blood.

Tobias Angel was already halfway to the wheel by the time the unhappy Harker had spun the spokes. A blow from the zealot's big fist sent the helmsman staggering into an inert heap in the scuppers. The *Argo* went about like a racehorse, sails all a-flutter.

"Let draw!" croaked Walberswick.

At the same instant, the schooner struck rock.

It was like—it was like no other sensation on earth. One moment, the *Argo* was a creature of the elements and at one with them: wind-borne, delicate as a hawk balanced upon its primaries, thrusting as a shark moving in to strike; next, she was just a hundred tons of nicely fashioned wood and non-ferrous metal, with two lines of wet washing flapping impotently on high; stopped still, as if by the hand of God.

"Let fly all your sheets! Let go the wheel!"

The order came from Cambronne. Lantern jaw agape, Tobias Angel did as he was bidden, and the men handling the sheets did likewise. Spilled of wind entirely, the sails lost what little impulsion they still possessed. Likewise the hull, freed of the discipline of the rudder, did what it wanted most, which was to slip back into deep water. With an audible sigh, the slim hull edged away from the rock on which the deep keel had been snagged. The sails, impatient to draw again, set up a frenzied cracking.

"Haul taut your sheets! Steady as you go, helmsman!"

The *Argo,* shaking herself like a dog newly emerged from a bath, bit her sharp stem deeply as the wind took her. Clear of danger, she went back to the way they had come. Cambronne met Walberswick's eye; the sick man's regard was grudgingly admiring.

"You're the captain, all right, sir," he said.

Cambronne watched the landscape fade behind him as swiftly as it had ever done in his twenty-two years at sea: the figures on the jetty becoming dots, then disappearing, the jetty itself gone, till all that remained was the humped island with the pointing finger of the lighthouse.

"She's a miracle," he murmured to himself. "And after all these years. A tyrant's whim. The dream child of a genius. And now she's mine—*all mine!*"

The summer's evening became over-clouded and they ran before the wind on the last leg of the voyage with the rain streaming down. Holt, Virginia and secretary Needham retired to shelter below, but Cambronne stayed on the upper deck with the rest. As also did shipbuilder Walberswick, hunched near the chart-table, skeletal hands clutching his coat-collar high against his scrawny neck, the better to keep out the sluicing rain, water pouring from the brim of his tall hat. Presently he was struck by a paroxysm of coughing, so that he had to cling to the chart-table for support in his agony.

Cambronne nodded to a seaman who stood by. "Get Mr. Walberswick below," he said. "Strip him and put him in a bunk with dry blankets."

"Aye, aye, Cap'n." The man went and took the shipbuilder by the arm. Uncomplainingly, he allowed himself to be led.

"Steady as you go, Bosun," said Cambronne. They were within sight of Nogg's Wharf.

"Steady she is, Cap'n," responded Tobias Angel. "Leave to speak out, sir?"

"Go ahead."

"Cap'n . . ." The man seemed to have difficulty in begin-

ning his speech, bereft, perhaps, of a suitably quotable text
from the Holy Book. "Cap'n . . . concerning what Mr.
Walberswick was saying to me a little back—about your
wishing to take me as regular bosun . . ."

"Mr. Walberswick has told you already?" asked Cambronne, surprised.

"That he has, Cap'n." The cadaverous gaze was fixed
appealingly upon Cambronne, the lantern jaw working from
side to side like a cow chewing cud. "And would you have
me, Cap'n, sinner as I am?"

"I don't give a damn for your sins," said Cambronne. "Just
as long as you do your duty and keep sober, you're my man."

"Cap'n . . ." Surely those burning eyes were not filling
with tears? Not a man easily embarrassed, Cambronne was
nevertheless constrained to look away. "Cap'n, there's an
evil demon within me, and that's the truth of it. And it's an
evil that only drink will release. When the evil boils up within
me, and there's that devil screaming to get out . . ."

"Steer two points to larboard," interposed Cambronne.

"Two points it is, sir. When the devil, he's screaming to get
out, sir, it's then I take to the drink. And it releases the
demon within me, Cap'n."

"Down mainsail, down foresail!" commanded Cambronne,
and bare feet pattered to do his bidding. "Steer for the jetty,
Bosun—and remember this, man." He faced the zealot
squarely and wagged a finger under the other's nose. "From
now on, you will keep away from the bottle. You will allow
that demon to remain within you, for he is your strength, your
power. Without him, you are a shiftless, drunken wreck.
Understood?"

"Understood, Cap'n. Understood, sir!" The uncomely face
was wreathed in a smile as if of deliverance.

The *Argo,* impelled by her headsails, glided sweetly toward
the jetty. The rain slackened, and Cyrus J. Holt came on deck
again, followed by Virginia and Needham.

"Well, Cambronne, and what do you think of your new
command?" demanded the ship-owner.

"Everything I could have wished," said Cambronne. "With
a hand-picked crew and a couple of weeks to work up, I'll be
able to report to you that we are ready for anything."

Holt shook his head. "A week, Captain!"

"What's this you say, sir?"

"A week from today," said Holt. "Whether you have secured a full complement of crew or no, you will sail the *Argo* to the West Indies, to Jamaica—there to await further orders from my agent resident in the British colony."

"And I am to accompany you, Captain." This from Uriah Needham, whose regarding eyes were fixed upon the Jerseyman with a secret communication which said clearly: "And you will be sorry, Captain Cambronne, if you pose any argument!"

"And I, also!" cried Virginia Holt. "Papa says it's high time that I traveled, and he has so many friends and connections in the West Indies that I am sure to have a most wonderful time." She pouted, seeing Cambronne's expression. "Oh, Captain, I beg you. Don't say that you subscribe to that silly, *silly* seaman's belief about women and parsons being unlucky travelers on shipboard!"

Before Cambronne could make reply, Uriah Needham intervened. This time, his communication was spoken aloud —and was subtly keen edged:

"Captain Cambronne will be delighted to have you aboard, Miss Virginia," he said. "That's plain to see. Indeed, why not the entire Holt family? Why not, sir?"—to his employer.

The ship-owner frowned. "Damme, Needham, you know well enough that I can't go haring off to the West Indies at the drop of a hat. My agent in Jamaica can very well look after the business interests. As for my lady wife . . ."

"Not Mama!" interrupted Virginia. "The voyage would upset her greatly. Besides—she has her work for the Anti-Slavery Society and—um . . ."

"Her *visiting*," supplied Needham. He gave Cambronne a guileless glance. "I refer, Captain, to Mrs. Holt's charitable visiting of the poor, sick and needy of our city. Though, thank heaven, Boston being a prosperous metropolis, there are happily few poor. But many who are sick. And many, Captain"—he let his glance linger—"many who are in need of solace and consolation."

"Well, that's settled," said Cyrus J. Holt. "Virginia, you will take ship, along with Needham here, in a week's time. And now, Captain Cambronne, since I observe that the gangplank is in place, my daughter and I will take our leave and proceed ashore, lest we be late for dinner."

Cambronne chewed his nether lip. And kept his peace.

* * *

Shocks for Cambronne. A shock, immediately following, for Cyrus J. Holt. In a thin splattering of rain, he and Virginia ran for their covered carriage which stood on the wharf. Cambronne and Needham followed after.

There was a messenger standing by the Holts' carriage. He had the appearance of those harbingers of ill tidings whom ancient tyrants used to put to the sword as a matter of policy. He carried an umbrella and looked as if he had been there all evening.

"Mr. Holt, sir," he essayed. "I . . ."

"Well, what is it, man?" demanded the ship-owner testily. "Can it not wait? Can't you see that my daughter and I are getting wet?"

"Sir, he's dead—dead!" cried the wretch.

"Dead—who's dead?" Holt paused in the act of leaping into the carriage ahead of his daughter.

"Why, sir—Mr. Winterburn, my master!"

"Josh Winterburn—*dead,* you say?"

"Hanged, sir!"

"Hanged?"

"Dead and stiff, sir. Found hanging by his neck from a beam in his own coach-house soon before noon today."

"Suicide, was it?" demanded Cambronne, who had heard it all.

"Why, yes, sir," responded the messenger. "What else?"

Suicide, indeed. But why, thought Cambronne, did Cyrus J. Holt turn ghastly pale, and why did his pudgy fingers stray to his own neck, as if in protection? Every man's death diminishes one; but the bell that tolled for Holt's former business associate seemed to touch Holt more nearly than most.

CHAPTER 4

Jason Cambronne had no traffic in protestations, explanations, pleas and the like. Needham had put him in check; but the game was only just begun. No Fool's Mate for any opponent of the tall Jerseyman. So it was that on their return journey he made not the slightest allusion to the fact that, by means of discreet blackmail, he had been obliged to take on two passengers, unwanted passengers at that. Indeed, he did not speak at all.

Needham gave Cambronne an uneasy glance as he alighted outside the Lincolnshire Arms, and wished him good night, to which Cambronne responded civilly enough.

Yet another shock for the captain of the *Argo*. Fate was dealing him all the low cards that eve . . .

He was thirsty, he was hungry. Above all, he was soaking wet. The prospect of a strip wash all over with warm soapy water, clean linen and a dry suit of clothes, followed by a bowl of good soup and some broiled ribs of beef, not to mention a bottle of claret, were uppermost in his mind—and to hell with Needham and the rest.

He bounded up the stairs to his chamber, passing a serving wench on the way, and instructing her to bring up a jug of piping hot water with all speed. The girl simply stared at him, open-mouthed. He half-noticed, and put it down to imbecility. It should have served him as a warning. It did not.

He paused on the top step.

"My God!" he cried. "What in Hades . . . ?"

The door of his room was open. His traps: sea-chest; a small, melon-topped chest; carpetbag; sword and pistol cases; hat boxes, were piled—none too tidily—outside the door by the landing rail.

His exclamation brought someone to the door of his room: a man of middling height, fair-haired, quirkish-looking mouth, searching eyes, powerful forearms. The latter were on view, since he was in shirtsleeves and wiping his wet hands on a towel.

"Good evening to you, sir," said the apparition. "Looking for someone? Can I be of any assistance?"

"You've a damned fine insolence," declared Cambronne, "to be making free of my room! And who shifted out my traps?"

The stranger smiled—a pleasant, lopsided smile. "*My* room, sir," he said. "As for your traps, 'twas the landlord who did it, on my instructions."

"What's going on then, Tom me darlin'?" a voice husky with a lifetime of gin and smoke-filled tap-rooms drifted out of the door, along with its owner, who was not to be designated a lady, save in the loosest possible terms. She was painted like a clown, patched on both cheeks, likewise on the upper slope of her bosom, which was generously on view. In her arms she carried a small pug dog with a red satin bow about its thick neck and a villainous mien.

"Nothing, Bridie," responded he addressed as Tom. "Slip out of your clothes and get into bed. I'll be with you just as soon as I've settled with this lunatic who thinks he's got a lien on my room."

"The room, sir, is mine," said Cambronne, folding his arms and regarding the usurper without heat. "And I am giving you notice to quit. Now! Without benefit of Mistress Bridie. You may take her with you and enjoy her elsewhere, dog and all."

"Gentlemen, gentlemen, what's all the fuss?" It was the innkeeper, he who had mulcted Cambronne a dollar for the privilege of entertaining a lady in his room, and had presumably taken a toll from the stranger on account of the strumpet with the pug. A man, thought Cambronne, who had his price.

"Get this gentleman out of here," said the Jerseyman. "And you may put my traps back yourself, since you took 'em out."

A cunning look came into the fellow's accommodating eyes. "A mistake has been made, Captain," he said. "Not by me, I hasten to add, but by my scrivener. This gentleman here booked the room well in advance. It's there in the ledger: 'Mr. Thomas Blackadder, paid in advance for room six.' You can't argue with that, sir."

"Damned if you can't!" snapped Cambronne. "Produce this ledger."

The other leered. "Office is locked, sir. Scrivener's gone home for the night. Don't know where he lives." He delivered it with the air of a man trumping an ace.

"You're lying," said Cambronne. "How much did he—this Mr. Thomas Blackadder—pay you to throw me out?"

The man looked pained. "Would I do a think like that, Captain? Would I, now? And, anyhow, 'tisn't a matter of throwing you out, sir. I was just awaiting a bit of help from the ostler's lad, to carry your things up to a very fine room in the attic."

Cambronne turned his back on the landlord and addressed himself to Thomas Blackadder, taking out his turnip pocket-watch as he did so.

"Sir, will you vacate my room, which, as I am now convinced, you have usurped by means of bribery?"

"No, sir, I will not," came the reply. Delivered with cheerful good nature.

"The attic room's very fine, Captain," pleaded the innkeeper, adding in desperation: "On a clear day you can see Deer Island, plain."

Cambronne flipped open the cover of his watch. It conveyed the menacing sound of a pistol being cocked.

"Mr. Blackadder," he said. "I give you one minute precisely. In one minute, you will be out of my room: traps, strumpet, dog and all."

"Sauce!" cried Mistress Bridie. "Will you listen to the feller? Who's he callin' a strumpet?"

"My apologies, ma'am," murmured Cambronne. "Righteous anger has clouded my civility. And you, sir—will you do as I say?"

"I will not," replied Blackadder, smiling still. He leaned back against the door jamb, draped the towel over one shoulder, folded his brawny arms.

"In that case," said Cambronne, "you force me to take steps."

"What steps, pray?"

"In one minute," replied Cambronne. "No—in three-quarters of a minute, now—I shall remove your traps from my room."

"But that will still leave myself in possession," said Blackadder. "Not to mention the strumpet and dog."

"Ooooow!" protested Mistress Bridie.

"Your traps having been removed, Mr. Blackadder," replied Cambronne, "I shall then proceed to remove *you*. The lady and her pet dog will doubtless follow of their own accord, since I have no use for either."

"I quite look forward to witnessing this event," said Blackadder. And he crossed one foot over the other, comfortably.

The thin ticking of Cambronne's watch filled the silence of the next half-minute, at the end of which he snapped shut the cover and replaced the timepiece in his pocket.

"You leave me no choice, sir," he said, and strode into the room—his room.

Mr. Thomas Blackadder, in addition to being a barefaced rogue, was also of an untidy disposition, as evidenced by the state to which he had already reduced the room. Clothes, books, toilet articles lay everywhere. Only the newly made bed was tidy and, but for the advent of Cambronne, Mistress Bridie and he would soon have reduced that to ruin, surely.

There was a large open chest. Into it Cambronne bundled as much stuff as it would hold, conscious all the time that its owner was watching from the door, a sardonic smile on his lips. The trunk having been filled and the lid secured, Cambronne bore it to the door, past Blackadder—who, indeed, moved aside to let him by—and to the head of the stairs, where he laid it down.

"Article one," he intoned. And with his foot shoved the chest down the stairs, toppling over and over, to land at the bottom.

"Divil take it, Tom darlin'!" cried Mistress Bridie. "Are you goin' to let him get away with that and all?"

Blackadder straightened himself up and pointed to Cambronne's sea-chest.

"Yours, I believe, sir?" he asked.

"It is," replied the other.

Blackadder nodded. He then stooped and, picking up the heavy chest as if it had been a ditty-box, hefted it over the landing rail. It fell with a crash in the stairwell below, bursting open to spill its contents.

"Article two," said Blackadder. "Your move, sir."

The pug dog set up a throaty yapping, the effort of which made its eyes stand out from their sockets like chapel hat-pegs.

With a set countenance, Cambronne re-entered the room.

Next to go was a sailcloth valise. Down the stairs it went to join its companion.

Blackadder responded by tossing Cambronne's carpetbag over the banisters.

The whore was by now helpless with laughter, choking on every breath and holding on to the wall for support. The pug, still in her free arm, kept up its continuous yapping. The innkeeper had made himself scarce, fearful that he might be drawn into the conflict that must surely follow.

Soon, it was all done. The last of Blackadder's traps lay at the foot of the stairs, Cambronne's in the stairwell. The protagonists faced each other: Cambronne grave-faced, the other still smiling.

"Now you must remove *me,* Captain," said the latter. And he resumed his leaning posture against the door jamb.

"I shall not enjoy doing it," said Cambronne.

"That you will not, sir," responded Blackadder. "That I promise you."

"I meant that you are a man of spirit," explained the Jerseyman. "One of the sort who, in happier circumstances, would have made an agreeable companion at dinner tonight. But you leave me no choice. Stand and defend yourself."

"Make your move, Captain," replied Blackadder, arms still folded.

Cambronne delivered a right-handed punch to the other's head, which, because he was reluctant to bring down a sitting bird, was slow in coming and signaled well ahead; nevertheless, if it had found its mark, Blackadder must have gone down like a poleaxed ox.

It did not find its mark. Blackadder's head shifted with uncanny speed, and Cambronne's bunched fist struck only against the plaster wall. Almost simultaneously, the captain of the *Argo* saw something come up out of nowhere and, taking him full on the tip of the jaw, drive him back three paces, where he reeled against the banisters, which rocked drunkenly against his weight—but held.

The whore gave a cheer. The pug set up another yapping.

"Extend no more consideration toward me, Captain," said Blackadder. "Fight with regard only to your own advancement."

Cambronne wiped blood from his lips with the back of his hand. "That I will do, sir," he responded. "You have my word on it."

He went in again. Made a feint. Seized Blackadder's left wrist (had reckoned that it was with the left that his opponent had delivered that first, shattering blow), and drove his right fist into the other's gut, following it up with another to the throat. Blackadder gagged, retched, and fell back against the wall. Cambronne took a pace back to await events—thereby putting himself in precise kicking distance. Blackadder's booted foot took him full in the groin.

"I told you not to give me any consideration, my friend," gasped Blackadder. "You have to put aside your gentlemanly scruples when you choose to tussle with old Tom." It was a remark to which Cambronne made no answer, being bent over in agony.

It was then that the pug dog, freed of its mistress's arms, took a turn in the fray. Small though it was, its jaws and teeth were by proportion monstrous, the latter as sharp as shipwrights' nails, the former of bulldog tenacity. It affixed itself to Cambronne's leg, in the fleshy part above the ankle, biting deeply and snarling all the time. And it was when the captain of the *Argo*, the seat of pain suddenly shifting from groin to leg, stooped to rid himself of the new menace that Mistress Bridie, who had dropped the dog the more swiftly to fetch an offensive weapon from the bedchamber, came up behind and brought a heavy chamber-pot down down upon Jason Cambronne's head, smashing the ceramic item to fragments and all but braining the Jerseyman.

He was lying on a desert strand, with the sound of waves beating upon the shore not far distant. The Holt women, mother and daughter, were bending over him and mopping his brow. Both were nude. It was diverting to see the resemblance between them: the one more overblown, but none the less alluring. A little more clarity, and both images fused together into one. And into the face and upperworks of his late adversary, Mr. Thomas Blackadder . . .

"My God, I thought Bridie O'Hagan had killed you!" said Blackadder. "Man, there's a lump on the back of your head as big as a galley kettle. Don't move, for I've a notion that she may have broken your neck, also. Ah, you can move it. You may live."

"What happened?" asked Cambronne, sitting up, wincing. "I lost the fight, did I?"

"That you did not," responded the other. "After the punch

you gave me in the tripes, I'd nothing left in me but that one kick. A babe in arms could have settled for me after that. No, it was Brian Boru and . . ."

"Brian who?"

"The pug dog. She names him after this ancient king of Ireland. Brian Boru."

"God, my leg!" Pulling up his pantaloons, Cambronne revealed two neatly disposed crescent-shapes: punctured, purplish, oozing blood.

"If you go rabid in consequence," said Blackadder, "I beg you not to bite me."

"But it wasn't this that laid me low," said Cambronne.

"No, it was Bridie, who felled you with a pisspot."

"Ah, no wonder." Cambronne lay back. He was on the bed in the bedroom—his bedroom. There was no sign of the whore, nor of his traps, nor of the other man's. Blackadder was sitting on the only chair by his bedside. He looked—considering everything that had happened—astonishingly agreeable.

"You can fight real dirty," said Blackadder, without resentment. "Where did you learn it?"

"Boarding parties," said Cambronne. "When you've nothing in your hands but a clumsy navy cutlass and an empty pistol, and you come up against a fancy fellow with a rapier who's learned his trade in some *salle d'armes* . . ." He shrugged.

"Navy—what navy?"

"The Royal Navy."

"A Limey!" Blackadder smote his thigh with the flat of his hand. "And to think I took you for a Frenchie. From your accent."

Cambronne explained his antecedents. And then: "Look, Blackadder . . ."

"Tom," said the other. "Call me Tom."

"Tom, when I came back here, my only thought was for a wash, a change into dry clothing, and then a slap-up meal. Will you not join me at dinner? For, as I've already said, I find you a man of spirit and, from the manner of your talk, not to mention the look of your traps, a seaman like myself. What do you say? And we can settle the matter of the room, amicably, over our meal."

Tom Blackadder offered his hand, which Cambronne took.

"Captain, I'm your man," said Blackadder. "For I have to

tell you that I never in my life did see a gentleman of such spirit and resolve—and all without bate, or malice, or fussing—as you presented this night, and taking into account the provocation I gave you. Add to that, I have a confession to make . . ."

"Speak on," said Cambronne.

"You were correct in your assumption that I slipped bright silver into the greasy palm of mine host, to secure this room over your head," said Blackadder. "By way of mitigation, I offer the fact that there is not a lodging to be had in this city, and it was only because I brought with me Bridie O'Hagan (who has a working arrangement with that pox-ridden water-rat of a landlord, you understand?) that I contrived to effect the arrangement. It was *my* night's sleep and a tumble on the mattress with a well-upholstered doxie, or the interests of a complete unknown. Can you really blame me, Captain?"

Cambronne reached out a clenched fist and, laying it against the other's jaw, gave it a gentle, joshing push. "Tom Blackadder," he said, "I think you are a devil—but I like you. Here's what we will do. Tonight, you may shift your traps in here, along with mine. The damned landlord can carry both lots, since you've already paid him—and handsomely, I shouldn't wonder. The bed's big enough for the two of us." He grinned. "From what I saw of Bridie O'Hagan, I don't think much of your taste in womanflesh, but at least she demonstrated which way your persuasions lie. Me, you'll just have to take on trust."

They both laughed.

Whatever the shortcomings of the Lincolnshire Arms, they kept a good table. Half an hour later, washed and changed, Cambronne took his place in the dining-room with his new friend, where, after pledging each other in several glasses of hot negus (for despite the time of year the night was wet and chill) they ate a good fish soup, followed by the Jerseyman's favorite broiled ribs. After the manner of seamen, for whom the frailties of wind and weather are a constant source of interruption, they ate swiftly and without wasting much time on talk. Like seamen also, and perversely, they scarcely touched any of the generous selection of fresh vegetables provided, augmenting their meat with bread alone, for constitution that has grown used to doing without will happily stay without. Only when the plates were cleared away and a new bottle of brandy was broached and both men were pulling on their cigars did they talk in earnest. And their talk was the same as that of seamen the world over, from time immemorial: 'old ships.'

"I did my time in the United States Navy," said Blackadder. "This was in the war of 1812, though I never did set eyes on a Limey in all my two years as a volunteer before the mast. Were you one of those who fought our lot?"

"Mmmm," replied Cambronne offhandedly. "More brandy?"

"Were you now?" said Blackadder. "As captain?"

Cambronne nodded.

"What ship?"

"Delight."

"Not the *Delight,* surely? Not the Limey that damn near sank our *Endurance* within sight of half the good citizens of New York so that she had to be beached on Long Island? Don't tell me that I'm sharing a bed with the skipper who did that?"

Cambronne shrugged. "We were very luck to catch *Endurance* with the weather gage. Your fellows fought and sailed well, but the odds were piled against them. Add to that, our first broadside brought down their foretop and killed half the officers. After that it was target practice."

"That's not the way I heard it, Captain," said the other, eyeing his companion over the rim of his brandy glass. "To think I kicked in the nuts the man who nearly sank the *Endurance!* But whyfor didn't they make you an admiral in the fullness of time? Hell, the British navy's record in the war of 1812 wasn't anything to write home about. Your feat was practically unique."

"In the fullness of time," said Cambronne dryly, "I misbehaved myself, was court-martialed and dismissed my command."

"Oh, I see," said Blackadder, and looked as if he saw very well. "And what now?"

"Now, I've got a new command." Very deliberately, Cambronne drew and exhaled a lungful of smoke before continuing. "And I'm looking for a crew."

The other's shrewd eyes narrowed. "Are you making me an offer, Captain?"

"I might. Tell me about yourself."

Blackadder refilled both their glasses. "Well, like I said, I shipped before the mast in the navy for two years. After that, I decided that the seafaring life was for me. I've had nine years in the deep-water trade. Topman. Bosun. Master's mate. List of old ships as long as your arm. The last was *James J. Walker* of Portland, Maine. She paid off for the scrapyard in Boston last week. So you see, Captain, I very much want a berth."

"And before you joined the navy. What then?"

The quirkish mouth twisted in a sardonic grin. "Damn me if I didn't think you'd ask me that, Captain."

"I'm still asking," responded Cambronne.

"I was a younker," said Blackadder. "You could say I got into bad company, only I wouldn't say it made a lot of difference. They gave me two years in Walnut Street jail in Philadelphia."

"For what crime?"

The grin broadened. "Captain, captain, you don't know the ground-rules. In jail, that's one question you never ask, and an answer you never offer."

Cambronne nodded. "I'll observe the convention. You say you're master's mate. I'm looking for a master. Do you think you could hold down the job?"

"You could try me, Captain. Where shall we be plying?"

"The Caribbean, mostly. Do you know it?"

"I know it well. Cuba, Haiti, Puerto Rico, Jamaica, Trinidad. Captain, I know the Caribbean from the Gulf of Mexico to Georgetown. I could navigate you from one end to the other without sighting dirt all the way and bring you a landfall up right on the tick of the clock. Were you ever in a hurricane?"

"Yes."

"Well, you'll know what I mean when I tell you that I was caught in a hurricane in '21. This was aboard the *James R. Stover,* out of Tampa. We were on passage from Curacao to Martinique when the blow hit us. We were with bare poles within minutes and the mainmast went soon after, braining the captain on the way. Three and a half days we rode it out at sea-anchor, till everything that was movable had been ripped off us: ship's boats, charthouse, wheel, charts, everything. At the end of it, I brought that hulk to St. Vincent under jury rig, with no charts, no sextant. Nothing. Yes, Captain, I know the Caribbean all right."

Cambronne nodded. "We sail next week," he said. "Be glad to have you aboard, Master."

They shook hands.

"What's to be the cargo, Captain?" asked Blackadder.

"No cargo."

"Passengers, eh?"

"There will be two passengers on our outward passage," said Cambronne. "The owner's daughter and his secretary. Normally, we shall carry neither passengers nor cargo."

A silence hung between them, substantial as the thin curl of smoke that rose from Cambronne's cigar.

Presently, Blackadder said: "May I put the question, Captain?"

Cambronne grinned. "You play *my* ground-rules now, Master. It's a question you don't ask—not yet—and an answer I won't offer—not till the times comes."

Blackadder rubbed the side of his nose and looked thoughtful.

"Put it this way, Captain," he said. "Am I right in supposing that the chain of circumstances which decided you to make me the offer—the fact that we fought together, ate and drank together, the fact that you like the cut of my jib as I like the cut of yours—am I right in supposing that the last gobbet of information concerning my early life which you prised out of me, far from going to my demerit, actually clinched the offer?"

"You could suppose that," conceded Cambronne. "If the fancy took you."

So on that auspicious day, Cambronne met his new ship and also appointed her master, the man who was to be his right arm—in charge of navigation, ballast, sails, cables, the provisioning of the vessel—and his deputy. They shared a bed that night and, despite the rigors of his day, Cambronne was happy to exchange anecdotes of "old ships" till cockcrow. They slept the morning through till noon.

Three days later, there took place the obsequies of the late Josiah (Josh) Winterburn, former vice-chairman and director of the Augusta Line, holder of numerous other directorships, as well as being a founder member of the Anti-Slavery Society, the possessor of a reputation that would have made a Borgia blench, and a supposed suicide.

On the day of the resplendent interment, at which the menfolk of Boston's top families followed the beplumed hearse, their wives and daughters took tea with the grieving widow in her black-draped drawing-room, for Bostonian high society followed the convention of the English upper and upper-middle classes, and anyone with pretensions to being a lady would as lief be seen coming out of a cathouse as out of a cemetery.

One male, alone, shared the ladies' company at tea instead of attending the funeral, and that was Jeff Carradine, who, by reason of his unmarried state, his charm, good looks and slightly raffish reputation, was allowed to be eccentric in most things—and that included not going to funerals. So it was Carradine who, scorning the presence of the servants, handed around cakes and thin cucumber sandwiches *à l'Anglais,* who was perfectly charming to everyone and commiserated with the widow, who, from her manner, had been secretly at the bottle all day, and was weeping quite unashamedly.

"My dear Lucy, of course you will miss Josh. How could it be otherwise?" If Carradine intended an irony, he gave no sign of it.

"He was a good man—at heart," sobbed Lucy Winterburn. "And much misunderstood."

Carradine may well have thought that the late Josh Winterburn had been very well understood by all who had had the misfortune of his acquaintance—but if he did so he kept the observation to himself and changed the slant of the conversation.

"My dear, you must allow a little time to go past," he said. "That being done, the mourning having been observed, you must look to your own life, your own future."

"Jeff!" Lucy Winterburn's slightly protruding blue eyes, swimming with tears, were turned upon the elegant *flâneur* with something like a wild and wayward hope. "You mean—I should *remarry?*"

Carradine, not a man to be embarrassed easily, regarded Lucy Winterburn's uncomely face and form for a few moments before replying.

"I do not entirely rule out your future remarriage, my dear," he said. "But what I had in mind was the more *immediate* future. I was speculating in terms of, say, a visit to Europe. An extended stay in Paris, perhaps. Or Rome, or

Venice. Though Venice can be trying in the summer
months . . ."

How can they go on so? thought Virginia, who sat with her
mother on a Louis Quinze sofa, a cup of tea in one hand, in
the other a thin sandwich from which she took small, nibbling
bites. Even Uncle Jeff, who was the soul of honesty, was as
hypocritical as the rest of them when it came to not speaking
ill of the dead. Everyone in the room knew that Josh
Winterburn had been a monster. His own wife, drunk and
sniveling over there, was supposed to have cut her wrists on
their wedding night. God knows what she must have had to
put up with in her nuptial bedchamber through all these
years. Papa was quite right: the dead man's reputation was
gossiped about in Miss Hornbuckle's dancing academy as it
had also been whispered at her kindergarten. It was common
knowledge that Mrs. Winterburn had never been able to keep
a decent-looking female servant in the house. Black or white,
young or old, they pretty soon had the master's hand upon
them, his foul breath gusting against their lips. She herself,
when her bosom had only just begun to bud, had been
"accidentally" touched there by that awful creature during a
picnic party on Beacon Hill. Thank God he was dead. Boston
would be a cleaner, safer place without him.

Her mother intruded upon Virginia's thoughts.

"Half past five," she said to no one in particular. "The
gentlemen will be returned at any moment."

Mama had changed, decided Virginia. Quite perceptibly,
in the last few days—since just after the birthday ball—she
had grown more—how to put it?—mellow. To start with,
there was now an end to her appearing at family breakfast in a
thin *peignoir* with nothing under it but drawers and stays,
which had been an embarrassment for all concerned, the
servants included, and had almost certainly not achieved its
pathetic object, which was presumably to lure Papa into her
bed. Virginia was well aware that her parents had not slept
together in her lifetime, for had Mama not said so many times
to her friends, forgetful of the little girl absorbed in nursing
her doll not *quite* out of earshot . . . ?

Gone the pink peignoir; in its place, a prim and sensible
housecoat with a high neck and long sleeves. And in black, of
all colors. Mama at breakfast in the past few days had looked
positively *nunlike*. Virginia knew all about nuns, for they had

taught in her kindergarten. Stealing a sidelong glance, she decided that Mama had a positive resemblance, in manner and expression of face, to the Reverend Mother Ursula: the same oddly virginal look, yet with an inner serenity that comes from—what?—religious experience? Had Mama had a recent religious experience? It seemed hardly likely. And the mourning-gown she was wearing: it was all of a piece with the clothes she had worn for the last few days. High in the neck, of course, being a mourning-gown. But so also had been the day-gown that she had worn on—was it Saturday or Sunday? A far cry from that blue and gold striped day thing that showed nearly down to her navel and brought titters of mockery from the girls at Miss Hornbuckle's whenever Mama came to fetch her in it. Very odd.

Footsteps in the corridor outside. Her father's throaty cough.

"Ah, the gentlemen have returned," said her mother.

"So it has been done!" cried Lucy Winterburn, dabbing her streaming eyes. "Josh has been laid to rest." She bowed her head and gave way to her emotions.

The mourners, when they entered the drawing-room, had none of the air of men who had been attending the last rites of a fellow human. Their attire excepted, one might have thought that they had just returned from their club after a good luncheon and a few rubbers of whist. Cyrus T. Holt, particularly, was looking decidedly rakish. During his long wait outside the Winterburn mausoleum, his spidery hair, buffeted by the unseasonable wind, had taken flights of fancy and stuck up in front like a cockatoo. He had also consumed, with the help of his immediate neighbors at the obsequies, the entire contents of a large hip-flask of brandy.

Jeff Carradine rose at the mourners' entry and shook hands with Holt.

"Been lookin' after the little ladies for us, Jeff?" said the ship-owner, who was drunker than he appeared. "Stout fella! Don't know what we'd do without our Jeff, hey, gennlemen?" A murmur of agreement greeted his announcement, and the bereaved widow gave tongue to a fresh outburst of sobs.

"Miss Virginia, your servant, ma'am." Uriah Needham glided to Virginia's elbow and took up his stand there. She, who well knew that he nursed a secret passion for her, and had not the slightest liking for him, nevertheless derived a tolerable amount of satisfaction from his attentions—living, as she did, a fairly circumscribed life, watched over constantly by either her mother or her maid Eloise. Needham she knew to be poor, ambitious, not tremendously attractive, devious. But he worshipped the very shadow that she cast before her. What, she asked herself, could be nicer?

"Good day, Mr. Needham" responded Virginia, adding, *sotto voce,* and with a quick glance toward Mrs. Winterburn, who was being comforted in her latest transport of grief by the ubiquitous Jeff Carradine: "How did it go? The funeral service, I mean."

"Well enough, Miss Virginia," said Needham. And, like her, he glanced to the widow and kept his voice low. "Naturally, given the circumstances of Mr. Winterburn's demise, the Reverend Tomlinson was chary about extending the full blessings of the church to the departed. There was more fanciful talk about Mr. Winterburn's good deeds while on earth than speculations about his prospects in the hereafter. Like a beggar, Miss Virginia, a suicide cannot be a chooser."

"Oh, dear," whispered Virginia. "And, do you know, Mr. Needham? I loathed the man. He was—like a walking corpse."

"Mr. Winterburn was not a gentleman to everyone's taste," responded Needham. "However, to change the subject, Miss Virginia, time is passing, and we shall soon be embarking upon our voyage to the Caribbean." His pale eyes shone with ardor, and Virginia reflected, with a dull sense of *ennui,* that Uriah Needham's adoration, constant, and at close quarters in a vessel the size of *Argo,* could very soon become like eating cream with cream.

"Yes, indeed," she replied. "We set sail on Friday next, do we not. I think that I . . ."

"Not you, Miss! No haring off to Jamaica for you!"

Her father's voice. Slurred. Bellicose. What had happened to Papa? she asked herself.

Silence in the room of mourning. Even the wretched widow ceased her sobbing, and Jeff Carradine tactfully avoided everyone's eyes by looking down at his well-kept fingernails.

"Not here, Cyrus," pleaded Augusta Holt of her husband. "Not on an occasion such as this."

"Today is as good a time as any!" returned the ship-owner, his fury fired rather than quenched by his spouse's intervention. He gestured to the portrait of the late Josh Winterburn, whose painted snake's eyes burned down upon the company from above the chimney-piece. "Josh wasn't one for beating around the bush. 'Out with it, Holt!' he'd say to me. 'Say what's on your mind and to hell with embarrassing present company!'"

"Excellent sentiments," commented Jeff Carradine, with the air of a man introducing a red herring. "I am put in mind of an occasion when . . ."

"Dammit, you're not going to Jamaica!" bawled Holt, pointing to Virginia. "Not without your mother to act as chaperone, and that's out of the question, as you well know, for your mother pukes at the very sight of a ship."

"But, Papa, I . . ." Virginia's eyes brimmed with tears, and not merely tears of anguish. A spoiled childhood, an only child, is not conducive to the acceptance of disappointment, as when a goody is promised and then withheld. Virginia was well on the way to anger.

"Enough! I'll have no more of it. You're not going, and that's an end," said her father.

"Mama, please . . ." Virginia turned to the nunlike figure seated beside her.

"And it's no use thinking your mother will side with you against me!" declared Holt. "It was she who put her foot down and said I was to forbid you!"

"Mama!" Virginia stared at her mother, who dropped her gaze to her own beautifully formed hands which lay folded piously on her black-clad lap. "Why could you do this to me—*why?*"

"Well, woman, will you tell her, or should I?" demanded Holt, and, getting no reply: "All right then, girl. Your mother informs me that your carryings-on with the young beaux of this town has become a scandal among the matrons and an embarrassment to her. That's the first thing."

"Mama!" cried Virginia yet again—and still winning no response, not even a glance. She was conscious also that Suzanne Duveen was eyeing her with malicious delight from the other end of the room, and that her former beau, Henry Davenport, was frowning at her disapprovingly. All at once she felt hemmed-in, trapped, friendless. Even Uncle Jeff was examining his fingernails again.

"Secondly, as your mother points out," resumed the ship-owner, "you threw yourself at Cambronne's head during your birthday ball. You insisted on monopolizing him and then, when he begged leave to depart, slapped his face. Now Cambronne, my girl, is not a man to be trifled with by an untried maiden. He's a man with a reputation concerning women, and a pretty gamy reputation at that. Your mother considers that you have shown a mite too much interest in him, and that, taking one thing with another, it would be highly undesirable for you to make the long sea voyage in his company. I agree with her, and in doing so I don't fault Cambronne as an officer and a gentleman. But he's a man, and a red-blooded man at that, while you are but a silly chit of a girl who'd play with fire."

"It's a lie! Mama, you've lied about me!"

Virginia was on her feet, pointing accusingly at her mother, while the latter stared at her daughter with something like alarm.

"Virginia, my darling," faltered Augusta Holt. "My baby . . ."

"Dammit, I am *not* your baby!" cried the other. "What mother would speak of her baby thus? You say that my carryings-on have become a scandal. I say that's a malicious lie!"

Virginia turned, and as she did so her skirts brushed against the delicate, spindly-legged table upon which stood an array of empty teacups and plates, all of the finest Sèvres. The table swayed and nearly fell. Impelled by a sudden notion to destructiveness for the sake of release, Virginia, as soon as the table had recovered its equilibrium, gave it a clout with her dainty, button-booted foot and sent it hurtling across the room, Sèvres porcelain and all, to land at the feet of its horrified owner. The widow Winterburn swooned clean away with alarm. Jeff Carradine led the effort to assist her with smelling salts and loosening of the bodice. In the pandemonium, Virginia made her escape from that house of mourning.

Cyrus J. Holt took out his hip-flask, shook it and, finding it indeed to be empty, growled at his wife:

"That was a damn fool idea of yours, woman! She'll make all our lives hell now, and there'll be nothing for it but to let her go."

"But, but . . ." essayed Augusta Holt, tearful.

"Very well then, she must have a chaperone," conceded her spouse. "And what's wrong with her maid, Eloise? Why in the blazes couldn't you think of that in the first place, woman?"

So it was that Jason Cambronne was informed, by means of a curt note from his employer, that he must make additional provision for another female passenger, the maid Eloise, during the passage to Jamaica, an item of news that caused Cambronne to curse all owners, for he had already apportioned the better of the two after cabins to Virginia and must now abandon the second berth to the maid and himself sling a hammock in the saloon, along with Tom Blackadder, the master. He gave orders to this effect, and Blackadder made the adjustment to his bill of complement.

As far as complement was concerned, the *Argo* was clearly going to be greatly, but not seriously, undermanned on her maiden sea voyage. Jack the Cat turned up at the Lincolnshire Arms with his six good topmen and a promise of four more, including, he said, "a cabin boy who might double for a powder-monkey one day." He flashed his hideous grin at Cambronne and Blackadder when he said this, and the latter raised an eyebrow but made no comment.

To the hostelry came also Tobias Angel. The zealot bosun, sober and quoting freely from the Good Book, informed Cambronne that the five shipwrights who had acted excellently well as crewmen during the sail in Boston Roads had expressed a concerted desire to be signed on the books of the *Argo*. Upon Cambronne registering some doubts as to the ethics of stealing Walberswick's hands, Tobias Angel gravely informed him that the shipbuilder, the last great work of his life finished and floating, had closed the yard and taken to his bed—there to await the coming of the Grim Reaper.

Tom Blackadder, too, went a-recruiting. And by the following midweek had run to earth no less than thirty hands from his last ship, the *James J. Walker,* all of whom he was able to vouch for as regards competence and tolerable sobriety. One of them was a cook.

The week passed quickly. By the Tuesday preceding the proposed sailing on Friday, all the crew save Cambronne were sleeping and working aboard the *Argo* at Nogg's Wharf. The schooner's captain went aboard every morning and received the master's report on the progress of victualling, watering, and all the hundred and one problems concerned with commissioning an entirely new ship with an entirely new crew. There were the usual frictions. Three men (from Blackadder's old ship) returned aboard drunk one night and were put on Captain's Report. Cambronne dismissed them instantly with a week's pay; likewise a man who was caught stealing from his messmates. For reasons of his own, which he did not confide to Blackadder, he also discharged a man who seemed to take more than a passing interest in the locked compartment that contained the wondrous suit of great blue sails. In the afternoons he himself supervised sail drill for all hands.

On the eve of departure, secretary Uriah Needham presented himself at Cambronne's lodgings with final instructions from his employer, or, as Cambronne knew, from the mysterious personage referred to as "The Man." The Jerseyman, constrained by a civility that, considering the circumstances between them, did him justice, felt obliged to invite Needham to dine with him. They spoke little over the meal; Cambronne's thoughts were largely on the coming voyage and what might follow after. His final instructions, contained in three lines on one sheet of paper, were simple in the extreme: he was to proceed with all speed to Kingston, Jamaica, and was there to present himself and the note to Mr. Percy Hetherington, agent of the Augusta Line, who would instruct him further.

On the morning of departure, after he had settled his score at the Lincolnshire Arms and put his traps in a hired carriage, Cambronne walked the two blocks to the jeweler's shop where he had left the pendant for repair, paid for it, and slipped it into his breast pocket.

They sailed on the evening tide, with only Cyrus J. Holt and his coachman to see them off. The ship-owner's wife, who had contrived to patch up the differences between herself and Virginia (having got her own way after all, Virginia was willing to concede that all the most eligible beaux in Boston were mad for her, and it was highly likely that some of the old biddies, jealous of their own homely daughters, might well have blackened her name to Mama), pleaded a headache at the last moment and did not accompany her husband to Nogg's Wharf.

The *Argo* stole like a white ghost down the silent, moonlit river, the ebb carrying her with scarcely a ripple underfoot; past the bulk of the city, rising in a coronet of a million winking lights to the summit of Beacon Hill; past the clanging bell-buoy that marked the end of the main channel, with the light on Long Island Head beckoning from the darkness beyond the bowsprit.

Cambronne stood alone on the poop. Blackadder, acting as officer of the middle watch (it was half past midnight) was stationed beside the helmsman, and all hands on deck were looking to the sails. Something stirred at the Jerseyman's side. Turning, he saw that Virginia Holt had emerged from the companionway and was standing there. He caught the soft smell of her, the wild violets and the rest, and felt his manhood stir.

"You should not be on deck at this hour, Miss Virginia," he said, with more gruffness than was called for under the circumstances. "The dank night air isn't healthy for young lungs."

"Why, Captain Cambronne," said Virginia. "I do declare that you are being avuncular, and that's nice. My mama, you know, was of the opinion that, far from being avuncular, you might seek to deflower me. Now, what do you think to that?"

He supposed she had been partaking too heavily of champagne at her farewell dinner with her parents. Indeed, come to think of it, he could smell wine on her breath. She was very close.

"Indeed, ma'am?" he said.

"Which is why I was obliged to bring a chaperone," said Virginia.

"No well-brought-up young lady should venture far without a chaperone," was Cambronne's comment upon that.

"But, you know, I don't think you would seek to bring about my ruin," continued Virginia. "Not when one remembers how you left me standing in the middle of the dance floor at my own birthday ball. Oh, and how angry I was. I broke my favorite jewel, my garnet pendant, did you know? And never found it again."

"It is a sad thing," said Cambronne, "to lose an item of which one has grown fond."

"And now we are on our way to Jamaica," said Virginia. "I am to stay with the Governor, who's an Englishman, of course. I don't suppose we shall be seeing each other very much after we reach Kingston. Still—there's always the days ahead. Good night, Captain Jason Cambronne."

"Good night, Miss Virginia."

She gave him a coquettish wave—at least, he supposed it was coquetry—and disappeared down the companionway. Cambronne put a hand inside his cloak, fumbling till his fingers closed about the pendant that hung, concealed from all eyes, on its mended chain under his shirt, and cursed himself quietly under his breath.

He stayed on deck till the *Argo* had passed Long Island Head and Deer Island, till the leadsman was calling ten fathoms by the mark and the cluster of islets and rocks named the Graves had fallen abaft the beam. It was then that the schooner's stem bit deeply into a gentle swell, and the thousand small noises of a sailing ship in motion began to make themselves heard.

"You have a favorable wind, Mr. Blackadder," said Cambronne. "Shape course, now, to weather Cape Cod by at least five cables, and have me called at eight bells."

"Aye, aye, sir."

The Argonauts were on their way.

CHAPTER 5

By midafternoon of the following day, *Argo* was speeding due south through a slight swell, with the accommodating Northeast Trades pushing her on and Nantucket Island a gray smudge on her starboard quarter. They had met bad weather off Cape Cod the previous night, and Tom Blackadder had thought it prudent to waken his captain. Six hours of beating into head seas, close-hauled, with the constant need to shift sails, had taken its toll of the green crew. Now, with the midday meal over, the hands off watch were sleeping below in their messdeck. Eloise, the black lady's maid—no sailor, she—was still confined to her bunk and being tended by her young mistress.

"Ten knots, sir," said Blackadder, coiling in the line. "She's a sailor, right enough. I never saw better."

Cambronne thought of the blue suit hidden below in the locked compartment and made no comment. The time had not yet come to show off the *Argo's* full capabilities. That must come later, when he knew, and trusted, every member of the crew, and every man knew, and accepted, the business they were on.

A quartermaster came on deck, squinting against the glare, padded over to the ship's bell and solemnly struck it eight times.

"Who's got the next watch?" asked Cambronne.

"Jack Smith," replied Blackadder. "Or 'Jack the Cat,' as the men persist in calling him. Not that he minds. A good man, that. Was he once an officer, do you think?"

"It's possible," said Cambronne. "But he'll not be telling. Keeps his own counsel, that one."

At that moment, the object of their surmise came on deck. Cat's eyes flickering this way and that: taking in the set of the sails, the state of the sea and the wind. He came over to where Cambronne and Blackadder were standing, close by the wheel, and treated the former to a sketchy approximation of a naval salute. And the hideous, wide-mouthed grin.

The remainder of the new watchmen were coming on deck, though merely to prove themselves to be awake and sober. There promised to be little work that afternoon, save a trick on the wheel, for any but Jack the Cat, the acting officer of the watch.

Blackadder handed over the ship to his relief in the time-honored manner: "Course, due south," he said. "Wind nor'-east. Under all plain sail and running at ten knots."

"Aye, aye," responded Jack the Cat.

Cambronne and Blackadder took a few paces together down the deck, turning when they came to the foremast. Neither spoke. Each was occupied with his own thoughts. Both were witness to the incident that followed.

Virginia Holt came up the companionway, a shawl about her shoulders, her hair unbound and streaming free in the wind, cheeks pink with the freshness. Jack the Cat was standing by the helmsman, his back to her, when, at the sound of her footfall, he turned.

Her scream, when she saw his face for the first time, would have struck terror into the heart of a brave man. Her expression, compounded of horror and disbelief, showed her to have been dragged on the instant to near-madness. She recoiled against the companionway rail, hand pressed to her mouth, eyes staring.

"Oh, my God!" breathed Cambronne. "That poor devil."

What to say? What to do? By the time Cambronne and Blackadder had joined the group, Virginia had retreated from the frontiers of insanity and was gazing at the object of her terror with a numbed acceptance. Jack the Cat was grinning at her. The helmsman was gaping from one to the other, open-mouthed.

"Watch your ship's head, man!" growled Cambronne to the latter, thereby breaking the spell.

"I—I'm very sorry," faltered Virginia. "That is, I . . ."

Cambronne cleared his throat noisily. "Miss Virginia," he said. "May I present Mr. Jack Smith? An Englishman," he added.

"Your servant, ma'am," said Jack the Cat, bowing.

The color was returning to Virginia's cheeks. She made to offer her hand to the hideous creature who stood before her, but thought better of it. She struggled to frame words that might soften the hurt that she must surely have offered to the disfigured man who was regarding her, still, with the enigmatic, catlike grin that must surely haunt her dreams forever. And struggled to no very good purpose.

"I didn't mean to—add to your misfortune, Mr. Smith," she whispered.

The answer came back sharply, and still with the grin:

"One is never as unfortunate as one imagines, ma'am," he said. "Nor, indeed, as *fortunate*—a precept that you might well apply to yourself, ma'am."

Virginia swallowed, nodded awkwardly, and retired back the way she had come.

"*Touché*, I fancy," murmured Cambronne. "Bad enough to commit an indiscretion, but then to have Rochefoucauld quoted against one in the bargain . . ."

Jack the Cat chuckled. "Helmsman, watch your ship's head," he said.

Another incident served to lighten the taste of ill omen that hung in the air after Virginia's departure. Cambronne and Blackadder had resumed their pacing when a young lad, barefoot, ragged-trousered, with a filthy seaman's jerkin, came from out of the crew's quarters carrying a bucket of dirty water, which he unhesitatingly threw over the side—into the wind. Captain and master received the benefits of the same in fairly equal portions. When both had finished cursing the lad and making certain specific assumptions about his parentage and prospects in the after life, Cambronne, seeing the object of their fury near to tears, addressed him more kindly.

"What name, son?" he asked.

"Dick Trumper, sir," piped the other.

"What's your task?"

"Look after the messdeck an' act as heads-boy," was the reply.

"First ship?"

"Second, sir." He had a starveling's face and a pudding-basin haircut that must have been done with a blunt razor.

"Did no one ever tell you, lad, to throw slops over the *leeward* side, so you don't get your own back?"

"Yessir, but I forgot, sir," said Dick Trumper.

"Then don't forget again, lad," said his captain, "or you'll spend a night at the masthead to fortify your memory. Get below."

"Yessir." The child fled. Cambronne and Blackadder resumed their perambulations.

"Young Master Trumper is one of Jack's acquisitions," said Blackadder. "The one who might—er—double for powder-monkey one day. If only we had cannons aboard."

Their eyes met. "He might at that," was Cambronne's bland retort.

Logging over two hundred miles a day, and with the favorable North-easter continuing to blow, they were soon moving into balmier climes. On the tenth day of passage, having safely negotiated the tricky barrier of the Bahama Islands chain, the *Argo* entered the Windward Passage that separates Cuba and Hispaniola, and there they ran into a blow. One minute the sea was bland, richly cerulean; next the tell-tale white horses were appearing on the crest of one wave in ten. Jack the Cat, keeping watch on deck, ordered the mainsail to be reefed down two points and the flying jib to be taken in even before he called Cambronne. It was two bells in the First Dog Watch, five o'clock in the afternoon, and the sky darkening ominously to the east.

A hoarse scream of terror, and then:

"Man overboard!"

Cambronne heard it as he bounded up the companionway, brushing past the messenger sent to fetch him, the change in the schooner's motion having alerted him.

"It's Jake Carter!" yelled someone from for'ard. "Fell off the bowsprit when he was taking in the jib. Went right under the stem. Christ, it was awful!"

Jack the Cat was barefoot. Barefoot, he raced to the taffrail, vaulted it, one-handed on the capping, and was plunging into *Argo's* creamy wake before Cambronne could open his mouth and shout the order to go about.

Virginia heard the order to go about as she came up the companionway. The first time the schooner had dipped and plunged under the rising sea, Eloise had vomited. Having made the negress comfortable on her bunk, she fled to the fresh air, herself sickened by the reek of vomit. She was in time to see the great sails flapping and the sky above her describing a spinning arc, the deck taking a new angle beneath her feet.

"What *is* it?" she cried. "What's *happened?* Are we—wrecked?" Her voice rose on a note of hysteria.

Cambronne pointed to a dot of red hair that—the schooner's turning circle being so dramatically tight—was scarcely more than half a cable distant and rapidly shifting for'ard as the vessel entered the last quadrant of her turn.

"That's Jack the Cat," he said. "The man who frightens you out of your wits. He's in the act of offering up his life for someone else's, and, if we don't pick up the both of them on this turn—the sea being how it is—the Almighty might well take up his offer. Steady as you go, helmsman! Stand by to luff!"

Virginia went for'ard with the others who were not engaged upon handling the ropes. She saw the red head disappear behind each white-capped wave, and reappear. She joined with the others, shouting and pointing, when another shape appeared some distance from the swimmer: the shape of another man lying face downward in the water, arms extended, clearly picked out by the bright yellow buff leather of his seaman's jerkin.

"There he is!"

"Right ahead o' you, Jack!"

"Jack's seen him!"

With consummate skill, Cambronne brought the *Argo* into the wind, and her sails flapped in irons at the moment that Jack the Cat's red head came abreast. Ropes were thrown over. A line of men stood ready to go over the side on ropes' ends and grab rescuer and rescued, both.

And then: *"They've gone!"*

No sign of the red head, no sign of the man Jake Carter.

"What happened?" This from Cambronne.

"Jake went under, sir. Then Jack, he dived for him and ain't come up."

The *Argo* was drifting rapidly downwind, away from the spot where the two men had last been seen.

"Take the ship, Master!" cried Cambronne. "Bring her round again."

"Aye, aye, sir," responded Blackadder.

"There they are!"

Full fifty yards away, Jack the Cat's hideous face emerged from behind a tossing wave, and with it the humped form in yellow. Even at that distance, those on deck could clearly see that the Englishman's countenance was white and drained with fatigue, dog-weary from his efforts against the unyielding sea. Even as he was kicking off his heavy boots, Cambronne was making the calculation that the *Argo* must take at least five minutes—given the luck of faultless tacking—to beat to windward that vital fifty yards. From the look of Jack the Cat, he did not have five mintues left of life.

"You have the ship, Master!" he shouted.

And vaulted over the side, feet first.

Into the deep green world and the sound of roaring in his ears. He saw the keel of the *Argo* quite clearly as she gathered way and sliced past. Next, he was rising to the light and the air. When his head broke surface, the schooner was slanting on a larboard tack that would bring her upwing to the men in the water. One more turn and she would be alongside again. Well done, Blackadder—so far.

He looked about him. Five waves away, a red head bobbed momentarily into sight. Cambronne struck out toward it. The sea plucked at his strength, denying him every inch. It was like wading through treacle. And what if that had been Jack the Cat's last appearance before the final plunge?

Where was Jack now? He trod water, rising on the crest of a comber. The red head was floating not five yards from him: face submerged, snaky tendrils of ruddy hair matted with sea salt. He reached out, took a handful of the stuff and jerked the hideous visage into the air. The slit eyes opened. The ghastly mouth parted in a grin.

"Hello, Captain," said Jack the Cat, in a voice so weak that one could sense the last of the man's strength ebbing out with his breath. "Once more, you seem to have cheated me of my purpose."

"You're not saved yet," said Cambronne. "Where's Carter?"

"Here—somewhere." A hand and an arm and a patch of yellow buff were floating close by Jack the Cat.

"Dead?" asked Cambronne.

"Unless he's learned to breathe under water."

"Hold onto my shoulders," said Cambronne. "I'll try and keep his face out of the water. The *Argo's* coming—see?"

Stealing every last inch of wind, close-hauled to extinction, Blackadder was bringing the schooner straight at them. Cambronne could see the men lining the rails, ready to leap down into the water on ropes' ends. The seaman Carter was a dead weight in his arms, and Jack the Cat was bearing him down. If Blackadder mistimed and had to go round again, there would only be one of them left alive at best by the time he came back.

"Put up your helm!" The shouted order came clearly to him across the tossing wavetops. The schooner faltered in her onward flight, stopped within yards of where he floundered. Two heavy bodies splashed into the water close by him, and the intolerable burdens were taken from his hands and shoulders.

They brought them inboard. Jack the Cat against the bulwarks where his shipmates gently put him, ghastly mouth agape, chest heaving with racking intakes of breath. The man he had rescued, the topman Jake Carter, they laid face downward on the deck and squeezed some of the water out of his lungs. Then someone noticed how the head lolled loosely.

"Jake is dead! Neck broken as clean as if he'd been topped from a rope's end!"

They all looked to Cambronne.

"It was the keel that killed him," said the captain of the *Argo*. "The deep keel. If she had been an ordinary schooner, she would have passed right over him when he took his plummet." It was the first admission Cambronne had ever made to his crew that their vessel was in any way different from what she appeared. Even Tobias Angel and the former shipwrights from Nogg's Wharf, who were in the know, had kept their counsel about the *Argo's* underwater secrets.

They wrapped Jake Carter in a seaman's coffin, which is six feet of sailcloth sewn with sailmaker's palm and waxed yarn. In the gloaming of that summer's eve, they gathered on the poop deck, and with the shrouded corpse lying upon a plank, all covered with his country's flag, Jason Cambronne intoned the prayers for committing the remains of a shipmate to the eternal deep, scarcely having to prompt himself from the old Church of England Book of Common Prayer that had traveled in his ditty-box from his first voyage as midshipman, so many times had he, as captain, performed that somber function:

"We therefore commit his body to the deep, to be
turned into corruption, looking for the resurrection
of the body, when the Sea shall give up her dead . . ."

The plank was lifted at the inboard end, and the remains of seaman Jake Carter slid from under his country's flag and made its last deep plummet, impelled by the pigs of lead attached to the ankles.

Tobias Angel pronounced a loud "hallelujah" and blew his nose noisily. A quartermaster folded up the flag. And Virginia Holt, who had watched the brief ceremony, made a certain resolve to herself concerning Jason Cambronne.

As the passage drew to its close, and the days ran out, and every hour brought a "Sail ho" from the masthead lookout as they entered the busy commercial lane of the islands, Virginia's resolve hardened. On a hot night off Cape Dame Marie, coasting Haiti, with pinpoints of light rising seven thousand feet into the inky blackness of the tropical night and the scent of hibiscus and honeysuckle heavy on the air, she called to Cambronne from her open cabin door when he came off deck shortly before Eloise laid places for dinner.

"Captain Cambronne, will you help me, please?"

She was making play with a bracelet, frowning prettily and juggling with the thin scrap of gold chain links. Her hair, gathered into a chignon at the crown, had a wanton disorder, and her eyes were avoiding his. She was wearing a scandalous gown of *tissue d'or,* and one plump young breast emerged so far from the scooped-out bodice as to command most earnest attention.

"Yes, Miss Virginia?" He paused on the threshold of the tiny cabin, that smelled so unfamiliar of wild violets and her.

"I can't fasten this wretched thing. Do it for me, please."

"Of course."

She gave him her wrist to hold, looking at him the while, her blue eyes shameless. He took it. Made no pretense of tarrying over the small task, but deftly drew back the tiny spring that secured the retaining link and let it slide back. Then he released her. Grinned.

"Is that all?"

She flushed most becomingly. Her eyes, suddenly grown less wanton, fell. Her hand went to her bosom. Somehow, the fugitive breast contrived to be covered.

"Yes—thank you."

"A pleasure, ma'am." He turned to go.

"Captain . . ."

"Yes?"

"We—we are nearly at Jamaica, are we not?"

He nodded. "If the wind holds, we shall raise the light-house at the easternmost point of the island before dawn, and be in Kingston by noon tomorrow."

"So soon?"

"So soon, Miss Virginia."

"Well, I must say," she declared, "I shan't be sorry. I haven't slept well aboard the *Argo,* do you know."

"I'm sorry to hear it," he said.

"My maid," she said. "That wretched Eloise." She made a small gesture toward the paneled partition that separated her cabin from the one next door. "She snores. All the night long."

"Inconvenient," said Cambronne. "And damnedly inconsiderate."

"All the night through," said Virginia. "As soon as her head touches the pillow at ten o'clock sharp. Never stops till morn."

"Tch, tch!" Cambronne shook his head.

"I shall never sleep a wink this night, I know it," said Virginia. "But, then, neither, I suppose, will you. You will be on watch, of course."

"Not till dawn," said Cambronne. "When they raise Morant Point, I shall be called. Till then, I shall be asleep in my hammock. Blackadder's snoring won't keep me awake. And in any event, he has the middle watch."

"I can't abide to lie awake in the dark," said Virginia. "If you see the chink of light under my door, you will know my candle's burning and I'm sleepless. I hope the light won't trouble you."

Cambronne grinned. "I'll tell you if it does," he said.

Her eyes, that had grown bold and wanton again, withdrew into confusion, and her gaze fell.

"Good night—Captain," she whispered.

Shortly before the change of watch at midnight, Cambronne went on deck for a last cigar. There was another vessel to windward, steering a slightly converging course. She was fast, not so fast as the *Argo,* but still a potential hazard for over an hour, making no attempt—as, since she held the weather gage, custom and common courtesy demanded—to steer further off the windward or shape course to pass under *Argo's* stern. There was never any real danger, for a brief order could have sent *Argo* streaking downwind; but it was a minor annoyance that was not terminated till the other's lights had passed abaft the beam. By that time, Blackadder had taken over the middle watch and Jack the Cat, whom he had relieved, had gone for'ard.

"Good dinner tonight," said Blackadder. "That nigger cook works wonders with hard tack and biscuit."

"Mmm."

"That Miss Virginia," said Blackadder. "Now, do you know, Captain, she almost makes me revise my opinion of the female of the species. With an untried girl such as she (I'm supposing she's untried, though one might get a surprise upon bedding her), a fellow usually feels like a ferret facing a rabbit. But most of the time with Miss Virginia—as tonight at dinner—I'm damned if I know who's the ferret and who the rabbit. Did you say something, Captain?"

"What's your course?" growled Cambronne.

"West-sou'-west, Captain. As I was saying, she's full of surprises, that one. Damned if I didn't think, only the other night, that she was setting her cap on me. You know? She had a way of saying 'please pass me the salt' that was like putting her hand into a fellow's breeches. Whereas tonight—well, I never had so much as a glance. She certainly demanded your attention, didn't she? The way she went on about the high old times she was hoping to have in Jamaica, and all the beaux she expects to meet and the balls she'll be invited to. In your place, Captain, I'd have thought she was trying to make me jealous. What do you think?"

Cambronne drew on the last inch of his cigar and, exhaling the smoke, flicked the butt over the side, so that it described an arc of brightness that was quenched in the white wake.

"I think you talk too damned much, Blackadder," he said. And went below.

Blackadder chuckled and shook his head. "Do as you please, captain mine," he said under his breath so that the helmsman should not hear. "Personally, I believe you won't tup that little white doe tonight. But I'm damned if I know why."

It was quiet in the big stern cabin: no sound but the gentle creak of the paneling under almost imperceptible stress from the tug of wind and water—that, and a steady snoring from the cabin next to Virginia's.

Quietly, Cambronne drew off his boots. Stealthily, and in

his stockinged feet, he went over to her door, under which there shone a thin streak of candlelight. His hand, raised to lower the latch, hung there for a full half-minute. And then fell to his side.

Cursing himself within, he went to his hammock.

Blackadder knew Kingston Harbor and its approaches; Cambronne did not. The master, it was, who piloted them in, passing the guardian gates of Gun Cay and Rackham's Cay and turning due north off Port Royal. And Blackadder was not so totally absorbed in his task that he was not able to instruct Virginia Holt on the passing scene. It was past midday. She had only just appeared on deck. Anyone with discernment would have seen that she had spent a bad night and had been crying. She had not greeted Cambronne, who was pacing the deck in his best broadcloth suit and the flat cap circled with tarnished braid.

"There you see Port Royal, ma'am," said Blackadder. "Wiped out by an earthquake, so they built Kingston, which you see coming up yonder, in the hope that it won't suffer in a similiar manner."

"Very interesting," murmured she.

On almost a beam wind, the *Argo* weathered a long spit of land that enclosed the great harbor, and a mass of white buildings on the shoreline stood revealed. Beyond that, a wide plain, and all beyond that, a range of craggy hills rising to high peaks.

"That's Mount James," said Blackadder, pointing. "I'm using that as my marker. Mount James, in line with that church steeple yonder, takes me right to the mouth of the deep channel, for, big though it is, Kingston Harbor has a front door that's only a bitty one-tenth of a mile wide, and the *Argo,* who draws a lot of water, could go aground real easy. It's been nice knowing you, Miss Virginia."

Cambronne, pacing past, said: "What's your head, Master?"

"Due north, sir," replied Blackadder.

"Make it so," murmured Cambronne, and went on past them.

"I *hate* that man," hissed Virginia.

"What was that you said, ma'am?" asked Blackadder.

She did not reply.

Presently, having negotiated the deep channel, the *Argo*

emerged into the wide benison of what is arguably one of the finest harbors on earth, and glided on her headsails to rest against a quayside teeming with life and commerce. The schooner—yet another vessel to swell the sum of schooners already gathered there—did not excite any special attention. The handful of loafers who had caught hold of her heaving lines and made fast her head and stern ropes picked up the coins that had been thrown to them and went back into the shade, flopped down, tipped their wide-brimmed straw hats over their eyes, slumbered on in the hot midday.

Virginia had ordered her maid to pack her things early. They were on deck, borne by two sweating sailors, as soon as the vessel touched dry land. Virginia, bonneted, prim, tight-mouthed, gave her hand—briefly—to Cambronne. The *Argo's* arrival, signaled ahead to Government House in Spanish Town across the bay, had brought a fine carriage with a fringed canopy and two spanking grays, Negro coachmen, footmen and outriders, not to mention a drawling young aristocrat who described himself as a First Secretary, to convey her and her maid, together with secretary Uriah Needham.

"Goodbye, Captain Cambronne," she said. "Thanks so much for your many kindnesses."

"Your servant, ma'am." As ever, he kissed the empty air an inch above her fingertips.

"Do we pipe the side, sir?" murmured Blackadder, as Virginia went down the gangplank on the arm of the young sprig from Government House. "The owner's daughter and all that, you know. Worth a salute."

"Shut your damned mouth," responded Cambronne without heat.

"Yes, sir," said Blackadder, grinning.

The carriage and grays, with the outriders to the fore, clattered away along the quay, scattering the motley noon-day crowd and disappearing from sight around the bend of a steep-sided rampart.

"Shore leave for off-duty watches, Mr. Blackadder," said Cambronne. "I am going to present my respects to the owner's agent, one Mr. Percy Hetherington."

The agent's address, limned upon the letter in Needham's tight, clerkish hand, was given as Liguanea House, and it was thither that Cambronne conveyed himself by hired carriage,

passing through the sprawling streets of Kingston and out into
the plain beyond, along rutted roads scored through high
hedges of sugarcane. They passed a gang of slave workers
trudging between an almost equal number of guards armed
with cruel whips and pistols tucked into their waistbands. The
latter struck Cambronne as the sort of men whom a prudent
ship's captain would as lief sail short-handed as sign on:
hard-faced, troublesome-looking rascals all.

It was stiflingly hot. The Jerseyman had taken off his thick
jacket and was mopping his brow by the time the carriage
turned in between a pair of identical gatehouses of white-
painted stone, with stately Doric columns at each portico.
There was a large sign attached to the right-hand building,
which, in a flowery italic script, announced that Mr. Percy
Hetherington was a Marine Surveyor, Honorary Consul to
the Sublime Porte of Constantinople, and Agent for the
Augusta Shipping Line. A man of many parts. And it was
obvious that one or other of Mr. Hetherington's activities—
perhaps all—enabled him to live in a style which approximated to that of an English country gentleman. The straight, long
carriage-drive that led to the house was graveled and swept
smooth. As Cambronne's carriage moved down it, a Negro
emerged from the shade of a eucalyptus tree, broom in hand,
and proceeded to obliterate all traces of the tire marks. The
Jerseyman's arrival was observed by an elderly black factotum who was seated, half-dozing, in a sentry-box close by the
porch of the house. Seeing the approaching carriage, this
party rose to his feet and, augmenting his tail-coat of blue
velvet and gold lace with a feathered bicorne hat, shuffled
forward to give greeting.

"Good af'noon, sah," he said. "May I have your name and
business, sah, please?"

"Cambronne. Captain Cambronne—to see Mr. Hetherington on business of the Augusta Line."

The factotum nodded, removed his bicorne, indicated
Cambronne to follow him into the house, which smelled of
wax polish and the heady scent of tropical flowers. Through
double doors, they entered a vast hallway whose parquet floor
was strewn with Oriental rugs as soft and faded as old
snakeskins. Cambronne's guide motioned him to take a seat
on a white-covered sofa and went on through an archway to a
further part of the building. The Jerseyman sat down and
gazed about him at the tell-tale signs of opulence none too

unostentatiously borne: the silver and the paintings, fine ormolu furniture, a crystal chandelier that would not have looked out of place in a royal palace. He scarcely had time to take it all in before the tap-tap of briskly moving feet announced the approach of someone other than the old Negro.

"Captain, I am so sorry you have been kept waiting. I had news from the harbormaster that your vessel had arrived, and dispatched a carriage immediately to stand at your disposal. It must have passed you on the way here. Did you have a good voyage? Will you take a drink? Of course, I am Hetherington. How d'you do? So nice to meet you. Let us go into the library, where it is cooler. This heat!"

The speaker was young, younger than Cambronne by five years or more, but he wore his age, every last month. The signs of dissipation were writ large in his pouched eyes, the jowelled chin, the paunch that overtopped the cummerbund at what was once his waist. He was florid of complexion and fussy of manner, and his berry-black eyes—calculating eyes that took in every detail of Cambronne's appearance and dress, reckoning the quality of the man and putting a price on the clothes—slid away when they met the other's steady gaze.

"And, speaking of coolness," he continued, leading Cambronne toward a door at the end of the hallway, "you must get yourself some light tropical clothes. Clothing is very cheap here. I will send my Indian tailor to call upon you." Hetherington wore a suit of white silk, with a shirt of the same material in pale lilac and a loose cravat to match.

The library proved, indeed, to be cool, though perhaps this was an illusion created by a fountain that plashed diamond droplets in a pool set in the center of the room. Motioning to Cambronne to be seated, Hetherington clapped his hands.

"It will be rum," he said. "The island's white rum is quite perfect, and I take nothing else. You will enjoy it spiked with lime juice, slightly chilled. Ah, here come Pushpam and Issy."

Two young girls entered. They wore flowers in their smooth black hair that reached to their slender waists, whose slenderness was plain because both were nude to the hips, below which they wore simple petticoats of patterned cotton. And they were barefoot.

"Indian girls," explained Hetherington. "Can't abide the stink of niggers. I import them from Bombay. They're not slaves, of course. I have to pay 'em wages. But not much. And when they become fat and overblown—as Indian women so often do—all I have to do is send them packing. A slave—a slave who won't fetch a price—one has to feed and clothe for life. Ah, the rum and lime juice!"

Smiling the while, pointed breasts swaying stiffly, one of the girls placed a tall, frosted glass on the table by Cambronne's elbow. Hetherington was similarly served.

The latter raised his glass. "Your very good health, Captain."

"And yours, sir," responded Cambronne. "And to the forthcoming enterprise of my ship, the *Argo!*"

It seemed to the Jerseyman that the form of his pledge caused his host certain surprise and puzzlement.

"Er—quite so, Captain," said Hetherington.

Cambronne was prompted to press home his point. "Do you have orders for me?" he asked. "Or instructions regarding the—additional equipment?" By that he meant guns and ammunition.

The other had recovered his composure. He smiled archly. "I can see that you are a man who likes to come to the point, Captain," he said. "Well then, to business. I think we can allow dear Pushpam and Issy to remain"—he nudged Cambronne's elbow and winked. "They are a pleasure to the eye, and, apart from the bare essentials of English, speak nothing but their own heathenish tongue. We can be quite frank and open. Let us begin with the complement of your vessel. You have no doubt had men fall sick on the voyage. Accidents, perhaps. Death?" He cocked his head on one side and regarded the other with a look of gentle encouragement.

"One man killed," said Cambronne. "And I had to discharge others before we left Boston. I shall have to take on more, many more, if we are to perform our duties as planned."

"Quite so," said Hetherington, looking wise. "What is your complement at the moment, Captain?"

"We left Boston with thirty-six hands," said Cambronne. "It was few enough, but adequate for a schooner of one hundred fifty tons burden."

"Oh no, no!" The agent raised his pudgy white hands in dismay. "You do yourself less than justice, Captain. You will need more, many more men. And *I* shall underwrite your demand and square it with the owners." He leered. *"And pay* their wages without demur. Come, now—*how* many? The decision is yours, all yours."

Intent upon his swift calculation of how many hands would—in the light of the experience he had gained of the *Argo's* performance on passage from Boston to Jamaica—be required to sail and fight the schooner, Cambronne did not notice the insinuating note in his companion's voice. Nor did he observe the other watching him from under his pouched eyelids; berry-black, cunning.

The *Argo,* thought Cambronne, had handled more easily than he had dared to dream. The blue suit of sails would make a difference, but not a great deal. The factor of five crewmen to a gun was the sticking point. And that did not count the swivel-guns. Dare he risk cutting corners? Certainly, so far as comfort and efficiency were concerned, the less passengers the better. Yes . . .

"I'll make shift with another thirty-two men, Mr. Hetherington," he said. "That gives me a complement of sixty-seven."

"You'll make shift . . . !"

Hetherington choked on his drink, retched, and took some little time to recover. When he did, he sat back in his chair, breathless, and regarded Cambronne as one would regard a particularly large and ungainly animal turned loose among one's more friable possessions.

"Are you mad, man?" he demanded at length. "Do you think I've got where I have, amassed all this"—he gestured to the contents of his library: the rows of gold-tooled leather, the bibelots, the fountain; to Pushpam and Issy, curled up together on a Persian rug like a pair of coffee-tinted gazelles —"do you fancy I've come *this* far by letting greed blind my caution? Another thirty-two men? You'd have us both in the dock for fraud! Five—ten—yes. Ten names on the ship's books belonging to men who don't exist; I pay their wages and each of us takes half share. But—sixty-seven men to crew a small schooner! You must be out of your mind!"

Mr. Percy Hetherington had betrayed himself out of his own mouth. He lived by fraud. The upkeep of the English country house set in the lush tropic island, the pictures and the bibelots, the black factotum in the cocked hat, the lovely creatures imported from Bombay, the ruination of his own self that was written large upon his countenance and his gross body—all were derived from defrauding his employers of the

Augusta Line. Not to mention the Sublime Porte, and whatever was to be had in the role of marine surveyor.

Furthermore, he knew absolutely nothing about the *Argo's* purpose in the Caribbean, nor that she was to carry guns and the extra men to serve them. A few more loaded questions settled that in Cambronne's mind. Hetherington knew no more about the illegal traffic that was carried on behind the bland innocence of the Augusta Line's house-flag (two clasped hands, white on blue, and the motto "Friendship") than did secretary Needham. At least Needham suspected, while Hetherington, living right in the heart of the slave-trade area, was totally unaware. His whole intent was upon squeezing every guinea he could—with a degree of prudence—from those who employed him.

Having admonished Cambronne—as he hoped—with some effect, and having taken a couple more glasses of rum with lime juice, he expounded upon the manifest advantages of prudence in the business that he—a dishonest shipping agent —and Cambronne—a demonstrably dishonest and over-reaching sea captain—were upon. The Jerseyman listened with less than an ear, while Hetherington explained how they would together rig bills of lading, demand payment for repair work that existed only on paper, cut corners on provisions, water the rum issue . . .

If this human wreck is not privy to the conspiracy, thought Cambronne, why was I sent to him? Why am I sitting here and listening to this blethering sack of guts? Mark you, the rum and lime juice is not to be sneezed at, likewise the wenches who're watching us from over there, whispering and giggling to each other. I almost fancy . . .

"Ah, I quite forgot. I have something for you, Cambronne." Hetherington broke in on his thoughts, rising to his feet a trifle unsteadily and crossing to a leather-topped rent-table, from a drawer of which he produced a letter, which he brought back, with a sly tap to the side of his nose. "I had no idea that—you will forgive me—a humble captain of the Augusta Line could be so well-connected." He held out the missive so that Cambronne could see the seal, which bore an elaborate armorial crest representing a falcon with hood and bells. "From Lord Basil Lasalle," he said, cocking a shrewd eye to see what effect the name had upon his guest.

"Very interesting," said Cambronne. "I have never had the

pleasure of the gentleman's acquaintance. Who and what is he?"

"My dear fellow, Lord Basil's connections, not to mention his wealth, make him one of the most influential men in Jamaica, in all the British West Indies," said Hetherington. "Whatever his business in writing to you, it can do no harm to your social standing in these parts. Not even if he's dunning you for a debt!" The shipping agent laughed, choked, and had to be ministered to by the Indian girls, who fussed around him, loosening his cravat, patting his back, while Cambronne took a few paces to the window and slit open the letter with his thumb.

The message was short—and answered the question he had been addressing to himself for the last half-hour.

Capt. Cambronne,

You will wish to be at Manatee at six of the clock, no later. You have much to do this night. No word of this to that fool Hetherington, but he will direct you here.

Basil Lasalle

Hetherington had responded to the tender ministrations of his enticing handmaidens and was watching him when he looked up from the paper.

"I am invited to visit him at six today," said Cambronne. "And he suggests that you will direct me there."

"Of course, of course," cried the shipping agent. "To Manatee, that's his plantation on t'other side of Spanish Town, the biggest and finest on the island. Six o'clock. You've plenty of time, my dear fellow, though not enough, I fancy, to return to your ship. Here is what you will do. I will have them prepare a bath for you, then I'll lend you one of the silk suits I had made when first I came here. They will all fit you as neat as a trivet, the suits I had made o' the Indian fellow when first I came here." He glanced wistfully at Cambronne, then down at himself, and sighed.

"That's very civil of you, Hetherington," said the Jersey-man, whose mind was racing. The most influential and richest man in the West Indies, and, by the peremptory tone of the letter, a member of the syndicate that employed him—and the *Argo*. The conspiracy in Boston, the masked personage they called "The Man," had a long and powerful arm indeed. "You have much to do this night"—that sounded promising. What matter of activity was he destined to perform that night?

Hetherington had tugged on a bell-rope and summoned a footman, whom he carefully instructed to take charge of Captain Cambronne: to convey him to the principal guest suite in the south wing, and there to cause a tepid bath to be drawn, and fresh clothing provided, which he himself would select from the recesses of his own wardrobe.

"You really are very kind, Hetherington," said Cambronne. He was aware that he had imbibed deeply of the white rum, and sincerely hoped that the intervening two and a half hours before he was due to confront Lord Basil Lasalle would suffice to blow away most of the fumes. Perhaps a cat-nap in the bath, or maybe he could get his head down atop of a bed for half an hour.

"A pleasure, my dear Cambronne, a very great pleasure. Any connection that the Augusta Line is able to establish with Lord Basil of Manatee can only be of benefit"—the shipping agent tried to look sincere, but failed—"to us both," he concluded, with a wink.

The suite to which the footman led Cambronne comprised a bed-chamber with four-poster bed, a dressing-room, sitting-room, and bathroom. In the latter, a procession of black scullery-maids was already pouring buckets of warm water into a high-sided copper bathtub which had been placed in the center of the tiled floor. The footman fussed and got in the way when Cambronne disrobed, and only when all the servitors had departed did the Jerseyman venture into the bathroom, naked as the day he was born, and lay himself into the suavely warm, scented water.

A tap on the door.

"Who is it?" demanded Cambronne, opening his eyes.

The question—interpreted as an invitation—prompted the entrance of one of the Indian handmaidens who had attended them down below in the library, the one Cambronne had divined to be slightly the older of the pair, with the more developed figure and the promise of ancient evil in the almond-shaped eyes that looked down at him along a very straight, delicately chiselled nose.

"Which of you is you?" asked Cambronne. "Are you Pushpam, or Issy, mmm?"

"I am being Pushpam, sair," she replied.

Cambronne held out a hand.

"Plenty of room in here for the both of us, m'dear," he said.

Pushpam, with breath-robbing elegance and a smile that would have turned an ascetic into a voluptuary upon the very sight, was already slipping the simple cotton petticoat down over her hips.

The road to Lord Basil Lasalle's plantation of Manatee took Cambronne through the broad, elegant streets of Spanish Town, capital of British Jamaica. Beyond the church spires reminiscent of Wren, the elegantly proportioned domes, the richness of city foliage, there rose to the illimitable azure sky the so-called Red Hills that form the steep edge of the southern coastal plain of the big island. In the languorous tropical late afternoon, Cambronne had no eyes for the passing scene. He felt refreshed, rested. The rum fumes were fading from his brain. With disturbingly vivid flashes of remembrance directed toward the delights of Pushpam's repertoire only occasionally intruding upon his mind, the Jerseyman contemplated the prospects that lay before him: the heady thrill of command, the delight of being the hand and brain that conned a fine ship, the lure of action and adventure, the siren call of success. This pleasant euphory was rudely shattered upon the carriage emerging from a shadowed street into the glaring sunlight of an open square, where a brutal reminder of man's mortality was displayed for all to contemplate.

The jail building was of white-painted stone under the tropic sky—that said, it was like every jail the world over, with eyeless windows and a great, iron-studded door set with a wicket and a Judas-hole. A red-coated British soldier, brick red of face, with sweat streaming from under his tall cap and descending to the tight leather stock that banded his neck, stood guard, long bayonet gleaming, at the gate. Ten paces from the gate, and so positioned that all who crossed the square must pass close by it, a wooden gallows rose roof-high, and another redcoat stood guard at its base.

Cambronne craned his head from under the canopy of the carriage and looked up. Carrion crows to the number of three wheeled unhurried circles about an iron cage set atop the gallows, and another was perched there. The cage was shaped

like a coffin—or roughly like a man. In it was the sun-
blackened semblance of a man, with a few rags of clothing to
cover its nakedness and a head—mercifully too high up and
too blackened for the observer to distinguish the features—
lolling brokenly on the leathery skin of the rib cage.

"Who was he?" Cambronne demanded of his coachman.

"One o' de crew of a slaver, sah," replied the other. "Wuz
taken by a navy ship. All of um wuz hanged 'cept the cap'n
what got away. Dis fella dey put up dah so's folks wouldn't
forget."

"I see," said Cambronne.

He sat back and closed his eyes. Gone the euphory. Gone
the heady thoughts of days ahead. The late afternoon sun still
blazed down and nothing had changed in essence—except
that the thing which had once been a man, and was now
crows' meat, now cast a wide shadow over Jason Cambronne,
reminding him of the price of failure.

If Percy Hetherington lived in the style of an English
country gentleman, with landscaped acres, gatehouses and
someone to sweep the carriage drive, Lord Basil Lasalle's
manner of living more nearly approximated to that of the
later Bourbon kings before the French Revolution. Manatee
was more of a town in its own right than a mere plantation,
and its acres of sugarcane stretched from the shores of
Galleon Harbor almost to the outskirts of Spanish Town; all
the last half hour of Cambronne's journey, though he was not
aware of it, he had never left Lasalle land.

His carriage passed unchallenged through the plantation
proper, and through the streets of shanties and dormitory
hovels that housed the slaves who worked on the estate,
though he won many glances from that curious breed of
men—the slave-drivers—who strode everywhere with whips
coiled in hand, pistols on show. Not till his carriage reached
the environs of the mansion known as Manatee Grange was
he stopped, his business demanded, his credentials checked.
In fact, he had only to state his name and show the outside of
the letter with the falcon crest (an insignia he had observed to
be emblazoned upon every building he passed, and which,
did he but know it, was also branded upon the shoulder and
buttock of every slave on the estate) to win complete
subservience from the hard-eyed white brutes who served and

guarded their aristocratic master. He was expected. As an expected visitor, he was escorted the last mile by two outriders on spanking big bays, both men carrying carbines slung from their shoulders. Within the confines of the mansion's grounds and gardens there was no sign of the squalor and misery that Cambronne had espied in the slave quarters: only rolling green parkland fed by man-made canals that ended in a vast water-garden in front of the baroque facade of Manatee Grange. There a hundred jets of bright cyrstal kissed skyward in ordered patterns of rainbow-hued confusion about a central feature, which comprised a vast circular fountain-bowl containing a heroic-sized group representing the sea-god Neptune, his queen, his daughters, and the tutelary gods and goddesses of the English rivers, all crowded into a sea-borne quadriga drawn by four high-prancing seahorses; and from every orifice—from the conch horns blown by Neptune's daughters, from wide-open mouths, flaring nostrils, proud nipples—another bright water-jet added to the display. A haze of cool dampness hung over the watergarden, and Cambronne, passing through it, was greatly refreshed.

Not one but a whole line of flunkeys greeted his arrival at the foot of the double curve of steps leading to the massive portals of Manatee Grange, on whose roof line a hundred classical statues posed and gesticulated. Commanding this small brigade of servitors was—who else?—a typical English butler in knee-breeches, powdered wig, tailed coat, and carrying a tall, silver-knobbed staff like a beadle's.

"Captain Cambronne, sir. Lord Basil h-is h-at present h-engaged h-upon h-other matters, but will h-attend you presently. This way, Captain Cambronne, sir."

Cocking a wry eye, greatly amused, Cambronne followed after the butler, whose minions came in single file behind the sea captain, taking their step from his. The ill-assorted procession passed through the great door and into a chamber that could have housed Percy Hetherington's abode, chimney-pots and all: a salon of such staggering proportions as to confound the eye, with a wide double staircase ascending in two noble curves to the upper story.

"Who is this gentleman, Cumberley?" The voice—deep, husky, sonorous—came from the top of the staircase, and echoed.

"H-it's Captain Cambronne, to see Lord Basil, madame."

"Lord Basil will be a little while yet. I will entertain the good captain till he comes. I shall find it—most agreeable."

The speaker descended. Slowly and with a languid grace that put Cambronne in mind of a predatory cat of the jungle: lithe and impeccably groomed, self-pampered and self-regarding; dangerous to the eye. She wore a riding-out costume of black velvet, which further contributed to the cat image. Upon her sleek black hair, which was drawn back in a severe chignon at the nape, was jauntily perched a truncated top hat garnished—shockingly—with a bandeau of violet taffeta. She descended like a dancer, placing each tiny, booted foot deliberately on each succeeding step, and pausing an instant before following it with the other foot.

Her face was flawlessly beautiful, with almond-shaped eyes and dramatic cheekbones. The lips a trifle full, and of a richness of color that owed something to paint. A mole subtly announced the corner of her mouth. And her skin—a shadowed magnolia tint—betrayed an admixture of Negro blood. A mulattress.

Upon reaching the lower step, she extended a small, gloved hand to the Jerseyman.

"How do you do, Captain. I am Alissa."

"Your servant, ma'am." The hand in his was as delicate as a bird, but communicated a strange and disquietening *frisson* of animal magnetism.

"You have been in Jamaica—how long, Captain?" Her dark-lashed eyes took in the details of Cambronne's costume. Poor Hetherington's silk suit fitted him to perfection; if anything it was a trifle tight, and subtly described the muscled breadth of his shoulders, the power of his loins.

"We arrived on the noon tide, ma'am," replied Cambronne. "And I was straightway summoned to attend Lord Basil."

"We shall walk in the gardens till he comes," said the exotic creature who called herself Alissa, taking from the breast-pocket of her habit an alligator-skin case from which she extracted a long thin cheroot. "Give me your arm."

From nowhere, one of the butler's acolytes produced a candle from which Alissa took a light, drawing deeply on the aromatic smoke and exhaling it through her finely fashioned nostrils. Then, taking Cambronne's proffered arm, she indicated that they must pass on through the great salon to an archway at the far end.

"Are you married, Captain?" she asked him.

"I am not, ma'am."

"Neither am I," said Alissa. She eyed him sidelong, the shadow of a smile touching the corner of her lips. "And in answer to the question that you are too chivalrous to put, my position at Manatee is that of châtelaine. Not—as you might report to your shipmates when you return aboard—mistress to Lord Basil."

"Ma'am, I would not dream of . . ."

She cut short his protest. "My dear captain, do not dissemble," she said. "It does not become you, whom I take to be a strong, forthright man. Of course you will talk about me when you return to your ship. I am a woman whom men do not overlook, whom men talk about, speculate about. Your guess, when you first saw me just now, was that I am Lord Basil's mistress. Correct? Come now, Captain Cambronne, if we are to be friends (and I hope we are to be friends), there must be frankness between us."

Cambronne grinned. "That was certainly my first thought, ma'am," he admitted.

"Then, as I have said, you are wrong," she declared. "Alissa is no man's mistress."

Cambronne made no reply to that pronouncement, and could only marvel at the advancement in intimacy that his companion's direction of the conversation had led them to achieve in the relatively short time it had taken to traverse the great salon and emerge, by way of a colonnaded corridor, into a garden at the rear of the mansion.

"Amuse me," demanded Alissa. "Tell me of your *amours*. When did you last lie with a woman?"

Cambronne all but laughed out loud at her question, but was oddly prompted to match frankness with frankness.

"This afternoon, ma'am," he said. "But an hour since."

"*Ma foi!*" exclaimed Alissa, miming alarm. "Hot, as you might say, from your jousting at the Court of Venus. Tell me, where did this—I am quite sure—highly satisfactory encounter take place, and in what circumstances?"

"At the house of Mr. Hetherington, who is agent to my employer," said Cambronne.

"Ah—Hetherington! The gentleman who imports young

ladies from Bombay. I remember him. Well, I take it you greatly enjoyed your Bombay lady, Captain. But you must be careful, lest the life of self-indulgence and dissipation that some European gentlemen lead in Jamaica brings you to the same strait as Mr. Hetherington, who was quite personable to look upon when first he arrived. Ah, here comes Lord Basil, which means that I shall be tactfully asked to leave. We must resume this most interesting conversation at another time and in another place, Captain.''

He entered the garden by way of a wide stone staircase that led down from a terrace that stretched the entire length of the rear of the mansion. He was clad all in white: white tail-coat and pantaloons, white frilled shirt and neckcloth to match. His hair, too, was of a startling blondness and worn long in the nape. Pale complexion, also. But, as he drew closer, it was to be seen that he was no albino; large and exceedingly lustrous green eyes met the Jerseyman, took him in from head to foot, then flashed to the woman at his side.

"Hello, my dear. Are you riding out? Don't let us keep you. Kiss me." Lord Basil was in his mid-thirties, and his voice had an edge of authority.

Alissa gave Cambronne the ghost of a wink and obediently kissed the aristocrat's proffered cheek. Both men watched her walk away down the sunlit path back to the house.

"Magnificent creature, isn't she?" drawled Lord Basil. "Her father was a Creole from Louisiana, her mother a half-caste from Trinidad. I sometimes think that Alissa possesses all that is most elegant and beautiful in the races that went into her make-up. And many of their shortcomings, I may add. She is quite indispensable to me in every way. Did you have a good voyage from Boston?"

"Excellent, thank you," said Cambronne.

"You met Hetherington. What opinion did you form of him?"

Cambronne replied guardedly. "He did not seem to be very well informed about—certain aspects of my business in the West Indies."

"He knows nothing," was the response. "The man's a fool and a libertine, and I haven't the slightest doubt but that he's robbing Holt blind. But he has his uses. No one here in Jamaica knows anything of the connection between the Augusta Line and myself, nor between myself'—here the regarding green eyes met Cambronne's eyes—"and the business we are about."

"I see," said Cambronne. "There's another employee of the Augusta Line, Uriah Needham, secretary to Mr. Holt, who also hasn't been admitted to the secret. I've asked myself many times what he is going to do out here."

The aristocrat shrugged. "He will confine himself to Augusta Line business and myself," he said, adding with a dry chuckle: "If he examines Hetherington's books and accounts, so much the worse for Hetherington, I shouldn't wonder. Let us go into the house. I've something to show you."

They entered the mansion by way of the terrace and a door that led into a high-ceilinged room which had the trappings of a gentleman's study. Lying upon a table by a wide window that commanded a view of the gardens was a nautical chart. As Cambronne approached it, he was able to see that it represented the isle of Jamaica, its longest axis lying precisely east-west. Glancing closer, his pulse quickened.

"By heaven, Lord Basil!" he exclaimed. "This chart makes great claims. These soundings in fathoms along every last yard of the shoreline out to the hundred-fathom line—can they be accurate?"

"Yes," replied the other. "And we have in our possession charts of most of the islands in the Caribbean, as well as a large part of the north and south American mainlands bordering upon that sea." He smiled—a pale, graveyard sort of smile. "We have been in business a long time, Captain. And before us there were the buccaneers and the pirates of the Spanish Main. A whole repository of seamanlike knowledge, carefully garnered and stored, kept from those outside the brotherhood. The fighting navies of the United States and England do not own such maps as the one you see here, Captain, as well you know. In addition to possessing your ship—the legacy of Vincenzo Alfieri—you have the means to take that ship where others dare not venture, to remote inlets and coves whose hazards are marked only upon our secret charts. You will be—inviolable. And that inviolability will commence—*tonight!*

"In your letter," said Cambronne, recalling, "you said that I had much to do this night."

"You have arrived here," said Lord Basil. "Another schooner, to swell the teeming fleets of similar craft that ply the Caribbean. Tonight, like the hunted fox with every man's hand against him, you will go to earth. See here"—the aristocrat's long, pale fingers flickered over the chart, along the southern shore of the island—"my estate extends to the edge of this bay, and the shoreline is patroled, day and night, by armed men and killer dogs. The approach from the sea, as you observe from the soundings, is by means of only one narrow channel. And here, close by the shore, is a rock which is the size of this very house. Between that rock and the shore is anchorage for one vessel and one vessel alone. That will be your earth, Captain. A safe hiding-place which you will only enter, and which you will only leave, after dark."

Cambronne's professional eye, taking in the configuration of the land surrounding the bay, and the sight-lines from seaward, already knew as much about the secret anchorage as if he had been there.

"As you imply, Lord Basil," he said, "a vessel the size of the *Argo* could remain there forever, unseen from sea or shore."

"Can you negotiate the approach by night, do you think?" demanded the other.

"With this chart—yes," said Cambronne. "But I should prefer to moor, rather than anchor."

"Mooring-buoys, spaced to take your ship, have already been laid, Captain," said Lord Basil.

"You have thought of everything, sir," said Cambronne.

"That is my business, Captain," said the blond aristocrat dressed all in white.

A Negro footman brought refreshments to the study: tea and coffee, rum and French wines, delicate sandwiches in the English manner. Lord Basil sipped tea from a porcelain cup and talked incessantly, while Cambronne twirled a glass of claret between his fingers and listened to every word, interjecting a question from time to time.

"Tomorrow, you must repaint your ship's side," said Lord Basil. "It must never again be recognized as the schooner that entered Kingston today under the command of a certain Captain Cambronne. What color is the ship's side now?"

"She is in natural oak," said Cambronne.

"I would suggest black," said Lord Basil. "Much of your work close inshore will be done under cover of darkness. Black will add to your invisibility."

Cambronne nodded.

"Tomorrow, also," continued the other, "you will take aboard ordinance stores. Your eight cannon and swivel-guns. Powder, wads, and shot of all types. Five racks of muskets and ditto of cutlasses. And crew. I will make up your tally of crew to the required strength. All of these men have worked in our trade for years and are to be trusted. What of your present crew—have you told them what their work is to be?"

"Not yet," said Cambronne. "I will do that tonight, before we sail for the secret anchorage."

"There are ways of doing it," said Lord Basil, "so that the faint-hearted or squeamish may have the opportunity to withdraw their services without actually becoming privy to your secret."

"I have thought of such a way," said Cambronne.

"I knew you were to be relied on," said the other.

Out in the elegant garden, from somewhere in the long shadows of the descending sun, a peacock's call shattered the stillness, the most eerie sound in all nature. Cambronne felt the short hairs prickle at the back of his neck. He took a long pull at his claret, and said, "When does the *Argo* sail upon her first voyage of escort, Lord Basil?"

"After provisioning, you will be at forty-eight hours' notice."

"So soon?"

"The *modus operandi* that I have devised," said the aristocrat, "is simple in the extreme. As soon as the merchandise has been assembled at one or other of our boarding-points in the Gulf of Guinea and is ready to be loaded aboard the ships, a fast dispatch vessel leaves Africa with the news that the convoy is precisely three days behind her. Upon receiving that information you will sail to a pre-arranged rendezvous with the convoy at sixty degrees west, on the edge of the Caribbean, whence you will escort the ships to their destinations in Cuba, Brazil and elsewhere."

"And what of the—opposition, Lord Basil?" asked Cambronne. "What ships of the Royal and the United States navies are doing anti-slaver patrol in the area, and what are their methods?"

The aristocrat laid his cup and saucer down and smiled thinly at his guest. "Tomorrow night," he said, "I am giving a reception in honor of the Governor of Jamaica. Present at the reception will be Commodore Harvey, Royal Navy, who heads the combined anti-slavery forces in the Caribbean. The good commodore is a garrulous fellow, and you, as a fellow member of the sea-going persuasion, will have his complete confidence. You will be able to pose your question to the man most fitted to answer it."

"I see," said Cambronne.

"You will gauge his temper and his quality," said Lord Basil. "And, as a man of perception, you will not be fooled by his bluff and simple manner. The fellow is shrewder than he looks. Not, I hasten to add, a great deal shrewder than he looks. But he has the stubbornness and persistence often associated with those of pygmy intellect, and they are qualities which may serve a man better than most. Were you aware that the Anti-Slavery Society—I refer to the *real* society and not Holt's sham—are on to us?"

"No, I was not," said Cambronne.

"We are definitely under suspicion," said Lord Basil. "Some of us. Not I—or so I fancy. The Boston end, certainly. But they can prove nothing. No connection between the slave trade and the Augusta Line, and, as I have said, no connection between the Augusta Line and myself. I have invited you here today, Captain, because your father performed various excellent services for my father the Duke—or that will be the story. Similarly, for the sake of past favors, you are coming to the reception tomorrow."

"I thank you, sir," said Cambronne. A pause. "Speaking of Boston . . ."

"Yes?"

"I suppose that you have met the personage we refer to as 'The Man'?"

"Yes I have. Many times."

"Do you know his true identity?"

"No, Captain, I am not to be drawn on that question."

"He is, perhaps—you, yourself, Lord Basil?"

The sidelong, green-eyed glance was sharp, dangerous. "No, I am not 'The Man,'" was the response. "And I warn you that you are fishing in perilous waters, Cambronne."

"Peril is my trade, sir," grinned the other.

CHAPTER 6

Cambronne took his leave without seeing the exotic Alissa again. He went with the chart of Jamaica rolled up under his arm, and reached the teeming quayside at Kingston in the purple-hued twilight. Tom Blackadder greeted his captain at the gangplank. Blackadder was seated on a bollard and smoking a cheroot.

"Call all hands after supper, Master," said Cambronne. "We sail on the tide, but I will first address the crew."

"A long voyage, sir?"

"No. An hour, perhaps a little less."

"Shall we be coasting? My knowledge of the south coast is good, but not all that good. Not for night work."

Cambronne grinned. "You will be astounded by your expertise tonight, Master," he replied, and had the satisfaction of seeing puzzlement in the other's countenance.

Blackadder had risen to his feet, was just about to precede his captain along the gangplank—as custom demanded—when there came a deep bellow from the quayside:

"TOM!"

And from out of the idling crowd there burst an apparition of a man: fully seven feet tall and built like a brick wall, with a domed, shaven head that rose from wide, sloping shoulders and a tree trunk of a neck.

"Oh, my God!" murmured Blackadder. "What have I done in my life to deserve *him* again?"

The apparition was carrying a kitbag, ditty-box and rolled hammock under one massive arm. Dropping these, he reached out two hamlike fists and, taking Blackadder by the head, proceeded to rain kisses upon the other's protesting lips, his cheeks, his brow.

"Ach, Tom! Tom!" bellowed the giant, whom Cambronne perceived to have only one ear, the other being reduced to a twist of shriveled gristle. "Tom—is gut! Gut!"

"Sure, it's good to see you again, Swede," replied the unfortunate, struggling to free himself, but only winning himself a place closer to the other's heart as he was embraced by those massive arms and hugged tightly.

"Friend of yours, Master?" asked Cambronne, amused.

"Shipped with him more than five years since," explained the other with an anguished glance. "He thinks I saved his life once."

"And did you?" asked Cambronne.

"Tom—is gut! Gut!" repeated the giant, lovingly.

"It was in a tavern in Valparaiso," explained Blackadder, still imprisoned. "They'd slipped something in his drink, and I beat them off him just as they started to go through his pockets. Then I dragged the brute by his heels out of there and ducked him in a horse-trough. Ever since then, he's loved me like a brother. Get off me, you damn fool Swede bastard! You're breaking my ribs!"

"What happened to his ear?" asked Cambronne, lighting himself a cigar.

"Chewed off by a Chinese whore in Cochin. Let go of me you brainless hulk! He speaks hardly a word of English, being a goddamned Swede. But he always seemed to understand me."

"Tom! Tom! Gut Tom!"

"Ask him if he's got a ship," said Cambronne.

"Swede, you stupid big bastard—do you have a ship?"

A mist of incomprehension clouded the pale blue eyes of the affectionate giant, and was only dispelled when the question was repeated twice more. Then a slow grin of delight cracked the bovine countenance.

"Swede ship mit Tom! Ja! Is gut!"

"He wants to ship with me," said Blackadder, rolling his eyes. "And to think I've been looking over my shoulder these five years in horror of seeing him again."

"Is he a good hand?" asked Cambronne.

"Dumb as an ox, as you can see," said Blackadder. "But you could tie a hawser to him and he'd tow the ship. Good man in a fight—but you can see that for yourself."

"We'll have him," said Cambronne. And, remembering, he added: "I thank God that he wasn't with you that time I tried to throw you out of my room at the Lincolnshire Arms in Boston!"

* * *

So Swede joined the *Argo* as topman, and slung his hammock for'ard with the rest. Supper over, and at two bells of the first watch, the schooner slipped her ropes and glided out into mid-harbor, where she dropped anchor. To Blackadder's puzzlement, Cambronne also gave orders for the jolly-boat to be lowered at the gangway. He had the lower deck cleared and the men mustered in the waist, betwixt the fore and main masts. He then addressed them:

"Lads, what I have to say is for your ears only, which is why we're out in the stream," he began.

Blackadder was watching him, arms folded, from the bulwarks. Jack the Cat and Tobias Angel were by the foremast: their eyes, like everyone else's, were unwaveringly upon him. He had his audience in thrall.

"There can't be a man among you," he continued, "who hasn't wondered what business this ship is bound upon, seeing as she carries space for neither passengers nor cargo. One or two of you"—he glanced from Blackadder to Jack the Cat and back again—"have a fair notion that we're bound for something out of the ordinary, and they are right."

Crossing to the gangway, Cambronne pointed down to the jolly-boat that bobbed at the end of its painter in the dark water.

"I will unfold to you gradually," he said, "what the *Argo* was built for and why she's here. If my story interests you, you will wish to stay and hear me out to the end. Any man who is not attracted by the work I offer is free to take his place in the jolly-boat, to be rowed ashore before we depart. Anyone who doesn't like the cut of my jib, or what I've said so far?"

No one answered, not a man moved.

"To begin," said Cambronne. "You will be asking yourselves: is what the *Argo* came to Jamaica for outside the law? The answer is: yes, it is outside the law. Do I see anyone making a move to go?"

Stillness. And total silence, save the lapping of wavelets against the schooner's stem.

"Is it piracy?" continued the Jerseyman. "No, it is not strictly piracy, but for all that it's a hanging matter. What are the rewards? The rewards are such that a poor seaman might

expect to retire within a couple of years and buy himself a tidy
tavern ashore on the proceeds. Do you want to hear more?"

"Keep talking, Captain," murmured Blackadder.

"There will be danger," said Cambronne. "And not only
the normal seafaring hazards of fire and tempest. And, as I
have said, you might end up on the gallows. Still I see not a
man making a move to leave. Well then, I must tell you what
our business is to be. But first"—he took from his pocket his
under-and-over pistol and thumbed back the hammers to full
cock—"I must warn you that any man who makes a move to
leave after he has opted to stay and hear me to the end will
have his head blown off his shoulders; and, likewise, any man
who betrays his ship and his shipmates at any future time will
be hanged from the mains'l gaff-end. This is your last chance
to get down into the boat. I will count to ten."

They stayed motionless to a count of ten. And then
Cambronne pocketed his pistol and told them all.

More or less.

They sailed on the tide, and all Blackadder's doubts were
put to rest when Cambronne showed him the chart, the like of
which he had never dreamed existed. Indeed, there were
hazards in the approaches to Kingston Harbor—hazards of
which he had many times and unknowingly stood in peril—all
faithfully recorded on the chart.

Less than an hour later, having safely negotiated the
approach to the bay that bordered the Manatee plantation,
and preceded by the jolly-boat, the *Argo* glided behind the
towering fang of rock that would be her safe haven from
henceforth. Her head-rope was taken in the jolly-boat and
passed through the ring of a mooring-buoy that had been
placed there; likewise, her stern was safely secured by
another buoy. And there she lay snugly, not two cables'
length from the dark shoreline. Blackadder, who shook his
head in disbelief, insisted on taking a sounding of the mooring
with lead and line, only to find that there were, indeed, two
clear fathoms beneath the *Argo's* deep keel—exactly as
recorded on the miraculous chart.

Cambronne slept well in his narrow cabin that night, with
the shore breeze coolly bringing the heady scent of honeysuckle through the open window. He dreamed of calm seas
and good landfalls, of fair women and staunch companion-
ship. At early dawn he woke and went up on deck, dived

nude into the transparent blueness, deeply and level with the schooner's keel, seeing it properly for the first time and marveling at the genius of the man who had designed the wonder-vessel.

The crew breakfasted off fresh grilled ham and eggs, washed down with strong coffee laced with rum. Scarcely had they finished before lighters put out from the shore and came alongside. The blacks aboard the ladened lighters attached brass cannon-barrels to the end of the tackle that *Argo* lowered to them, and these were hauled inboard: eight 12-pounder barrels of the latest, post-Trafalgar pattern, from Portsmouth Dockyard by heaven knows what means. They were followed by carriages of seasoned English oak bound with steel, together with side-arms of rammers, sponges, ladles and worms, as well as flintlocks to ignite the charges, all packed in fine mahogany boxes of high polish. Next came the racks of rifled muskets after the pattern of the famous Kentucky rifle, and racks of heavy cutlasses that would lop off an arm or a head with the lightest of blows. After that, kegs of powder that were immediately taken below the waterline for safety's sake, and shot of all sorts: round, bar, chain, grape, faggot and elongating. It was past noon before the ordnance stores were all taken in and lighters returned to shore for another load of cargo—this time, human cargo.

Cambronne was greatly interested to observe the demeanor of the newcomers—the remainder of his crew—and also to see his old hands' reactions to them. The new men, who—as Lord Basil had told him—had crewed in slave-ships, were not particularly hard-bitten, nor brutish-looking, for all that they had been following one of the vilest trades on earth. They were spruce and well-barbered, with good traps in the way of brass-bound sea-chests, hat-boxes, waterproof hammock-covers and the like. They carried themselves with the careless ease of men with money in their pockets and the prospect of plenty more to come. On closer examination, the observant and sensitive might have noticed a certain coldness of eye in some of them, as if they had grown accustomed to sights and sounds against which the human mind has no defense but first to ignore, then to accept, then to embrace as a way of life.

Their effect upon the old hands of the *Argo* was very marked. If there were any who had, by their silence, pledged themselves to a course of action of which, in the dark hours of the night, they might have had second thoughts, the sight of the newcomers, their brash and confident talk, their cool assurance, not to mention their manifest affluence—must, surely, have quietened their uneasy consciences. Old crew and newcomers had midday meal together on the mess-deck, and many were the tales told over rare cold roast beef and candied yams, sweet potatoes and black-eyed peas, supplemented with ample rum and lime juice.

Jack the Cat sought out his captain on the poop-deck that afternoon, while the rest of the crew were at make-and-mend after their exertions of the morning. The Englishman's disfigurements stood pitilessly revealed in the blinding sunshine: the scarred surrounds to the eyes that gave them the catlike look; the wide slit of mouth reaching almost back to the jawbone each side. And he smelt strongly of rum.

"Permission to speak, sir?" And he gave a travesty of a naval salute.

Cambronne frowned, sensing trouble in the other's demeanor.

"Carry on, man," he said.

"Captain, I made a compact with you back in Boston, and nothing you told us last night makes any difference."

"But . . . ?"

"But, Captain, I now have a certain reservation."

"Out with it."

"I have been eating—and drinking—with our new shipmates," said Jack the Cat. "Good fellows, all. None too proud of the trade they've been following, but not mealy-mouthed about it, either."

"Come to the point, man!" demanded Cambronne. "What's your reservation? State it—then go pack your kitbag and be gone!"

"My reservation, Captain, is—Lord Basil Lasalle, rot his guts!"

Silence—and then: "Where did you hear that name?" demanded Cambronne.

"Most recently," replied the other, "I heard it down on the mess-deck. Our new shipmates let drop that we all work for 'the man up at the big house.' And they gave his name. It is a name I know well from the past."

"Go on."

"Captain, our compact stands—on one condition."

"State your condition."

"That you listen to a warning," said Jack the Cat. "Pay heed to it or not as you will. But give me leave to state it."

"I'm listening."

The Cat's eyes slid sidelong to the shore, where the waving crests of the sugarcanes stretched like an ever-moving ocean as far as the foothills of the mountain range in the heart of the island.

"I'm warning you against a human devil," he said. "Take all that's worst in a snake and you've got Lasalle. Add the mentality of a man who'll torture and kill for pleasure's sake and you've got Lasalle."

"You have proof?" demanded Cambronne. "What has he done to you?"

The other sighed. "To me—nothing," he said. "I was of his age, and his equal, in the community in which we lived, so I had nothing to fear from him. Others—the younger ones—were not so fortunate."

"You are speaking of a school?" said Cambronne.

"Yes. We were—at school together."

"Were you, indeed?" said Cambronne. "Interesting. Do continue."

"I could give you a hundred instances," said Jack the Cat. "I will confine myself to one. The climax of that devil's school career. There was a youngster who dared to stand up to him. I was not present at the time, or by God I would have prevented the outcome. Lasalle ordered his cronies to string the lad up from a beam by his thumbs and strip him. And then, as punishment for defiance, Lord Basil Lasalle took a knife, and with his own elegant hands, he gelded the offender as one would geld a calf."

"Suffering Christ!"

"The lad died," said Jack the Cat. "He was an orphan, with a guardian who stood to inherit a large fortune upon the demise of his ward; Lasalle is the younger son of a duke: a fortuitous conjuncture that permitted the whole affair to be hushed up, and to everyone's—almost everyone's—satisfaction. That is the man for whom we work, Captain. And this is my warning: beware! You are supping with a devil. Take heed that you eat with a long spoon."

A touch of the forelock, a rictus grin—and Jack the Cat went for'ard.

* * *

That night Cambronne was rowed ashore, where a carriage
waited to convey him to Manatee. He was driven through
long lanes carved between the high walls of sugarcane and
through the landscaped parkland to the great house all lit up
and pulsating with music.

"My dear Cambronne. How nice you could come. Miss
Holt you know, likewise Madame Alissa. I should like to
present you to His Excellency the Governor and Lady
D'Eath." Lasalle was in white again, and Cambronne
searched in vain to read any sign of depravity in that smooth,
bland countenance. Could this be the cool voice which had
ordered the stringing-up of that tragic lad? he wondered. And
this the smooth hand that . . . ?

"Delighted to meet you, Captain." His Excellency the
Governor was short and round, his lady wife tall and thin.
Cambronne looked beyond them to Virginia Holt, who bit
her lip and quickly addressed a remark to Uriah Needham,
who stood beside her. Secretary Needham had greatly grown
in confidence from the pale and awkward youth whom
Cambronne had first met so short a while ago—a fact
that the Jerseyman registered with a wayward twinge of
unease.

"And here," said Lord Basil, completing the round of
immediate introductions, "is Commodore Harvey. Harvey, I
should like you to meet Captain Cambronne of the Augusta
Line, formerly Royal Navy. I will leave you two nautical
gentlemen to your arcane discourse." The master of Manatee
raised an elegant eyebrow to Cambronne and went to attend
his other guests.

"Cambronne . . . Cambronne . . ." The commodore's
complexion was the color of port wine, and his voice was
fruity to match. He was a few years older than Cambronne,
and the Jerseyman was relieved to confirm that they had
never met before. "Don't seem to recall the name, Captain.
When did you leave the navy?"

Cambronne told him—or as nearly as made no matter. He
fended off further and more particular details regarding his
career—as, for instance, what ships he had commanded—by
vehemently raising a matter that he gauged to be close to his
companion's heart.

"Tell me, sir," he demanded, "is it true what I hear, that a navy ship was fired upon by a damned slaver, and her captain killed?"

"It is, sir. It is!" Commodore Harvey's complexion grew, if anything, even more choleric. "Every word is true!"

"Has it come to this, then?" cried Cambronne. "Is it for this that we fought and won at Trafalgar? Are the seas not even safe for an armed vessel of the Royal Navy?"

"My God, sir, your words cut me deeply," declared Harvey. "I knew him well, Makepeace, the captain of *Circe*. An officer of the old school. We'll not see his like again among the young whippersnappers who're coming into the service today. Killed, as you say, by a shot from the slaver. A pure fluke of a shot, of course. Those devils know nothing of gunnery. And they were hanged for it, every one. Save the damned captain, who managed to escape from Execution Dock. Terrible business. Terrible business. And I hold myself responsible."

"You should not blame yourself, Commodore," said Cambronne. "The hazards of war . . ."

"Never should have let *Circe* patrol on her own," declared Harvey. "Learned my lesson now. Ever seen a pair of greyhounds run down a hare, Cambronne? That's the way we shall be doing it from now on."

"Ah! Your ships are patroling in pairs?" said Cambronne. "But do you have sufficient frigates, sloops and so forth to cover so vast an area?"

Harvey winked and looked wise. "The Yankees are taking their share of the burden," he said. "Everything north of the twentieth parallel is their hunting-ground, everything south, ours. *And* I've demanded—and got—six more frigates from England, who'll be arriving on the station by the end of the month. Mark my words, Cambronne—by the end of this year, the slave trade will be as dead in fact as 'tis supposed to be on the statute books."

"Your analogy with greyhound coursing was very illuminating, sir," said Cambronne. "As regards your methods . . ."

"As regards the methods I have laid down for captains to follow," said Harvey, "they are largely dictated by the central problem, which is to capture intact a sizable armed ship without causing undue harm to the poor black devils shackled below. Had poor Makepeace stood off and fired round-shot, he could have driven that slaver to surrender with ten minutes' hard pounding.

"But at considerable cost, perhaps, to the slaves," said Cambronne.

"Quite so. Instead, he went in close and went for her rigging with chain-shot." The commodore spread his hands and hunched his shoulders. "Thereby getting himself killed by a fluke."

"And so . . ."

"And so, Cambronne, I have given orders to my captains to stand off and pound the devils with round-shot."

"And the slaves?"

Commodore Harvey's choleric countenance assumed an expression that approximated to the pious. "We must regrettably accept a certain proportion of casualties among those unfortunate wretches," he said. "But they are, after all, what they are. And I'll not have the life of one British seaman, be he captain or Jack Tar, put to hazard when there's a better method at hand."

So that's it, thought Cambronne. The navy's opting for safety. Where is the spirit of Trafalgar? Stand off and pound, and to hell with the poor black wretches—men, women and children—huddled down in the dark holds, while the round-shot comes bursting in, turning every oak sliver into a razor-edged killing knife that will tear and rend their shrinking flesh.

If the hunters opt for safety, then the hunted must follow the precept of the dictator without whom the *Argo* would never have been dreamed of:

"Encore de l'audace! Et toujours de l'audace!"

There was a five-piece orchestra playing in the minstrel gallery at one end of the vast salon, and a few of the younger guests were dancing.

Virginia had several times been ogled by an exceedingly handsome young Guards ensign—an aide to the Governor, Hatchwell by name—who had not yet found the temerity to break through the distinguished company surrounding her and request a dance, but looked as if he soon might. On the whole, she hoped that he would not, for she was fascinated by Lord Basil.

A product of rich and snobbish society, Virginia was totally entranced by the notion of the British aristocracy, and the very idea of sitting and talking to a living, breathing lord (Lord Basil had made it plain that he did not dance, and they had retired together to a corner of the salon) left her with the dizzy feeling that, as soon as it was over, she must instantly write home to all her friends in Boston about it. And what would silly Suzanne Duveen think to that?

Surprisingly, as her companion explained to her, he was not really a lord at all, since, as a younger son of a duke, he held the title by courtesy and was reckoned only as a commoner. But to be the son, albeit only a younger son, of a duke! Yes, she would write to silly Suzanne that very night, however late.

He—Lord Basil—was recounting to her an extremely amusing anecdote concerning an ancestor of his, the fifth duke, who had been a crony of King Charles II, when her attention was drawn from the doings of that libertine monarch and his circle to an encounter taking place across the room. Jason Cambronne was talking to the creature known as Madame Alissa.

She—Virginia—had scarcely acknowledged Cambronne all evening, and was fearful that he would approach her. The very thought of having to face those mocking, blue-gray eyes with their message that he was recalling that night in her cabin aboard the *Argo* when, after drinking too much wine at dinner, she had gone so far as to . . .

Not to think of it!

She turned her attention back to Lord Basil, who had come to the point of his story about the Merry Monarch and the fifth duke, which appeared to turn on the fact that the king had mistaken the duchess's bedchamber for that of his own wife, and his droll comment upon realizing this. She just had time to assemble a laugh.

Lord Basil, observing that he had pleased his lovely companion, embarked on another tale. She gave him her full attention for a few moments, then again let her gaze slip over his shoulder to the two figures opposite.

The Alissa creature was a walking scandal. She supposed that the woman was Lord Basil's mistress, which only went to show how lax were the social mores in the West Indies. She was dressed in a single sheath of patterned silk that left bare one shoulder and was swathed about the convolutions of her figure in such a manner as to suggest that there was life within that was bursting to get out. On her head was a turban of a similar material, atop which, secured there by a brooch of diamonds, was an aigrette of bird-of-paradise plumes. Her

feet were bare, the toes banded with jeweled rings, likewise
her ankles. One hand on hip, the other holding a long cigar
which from time to time she put to her painted lips, she
was—seemed to be—holding Cambronne enthralled. The
man was looking down at the creature with a half-grin—that
maddening half-grin that seemed to be his stock-in-trade for
dealing with women. Virginia drew a sharp intake of breath
from sheer distaste when the colored woman reached out and
laid a hand, briefly, upon his forearm, in a gesture that might
have been meant to emphasize the remark she was making,
but which Virginia knew (any woman would know, it was so
obvious, was it not? she asked herself) to be sheer coquetry.
And, as if by some curious magnetism, the creature seemed
to divine Virginia's spark of abhorrence, for the dark,
almond-shaped eyes flashed sidelong, and, seeing the girl's
gaze upon her, she smiled. It was a mocking, feline smile that
sent Virginia's attention scurrying back in confusion to what
her companion was saying.

The episode that followed, the incident that turned the
event into a legend that was spoken of in smart Jamaican
society forever after, began, like a mummers' play, with a
shifting and a reassembling of the characters involved; and
Virginia stood at the center of it all, the unwitting catalyst,
the innocent whose dew-fresh loveliness caused the sable
wings of Death's dark angel briefly to overshadow that
brilliant gathering.

First, Lord Basil was summoned to attend upon the Governor's lady, who wished him to counsel her on some trivial
matter. Lord Basil raised an eyebrow but went amiably
enough, first enjoining Virginia to stay right where she was
and not go away, for he had more, much more, to tell her.

Next, by chance, Lord Basil's butler—he of the powdered
wig, silver-knobbed staff and laborious aspirates—found
need to consult Alissa, as châtelaine of the establishment,
about a minor domestic crisis. She departed with him, leaving
Cambronne alone and with no one to talk to but Virginia,
with whose eyes he locked on the instant, till she lowered her
gaze and tried to summon up the will to run. She heard his
tread as he crossed the parquet, and saw that her gloved
hands were trembling. God, what a fool, what a debauched
and silly fool she had been that night on the ship! Would he
mock her with it? Would he . . . ?

"Miss Virginia, ma'am. May I have the pleasure of the next dance?"

With a start, she looked up into the handsome, vacuous face of Mr. Ensign Hatchwell, who had the manners and appearance of a well-bred racehorse: all fire, brilliance and blunder. She had—rightly—mistrusted him and his motives toward her; but at this juncture he promised all the blessed release of a St. Bernard dog on a high pass in the snowbound Alps.

She took his hand and advanced with him to the dancing floor, passing Cambronne on the way, not daring to look into his face for fear of what she might see there. He paused at her passing and she saw from the corner of her eye that he inclined his head in a bow.

They danced a valse, she and Ensign Hatchwell, and a fine pair they made, natural aristocrats both, and both in the springtime of their youth and beauty. The Governor's lady observed as much to Lord Basil, pausing in her long-winded prattle concerning her arrangements for the forthcoming Government House ball to comment on how nice it was to see that the little Yankee gel had found herself a beau of her own age—thereby going some way to impel the incident that followed.

The valse ended, leaving Virginia glowing most becomingly, and Ensign Hatchwell with the firm, if erroneous, conviction that he had scored a palpable hit with the little colonial filly, and that one only needed to press home one's advantage and there might be a tale to recount to one's messmates on the morrow.

He escorted Virginia back to her seat, then went off to fortify himself with a large rum and lime juice in preparation for the second assault upon the crumbling edifice of her chastity. And stayed to have two—thereby further contributing to what followed.

Lord Basil joined Virginia almost immediately after, and continued his tale where he had left off. She, finding his matured charms and cool assurance markedly more agreeable than Ensign Hatchwell's coltish brashness, relaxed in the glamour of his presence and was as annoyed as he when an importuning voice at her elbow requested the pleasure of yet another dance.

"Thank you, no sir," responded Virginia.

But Ensign Hatchwell, fortified by his conviction that he had made a hit, and also by two large rums, was inclined to quibble. This he did by remaining where he was and cocking a warm glance down at his intended victim.

"Come now, Miss Virginia, ma'am. Not one more valse? Why, I have been watching you and you've scarce danced all evening."

"Young man, you heard the lady's answer. Take it and be gone." So spoke Lord Basil, who not only disliked the young guardsman for being young and beautiful, but knew full well what Hatchwell was after.

"That young lady can speak for herself, sir," was Hatchwell's retort.

"The lady has spoken," said Lord Basil. "And I also have spoken. Now be off with you."

The young man flushed as scarlet as his coat. "Sir, if you were not my host," he said, "I would not have you speak to me so!"

Lord Basil's pale countenance was quite expressionless, save for a narrowing of the eyes that might have warned a more prudent man.

"Would you not so, sir?" he murmured. "Damme that's mighty interesting. And what *would* you do, pray? Would you—take me out, perhaps?"

Hatchwell, remembering that he was a Guards officer, stuck his chin out and puffed out his chest.

"I might well at that, sir!" he responded.

"Would you so?" said Lord Basil. "But you might need a little more encouragement, perhaps. As for instance—*this!*" He had taken off the white velvet glove from his left hand. Suiting the action to the word, he reached out and lightly struck Hatchwell across the mouth with it, in full view of all present.

"He'll kill the young sprig." Alissa had returned.

She murmured the comment at Cambronne's side, and as casually as if she had been making a remark on the weather.

"Perhaps one should intervene," said Cambronne.

"It would be imprudent," said she. "Possibly dangerous, and certainly useless. I know him. He wants that boy's blood. And he will have it."

Ensign Hatchwell's lower lip was trembling with emotion that was a piece beyond his control. Personal inadequacy leaving him incapable of dealing with the plight in which he had landed himself, he nevertheless had recourse to the inculcated shibboleths of his caste.

"I will have satisfaction for that, sir!" he cried.

"Oh, my God!" murmured Cambronne.

"Name your weapon and choose your seconds, sir," continued Hatchwell. "And the time and place."

Lord Basil uncoiled himself from the sofa and stood up, a thin smile upon his pale lips.

"My weapon, sir, is the sword," he said. "As to time and place, it shall be here and now. As to seconds—Cambronne, stand for me, I beg you."

They brought duelling rapiers: fine killing weapons of Toledo steel, blued, and chased with gold inlay, with grips of ivory and quillons fashioned in the fanciful Spanish style of the sixteenth century. The points were unguarded and needle-sharp.

"Must this happen, Lord Basil?" asked Cambronne, as he helped his principal off with his coat. "I take it that you are an accomplished swordsman. While that brash young cub . . ."

"I am, arguably, one of the finest swordsmen alive, my dear Cambronne," replied the other. "And I am determined upon leaving my mark on that puppy!"

Cambronne made no reply.

The principal military attaché—a veteran of Waterloo and stern pillar of the church—had taken upon himself the role of president. He called the two disputants together, shirtsleeved and armed as they were, and instructed them in the few and simple rules surrounding the "affair of honor," which, though outlawed in England, was by no means dead there, and certainly flourished in the colonies. This being done, he parted their swords and bade them set to.

At the first parry and riposte it was apparent that, gauche or not, coltish or not, Ensign Hatchwell knew how to handle a blade. He was quick, neat-wristed, spare in his movements and aggressive. Cambronne, who readily acknowledged himself to be no better than a fair to middling cut-and-thrust man, quickly formed the opinion that, notwithstanding Lasalle's boast, the older man had picked himself an opponent of mettle.

The movement was swift, with the master of Manatee retreating all the time, back and back along his great salon, between the two lines of wide-eyed guests and servants. The ring of blade on blade (a homely sound, reminiscent of a carving knife being sharpened on a steel), the labored breathing of the two opponents, and the slithering of their dancing pumps on the parquet—no other sounds intruded. No one spoke a word, or offered any encouragement.

Presently there began a scarcely perceptible change in the fortunes of the two swordsmen. A discerning eye would have noticed that Ensign Hatchwell was doing the most work—and was growing tired of consequence—while Lasalle, though successfully parrying his opponent's every thrust, was doing so with a remarkable economy of effort. Furthermore, by allowing the other to take the early initiative he had quickly learned Hatchwell's repertoire of fence. And a more expert eye than Cambronne's would have known that the young guardee's repertoire, though impressive, was limited.

Having backed the whole length of the vast chamber, Lasalle stood his ground, nor could all Hatchwell's efforts shift him, though the younger man tried every means. With his opponent's blade bursting like fire all about him, the master of Manatee plucked safety out of the air with devastating ease.

And then—he began to advance.

"The brat is as good as dead," murmured Alissa.

Ensign Hatchwell's deterioration was slow—at first. No more than a lock of sandy hair overhanging his brow, a slackness of the lower lip, a wider look to the eye betrayed his state. But the next time he retreated past Cambronne, the Jerseyman was carried back twenty-odd years to his first experience of a sea battle, off Ushant, when a midshipman. There had been a topman serving one of the guns of Cambronne's battery: a big fellow, popular with his mates, a good man in a fist fight, but untried in battle. The moment the French opened fire, this man ran for cover, tried to get below and was bayoneted to death by the Marine sentry put there for that purpose. In the agonizingly long minutes before the firing started, as the enemy drew closer, Cambronne had detected a curious stink emanating from the topman: the stink of naked fear and the dread of death.

He smelled the selfsame odor coming from Ensign Hatchwell!

With only fear to sustain him, with all hope of besting his opponent gone, the youth was now literally fighting to protract his life. And it was obvious to Cambronne that, having allowed his opponent to display his repertoire, Lasalle was now playing with him, cat and mouse. Why else, when Hatchwell's body lay open after a fumbled parry, did Lasalle not pink him through? And why, when the young guardee backed against the lowest step of the staircase and nearly fell, did the master of Manatee take a pace back and lower his point? Not out of any chivalrous impulse, surely, not if the horrendous tale purveyed by Jack the Cat was even halfway to the truth.

No—Lasalle was letting the boy die by inches. It was torture without the rack, burning alive without fire, dry drowning.

When he had had his sport, when Hatchwell was scarcely doing more than make simple parries in his constant retreat, the master of Manatee brought it to an end with a brilliant disarming movement: locking quillons with his opponent's weapon and ripping the ivory grip from the other's fingers so that the rapier was carried half across the chamber.

He then extended his point at Hatchwell's heaving breast.

"No, Lord Basil—I beg you—don't!" It was Virginia who pleaded, a blond Portia at the bar of Death. If he heard her, Lasalle paid no heed; his attention was all upon the sweat-dabbled, slack-mouthed countenance of the wretch who stood before him, arms extended, breast open to the needle point of the rapier.

As if to prompt a response, Lasalle jerked the point forward, swiftly, brutally, feigning a thrust. The movement had its desired effect. One word was wrenched from Ensign Hatchwell's lips:

"Please . . ."

It won him his life, but at what cost! Even as Lasalle tossed his rapier to a footman and turned on his heel to rejoin Virginia, the young man knew that he had betrayed his honor, his manhood. There are more ways of marking a man than cutting his flesh. Lord Basil had made his mark—and turned a brash youth into a spiritual gelding.

The evening went sour on Cambronne after that. Nor did the dancers show any great animation, but mooned to and fro like mutes at a funeral. Lasalle had taken Virginia in to the supper buffet, Alissa was nowhere to be seen. When the Jerseyman espied Commodore Harvey moving in his direction with the jovial, buttonholing look of a man who wants to swap yarns about "old ships," Cambronne had an impulse to make himself scarce.

One of Lasalle's private carriages took him back to the jetty. A hail across the dark waters, to where the *Argo* lay like a sable funeral barque, swiftly brought the jolly-boat.

A long and hard-working day (they had spent the dog watches in painting the ship's side a dull black) had taken its toll on the men. Only a single duty quartermaster had been awake to arouse the boat's crew. Cambronne said good night to the fellow and went aft. Tom Blackadder's gentle snoring came from beyond the closed door of his cabin.

The Jerseyman poured himself a nightcap, slumped down in the stern window-seat and looked out across the dark, oily-smooth water. He was still looking, and contemplating, when a lithe form swam into view. A porpoise? Dolphin? No, it was human. An escaping slave? Small comfort could a slave hope for aboard such a vessel as the *Argo!* But whoever it was was certainly coming straight at the schooner's stern.

A hand reached up and seized the sill of the open window. A small, slender satin-skinned hand. A moment later, Cambronne was assisting Alissa to climb in through the window. The gorgeous mulattress was wearing the same silk sheath in which she had scandalized the *bon ton* of Jamaica that evening. It was clinging to her wetly and the more revealingly. She peeled it off, announcing herself to be totally nude beneath, wrung out the dripping cloth and hung it to dry over the sill.

She ran her fingers through her gleaming hair. "Light me a cigar and pour me a glass of rum, Cambronne," she murmured.

That night, the Jerseyman and Alissa together went far beyond the set frontiers of bodily desires, to the ecstatic country where only the abandoned may enter. Upon their third return from unimaginable delights, she lay in the crook of his enclosing arm and smoked another cigar. And talked.

"I think I loathe that man," she said.

"Lord Basil?"

"Two years I've been at Manatee. There are no strings binding me. I made that clear to him when I came, and he accepted the arrangement. Not mistress, but companion."

"And now?"

She exhaled a smoke ring, watched it rise to the deckhead and fade into the darkness.

"Now I think it's time for Alissa to move on."

"Because of what he did tonight?"

"Perhaps. Yes. I think the destruction of that boy was, in a curious way, one of the cruellest things I've ever seen him do. And, Cambronne, I have witnessed things in Manatee that would make your heart turn sick. Slaves who attempt to escape are given into the tender care of the chief overseer, who is more like a wild animal than a man—save that no wild animal would treat its own kind so. And Lasalle invariably stays to watch from the shade of an umbrella, comfortable in a big wicker chair. Particularly if the poor wretch is a woman. Yes, I think Alissa will move on, especially since it's clear that she is about to be supplanted."

"Supplanted?"

"By the little Yankee chit. Did you not see the attentions he was giving her? Oh, I promise you, Basil Lasalle does not take such pains with a woman unless he is greatly attracted."

"But heavens, Virginia's only just past eighteen," said Cambronne.

"So? My mother was wed and brought to bed of three children by the time she was eighteen," said Alissa. "Lasalle has taken young girls of good birth and social standing as his mistresses, nor has it done any harm to their reputations. We live very broad-mindedly in Jamaican high society. Oh, the fond mammas would greatly have preferred dear Lord Basil to extend the benefit of clergy to their darling offspring, but he is simply not the marrying kind, so a girl must be content with the social cachet of being mistress to the most influential man on the island, or, as in my own case, companion."

"And where shall you go, Alissa?" asked Cambronne.

"Back to Louisiana, perhaps. Perhaps even to England. Do you think I would cause an éclat in London society, Cambronne?"

"You would be quite sensational," he said.

For that, she kissed him full on the lips, and, finding him oddly unresponsive, essayed further and more explicit overtures, till, in the course of her varied and protracted dalliances, she chanced to touch the pendant that hung about his neck on the gold chain.

"What is this, Cambronne?" she asked.

"Birth stone," he replied. "Garnet. For the month of January."

"Mmmm." She released him, pillowed her arms behind her head. "Cambronne . . ."

"Yes?"

"Oh—nothing."

Presently, aware that his breathing had become heavier and more steady, she turned over in the narrow bunk and faced the wall, closing her eyes. Within minutes she was asleep. It was then that Cambronne roused himself and, moving gently so as not to waken his companion, slid from the bunk and out into the main cabin, closing the door behind him.

He went to the stern window, to the spot where he had begun that night's adventure with the beautiful mulattress, and looked out to the dark shoreline, beyond which lay Manatee. It may have been a fluke of the wind, but for a moment it seemed to him that the sound of a valse was borne to him on the night air.

The eight bells telling the end of the morning watch woke Alissa in time to receive Cambronne when he entered with a pot of coffee that he had himself prepared in the galley. On the way, he had informed Tom Blackadder that he was entertaining a lady aboard, and the *Argo*'s master had tactfully left the stern quarters to his captain's sole charge.

"First coffee, then breakfast," said Cambronne. "Your— clothing is dry." He laid on the bunk the scrap of patterned silk in which she had swum from the shore.

She met his eyes. Smiled. Reached up and, wrapping her bare arms around his neck, pulled his head down to her yielding breasts. And, with the morning sun streaming through the open window, she and the Jerseyman journeyed once again into the forbidden land beyond imagining, with the lapping of wavelets at the waterline mingling with the many sounds of their concerted passion.

"Cambronne! Cambronne, are you there?"

Alissa opened her eyes and sat up.

"Good God—it's Lasalle. What's he doing here at this hour?" She did not sound greatly concerned.

Cambronne peered through the window and down. A barge rowed by six Negroes stripped to breech clouts was halted a heaving line's distance from where he stood. There was a carved and gilded canopy in the stern, and plenty of gilt dolphin decorations, Turk's head knots and the like. A very tidy craft. Seated under the canopy and waving a wide-brimmed straw hat up at him was Lord Basil Lasalle, dressed all in white as ever, and seemingly in a high good humor.

"We've come for breakfast, Cambronne!" he cried. "And to bear great news. Ah, good morning to you, Alissa my dear. You're looking well rested."

Cambronne was aware that Alissa was standing at his elbow and looking down at the barge. She had wrapped the scrap vestigial silk garment about her nudity—just. She waved back to the blond aristocrat.

"Good morning, Basil!"

At the sound of her voice, another face appeared from under the canopy of the barge.

"And good morning to you, also, Miss Virginia," said Alissa, with laughter in her eyes. The other made no response —except to stare.

"Take us alongside, you black devils,'" said Lord Basil. The Negro coxwain put a rope's end to his oarsmen's backs and the stately barge was rowed to the *Argo*'s gangway in time for her captain to put on his coat and hat and be on deck to receive his guests.

Virginia Holt was handed up by two grinning sailors who climbed down into the barge for that purpose. She greeted Cambronne with a pinch-mouthed "good morning," took Lord Basil's proffered arm, ignored Alissa completely when they met face-to-face in the stern cabin, and declined any breakfast.

The master of Manatee, before he sat down to eat, took Cambronne to one side.

"Cambronne, you dog, I have a mind to have you thrashed," said the aristocrat, "but it seems to me that I should thank you instead. How did you find her, hey? Did she perform up to your expectations?"

"Indeed she did, sir," replied Cambronne, poker-faced.

"Well, then, I will forgive you for cutting my reception and chasing off to bed the wench on whom I had a lien. There are matters more important to attend to. I told you that I bear great news, and here it is." Lasalle glanced over his shoulder at the two women seated at a table just out of earshot: the lovely blonde with the pursed lips and disapproving eyes; the exotic mulattress amusedly picking at a piece of fruit. "Cambronne, the dispatch vessel arrived in Kingston late last night. What do you think of that?"

"The convoy's at sea!" Cambronne felt his pulse begin to race.

"You must sail today," said Lasalle. "The dispatch vessel gives you an exact position to rendezvous with the three ships of the convoy, together with their destination. You will have little enough time during the passage eastward to train your men to the blue suit of sails, not to mention gunnery. Think you can do it?"

"Yes."

The testing time had come!

CHAPTER 7

The *Argo* sailed on the evening tide. Taking advantage of the persistent North-east Trades, she made good progress through the night and was heading east, with the Haitian coast fifity miles on the larboard hand, by noon.

At noon, Cambronne sent a man to the masthead with his own telescope, to search the horizon all around. Upon receiving no report of sail, he summoned Tobias Angel.

"Bosun, you will bend on the blue suit of sails," he said.

The light of true fanaticism burned in the hooded eyes of the cadaverous zealot.

"'Fine linen with broidered work was that which thou spreadest forth to be thy sail,'" he declaimed. "'Blue and purple from the isles of Elishah was that which covered thee. The inhabitants of Zidon and Arvad were thy mariners.' Ezekiel, Chapter 27, Verse 7 and part of verse 8."

"Quite so," said Cambronne. "And look lively about it, Bosun."

"Aye, aye, sir!" Tobias Angel touched his forelock and departed at a swift trot, bearing with him the key of the saillocker that Cambronne had handed over.

The entire crew of the schooner came on deck, so swiftly did the news get around that something very out of the ordinary was about to take place. There was much speculation when Tobias Angel and his former workmates from Nogg's Wharf, Ebenezer Harker and the others, dragged long coils of parceled blue canvas on deck and opened them up. While the *Argo* becked and nodded in the gentle swell, they stripped her poles clear of the plain white sails and bent on the blue. Ebenezer Harker—primed in his risky task by an exhortation from the bosun—swarmed out onto the bowsprit and rigged the extensible jib-boom that increased the schooner's length overall by ten feet. Similarly, the booms and gaffs of main and foremast were extended to accommodate the

greater length of sails at foot and head. In an awed silence,
with every eye upon him, Tobias Angel inspected every
lashing and pronounced that the blue suit was well and truly
bent on—a fact which he then reported to his captain.

"Hoist all sail, Mr. Blackadder!" said Cambronne. "And
stand by to count her knots!"

With the creak of block and tackle, and the urging on of
bosun's mates, the great gaff of the mainsail was hoisted, and
after it the foresail. Then there was the blue blossoming of
the huge jib and then the flying jib, scarcely less large.

"Haul taut and belay!"

As the wind filled the giant sails, the *Argo* heeled gently
underfoot, but not much, for the great area of keel kept her
taut and stiff. The faint creaming at the bows mounted into a
rushing torrent and white water trailed from her speeding
stern. Cambronne, standing by the wheel, was reminded of
what the consumptive Walberswick had said: "The blue suit,
which acts upon her hull like an orange pip squeezed between
finger and thumb . . ."

Blackadder was at the taffrail with knotted line and piece of
wood, which he caused to be thrown over at regular intervals.
With every succeeding report from the man who told the
knots, the master's expression grew ever more disbelieving.
Finally, he went up to Cambronne.

"Sixteen knots, as I live and breathe, Captain," he said.

"We have a ship underneath us, Master," grinned Cambronne.

"My God, that we have, sir!" replied the other.

Close-hauled, the *Argo* maintained that steady sixteen
knots for over an hour, and every man in the ship would have
given his day's grog issue for a short trick at the wheel. Like
schoolboys enviously regarding a fellow with a new cricket
bat, they huddled in groups about bosun Angel and watched
him handle the speeding schooner with ease; for Vincenzo
Alfieri's inspired design was built around the suit of blue sails
and the keel, and the combination of the two factors permitted the helmsman, even at high speed and in a blow of wind,
to hold the vessel on course one-handed.

After an hour of maneuvering at all points of sail, Cambronne gave the order for the plain white suit to be bent on
again. Over their midday meal he expounded to Blackadder
his philosophy, which was to keep the secret of the blue sails
for as long as possible; therefore he would only use them

when in company with a convoy he was protecting. Inevitably, the secret would come out and every seaman in the Caribbean would be aware that a fantastic schooner with a black hull and giant blue sails was running rings round the navy ships on anti-slave patrol. But, for the present, the *Argo* would keep her own counsel.

In the dog watchers they practiced gunnery. The crewmen whom Lord Basil Lasalle had provided were all trained gunners who had handled ordnance on slave-ships. The best of these was a crew of Britishers captained by one Stokes, a man with the look of a rural dean, with a fringe of sandy hair encircling his bald pate. Though barely literate, Stokes had a fine fund of well-turned invective at his command, and a clear and articulate way of expounding the intricacies of his craft. A twelve-pounder muzzle-loading cannon demanded a crew of five to serve it. Stokes's acolytes were two giant fellows known as Black Dick and Turnip (the former a free Negro born and bred in Bristol, the latter a peasant from Gloucestershire), an East Anglian with a line of broken teeth like the machicolations of a castle wall who rejoiced in the name of Christmas, and a Scot called Angus Dunbar. These five, working as a team, could load, fire and swab out their piece in under a minute, and were a joy to watch.

The first round fired from the *Argo*'s deck sped two hundred yards to land within a foot of an empty powder keg floated out for a target. The third round—still from Stokes's gun—sank it cleanly, to a chorus of cheers from his shipmates. Cambronne resolved to rate Stokes master gunner, responsible for the training and organization of ordnance, a position that he accepted with quiet pride. Throughout the rest of the watch the cannons were fired, singly, in rolling volleys, and in concerted salvoes. The shooting was ragged, particularly as regards salvoes, since most of *Argo*'s crew had never laid eyes on a twelve-pounder at close quarters, but the cadre of experienced men, led by Stokes, had the eight pieces served tolerably well by suppertime, when they were all swabbed out and secured, the flintlock firing mechanisms carefully boxed, burnt powder scrubbed away and the long brass barrels polished to a mirror finish.

Cambronne was well satisfied with the *Argo*'s first day's work-up as a fighting ship. About a week's cruising would bring them to their rendezvous with the convoy—a point where the longitude of sixty degrees west crossed the twentieth parallel, approximately two hundred miles north-east of Antigua—and in that time he would work the crew till they dropped, summoning all hands on deck right around the clock for gun drill, sail drill, fire-fighting drill, laying out a sea anchor, patching a hole below the waterline, rigging jury sail, sending away the boats, even abandoning ship—all the thousand and one evolutions that are a sea captain's defense against ill chance, ill weather and the violence of the enemy.

That night, after supper, he went up on deck. Jack the Cat was just relieving Swede at the wheel. The one-eared seven-footer had early proved his worth by demonstrating that he was well capable of hoisting the mainsail single-handed and likewise running out a twelve-pounder all by himself. He treated his captain to a pulling of the forelock and a bovine grin as he went below.

"Well, Jack," said Cambronne. "Did you see our mutual friend Lasalle when he came aboard? And, what's more to the point, did he also see you?"

"I saw the bastard," said the other without heat. "And he hasn't changed a lot in the years between." The hideous mouth stretched in a grin. "But he would have his work cut out to recognize the *joli garçon* I used to be, nor did he. I was sorry to see Miss Holt traipsing round with him, for I've always regarded her as a most superior young lady, don't you agree, Captain?"

"Watch your ship's head!" growled Cambronne.

"Aye, aye, sir."

Presently Cambronne broke the silence. "I don't think you need have any cause for concern over Miss Holt. She is young and a mite impetuous, perhaps, but she's not likely to have her head turned by the likes of Lasalle."

"I'm sure you're right, Captain," said Jack the Cat.

"I mean," said Cambronne, "for a young woman to—say—accompany a man to breakfast aboard a ship without a chaperone might be frowned upon in Boston, but it would pass unnoticed in Jamaican society."

"I totally agree, sir," said the man at the wheel.

"What the devil happened to that chaperone of hers, that nigger woman?" demanded Cambronne, half to himself.

"Watch your ship's head!"

"Aye, aye, sir."

Jack the Cat watched his captain pace restlessly to the bow and back down the deck again, hands clasped behind his back, head stuck slightly forward on his chest, face set and stern, the deeply scored lines on his cheeks more prominently displayed than usual. Reaching the companionway, he seemed to be of a mind to go below, but hesitated and looked irresolutely toward the man at the wheel.

"Damned if I feel tired enough to turn in," he said.

"With respect, I'm grateful for your company, Captain," said Jack the Cat. "Spinning a few yarns will make eight bells come all the faster for me. What's the topic to be? Not Lasalle and his doings, I fancy. Shall we speak of women? Shall I tell you of the black girl I had in Kingston on our first night ashore? Would you like to hear the details of the encounter, Captain?"

"Not greatly," said Cambronne. "But I am glad, in any event, that you bedded a woman instead of pursuing your tryst with violent death. I see no fresh scars on your face."

Again the hideous grin. "There is scarce room left on my face for new scars, Captain."

"Why did you do it, Jack?" asked Cambronne. "How did—that"—he pointed to the other's grotesquely mutilated countenance—"begin?"

"You turn the knife in the wound, as ever, Cpatain," said the other. "Am I to tell you my life story? I think not, not on this occasion, at any rate. Perhaps one day. But shall I tell my captain how I was first disfigured? I think so. It will while away the dark hour, the last and longest hour, of my watch. And also divert my captain, who finds he cannot sleep."

"Less of the prattle, man," said Cambronne. "Come to your tale."

The *Argo* sauntered a point off course from a wave's buffet. Jack the Cat deftly brought the compass needle back to where it had been.

"My tale begins," he said, "with the *joli garçon* whom Lasalle (again that name! I am sorry) would instantly have recognized when he came aboard the *Argo* for breakfast. Young. In great demand from the exquisite, pampered ladies of his caste and kind."

"There's a woman at the back of your misfortunes," declared Cambronne. "I might have guessed it."

"Not any one woman, Captain," responded Jack the Cat. "I have known many women, but I have never placed myself in the jeopardy of loving, for if one judges love by the majority of its effects, it is more like hatred than friendship—

and I value friendship highly. No—the cause of my downfall and inevitable future destruction was something quite different from the agony of loving a woman, and that is the part of my tale on which even the desire to shorten my watch and divert my captain will not draw me out."

"I would not have you agonize yourself to divert me," said Cambronne. "The plain and unvarnished tale of how you arrived at your present state will suffice."

"My present state," said Jack the Cat, "began with a tragedy of which, as I have said, I do not wish to speak. A tragedy which, despite the intensity of my agony at the time, I might well have surmounted, but for my weakness of character. I do not whine, Captain. There is no self-pity left in me. I have looked into my heart and I know myself for what I am."

He was silent for quite a while, so that Cambronne was constrained to prompt him:

"And . . . ?"

"Not even the arms of fair women, hitherto my great consolation, could help me," said Jack the Cat. "Instead, drink, which had been my servant, took a turn at being my master. And after drink, the rarer delight of opium. It was while smoking opium in a hell-hole down by the docks in east London that I fell foul of a Chinese, a creature of great stature among his own people, the leader of one of their 'tongs' or secret societies. Sodden with drink and opium, my reason shattered by agony of mind, I took offense at this fellow's calm arrogance, his assumption of a power that I did not see him to deserve. I cursed him for a yellow heathen and struck him across the mouth, as I would have horse-whipped any one of my father's lackeys who presumed to rise so far above his station as to treat me with contempt . . ."

Silence. Cambronne said: "Continue."

"This fellow, this big Chinee," said Jack the Cat, "who wore an embroidered coat and a hat with a peacock feather, did not return blow for blow, but regarded me for some time, and then he said, in English as clear and perfect as my own: 'After the custom of my people, that mouth which spoke an abomination will itself become an abomination.' And then he left the place without another word or sign."

"And then?"

"And then"—Jack the Cat drew a shuddering breath—"I finished my pipe and called for my score. I weaved my way out to the night and the fog. They were waiting for me in the next alleyway: four Chinees, all big fellows. Drugged as I was, surprised as I was, I had no chance either in fight or flight. Two of them pinioned my arms. A third dragged back my head by the hair. And the fourth—he slit the corners of my mouth back to the jawbone, as you see it."

"Good God!" breathed Cambronne. And again, "Good God!"

"I ran from them." continued Jack the Cat, "and they made no move to prevent me. Streaming with blood, screaming in my agony, I burst into a dockland tavern where, by good fortune, there was someone with the charity to take me in, to staunch the bleeding, to shelter me till my strength had returned (for I was by then 'sleeping rough' as the saying is) and I was able to go out into the world again. It was only then that I appreciated the import of the Chinee's words: I had become an abomination.

"The first woman to confront me after my disfigurement screamed as if she had trodden on a venomous reptile. I do not have to embellish the scene further; you saw the similar effect I first had upon Miss Holt. She was a pretty woman, of the sort that the *joli garçon* had formerly taken at his pleasure. That night I stared down the barrel of a loaded pistol and willed myself to pull the trigger, but I could not, since the faith in which I have been reared teaches that self-destruction is a mortal sin. And though I have long since departed from that faith, I cannot rid myself of the vision of the hellfire eternal that awaits suicides."

"And so," said Cambronne, "you have trailed your cloak for someone to do the business for you."

Jack the Cat stroked his scarred and pitted face, one hand on the wheel. "And have come close to finding him, many times," he said. "You saw me in the Lobster Pot in Boston. That was a repetition of a scene that had been played out a score of times in the seaports of the world, wherever violent men drink hard and look for trouble. I came very close to fulfilling my death-wish that night, and only your intervention prevented it. But, do you know? I have been more contented since. And that little black girl in Kingston, now, she scarce seemed to notice how I looked, or, if she did, she cared not a damn, but took a delight in my bedding her, so that I was almost persuaded that I was that *joli garçon* of long ago. You have brought me luck, Captain. I hope, in return, that I have been able to divert you with my tale."

"That you have, Jack," said Cambronne. "It's seven bells and I'm away to my bunk. I'll leave a note on the slate that I'm to be woken at dawn."

"I'll draw my relief's attention to it, Captain," said the other. "Good night, sir."

"Good night to you."

When Cambronne's footballs had faded away down the steps, Jack the Cat shook his head.

"Poor devil!" he murmured to himself. "It's a sorry state, to be besotted by a chit of a girl and scarcely able to admit it to himself."

The third day of the *Argo*'s eastward passage brought them abreast of Puerto Rico, with a fair wind all the way and a steady nine knots told off every watch. Cambronne had kept the crew at it, as he had determined. Indeed, Tom Blackadder had protested to him that the hands were being pushed too hard and too fast. Cambronne would have none of it, and argued reasonably that drill, more drill and even more drill is the fighting seaman's sheet-anchor, the credit balance of expertise upon which he can draw when all hell is let loose and even blind courage is not enough. So lower deck was cleared every forenoon and afternoon. The suit of blue sails was bent on daily, till the evolution was encompassed in half an hour, then twenty-five minutes, then ten. The ample stocks of black powder, made up into silk cartridge-bags to the amount of half a pound a bag, were expended with the profligacy of a Pall Mall clubman at the faro tables. Gun crews were formed in their fives, tried, tested, broken into different combinations, tried again. Only one crew remained intact throughout the working-up, and that was number three larboard gun, captained by Master Gunner Stokes, along with Black Dick and Turnip, Christmas and Angus Dunbar, to whose number was added the insignificant form of the lad Dick Trumper, the same starveling who had thrown slops to windward and all over his captain and master. Young Trumper turned up trumps as powder-monkey, being smaller, quicker, more frightened of failure than any other, and was adopted by Stokes and his crew as both acolyte and mascot. Poor little Trumper, alas, was much put upon by certain members of *Argo*'s crew on account of his age and—despite the hideous pudding-basin haircut—not unpleasing appearance. His task as heads-boy not surprisingly enhanced the danger in which he stood, for it meant he had to assist in the natural functions of the watch on deck, who, having handled tarred rigging, were blackened to the elbows. Little Trumper, standing attendance in the ship's heads for'ard, had early on undone the breeches lappets and directed the private parts of every topman aboard—at occasional hazard to his own virtue.

On the third night of the passage, the off-watch crewmen were gathered in the bows, drinking the grog that they had saved from the midday issue and listening to the sweet voice and guitar of Jack the Cat, while the *Argo* cruised sleekly through the ink-black, moonless night.

> "*Here, a sheer hulk, lies poor Tom Bowling,*
> *The darling of our crew . . .*"

Cambronne heard it from his narrow cabin, where he was studying one of the secret charts with which Lasalle had provided him: a hitherto unknown guide to the complex of islands and islets, banks, deeps and shoals known collectively as the Virgin and Leeward Islands and Lesser Antilles. They were all there in tantalizing particular, the hazards that lay ahead of him, with every island and islet clearly indicated, each bank marked with soundings in fathoms, likewise deeps and shoals. All gathered, in penny packets, since the days of Francis Drake and even before, a compendium of maritime knowledge added to by buccaneer and cut-throat, slaver, pirate; denied to the forces of law and order by a centuries-old conspiracy of mutual self-interest, of which he and the cabal that directed the illicit slave trade were the sole beneficiaries.

He looked up from the chart as the voice died and the guitar ended in a nervous jangle. There was a shout of pain, a concert of voices raised in what sounded like acclaim.

Tom Blackadder stuck his head in the cabin door, jerked a thumb.

"Fight down in the mess-deck, Captain. Do we ignore it, or . . . ?"

"We're not in business to fight each other!" snapped Cambronne, laying aside the chart. "We'll stamp it out. Let's go!"

The men on watch on deck were clustered at the foc'sle gangway, trying to look down and have some part in whatever was going on. Cambronne elbowed his way through them, with Blackadder ordering them to return to their duties.

It was hot in the windowless confines of the mess-deck, which stank of sweat, grog and stewed meat. Upon reaching the foot of the gangway, captain and master were presented with a row of backs. Everyone was shouting encouragement.

"Go at it, young 'un!"

"Swipe him again like you did before!"

"Jesus, what a sprig of a gamecock!"

"Stand aside, there!" barked Cambronne, thrusting through.

They were none too ready to give way, even to their captain, for the spectacle of view had touched the main-springs of their imaginations and they would as lief have been flogged for disobedience as miss a moment of it. Only by the exercising of main force was Cambronne able to gain the front of the onlookers, arriving there in time to see the boy Dick Trumper squaring up to a big fellow by the name of Hopper— a surly, glowering sort of individual whom Cambronne had been in two minds about dismissing in Boston. Hopper was in a black fury.

"By hookey, I'll mark you for that, you little bastard!" he swore. "And when I've done that, I'll have my way with you before all here!"

"Stop that!" ordered Cambronne. But his cry was lost in the yells of encouragement as Hopper moved forward to accomplish the first installment of his threat, reaching out one big fist to grab the boy by the shoulder and bunching the other fist to strike. Neither ambition was achieved.

The boy Trumper, who was backed against the bulkhead awaiting his tormentor, suddenly brought up one bare foot and drove it like a whiplash—first bent sharply at the knee then straightened—at Hopper's guts. The big man retched and clasped at himself. Before he had time to draw breath, before Cambronne had time to intervene, the boy's left hand sliced round, took his oponent at the side of the neck and felled him to the deck.

The applause rang out deafeningly in the confined space. Cambronne had to shout for silence, and wait a while till he was obeyed by all.

"What brought this about?" he demanded when all was still.

"He . . ." began Trumper, pointing to the fallen man.

"Hold your tongue!" snapped Cambronne. "You'll have your turn later. You, Stokes, you're a petty officer. What do you mean by allowing a brawl on the mess-deck?"

The master gunner, looking notably less like a rural dean when stripped to the waist and in a nightcap, had the grace to avoid his captain's eye.

"'Twere begun so quick that it were half done, like, afore it were begun, sir," he offered.

"He tried to—to rape me!" cried Trumper, in tears.

"Hopper, well he's been bottling his tot, sir," said the master gunner. "Got a bit excited, like, started skylarking with the lad, that was all."

"Jesus, you should have seen the way the kid threw him off!" interjected someone.

"He tried to rape me!" wailed Trumper, appealing directly to Cambronne. "Do you think I don't *know?*"

Cambronne drew breath sharply.

He pointed to the bulkhead. "Get back against there!" he ordered Trumper. "And don't try any of your fancy fighting tricks on me, or I'll have you hanged from the main gaff. Right, now spread your hands and arms wide. Touch the woodwork both sides."

Trumper obeyed and stood facing Cambronne, eyes wide and frightened, arms spread in the attitude of crucifixion. Cambronne approached.

Alone of all the inhabitants of the mess-deck that hot, tropical night, Trumper was wearing the traditional seaman's leather jerkin with shirt under. Cambronne's hands came up, took hold of the edges of the jerkin and wrenched them apart. This action won something like a sob of anguish from the other.

"I think we have met before—miss!" said the Jerseyman, and he tore open the shirt, revealing very pink nipples atop girlish breasts.

"By all that's holy—he's a wench!" someone cried.

"We've had a young wench a-sleeping among us all this time!"

The girl was trembling all over, her arms still spread wide, bosom still bared to the eyes of all.

"Cover your nakedness," said Cambronne, "and follow me aft." He pointed to the unconscious Hopper. "Get this wretch up on deck and throw a bucket of water over him. Master . . . !"

"Sir?"

"When they've brought him round, put him in irons."

"Aye, aye, sir."

"There'll be a charge brought against Hopper tomorrow morning, and it'll probably be attempted rape. Clear lower deck to witness trial and punishment at eight bells of the morning watch."

"Aye, aye, sir."

Cambronne nodded to the trembling girl. "Well then—follow me," he said.

On the way to the gangway he passed Jack the Cat, who was still holding his guitar.

"Well, and what do you make of this?" murmured Cambronne. "Who would have thought *she'd* turn up again? Did it never cross your mind?"

"Not once," replied the other. "Not till I saw the way she threw that pig when he fell upon her—then I was transported straight back to that night at the Lobster Pot!"

With the eye of faith, he could just about picture the girl as she had been that first time. Making radical allowance for the pudding-basin haircut, he could see how the dark tresses had fallen and covered most of her brow and cheeks. The cheeks, pale now, but painted then. Likewise the mouth.

"Where did you learn to fight like that?" he asked her.

She was sitting at the table in the main cabin, a cup of coffee between her grubby fingers, looking like a waif in a workhouse.

"I learned the art from my father," she said. "He was bosun in an Indianman, trading to Ceylon and China. I was alone when he was away at sea. No other family. Father said a girl alone should be able to defend herself. God, how right he was!" She bowed her tufted head, and a tear coursed down each pale cheek.

Cambronne held his peace for several minutes, till she appeared somewhat to have composed herself. Then, gently: "Leaving aside for the moment how and why you are aboard here posing as a lad, what exactly happened tonight between you and that man?"

Her eyes flared, and he knew that there was spirit there.

"He isn't a man!" she hissed. "He's an animal! An *animal!*"

"He's a wrong 'un," conceded Cambronne. "I guessed as

much in Boston, though he gave me no real cause to do so. Continue. What happened?"

"I've told you what happened!" she cried. "The brute came upon me when we were alone together in the heads. He tried to seize me. He was drunk. I avoided him and ran down to the mess-deck, but he came after me. He was mad for me. And, like I told you, he was for raping me there and then. Tried to tear off my breeches before them all!"

"He had discovered that you were a girl," said Cambronne.

"That he had not!" she flared.

"Oh—I see."

Silence.

Presently, she said: "I hated being a woman. God, how I hated it! When Father was lost at sea, and I had to fend for myself, I learned soon enough what it is to be a woman and penniless. You try to be honest, but they won't let you. I tried for a post as kitchen girl in a tavern down by the docks, along with twenty other women. I didn't get the job. As soon as the tavern-keeper set eyes on me, he said I'd be more use to him serving the customers in the taproom. It was—a very cheap, rough tavern. The girls, the serving girls, they had to put up with being mauled as they went about with the trays of drink. On my second day at that place, a customer complained to the boss that I was wearing drawers under my skirts. It was against the house rules, you see. I was dismissed on the spot, and without the wages owed to me. That's what being a woman's about, Captain, when you're penniless."

The schooner yawed slightly on a wave-crest and the paneling creaked, accommodatingly filling the silence.

"Have some more coffee," said Cambronne, rising.

"Yes, I will," said the girl.

"Spot of brandy in it?"

"I won't say no."

He poured coffee and added a nip of spirit.

"What's your name—your real name?" he asked.

"Meg," she said. "Meg Trumper."

"We'll continue to call you Trumper," said Cambronne. "And for the rest of this voyage you'll continue to wear boy's clothes. You'll act as cabin-boy to the after quarters and sling your hammock in the main cabin here. Have as little to do with the men as possible. You must know the decent fellows among them: Jack the Cat, Tobias Angel, the master—plenty of decent fellows."

He made as if to leave.

"Don't you want to hear why I shipped aboard the *Argo* as a boy?" she asked.

"It will wait," he told her. "It seems to me that you have taken quite enough stick for one day. Besides, it's time for night drill and evolutions. Pay no attention to the call to clear lower deck." He paused at the door. "And particularly don't answer the call to clear lower deck at eight bells in the morning. Sling your hammock and get your head down is what I advise."

"Captain, sir," she said hesitantly. "I—I suppose you'll put me ashore when we get back to Kingston?"

"We'll cross that bridge when we come to it," said Cambronne. "Good night, Trumper."

The morning dawned with a sullen sky, not much wind, and a surly drift of light rain. And it was steamingly hot, so that the men stood in their watches on the upper deck and were wet with an amalgam of rain and salt sweat.

Cambronne, with the sense of occasion instilled in him by a distinguished career in that most formal of all navies, was sweating in his best blue serge frock-coat and pantaloons, with his gold-banded cap pulled low over his brow. He stood at the small table that had been brought on deck and placed before the capstan. Blackadder, as master, stood on his right, Bosun Tobias Angel on his left. The prisoner was brought on deck between two of his shipmates. His manacles had been replaced by ropes knotted about his wrists. He was slack-mouthed, bewildered, still somewhat drunk.

"Read the charge," said Cambronne in a very flat voice.

"Aye, aye, sir," responded Tobias Angel. Adjusting a pair of steel-rimmed spectacles more advantageously upon his nose, he proceeded to read the details of Hopper's crime, blessedly—considering the circumstances—without prefixing the charge with suitable texts from the Holy Book, as was his habit.

". . . did unlawfully and feloniously attempt rape upon the boy seaman Dick Trumper, by means of the atrocious crime of buggery." The wording of the charge had been carefully cobbled together, overnight, by Cambronne and Blackadder, relying upon their respective recollections of the laws and provisions regulating both their countries' navies. The wording was also slanted in a particular sort of way. And for a particular reason.

"What do you plead?" demanded Tobias Angel. "Do you plead 'guilty' or 'not guilty' to the charge?"

"I never laid a hand on the little bastard!" cried Hopper.

"Enter that plea as 'not guilty,'" murmured Cambronne. "Proceed."

"Call the first witness," said Blackadder.

"Step forward Master Gunner Stokes!" cried Tobias Angel. "Salute the Captain. Stand at your ease. Answer the questions."

"Recount the event that took place on the mess-deck last eve," said Blackadder, referring to his notes.

Stokes, the rural dean, was far from happy. The rain had plastered the fretted fringe of gray hair around the limits of his bald pate. He licked his lips.

"Well, sir," he began, "there was this a-thundering on the gangway stairs, and down comes the—the lad—and Hopper on his tail. Afore we can do anything, and Jack the Cat, he's still a-singing 'Tom Bowling' and scarce notices the affray, Hopper tips the—the lad—onto the floor, and he's working at the belt o' the lad's breeches . . ."

"One moment!" interjected Cambronne. "Did the prisoner say anything at this juncture. Think carefully, man. Tell me straight."

"Why, yes, sir, so he did," responded Stokes. "Now, let me get it right"—he looked across at his crewmen of larboard number three gun—"Black Dick, Turnip, one o' you—do you recall exactly . . . ?"

"Don't seek to be prompted!" interposed Cambronne. "Their corroboration will be sought afterward. Give it in your own words, as best you remember."

"Yessir," replied the master gunner." "As well as I remember, that Hopper, when he were fighting the—the lad—out of his breeches—and afore the lad threw him in the most astonishing manner as I have ever seen—said words somewhat to this effect: He did say: 'Damme, if I don't have you this night, you young devil. Who do you think you are, to refuse the likes o' Nat Hopper?'"

"'*Who do you think you are, to refuse the likes of Nat Hopper*'—his very words, as you recall them?" demanded Cambronne.

"Yessir, Cap'n," affirmed Stokes.

"It's a lie! Stokes is lying, damn his hide!" The prisoner, spluttering in his fury and struggling between the guards who restrained him, pulling at his pinioned wrists, broke in on the proceedings.

"Silence!" shouted Blackadder.

"Let him speak!" said Cambronne. "Go ahead, prisoner. Set out the facts of this lie that you allege to have been made before this summary court-martial."

Hopper's sour face grew cunning, wheedling, persuasive. With a sick feeling of revulsion, Cambronne saw the man ashore and in his cups, mellowed from his habitual sourness by a desire he could not deny, importuning some painted, wretched creature . . .

His appeal was not made to his captain, but to his shipmates; and the appeal was to the solidarity of the hard-handed sons of toil, the tarred-to-the-elbows topmen who risk their lives aloft in all weathers, while They—the Others—lie aft in pampered splendor.

"Lads!" he cried. "How can it be so, that I would declare such a thing? Why, you know this lad, this Trumper. As saucy a piece as ever trod a deck. Refuse the likes o' Nat Hopper? Why, Nat Hopper had only to go into the heads and this little Jezebel would be sidling up, making free with his hands and eyes. And did I not tell you, only t'other day (I don't remember if it were Black Dick as I told, or mayhap it were Ebenezer Harker, I don't recall), how I came across him in the forepeak, naked as the day he was born, and prancing around like some strumpet in a dockland tavern concert, and all for my benefit, for to entice me. Refuse the likes o' Nat Hopper? Where's the refusal there, I ask? I tell you . . ."

He looked about him, into the faces of the crew, drawn up in two files, larboard and starboard—and the words died in his throat. There was no solidarity with a fellow tarred toiler, only a silent loathing that was manifest in every glance.

"Lads!" croaked Hopper, "I look to you for support. I have been lied against, I tell you. Not a man here will contradict me when I say that I did not try to take the lad by force, but was enticed. *Enticed!* Ain't that so, Black Dick?— Ebenezer?—Toby Jones?—*Any of you!*"

Cambronne cleared his throat.

"Is there any man present," he said, "who disagrees with the testimony of Master Gunner Stokes?"

Not a man spoke, or moved.

Addressing the prisoner, Cambronne said: "I find you guilty as charged. Condemned out of your own mouth. The person you know as Dick Trumper is not male, but female—a fact of which every man on this ship but yourself is now aware . . ."

"You're saying it's a wench?" cried the wretched Hopper. "It ain't so! I say the brat flaunted himself afore me mothernaked! You're trying to trick me, you . . ."

"Silence!" shouted Blackadder.

"As to the charge," continued Cambronne. "Rape is rape, no matter against whom it is directed, be it male or female. And attempted rape is attempted rape—by the same criterion."

The ship's bell rang once for the first half hour of the forenoon watch.

"Hang him from main gaff!" said Cambronne.

On the fifth day, they negotiated the perilous barrier presented by the islands and shoals of the Lesser Antilles, with "Sail ho" all round the clock, and the leadsmen constantly in the chains. The miraculous chart saw them through by the quickest and most advantageous course, which is to leave Anguilla and its necklace of islets and rocks well on the starboard hand. Beyond Anguilla, the full force of the north equatorial current would have set any other vessel far to the west, but the *Argo,* battling through heavy, beam seas with a fair wind, went straight as an arrow to its mark. Next day, she reached her rendezvous and hove to. After nearly a week of back-breaking activity, Cambronne allowed the crew to make-and-mend. The schooner lay at sea-anchor under bare poles, and the sound of Jack the Cat's guitar drifted over a glassy calm.

That afternoon, the masthead lookout sighted three sails to the east. The rendezvous had been effected.

They were an oddly assorted trio. The convoy leader was an East Indianman of seven hundred tons. Her consorts were a brigantine of a hundred and fifty tons and a three-masted merchantman of three hundred. The foul miasma of their trade hung heavily in the air at a cable's length as they hove to and the East Indianman lowered a boat to bring her master over to meet the captain of his escort. Cambronne put on his best suit for the occasion.

Bosun Angel and his mates piped the side for the visitor, who proved to be a villainous looking creature whose greasy locks were drawn back in a pigtail, whose shifty eyes lingered too long upon Meg Trumper when she served them in the main cabin, and who opined that they would all be million-aires within the twelvemonth, or his name was not Jabez Fowler.

"How many slaves do you carry, Mr. Fowler?" asked Cambronne.

"There's over a thousand aboard me," said Fowler, "and nearly half as many again aboard the others. Call it fifteen hundred in all when you count the losses from various ills. If we make a swift passage onward to Cuba and stay free of cholera and the yellow jack, this convoy will be the biggest cargo in the history of the trade. I'll take another glass of your very fine rum, Cap'n."

Meg served him. Since shifting her billet aft, she no longer affected to be a boy. Though still wearing breeches, she had put off the thick jerkin and her small bosom jounced visibly under her cotton shirt; moreover, she had taken to covering the unsightly stubble of hair with a colorful bandana tied at the nape, after the manner of the island women. Altogether her appearance was—as Tom Blackadder had remarked to Cambronne on several occasions during the past couple of days—really quite appetizing.

"As to our movements, Mr. Fowler," said Cambronne. "We'll sail at once and lie off Anguilla Bank till nightfall tomorrow, since I want convoy and escort to make the dash through the islands into the Caribbean under cover of dark. Once through, and without pursuit, we have the whole wide sea in which to maneuver."

Fowler drained his glass and held it out for more, watching Meg lustfully as she performed the honors. The man's a drunken sot, thought Cambronne, but something of a sea-man, or how else would he have made the rendezvous so neatly?

"I want straight to Cuba, Captain," said Fowler, "and no maneuverings. Those thousand damned blacks have been in irons, ashore and afloat, for nigh on two months, and I doubt me we shall find a single sucker alive when we open up the holds. Make straight for Cuba, I tell you. We all four of us carry guns. Let the damned navy fellers show their faces and we'll blast our ways through 'em!" He took another deep swig of his rum and belched.

"There will be no blasting through, Mr. Fowler," replied Cambronne. "Your ships will not fire upon the navy."

"How so, sir?" demanded the other, narrow-eyed.

"Earlier this year, as you may or may not know," said Cambronne, "one of the slavers opened fire on a British warship, as a result of which her captain was killed. That single round of cannon did more harm to your trade than all the anti-slavery societies of Europe and America, William Wilberforce and all."

"Have you no taste for powder and shot, Captain?" sneered Fowler.

He really is a most unpleasant swine, thought Cambronne, but there is no point in losing one's temper with him. We are in this business together, and we must sink or swim together.

"Listen to me, Mr. Fowler, and listen to me well," said the Jerseyman. "The sea between here and the south coast of Cuba is patroled by the British under Commodore Harvey, whom I have met. From Harvey's own mouth I have heard his tactics, which are as follows: his ships patrol in pairs and will stand off and pound slave-ships with roundshot, and to blazes with the lives and limbs of the poor damned blacks. It follows, then, that your lumbering merchantmen will never get close enough to those frigates and sloops to return fire. So here is what you will do: upon sighting a navy patrol, you will immediately turn tail and head for the opposite horizon at your best point of sail, leaving the *Argo* to cover your retreat."

"And what will you do, Captain?" demanded Fowler, with rather less sneering contempt than formerly.

"You will have to wait and see, Mr. Fowler," said Cambronne.

It was an auspicious meeting. Fowler drank the best part of a bottle and a half of rum and had to be assisted up on deck and down into his waiting boat. He buttonholed Cambronne at the gangway, just as the *Argo*'s bosun and his mates were piping him over the side.

"I'll come over an' see you again, Cap'n," he said, winking. "Do a little trading. That little filly who served the rum for a couple o' my prize black mares. Always pick out half a dozen o' the handiest-built nigger gals for me own use. Master's privilege. Any time you want to ring the changes, as the saying is." He winked again, hiccuped, and nearly fell over the side.

"I'm afraid that's out of the question," said Cambronne, straight-faced. "The girl is my niece, my brother's girl, and I've sworn on our dead mother's head that I'll bring her home a maid."

The slaver's master looked disappointed, but was fast asleep by the time his men had laid him in the stern sheets of the boat.

"Don't care for the cut of his jib, Captain," was Blackadder's comment as they watched the boat rise and dip over the carpet of waves that separated the schooner from the big merchantman.

"We're going to have trouble with him," declared Cambronne. "I can smell it coming."

Chapter 8

They were under way again, the *Argo* leading and the others following in a ragged line, with all sails trimmed to keep pace with the slowest sailer, which was the East Indianman.

Cambronne and Blackadder dined together early, since the latter had the first watch from eight till midnight. They ate boiled salt pork, sweet potatoes and black-eyed peas, and drank a bottle of tolerable claret—the last of a shipment that had been purchased in Boston. The rendezvous having been successfully effected, Cambronne felt relaxed, notwithstanding his grave doubts about the convoy leader. Meg was serving them at table. The Blackadder was quite right, he thought: a toothsome little morsel, now that she was cleaned up a bit. She was taking quite a pride in her appearance, had even made a paper flower and stuck it in the bandana, over her right ear. How long, he wondered, had she been in the whoring game before she came to challenge that black woman at the Lobster Pot? And what had decided her to turn from whoring and prizefighting to shipping aboard the *Argo* as a lad? One day he must ask her, get the rest of her story. Better not leave it too long, for he must certainly put her ashore when they got back to Jamaica. Women are a bad influence in a ship—and she particularly, if she should happen to take up her whorish ways again. He had had to hang one man for her already.

"I'm for the deck," said Blackadder. "Any particular instructions for tonight, sir?"

"We'll bend on the blue suit of sails at dawn," said Cambronne, "and keep them on, well reefed down. From dawn, we can consider ourselves in a zone of war, with every man's hand against us. I hope to God that we don't run into the navy before we're through in the Caribbean. There's not enough room for maneuver among the islands for my liking. Good night to you, Master. Have a good watch."

"Good night, Captain."

Meg took away Cambronne's plate.

"Will there be anything else, sir?" she asked.

"You can bring me a cool rum with lime juice in about an hour," he replied. "I shall be doing some chartwork on the table here. You can clear the things away."

The glass was falling and it was as hot as fire. Though he opened the stern windows as wide as they would go to catch the last breath of night air, it stayed hot. Before unrolling the next day's chart on the table-top, he stripped himself to the waist. Beyond the screen door, out in the lobby at the foot of the companionway that served as wardroom pantry, he could hear Meg clattering dishes. Dismissing the sound, he addressed himself to the chart and the problem of guiding his charges, by night, through one of the trickiest passages in the West Indies. It would have to be done without lights, for a string of four lit-up ships must surely call for the attentions of any lurking navy cruiser. No more than a shaded stern lantern to guide the following ship. And woe betide any ship that fell out of station. He wiped his brow with his balled-up shirt and took up his rule and dividers . . .

Back the way they had come: sou'westerly, so as to leave the Anguilla Bank well on the larboard hand. It shoaled steeply there, with bare rocks damnably close to the hundred-fathom line. Thank God for the miraculous charts. Why had he not asked that girl to bring his rum and lime earlier . . . ?

Di-ding! The double-double beat of the first bell of the first watch. Damned if he was going to wait another half hour for that cool drink.

"Trumper!"

She came in. "Yessir?"

"I'll have it now—the drink."

Back to the chart. Once through the passage of the islands, he fancied a southerly course toward the central American mainland. With Brazil and Cuba the prime markets for the slave trade, the Royal Navy, and Commodore Harvey in particular, might well consider that area to be dead ground. Yes—marching across the chart with his dividers—once through the islands, we go due south to, say, the fourteenth parallel, then turn due west. Blessedly, the South-east Trades will blow favorably and persistently all the way, and we shall have the westerly set of the Caribbean current in our favor.

North again, to pass between Jamaica and Haiti. Where's that damned girl?

He looked up, as a shadow passed across the overhead lantern.

"Oh, it's you."

"I've brought your rum and lime juice. The lime juice I got from the cook. He had it in a stone jar. Said he's been trolling this jar all day in the sea on the end of a line to keep it cool. I think that was the word he used. 'Trolling.'"

"That's right," said Cambronne. "Trolling. It's a way of catching fish."

He took the glass, which, in that heat, had the suspicion of frosting on its outside surface. He was amused to see the girl's eyes upon it, and marked how she licked her lips.

"Sippers," he said, and held out the glass.

"I—I don't understand," she said.

" 'Sippers,' that's an expression used in the Royal Navy," said Cambronne. "On the lower deck, the only currency is the daily grog issue. If a sailor wishes to make a gesture of friendship to another, or to repay a favor, he hands his tot to that person and says, 'Sippers,' which is an invitation for the other fellow to have first sip at the tot. Of late, since Trafalgar, which greatly puffed up the arrogance of Jack Tar, there has grown a custom of offering 'gulpers,' which is to say that the recipient may take as big a mouthful as he can manage. But for you, tonight, Trumper, it's 'sippers.' Here, take the glass."

She obeyed, held the vessel to her lips two-handed, the way a child will hold its beaker of milk. Her dark eyes looked at him shyly over the rim.

"Thank you, sir," she said, giving it back to him. "I'll go back and finish my chores."

"That's the idea," said Cambronne. "And I'll finish mine."

Halfway to the screen door, she paused, turned.

"Sir . . ."

"Yes, Trumper—what is it?"

"You needn't have hanged that man for my sake."

"Not for your sake," said Cambronne. "For everyone's sake. For the *Argo*'s sake. You heard me address the crew in Kingston, when I revealed what business we were at. I said that the penalty for betrayal would be hanging. In fact, hanging is the *only* punishment in this ship. What use to flog a man? He will only desert at the first opportunity. Pack him off ashore, bag and hammock? A good, quick way to have us all in chains in Execution Dock, with him turned King's Evidence and laughing at us as Jack Ketch ties the noose. No, Trumper, the only punishment in this ship is hanging, and the only means of discharge is feet first, weighed with old chain, wrapped in sailcloth, over the taffrail."

"Then you'll not be putting me ashore when we reach Jamaica again?" she asked.

He regarded her a few moments before replying. The dim light in which she was standing, beyond the loom of the overhead lantern, played kindly with her appearance, softening the *gamine* perkiness of her face, shadowing her eyes mysteriously. She had unfastened the top buttons of her shirt, doubtless against the heat, and the gentle cleft of her bosom was only subtly suggested. She looked as much unlike a whore as any woman he had ever clapped eyes on. He felt his manhood stir.

"Come here, Trumper," he said.

She obeyed him. Stood a respectful distance.

"No. Closer," he said.

She moved two paces. At close quarters, he could see a slight freckling about the bridge of her nose. She smelled clean. Her breath was sweet.

"I had an offer for you today," said Cambronne. "Would you believe? The skipper of that East Indianman who came aboard offered me two prime nigger wenches in exchange for you. I was sorely tempted."

Her eyes flared fearfully. "That man!" she breathed. "The way he looked at me! It—it was like I'd been vomited over, so I felt like I needed a bath." Her eyes fell. "Thank you for—for not accepting his offer."

"I might reconsider," said Cambronne.

"Then I must do everything I can to persuade you otherwise, mustn't I, sir?" she said.

Her hands were quite steady as they stole to the remaining fastenings of her shirt; she unbuttoned them one by one, slowly. She shrugged out of the thin cotton garment and it fell about her hips.

Reaching out, he drew her to him.

"So now you've bedded three women in this very bunk."

She was lying atop him and had taken off the bandana, so

that her rough-cropped hair stood out all around like a chimney-sweep's brush. She was tracing a pattern on his chest with her fingertip.

"Your arithmetic is at fault," he said.

She held up one finger. "Well, you've just had me. That's one."

"True. So far, your addition is faultless."

"Before me, the blackie-white woman who swam aboard. Did you know that the watch on the gangway saw her, reported her to Jack the Cat, who was standing as officer of the watch, and Jack said she was a present for the captain and they were to forget it?"

"I must remember to thank Jack," said Cambronne.

She held up another finger. "That makes two. And then there was Miss Virginia."

He shook his head.

"You didn't bed her? Why?"

"Miss Virginia is a lady."

"And I am *not* a lady?" She raised herself up, sharply.

"Do you lay claim to being a lady, Trumper?"

She sagged back against his chest. "No, I don't," she murmured. "But I was never a whore."

"You gave an uncommonly fine imitation of a whore when you came into the Lobster Pot that night, Trumper."

"The paint, you mean? That was so men would know what I was supposed to be at. I tried to be a whore, you see? But it wouldn't work. I even got as far as taking a man's money, but as soon as he started his fumbling around, I threw down his money and ran off. Men! Ugh!"

"Have you been very ill-used by men, Trumper? Is that why you ran away to sea as a boy?"

"I was raped once," she said.

"Not a good recommendation for the oriental expertise that you learned from your father," he said.

"I never had chance to use it," she said. "There were six of them. And they made their task easier by bludgeoning me over the head from behind. By the time I came to, they had all taken me once and were ready for the second time around!"

"I see," said Cambronne.

"Do you see, Captain, sir?" she flamed, sitting up and shaking her ill-cropped head furiously. "You have just bedded me, and—I have to say it—with great courtesy and consideration, as befits an English officer and gentleman . . ."

"Jerseyman," corrected Cambronne. "I am a Jerseyman born and bred."

She waved it aside. "But for all that, Captain Cambronne, for all your courtesy and consideration, you nevertheless used me as a whore. Not the cheap sort of strumpet I tried so hard to be back in Boston, the sort who lifts her skirts in a side alley for twenty-five cents and don't waste too much time, dearie, for I'm a busy girl. You used me as an English officer and gentleman—sorry, a Jersey officer and gentleman —would use a high-toned strumpet who lives in a fine town house with a carriage and pair in the mews behind and a rich protector who calls Mondays and Wednesdays at three precisely and other times by appointment. Why are you laughing?"

"I'm not laughing," said Cambronne presently. "I swallowed a mouthful of spittle the wrong way. Do continue, you are most diverting."

She slumped back against his chest and he felt the whole weight of her slight, soft body against him.

"I've forgotten what I was leading up to," she said. "All I know is I sickened of trying to be a whore, so I determined that, since I couldn't be a woman according to my own lights, I'd take a chance at being a man. Which meant to be a sailor. It was to raise the money to buy a set of traps as good as those my father took with him when his ship sank with all hands off Cape Horn that I went to the Lobster Pot and challenged Dutch Olga. Thanks to you, I walked away with my eighty dollars, and with it was able to pay off the arrears on my room and get myself the best set of traps of anyone in this ship. You know all the rest, Captain Cambronne."

"Not all, I don't," said Cambronne. "By what odd coincidence did you ship aboard the *Argo?*"

"It was simple enough and easily explained," she said. "Word moves fast in the dockland. There was this talk of an English sea captain (they didn't know about your being a Jerseyman), who was searching for a crew. You were the only man I'd encountered in the dockland who looked like an Englishman, and it was Jack the Cat who had spread the news, so I sought him out, told him I wanted a berth."

Di-ding! Di-ding! Di-ding! Di-ding! Di-ding! Di-ding! Di-ding!

"Good God!" exclaimed Cambronne, starting up. "It's seven bells. I must have slept, dammit!"

"That you did, Jason," said his bedmate. "As soon as you had had your wicked way with me—twice over, I may add—you fell asleep. *And* snored like a pig. Yes, you had better rouse yourself before Blackadder comes off watch and finds you tumbling the cabin-girl—*Eeeeeh!*"

Her screech was occasioned by Cambronne's taking her, two-handed, by the waist and lifting her up to the deckhead, where he held her, nude and squirming, while he delivered his homily as follows:

"Firstly, Trumper," he said, "you will understand that I do not give a damn if the master catches me in bed with the cabin-girl, or anyone else for that matter. Secondly, if you ever again address me by my given name, I will make an exception to my rule that hanging is the only punishment in this ship and will have the bosun flog you at the mainmast chains. Thirdly, you will refer to the master as *Mr.* Blackadder. Lastly, you will brew me straightway a cup of hot coffee, before I go up on deck and put this little fleet of mine through some night maneuvers. Did you take all that in?"

"Yes, Captain," she said with contrition.

He set her back on her feet. Slapped her pert rump.

"Then be off with you, Trumper," he said.

He put his "fleet" through night maneuvers of a sort. Postulating that they had been sighted by British cruisers (it was bright moonlight), he wore ship and, passing swiftly down the line of his consorts, shouted orders through the speaking-trumpet for them to turn ninety degrees to starboard in line. The ensuing confusion provided ample evidence of their need to exercise. The leading ship, which was the East Indianman, made no response at all to the order, but sailed stolidly on. The brigantine, who came after, turned not to starboard but went about, thereby coming into slight collision and locking bowsprits with the other three-master. Dawn found the whole fleet wallowing in a heavy blow of wind, with shipwrights still hacking away at tangled sail, spar and cordage to separate the two vessels.

It was then, a bare twenty miles from the fringe of the islands, with the wind freshening by the minute, with two of his convoy helpless as a pair of Stags with their antlers entangled, that Cambronne's masthead lookout shouted for a sail to the southward, and afterward another sail. And then the White Ensign.

The Royal Navy had caught Cambronne—almost literally —with his breeches down.

To give Fowler his due, he was quick to remember Cambronne's instructions in the event of such an occurrence: he put up his helm and high-tailed it toward the east. The other two had no option but to remain and wallow. The *Argo* beat to quarters, and the special bosun's party had the schooner stripped to bare poles and the blue suit half bent on by the time the guns had been loaded, primed and run out ready for firing. The navy ships—a frigate and a handy-looking sloop— were five miles to the south and coming on fast.

"*How long?*" The call went across to the two entangled ships.

"*An hour! Any minute now! How the hell do I know?*" The reply came from a tall, gawky individual with a beard who was standing, with commendable nonchalance, on the wildly dipping and rising bowsprit of the brigantine, axe in hand.

"*Give it ten minutes. After that, chop away everything in sight and get the hell out of here!*" shouted Cambronne.

The other acknowledged with a wave.

"How are we loaded, Mr. Blackadder?"

"Chain and bar alternately, from fore to aft, sir. And the blue sails are ready to hoist."

"Hoist away."

"Aye, aye, sir."

It had been a long time since Algiers, a long time since his fight with the U.S.S. *Endurance* in New York Roads. A long time since those tussles in the Channel with the Revenue cutters, with only an over-sized punt-gun for armament. Cambronne took a squint at the oncoming warships through his telescope. The frigate had lowered her mizzen—a fairly standard practice in the Royal Navy when going into battle, for a ship may go far with a mizzen when all else has been shot away. Prudence, clearly, was the keynote on the West Indies station with Commodore Harvey flying his broad pennant.

The blue sails bellied forth in the freshening wind. Even the rock-steady *Argo* heeled wildly as she was taken in its grip and impelled forward. From the direction of the after companionway there came the crash of broken crockery. That damned girl, thought Cambronne, hasn't thought to secure everything in the pantry and we'll probably be eating out of saucepans for the rest of the voyage.

"Steady as you go!"

"Steady she is, sir."

Argo was running before the wind with the navy ships on an approaching course, fine on his starboard quarter, the frigate leading and both close-hauled. They were heading straight for the two entangled slavers, and it was clear that they intended to pay little regard to the schooner which was presuming to close with them, but would possibly throw her a broadside *en passant*. So far, no challenge had been made, but this would undoubtedly precede any serious shooting, even though the fact of four ships proceeding in convoy—an unheard-of thing in peacetime—betrayed them beyond all doubt for what they were.

Standing by his helmsman, one eye forever straying to the sails, to the two slavers behind him and the other one vanishing to the east, to the warships drawing closer by the minute, Cambronne enjoyed a curious calm. The die was cast. He would have preferred a better choice of options. Even supposing that he was able to beat off the warships and save the two entangled slavers, there would be the devil of a task to find Fowler, and the sea was mounting all the time. Was it likely that they were in the path of a hurricane? That was the nub of it, of course. He was badly placed as regards his allies, and things could get very much worse. On the other hand—hence his eager confidence—in a short while things might be going very well for him indeed.

"Be ready to give fire when I order, Mr. Blackadder," he said. "Larboard side in salvo. Aim for sails and rigging. I want as few navy casualties as possible." He saw the men's eyes stray toward him, and read the question there. "I do not expect to have so much as a musket-ball come aboard the *Argo*," he added.

They all grinned. He had them with him.

The range was closing. He could see men's heads above the frigate's bulwarks. If neither they nor he changed course, they would pass each other at a range of something like a hundred yards, which, in gunnery terms, was like dropping bricks into a bucket.

"She's firing!" This from Blackadder, who had actually spotted the tiny, tell-tale puff of white smoke made by the discharge of a priming pistol. Almost immediately afterward, the frigate's bow gun emitted a cloud that rose to the foreyard and was instantly ripped away by the wind. The dull crash of the discharge followed. And then a small waterspout was kicked up fifty yards off the *Argo*'s bow. It was a warning shot: a call to heave to and be boarded.

"Heave to, Mr. Blackadder," murmured Cambronne. And when he saw the astonishment in the other's shrewd eyes, he added: "I want her nicely in irons—and you may make as clumsy job of it as you choose—when that following sloop comes abreast."

Blackadder grinned. "Aye, aye, sir." He had taken the point.

Argo was running with the wind on her starboard side. First, Blackadder gybed her. The great booms crashed over with a force that would have dismasted a ship of more homely lineage. By the time the frigate was sweeping grandly past, he had managed to get the wind on his larboard side, though the sails were still flapping like wet washing. They could almost hear the Jack Tars' mocking laughter coming across the wavetops. And not a shot to spare for such a contemptible crew of performers.

"Stand by larboard broadside," said Master Gunner Stokes, for no good reason, surely, but to relieve his feelings.

Cambronne identified the frigate's captain, a tall fellow well endowed with gold lace and an old-fashioned bicorne, who was staring after the floundering schooner, and no doubt wondering how she could possibly carry so much sail. A shrewder man might have stopped to inquire . . .

The sloop came up fast behind her consort, and both of them were clearly off to pound the entangled slavers with round-shot at safe range, according to the dictum of Commodore Harvey.

The sloop was nearly abreast. Blackadder had the *Argo* in hand and ready to move in either direction. He looked to his captain for the order. Cambronne was watching and waiting for the instant to pounce and strike. He raised his hand.

"Now!" He brought his hand down. "Take me under her stern, Mr. Blackadder!"

It was done before those aboard the sloop had time to appreciate their peril. Indeed, there were many on her decks who, being concerned with their tasks, did not know what was happening till metal started coming aboard.

One minute the schooner was halted, hesitating in the

wind, her sails flapping impotently. The next she was reaching with the wind on her larboard side, a bow-wave creaming aft as far as her waist, yet with Vincenzo Alfieri's great iron keel holding the deck, the gun-platform, as steady and level as a rock. With the sloop's captain in the act of opening his mouth to shout, the *Argo* "crossed his T," slicing past his unprotected stern. And, in passing, fired a broadside of twelve-pounders into his sails and rigging: a half-hundredweight of ill-shaped metal tearing through sailcloth, spars, cordage. Most of the shots passed the entire length of the vessel from taffrail to bowsprit, piercing on the way mizzen, main, fore and jibs, and their attendant ropes. There were no men aloft, and a severed spar fell into the well of the gun-deck without causing any hurt. Not one sail escaped damage from that single, devastating *coup de main*, and the mizzen (which the vessel's captain had imprudently not furled on going into action against the suspected slavers) was in rags, likewise the mainsail and main topsail, the principal driving sails. In that one stroke Cambronne had turned a fighting ship into a liability.

After firing, the *Argo* moved downwind, a gesture which, with her vastly superior sailing quality, she could well afford to make, since it placed the injured sloop between herself and the attendant frigate, which still posed a considerable menace. And there Cambronne waited for his opponent—the frigate captain—to make the next move.

His opponent had two options: either to press on and bombard the helpless slavers or to return and deal with the strange schooner which, with one broadside, had turned a vessel of three times the fire-power into a lame duck. In the event, he fumbled both options. The temptation to make an easy killing of the slavers was too great to miss, so he went on for a while. Then prudence prevailed and he thought of how he would plead at his court-martial to the charge of deserting his damaged consort to the mercy of an enemy of proven might, so he wore ship and came back. But by that time the wind had worsened; the sloop was wallowing and in quite serious danger of being broached to and capsized.

Neither the sea—that hard taskmaster—nor the rigorous game of making war have any mercy to spare for the hesitant, the over-prudent. Having wasted time and distance, the frigate captain's misfortunes began to pile up like dunning creditors at the door of the near-bankrupt. The sea worsened.

The two slavers finally managed to disentangle bowsprits in reasonably workable order and set off with all speed after Fowler's East Indianman. One close look at the sloop was enough to tell him that he must forget all hope of following either the slavers or their escort, but must tow his comrade to Anguilla before—as seemed possible—the gale blew up to a hurricane. He was sourly putting a line over to the sloop when his attention was called to the strange blue-sailed schooner, which was shaping course to follow after the slavers. And at a miraculous speed, cleaving through the heavy seas like a dolphin.

There was triumph aboard the *Argo*. All looked to their captain who nodded to the master.

"We've a long haul ahead of us, Mr. Blackadder," he said, "and the lads have done well. Splice the main-brace."

So, with the traditional double issue of grog, the *Argo*'s crew celebrated their first victory.

Cambronne's troubles were far from over. He overhauled the brigantine and the three-master by noon, ordered them to follow, and himself shortened sail to accommodate their speed.

The problem was to find Fowler, who was hull down over the horizon and could have turned in any direction, believing, perhaps, that things had gone badly with the convoy and that he would now have to make what shift he could on his own. Cambronne went below and studied his charts—the miraculous charts of the Antilles, which, so far as he knew, Fowler would not possess. The particular passage through the chain of islands which they had intended to make that night was now well to the westward and—as Fowler might well think—dominated by the navy ships. It seemed likely, thought the Jerseyman, that the slaver's master might attempt the next option, which was to leave the Anguilla Bank and St. Bartholomew to starboard all the way, round the island of St. Eustatius, and steer due south into the Caribbean. It was a tricky passage but reasonably direct, and, assuming that Fowler had some local knowledge and respectable charts, the obvious choice. He resolved to take the convoy that way also, in the expectation of coming upon the missing slaver.

He and Blackadder saw to their own midday meal. The motion of the vessel being too violent to allow the galley stove to be lit, the crew ate cold hard tack and biscuit. Meg

Trumper was seasick, so captain and master were obliged to serve themselves, braced hard against the firmly fixed table as they sawed at their salt pork and gnawed at the weevily biscuit. They pledged each other and the continuing success of their voyage in issue grog, and had scarcely come to the last mouthful before the cry went up on deck: *"Sail ho! It's the East Indianman! She's struck!"*

It was a lee shore: the edge of the Anguilla Bank, round which Fowler had clearly been feeling his way, sounding all the time. Cambronne could have told him, the miraculous charts would have shown him, that the bank shoaled from unfathomable deep to certain danger in a ship's length around its perimeter. Fowler, obviously, had trusted to his seaman's eye. The trouble was that the clear demarcation between deep water and shoal which would have been clearly visible in fair conditions just did not obtain that day—everything was white water.

"She's leaning against a rock and probably holed below the waterline," said Cambronne, lowering his telescope and passing it to Blackadder. "See how she rises and falls freely? She'd not do that if she were hard aground. My guess is that there's water under her keel and she's broached to against a fang of rock. In which case we can haul her off."

"Captain, I think you're right," said Blackadder, squinting through the instrument. "And I've a notion that friend Fowler has made the same appreciation. By the look of things, they're about to lower a boat and lay out a kedge-anchor to haul themselves off the rock."

"I was mistaken in Fowler, perhaps," said Cambronne. "Not a very personable character, but a competent seaman. It's to be hoped he kedges her off before she breaks up and sinks."

"Along with those thousand blacks manacled down in the hold," said the other.

"Quite!" said Cambronne. "I think we will move in and give her a tow also. Lower the fore and main, and we'll drift down on the headsails. Make ready a line to pass over to them."

"Aye, aye, sir."

The crew moved steadily, unhurriedly, about their tasks. The evolution—the passing of a tow-line to a ship aground on a lee shore—was one of the innumerable exercises that

Cambronne had demanded of his men, day and night, during the passage from Jamaica to the rendezvous. His prescience had borne fruit. The men on the fo'c'sle who were flaking down the lines had done it in the dark; they found it easy to do in broad daylight—even with a gale of wind blowing. First a length of grass line, which, being buoyant, could be floated down to the stricken ship from a safe distance to be taken up; next the stout tow-rope itself; and all the time the *Argo* was gliding easily downwind, propelled only by her headsails (but with all others ready to be hoisted up and away!) toward the big East Indianman.

"They're lowering the boat now," said Blackadder, still with the telescope."

"Very prudent of Fowler," said Cambronne. "Every little bit will help to get her off. I wonder that he's found men willing to risk themselves in the sea about that rock."

"There appears to be no shortage of volunteers, or pressed men either," said Blackadder. "My God! That cutter's stuffed as tightly as Mother Purdy's on the night the fleet comes in!"

"Give me that!" demanded Cambronne.

"Sir, you don't think . . . ?"

Cambronne had the glass. "They're all there!" he said. "And more jumping down into the boat at risk of their necks!"

"Fowler?"

"Fowler most of all!" said Cambronne. "He's at the tiller, and beating off the fellows who have landed in the water and are trying to scramble aboard!"

"They're abandoning ship!"

"Every man jack of them!"

"But what are they doing about the blacks in the hold?"

"When a man's in that much of a hurry to save his skin," observed Cambronne, "the fate of a few blacks doesn't unduly burden his conscience. My God, look at that cutter now!"

The cutter—a large pulling boat—was crammed from stem to stern with a score of hands clinging to its washstrake and fighting to get inboard. From the *Argo*'s deck about a quarter of a mile distant they could see the wild figure of the East Indianman's master, his long pigtail sticking out like a pump handle, belaboring the would-be boarders with a boat-hook.

The boat was still wallowing in the turbulent water close by the ship's side, rising and falling on every white-crested wave, and no one had yet made any attempt—indeed, it would have been out of the question—to ship oars and pull away.

And then it happened!

A monster comber took the cutter in its grip and dashed it against the high side of the East Indianman, spilling despairing men from its washstrake and toppling others from within, lifting it higher, ever higher, turning it on its beam ends.

"She's going over!" cried Blackadder.

The doomed wretches were spilling from the cutter like ants from an overturned nest. Fowler alone remained, clinging to the stern sheets and screaming soundless imprecations to the dying men about him. He was still clinging, still screaming, when the boat filled and went down by the head, taking him with it.

As the *Argo* glided closer on her headsails, with great combers passing beneath her, they heard the cries of the men in the water, but they grew ever fewer, ever fainter. And then, as the schooner came within a cable's length, another sound took over, the like of which, once heard, a man will remember for as long as he lives, and it will haunt his dreams and unquiet hours. It was the keening cry from a thousand throats, raised on high in despair and the knowledge of sure death, and it came from deep inside the hull of the stricken ship.

"The poor damned blacks!" said Cambronne. "Their hold is probably flooding. They're dying by inches. Somehow we've got to tow them off!"

"No ship's boat could live in that, sir," said Blackadder. "If it reached the slaver, it would be dashed against her side, just like the cutter. But . . ."

"But what?"

"But a man might swim over."

"What man could swim in *that?*" Cambronne gestured to a comber which, having passed under the *Argo*'s counter and lifted it skyward, was passing down the length of the vessel at the height of the bulwark capping.

"Swede—he would survive," said Blackadder.

"Swede? But I would never ask any man—even him—to go into that water."

"I would," said Blackadder. "And he'd do it for me. He'd dive stark naked into a snake-pit for me. Do I have your permission?"

The howls from the living grave within the slaver grew ever louder. But there was no sound, and no sign, of the men from the wrecked cutter.

Cambronne nodded. "If the Swede's willing to take a line over, he goes with my blessing. I think he'd be insane to attempt it, but it's his life."

Blackadder grinned. "Swede doesn't have a brain, sir. Only a will. And he's happy to hand that over to my keeping."

"We're getting close," said Cambronne, squinting against the spindrift that showered them with every passing wave. "I'll have the headsails down to take the way off her and we'll ride to sea-anchor till the line's secured."

The giant topman was working for'ard. Cambronne watched as Blackadder approached him down the everslanting deck, laid a hand on the big man's shoulder and shouted above the howling of the wind into what remained of his ear. The communication, obviously repeated several times, finally won a slow grin from the other and a vigorous nodding of the great domed head. Swede was willing.

With the headsails off her, and a huge canvas bucket of a sea-anchor streamed out from the bows, *Argo*'s forward pace was reduced to a crawl, though the pitching grew even more violent as every passing comber had its way with her sleek hull.

"Away with you, Swede!" shouted Blackadder. "I'll buy you the fattest whore in Kingston if you win through."

A last grin at his mentor and the giant threw himself feet first into the maelstrom, landing in the trough of a comber, so that the next one took him up in its maw and bore him onward. The watchers on the fo'c'sle saw the domed head vanish from sight. The heaving-line—the other end of which was tied about the swimmer's waist—payed out with a rush as if a swordfish were hooked on to it.

"He's gone, poor bastard! It's taken him right down and burst his lungs!"

"No—he's up again!"

Like a pink-topped buoy, the shaven head emerged in the trough of a wave and was immediately engulfed in the foaming crest of another. But now Swede had tuned his strokes to the rhythm of the storm and was moving with the inexorable force, using it to his advantage. Brute instinct was serving him well, where intelligence would have destroyed a man of more refined temper. Rising and falling from view, sometimes disappearing inside a comber for breath-robbing minutes on end, he was soon far ahead of the *Argo* and halfway to the wrecked ship.

"I think I shall be buying him that fat whore," was Blackadder's comment. "Stand by for'ard to float down the grass line as soon as he's aboard the slaver!"

They thought they had lost him on the last fifty yards to the East Indianman, when he went from their sight for longer, surely, than any man could survive without breath. Cambronne knew that, with the giant Swede gone, they could do no more. He could not ask another man to attempt it and was too realistic to try the game himself. If the storm increased, as well it might, the slaver would be pounded to pieces on the rock that supported her by nightfall. If it grew no worse, she could scarcely last till the following dawn. A thousand blacks would die. A thousand souls released from a lifetime of unremitting toil—that was one way of looking at it. Those who employed him would see it otherwise: as red ink on the debit side of their ledgers.

"There he is again!"

"He's almost there!"

Swede was rising and falling in the wild water at the foot of the Indianman's steep tumble home. There was a line trailing in the water, pathetic testimony to the many and frantic attempts on the part of the panic-stricken master and crew to lower the whole complement of ship's boats. And it was to this that the swimmer addressed his efforts, brute instinct guiding him as to when to lay back and when to advance, brute instinct informing him that to be dashed, even momentarily and lightly, against that barnacle-encrusted side was to be half skinned alive.

Brute instinct dictated the moment. On the high rise of a spent wave, and when he was higher than the line of barnacles, Swede grabbed the line and held fast. When the waters receded he was hanging, high and dry, and already beginning to swarm up the rope like a monkey up a pole. The cheers from *Argo*'s deck must surely have resounded heartily in his mutilated ear.

"Float the grass!"

After the light heaving-line, the rope of coir, known as "grass," made from coconut fibers grown in Ceylon. Hairy and brown. The weakest of all cordage, but possessing the inestimable advantage of buoyancy. The giant Swede, safely aboard the slaver, had the thick and comfortable grass in his massive hands, with the long, floating snake of it part-supporting the heavy tow-line that came after. The task of hauling inboard a tow-line generally called for clearing lower deck of all hands—particularly in conditions like that; in full view of his shipmates aboard the schooner, the big man performed the Herculean task alone on the heaving deck, braced against the slaver's bulwarks, with a thousand voices raised in panic and dinning in his ears. And he grinned all the while.

They cheered him again when he had performed the most demanding part of his haul: lifting inboard the heavy noose of the tow-line, thick as a man's forearm and a dead weight of sodden hemp, slotting it into a fairlead and happing the noose over a fo'c'sle bitt.

The two vessels were connected!

"Hoist all sail! Trip the sea-anchor and retrieve! Lay her on the starboard tack!"

The *Argo,* now perilously close to hazard, blossomed her suit of blue, bit the wind as she came about, rose high on the first comber to strike her fine on the starboard bow (and Vincenzo Alfieri must have stirred in his pauper's grave in Brooklyn as she was nearly laid on her beam ends), recovered her equilibrium, gained power before the next assault, sliced through it and forged on, close-hauled and triumphant.

The testing time came with the tautening of the tow-line, which, subjected to the sort of power that might be needed to dislodge the big East Indianman, could well part on the first shock of strain.

It held. The *Argo,* checked in her onward surge as if by a giant hand offered against her prow, wavered and all but luffed impotently into the wind, from whence she must surely have been carried down to join the slaver in mutual destruction; but the check was only momentary. The spirit of Vincenzo Alfieri, whose remains lay in that humble Brooklyn plot (and perhaps that of his master, at rest beneath the great dome of Les Invalides), may have inspired her to the sublime effort. In any event, she recovered, pointed full and by in answer to the helm and remained on course.

"We have her in tow!"

A ragged cheer from the deck of the schooner. They could see the giant Swede aboard the slaver capering like a madman and waving his arms as the big East Indianman, reluctant as a drunkard prised out of a tavern, edged slowly off the fang of rock, nose first as her tow demanded, and came after her guide and lead. God! Do I have it aright? thought Cambronne. Did she have water under her keel, or is her bottom ripped out? Will she settle down before my eyes as soon as she makes deep water, and will those thousand poor black devils be swallowed up in their own stink till the end of time?

"Steady as you go," he said.

"Steady she is, sir," responded Jack the Cat at the wheel, with Bosun Angel at his elbow nodding approval.

The *Argo* was in her best point of sail, which is to say that she was close-hauled and nicely full and by, her decks slanting no more—despite the gale—than any schooner afloat would have shown in a brisk blow of wind And the East Indianman was following her on the taut tow-line. Paying off to one side and the other as wind and sea hit her towering bluff, reluctant as some big booby of a schoolboy to be led to enlightenment, but going nevertheless.

The other two slavers, the brigantine and the three-master, were hove-to at a safe distance from the edge of the bank, as Cambronne had ordered them. They had seen a certain amount of the activity, but, like far-off observers of a battle, were confused as to the details. Not near enough to see the tragedy to which the cowardice of Fowler and his crew had brought them, they naturally thought that the *Argo* had floated a line down to the East Indianman and that her crew had picked it up Only after a shouted conversation through speaking-trumpets did the full horror break upon them, that their consort was now crewed only by one man—and a thousand manacled blacks.

"What now, Captain?" asked Blackadder.

"To Cuba," responded Cambronne.

Chapter 9

In the languorous late summer's afternoon, Manatee Grange, with its gardens, its water and its gesticulating statuary, could have been a painting by Watteau. The profound sense of unreality was emphasized by the stillness. Nothing stirred, not so much as the uppermost tips of the tall cypresses. Even the bright fountains seemed to be frozen in an instant of time.

Enter the English butler with his powdered wig and knee breeches and it was not Watteau, but Hogarth, who had made the painting.

"Will you h-attend h-upon Lord Basil now, Captain? This way, h-if you please."

The butler led the way, Cambronne following, with the line of flunkeys bringing up the rear as ever. Through the great salon, along a colonnaded corridor whose long windows looked out over the water garden, to a bijou classical temple of glass and marble with a gilded dome. Inside was all green coolness of waxen-leaved tropical plants, rising dome-high. It was these which, stealing heat and moisture from the air, made the delicious contrast with the cloying humidity of the Jamaican afternoon outside.

"Ah, Cambronne. Welcome back from sea. I have heard much of your exploits already. Pour yourself a drink and one for me also. Then sit down and give me your report."

Lord Basil Lasalle of Manatee was in his bath. His bath was a sunken marble pool in the center of the conservatory. The blond aristocrat lolled against a silk cushion set against the edge of the pool. The water was cold, as evidenced by lumps of ice that floated, together with rose petals, in the limpid water. A Negro boy, nude to the waist and wearing a Turkish fez, squatted, grave-faced, by the edge of the pool. As Lasalle spoke, the boy took out of a covered basket another large piece of ice and laid it gently upon the surface of his master's bath.

"The only confounded way I can abide this damned climate is to spend half my time in here," said Lasalle.

Cambronne grinned. Poured rum into two glasses at a side table, added lime juice, ice. Handed one glass to the master of *Manatee* and took a seat in a reclining chair close by the pool.

"Where shall I begin my report, Lord Basil?" he asked.

"In a word, was it a success, the voyage?" demanded Lasalle.

"Did we deliver all, or most, of the—er—merchandise, you mean?" He glanced significantly at the boy.

"Don't mind him," said Lasalle. "He's a deaf-mute. The most valued kind of houseboy in Jamaica. Cost me a pretty penny, too. Please continue. Yes, did you deliver the slaves to Cuba?"

"We did."

"Excellent. Excellent. Any losses?"

"When we had towed the East Indianman off the rock," said Cambronne, "and when I had put a prize crew aboard her to sail her on to Cuba, they found that her planks were sprung below the waterline and the slave hold was flooded breast-high. That's to say *male* breast-high. The smaller women, and most of the children who had not been lifted up, were drowned."

"Numbering—how many?"

"About a hundred."

"And losses on the other ships?"

"Negligible."

"Excellent."

"There is the matter, Lord Basil, of Fowler and his entire crew," said Cambronne.

Lasalle shrugged his naked shoulders. "The likes of Fowler are eminently expendable," he said. "He and his men made fortunes, every one. They knew the risks involved. There will be no shortage of men to take their places."

Cambronne eyed him over the rim of his glass, this English aristocrat turned mandarin of a slave empire. "When my time comes, Lord Basil," he said, "when the navy finally gets the first shot in and carries away my head, shall you say that I, too, am 'eminently expendable'?"

The lustrous green eyes narrowed. "Listen, Cambronne," said Lasalle, "and listen well. No man is indispensable. That is my philosophy of life. I am not indispensable. Certainly you are not indispensable. Even He whom we coyly refer to as 'the Man' is not indispensable. Do I make myself plain?"

"Perfectly plain, Lord Basil," said Cambronne. "Shall I continue with my report?"

"Please do. As I told you, I have heard much of your exploits already. The excellent Commodore Harvey was here to dinner the night before last."

"Oh, my God!"

"Well may you invoke the Almighty, Cambronne. Harvey had the report of your action off Anguilla back here in Jamaica while you were still off Cuba. Did you know that the sloop you damaged broke her tow-line and was wrecked off Anguilla island?"

"I did not, sir!" exclaimed Cambronne. "Were there any casualties?"

"There were not. Everyone was brought off, Harvey tells me. Even the ship's cat. The frigate captain's court-martial, by the way, is set for Thursday next at 2 p.m. I take it you will not wish to attend. May I trouble you to pour me another drink?"

Good-humoredly, Cambronne served Lasalle and himself. Swine and pervert though the master of Manatee might be, he had a personable side to his nature and the Jerseyman, who liked people, found the man—though potentially evil—superficially attractive. Cambronne felt much the same about colorful, venomous reptiles.

"So I take it that Commodore Harvey is much put down?" he said.

"I would put it much higher than that," replied Lasalle. "And what is most gratifying—from our point of view—is that your exploit off Anguilla has made a rift in the formerly excellent relationship between the Royal and United States Navies. I may say a most gratifying cooling-off, which could well spell the end to their recent collaboration against our activities."

"Is that so, sir?" commented Cambronne. "And in what form, pray, has this rift manifested itself?"

The master of Manatee, prompted by the question, choked slightly on his drink in risible recollection. When he had entirely recovered himself, he said, "I will put it to you this way, Cambronne. Present also at my dinner party the night before last was the U.S. Navy's resident liaison officer in Jamaica, one Lieutenant Slight. Mr. Slight, by reason of the

fact that his father owns three-fifths of the beef that comes
into Chicago, does not put too high a premium on tact and
diplomacy as levers to further his naval career, and was
extraordinarily outspoken about Commodore Harvey's methods against the slave trade."

"Was he now?"

"That he was. While the rest of the table listened in
horrified silence (I except myself, who was silently amused,
and Madame Alissa, who was laughing openly—but you and I
know, do we not, Cambronne, about Alissa's total scorn of
any self-restraint?), young Mr. Slight, fortified by my excellent claret and the knowledge of all that beef, suggested that
the present tactics of the Royal Navy against the slave trade
smacked of cowardice."

"Cowardice? Surely he didn't dare . . . ?"

"That he did, and more. While Commodore Harvey was
already choking on his Chicken Marengo, our fine Yankee
sprig implied—nay, he scouted it openly—that, had the war
of 1812 happened seven years earlier, and had the Americans
possessed line-of-battle ships, and had they thrown in their lot
with France and Spain against England, then Nelson must
have lost the battle of Trafalgar and lived to be an embittered
old ex-admiral. Now, what do you think of that? And what do
you think that the excellent Commodore Harvey thought of
that, hey?"

"I can't begin to think," said Cambronne. "To impugn the
immortal memory of Nelson and Trafalgar—why, to a navy
man that's like—what?—raping one's mother-in-law, farting
aloud in church? I simply can't draw a parallel."

"Nor I, Cambronne," said the master of Manatee. "Nor I.
But I tell you that I do not remember when I enjoyed an
evening more."

They laughed together. The black boy dropped more ice
into his master's bath. Cambronne poured them both another
drink.

"Who captained Fowler's ship on to Cuba?" asked Lasalle
presently. "I will see to it that he gets a handsome bonus in
addition to his share of the profits."

"That was Tom Blackadder, my master," said Cambronne.

"A good man?"

"One of the best. Fit for a command of his own—if we ever
thought to extend the scope of our convoy protection and
build another *Argo.*"

Lasalle raised a blond eyebrow. "That, I should tell you, is not beyond the bounds of possibility, Cambronne," he said.

"The man who carried the line across to the East Indianman, without whom the ship would have been lost and the slaves with her, is a fellow we call 'Swede,'" said Cambronne. "I should like to recommend him for a bounty, also."

Lasalle nodded. "Done," he said. "What do you think? Five to them each?"

Time for Cambronne to raise a quizzical eyebrow.

"Five pounds?" he asked, with a note of contempt.

"Five hundred!" snapped Lasalle.

"My God—there's money in slaving!" exclaimed Cambronne. "Why, with five hundred English pounds, a man may set himself up for life. Buy a tavern or a small business. Or, if he chose to remain in the seafaring trade, a fishing boat or a coaster. Is this wise? How can you keep men when you throw a life's fortune at them for one voyage?"

The thin, aristocratic lips sketched the approximation of a smile, and it was as dry and bitter as a suck at an unripe lemon.

"Seamen," said Lord Basil, "forever, in my experience, dream of buying themselves a tavern, or setting themselves up in a small business, or what have you. In our trade, that worthy ambition is swiftly made available. But there is the ancient principle, Cambronne, of the donkey and the carrot. Extend the lure of the carrot into infinity and the donkey will forever continue to carry his burden. In my experience, men of the sort who are most useful in our trade—rogues like the late unlamented Fowler—never amass any savings, no matter how much they earn, but squander every penny on drink, whores and gambling. They always sign up for one more voyage. I wonder about you, Cambronne. Does the donkey and carrot principle apply to you? And, by the way, your share of the recent affair will run into several thousands."

Cambronne shrugged. "I wouldn't say that money lures me very far, Lord Basil, nor do I have expensive tastes. No, I think I seek other goals. . . ." He let the comment hang in the air.

"Power, perhaps?"

"Power—certainly. Yes. You read me very shrewdly, sir."

The black boy quietly laid another piece of ice in the bath. Lord Basil stretched himself luxuriantly.

"Cambronne, I shall be forwarding a complete—and highly

favorable—report upon your first voyage to The Man," he said. "If you continue as you have begun, you can expect great advancement in our organization. It is even possible that you could become a member of the inner council. Would that be to your taste? Is that the sort of power you seek?"

"That would suit me admirably, sir," said Cambronne.

"Well, then, pour us both another measure and let us drink to your continuing success. Oh, and by the way, we have another cause to offer a toast. Virginia Holt and I are to be married."

A glass fell from the side table and shattered to fragments at Cambronne's feet.

"Clumsy of me," said the Jerseyman, stooping to pick up the pieces.

"We had hoped to set the day of the nuptials for the end of this month," continued Lasalle, "but last week a certain Mr. Carradine, a friend of the family, arrived from Boston with the sad news that Virginia's mama had passed away, so a decent period of mourning must be observed."

"Mrs. Holt—dead, you say?"

"Yes. Were you acquainted with her, Cambronne?"

"We met on—a couple of occasions," said Cambronne. "She was a lady of some—grace and character."

"Well, the Grim Reaper has claimed her," said Lasalle. "According to Carradine, she took the fever and died within days. However, let us drink our toast."

Cambronne filled himself a fresh glass, handed Lasalle his.

"To you, Captain," said the aristocrat. "And to your continuing success."

"To Miss Virginia," responded Cambronne. "And to you also, Lord Basil."

"One thing else," said Lasalle. "The Man is here, in Jamaica."

"Is he, by God?"

"And will wish to see you at an early date, Cambronne. So hold yourself in readiness at a moment's notice—at any time."

Before the Jerseyman could comment upon that, Alissa entered the conservatory like a parakeet descending, a riot of color and feathers.

"Cambronne! Kiss me on the cheek. How splendid to see you again! My dear Basil, how are you?"

Having accepted Cambronne's salutation, Alissa stooped

to kiss Lasalle, not one whit put out that he was stark naked under the pellucid water. Her costume was outrageous to the point of barbarism, being composed of the breast feathers of colored birds: thousands of multicolored scraps were sewn onto wispy silk, scandalously cut at the bosom and slashed at the skirt to show one shapely leg to the thigh. A whole tropical rain forest must have been denuded of its exotic birds to have achieved the vision she presented.

"I greatly enjoyed your dinner party of the night before last, Basil," she said, and, turning to Cambronne, "Have you heard the joyful news of the forthcoming marriage?"

"Lord Basil has just informed me," said the Jerseyman, searching her face, which told him nothing.

"I am so happy for them both," declared the beautiful mulattress. "She is so young, and in need of the steadying influence of a mature man. The more so now that she is motherless, poor child. When shall we see her again, Basil dear?"

"Virginia is coming to luncheon," said Lasalle. "Will you join us, Alissa? And you also, Cambronne?"

"I'm afraid that I . . ." began Cambronne, but Alissa forestalled him.

"What the gallant captain was going to say is that he must get back to his beloved ship—but he will do no such thing. I—Alissa—have spoke!" And she folded her arms across her commendable bosom.

"There's no escape for you, Cambronne," said Lasalle. "Alissa is not to be disobeyed, so you might as well accept with a good grace. Now I must go and get dressed. I'll leave you two to drink and chat. Luncheon is at one o'clock in the Chinese dining-room. I will see you there."

"The blond aristocrat emerged, dripping, from the bath, and was handed a silk robe by his little black deaf-mute. He nodded to them both and went out, with the boy padding at his heels.

"Well, and what do you think about that, Cambronne?" she demanded.

"About—what?"

"Come, come, don't prevaricate with me," she said. "You know very well what I'm referring to. The fact that that whey-faced chit of a Yankee girl has managed to achieve what every eligible female in Jamaica has held dearest to her heart, which is to become Lady Basil Lasalle of Manatee."

"How did she—bring it off?" asked Cambronne.

"Pour me a drink, give me a cigar, and I will tell you the story," said Alissa. "And while I'm doing so, I shall avail myself of dear Basil's tempting cool bath."

One hand to her shoulder, and she undid the sole fastening of the outrageous garment, so that it whispered down her body and fell in a dazzling pool at her feet. She was entirely nude beneath: a sweep of magnolia-tinted flesh adumbrated by the dark nipples and a splash of sable at the loins.

Cambronne gave her a tall glass of rum and lime juice, lit one of his own cigars and transferred it to her painted lips. Alissa lay back against the silk cushion and watched the water eddy about her superb breasts.

"You will remember, Cambronne," she said presently, "the night when I told you Basil had become attracted to the little bitch. Heavens, I had no idea then that he was so besotted by her. Of course, being Basil, he no doubt tried to bed her, but madam would have none of it." She laughed. "To think of the almighty lord of Manatee being refused a maidenhead! The sheer novelty of the situation must have been a revelation to him, and no doubt drove him to covet her the more, so that in the end he was driven to offer her his hand, his title, his fortune—everything, for desire of that scrawny little body. What did you say?"

"It was nothing," said Cambronne. "Please go on. When did it take place, the betrothal?"

"Very soon after you left," said Alissa. "I don't doubt but that Basil invited the little Yankee into his bed on the night of the reception; the fight with that wretched youth would have made him outrageously prideful and lusty. But, having been refused, he was offering to marry her within the week, and she was accepting. But, you know, he's got you to thank for what he may consider to be his present good fortune—though I personally think he will live to regret it."

"Why so?" asked Cambronne.

"Because of me," said Alissa. "She assumed that I was Basil's mistress, but, when she found us together on the schooner that morning (and it was obvious, I should think, that *I* hadn't just gone over for breakfast!), I ceased, in her mind, to be a mistress and became a whore. Whores, to nice young ladies of Miss Virginia's upbringing, pose no threat to decently married women."

"You think, then, that she accepted his hand because she

discovered that you and I had spent the night together?" asked Cambronne.

"I know it, my dear," responded Alissa. "I'm a woman too, remember, and know another woman's mind as well as I know my own—as regards men, that is.

"And now, Cambronne, I am getting out of the bath. I think I should like you to dry me with one of those towels hanging over there. And after that"—she reached out a hand and took hold of his—"I think we may find better ways to kill the hour before luncheon than speculating about that whey-faced Yankee chit."

The Chinese dining-room, to which Cambronne and Alissa repaired at exactly one o'clock, was an oriental extravaganza set inside the baroque shell of the great mansion. Designed by a pupil of John Nash after the manner of the Master's interior decoration of the Brighton Pavilion for the then Prince Regent, it loudly stated the conceit that one was inside a bamboo cage full of parrots and parakeets, for the wallpapers were painted to resemble bamboo, likewise the domed ceiling, while colored birds—stuffed and alive, the live ones in cages and the stuffed ones on perches—abounded everywhere. And the floors were scattered with an emperor's ransom in Chinese silk carpets. It was a setting that became befeathered Alissa as a sheath becomes a sword.

Not so Virginia Holt, who sat among that decadent splendor like a forlorn little blackbird waiting for a crumb. Dressed in full mourning and veiled, she looked—as far as one could judge through the veil—as if she had been crying. And it seemed to Cambronne that she was pale and must have lost weight. She was already seated when they entered. The master of Manatee rose and greeted them, waving them to their places at an oval table at which they were seated, male and female alternately. Cambronne was on Virginia's left, with Alissa opposite.

Alissa immediately set her mark upon the tone of the proceedings: the younger woman was to have no say in dictating the course of conversation. Cambronne had scarcely had time to kiss Virginia's hand, and was interrupted while murmuring a few words of condolence about her mother's death, when Alissa loudly announced:

"Another thing that happened while you were away,

Cambronne. Your Mr. Hetherington, he who was so accommodating with his Bombay lady, blew his brains out!"

Cambronne paused in the act of taking a slice of candied ham from a dish presented to him by a Negro lackey.

"Good God!" he murmured. "You don't say so. Why did he do that?"

"Let his example be a lesson to you, Cambronne," said Alissa archly, wagging a taloned finger at the Jerseyman. "Your Mr. Hetherington arrived out here a fit, whole man, but the lure of high living destroyed him."

"Young Needham had instructions from Virginia's father to inquire discreetly into Hetherington's finances," supplied Lasalle. "As anyone in Jamaican society could have told him, he found the agent of the Augusta Line to be in debt to half the island: wine merchants, tailors, gamblers, tradesmen, money-lenders. On learning which, Needham produced a letter from his employer authorizing him to examine the books of the agency. Hetherington gave up the books on demand, then went into his library and put a pistol into his mouth."

"How awful—awful!" breathed Virginia. "Whatever his faults and transgressions, to be driven to—*that!*"

"Amusingly, I can see young Mr. Needham going the same way," said Alissa. "He's a deep one, that. And, would you believe it? Dear Basil has set him up in the dead man's mansion, where he now enjoys the benefits of an English country gentleman. Plus the delights of the Bombay ladies, I shouldn't wonder."

"Hetherington's place is owned by the Augusta Line," explained Lasalle. "I presumed to advise Needham to occupy it, subject to the approval of his principal in Boston. A useful man, that young fellow. Alissa is quite wrong; he won't make the same mistakes as Hetherington."

"Quite so," said Cambronne, who had views of his own about Uriah Needham. "Still, I'm sorry to hear about Hetherington, particularly since I am still in possession of one of his suits. And I don't suppose it's paid for."

Alissa laughed at that. "I don't suppose the Bombay ladies are paid for, either," she countered. "My dear Basil, do you think they will be included among the effects to be sold off in settlement of Hetherington's debts . . . ?"

She was soon well on her way with bawdy speculations, and

it was clear that the master of Manatee, for all that he was now affianced, had not lost the capacity to be amused by her. Cambronne seized the chance of the diversion to address himself to Virginia, who, having raised her veil to eat, showed herself to have indeed lost the bloom of wild roses from her cheeks and to have a suspicion of a shadow under her eyes.

"Miss Virginia," said the Jerseyman, "I should like to offer my deepest condolences to you upon the sad loss of your mother."

Her eyes instantly brimmed with tears. "Thank you, Captain Cambronne," she murmured, not looking at him.

"She was—a very fine lady."

"Yes. Taken of the fever."

"Very, very sad. I trust she didn't suffer."

"Oh, but she must have, Captain!" The lovely, tearful eyes rose to meet his gaze. "You don't know what a terrible thing is the fever. Mama's sister, my Aunt Amy, went the same way. I helped nurse her with my own hands. It was terrible to see her fade before our eyes. The suffering was pitiful, yet in spite of it she found strength to take from her neck her pendant, her garnet birthstone, and place it around my neck. I wore it ever after, till—one day, I broke the chain and lost it. I think you remember the occasion, Captain." She looked down at her hands.

"Er—yes," said Cambronne.

"So there it is," said Virginia. "Having seen Aunt Amy's sufferings at first hand, I cannot offer myself the consolation that Mama perhaps had an easy end. But that she—she . . ."

"My dearest . . ." Lord Basil Lasalle rose from his seat, dabbed his pale lips with a napkin and hastened to the side of his betrothed; he took her hand and pressed it between his, offered her his handkerchief and himself wiped away her tears.

Alissa met Cambronne's gaze. Her eyes were dancing with secret amusement.

"Oh, how very sad, don't you think, Cambronne?" she declared. "Poor Mama. Poor Aunty Amy. Dear me."

It was a thoroughly wretched meal as far as Virginia was concerned, and an embarrassment for her intended, who did not like to see women giving way to their emotions—some of their emotions. For Cambronne there was a deep feeling of unease, which was in no way lightened by Alissa's attitude throughout the remainder of luncheon, when she kept slip-

ping him sidelong glances from under her wicked, upswept
eyelashes.

"Upon my word, Cambronne, you had me fooled completely. I would never have guessed it of you—never!"

He was with her in her landau, being driven to her house,
which was at the far end of the Manatee estate, on the edge of
a lake, and called Le Petit Trianon—in imitation of Marie
Antoinette's retreat in Versailles. He had come with her at
her request. More a demand than a request.

"May we change the subject, Alissa?" he asked. But she
would have none of that.

"You have been nursing a secret passion for her all this
while," she said, laughing. "Like some love-sick, mumbling
country lout. Making sheep's eyes at her from afar. Wearing
her token. Don't deny it, you wore it that night we bedded
together on the schooner, and you wear it now . . ."

Her hand, moving like a striking snake, tore at the buttons
of his shirtfront and brought out the tell-tale garnet pendant
on the gold chain.

"Poor Aunt Amy's birthstone. Do you deny it, Cambronne?"

"I deny nothing," said the Jerseyman, replacing the pendant inside his shirt and re-buttoning it. "And I admit
nothing."

"Well spoken," said Alissa, making mock of clapping her
hands in approval. "Spoken like a sea captain. At least I am
not to be treated to drooling confidences. Thanks for sparing
me that, Cambronne."

"May we now change the subject?" he repeated. They had
come to the gates of her home, and to the end of a long drive
that led to the portico of a pretty villa, all turrets and
machicolations in the Gothic manner, whose white walls were
reflected from the surface of the lake like some fairytale
castello.

She persisted. "And is this secret passion returned, I
wonder?" she mused. "Does *la belle Yanqui* similarly wear
your token, all unbeknown to you? Ah, I see it all now. How
wrong I have been. How wrong!"

"What do you see, Alissa?" asked Cambronne with a note
of weariness. "What is going on in that clever, beautiful head
of yours now?"

Alissa pointed to him. "Not because she had ceased to

regard me as a mistress, but merely as a whore—not for that did she accept Basil's proposal," she declared. "It was done out of pique, out of blind, unreasoning jealousy, out of despair from knowing that the man she craved for had taken Alissa to his bed—that was why she is shortly to become Lady Basil Lasalle of Manatee!"

"Now you are being ridiculous," growled Cambronne.

She shook her head. "I *have been* mistaken, but now the scales have fallen from my eyes," she said. "I see it plain. But there is no profit in it for you, Jason Cambronne. No turning back the pages of time. You have lost *la belle Yanqui*. He will never let her go—not till he has wedded her, bedded her, and grown tired of her, at any rate. And if you tried to cross him over her, he would squash you like a mosquito! *Like a mosquito!*"

The coachman was checking the onward pace of the magnificent pair of blacks that drew the landau, directing them with the lightest touch of the rein to traverse the half-moon of crisp gravel that fronted the villa's portico. A Negro butler and a maidservant—a mulattress like Alissa herself—came out to greet the return of their mistress.

The conveyance halted. Cambronne alighted and handed Alissa down; he bowed and allowed her to proceed him into the villa, through a cool hallway and into a sitting-room of duck-egg blue with a view over the lake, where noble swans glided in pairs, great wings arched like sails.

Alissa dismissed the servants. She and the Jerseyman faced each other.

"I mean it, Cambronne," she said. "You should have taken her earlier. On the voyage out here. In Boston. When she was yours for the asking. Now it is too late. Now she could be the death of you." She reached out her arms. "Come to me, Cambronne. Come to Alissa. Forget the little Yankee . . ."

As Lasalle had warned him, the summons came at a moment's notice. It happened the following evening, shortly after sunset. Lasalle, who must have been aware—and uncaring—that Cambronne was staying with his former "companion," sent one of his overseers to Le Petit Trianon with a spare horse and a message: Captain Cambronne was to ride forthwith to Gallows Corner, two miles from the Manatee main gates on the Spanish Town road, and wait there.

Alissa was resting. He did not disturb her, but mounted up and rode through the gentle gloaming of the tropic night, past the gesticulating bulk of Manatee and down the long road to the ornate gates. Two miles on, the sun having by that time set with dramatic suddenness, he came to the spot designated Gallows Corner: a place of shadows and lowering palms, silence, and the stink of decaying vegetation. As token of the forbidding name, a disused gibbet stood up against the sky of stars, gaunt as death itself. Cambronne drew rein, shivered and pulled up the collar of his coat. Unaccountably, it was as cold as a stone mausoleum in that unsavory spot.

His mount snickered and pawed the dirt road with a forehoof. Cambronne patted the creature's neck. A long time passed—perhaps an hour. And no sign of a moon.

Then he heard it: the sound of a conveyance approaching down the road from Spanish Town. A coach and horses. His mount heard it and tossed its head.

The coach came in and out of the shadows toward him, flanked by two outriders in caped coats and pulled-down hats. The coachman was similarly attired. From first to last, Cambronne never saw their faces, though he was soon aware that the horsemen carried carbines, which, having halted close by him, they soundlessly unslung and laid across their saddle-bows, the muzzles pointing in his direction.

Not a word from outriders or coachman; only the menace of the dark muzzles. The windows of the coach were closed and draped on the inside with black stuff. Cambronne tensed like a hawk unhooded as a hand drew aside the curtains and pulled down a window halfway. The hand was gloved in black.

"Approach me, Cambronne." The voice from within the coach was muffled and indistinct—as it had been on the previous occasion.

Cambronne urged his mount forward the two or three paces that separated him from the conveyance. He was aware that the two outriders' carbines followed his every movement.

"So, Cambronne. We meet again." There was nothing to be seen inside the dark maw of the coach's interior, not even a shadow or a silhouette, but the gloved hand remained upon the ledge of the lowered window, smoothly reposed. "You have made a good start, Cambronne," the voice continued.

"But there is much more to be done. The super-vessel will be called upon to perform great feats in the coming months. Are you equal to the demand?"

"I will do my best," replied the Jerseyman.

"That will be better than most, I know," came the reply. "Succeed, and great advancement is open to you."

"I thank you."

"Fail, and you will kipper in the gibbet like that fellow outside the jail—unless I am able to intervene and save you."

"I understand that," said Cambronne.

"Play me false, on the other hand, and nothing will save you," went on the voice, and, muffled though it was, it carried a timbre of total menace. "Play me false, Cambronne, and were better that your mother had throttled you at birth—that I promise you."

Cambronne said nothing.

"Drive on, coachman! Cambronne, *adieu!*"

The coachman flourished his whip and shook his reins. The conveyance started forward and the outriders with it. As the horsemen cantered past the Jerseyman, they kept their carbines trained upon him. Not till they and the coach were vanishing into the darkness of the palm-hung road did they turn to face the front and sling their firearms.

Cambronne wheeled his mount and set off back the way he had come, none the wiser after his fresh encounter with The Man—and charged with an indefinable unease.

Which, it occurred to him, might have been the object of the summons . . .

Jason Cambronne stayed for some days—and nights—at the villa called Le Petit Trianon, which Lord Basil Lasalle had given to his erstwhile "companion," first as a grace-and-favor residence, then freehold and unencumbered—as she explained to the Jerseyman. After the largely one-sided conversation that had followed the revelation about the garnet pendant, the subject of Virginia—her forthcoming marriage to the master of Manatee, the truth or otherwise of Cambronne's secret passion for the young Bostonian—was not raised between them. Every day, by arrangement, Tom Blackadder presented himself at Alissa's villa, where he was received alone by his captain in the duck-egg blue sitting-room. Civilities were exchanged, they drank a glass of rum apiece, Blackadder reported on the progress of things aboard the *Argo:* of a new re-painting of the ship's side, the better to confuse their opponents (this time it was colored a deep green); of the taking on of stores, both victuals and ordnance; the tally of sick and lame. And always Blackadder had some tale to tell—a tale picked up in a dockland tavern or whorehouse by a member of the *Argo*'s crew—of the miraculous schooner with the suit of blue that had literally run rings around a Royal Navy anti-slavery patrol and caused the sinking of a sloop-of-war. The senior officer of the small squadron, rumor said, had been court-martialed, found guilty of negligence and severely reprimanded, with all hope of future advancement finished.

On the fifth day Blackadder came early, and Cambronne received his master in a Chinese silk dressing-gown which brought a raising of the other's eyebrows. A message had arrived aboard the *Argo* at first light. Another convoy was on its way from the African coast and would rendezvous at a given latitude and longitude a week hence. Tarrying only to bid farewell—thanks to the state of the tide, a fairly protracted farewell—to his hostess, bedmate and (Alissa's own felicitous phrase) "partner at the Court of Venus," Cambronne rode in Alissa's own landau to where the *Argo*'s jolly-boat awaited him, with the mulattress's parting words nagging at the edge of his stern resolve:

"Trust me, Cambronne. I will keep your tender secret close to my heart, *cheri*. But if you cast aside Alissa, you will be sorry . . ."

It was more than three months before the *Argo* came back to Jamaica. In that time, Cambronne wrought for himself and for his ship a reputation in the Caribbean that eclipsed the half-legendary feats of the old pirates, of William Kidd, Blackbeard Teach, Calico Jack and the others. Most of it was exaggerated hearsay, some of it the lies of the waterfront. Back in his office at Navy House in Kingston, Commodore Harvey, R.N., was able to winnow the true from the false. His maps and wall charts told him a tail of failure . . .

They told of a slave convoy, the second to be escorted by the miraculous schooner with the blue suit of sails. (A note in the margin of the report from the captain of the patroling force: "Now painted deep green overall, and first showed in white sails, the which she changed to blue in less than a quarter of an hour as we approached.") This convoy the slavers' escort had snatched from under the nose of the Royal Navy off St. Lucia and taken down to Brazil in seas that had sent the navy ships scudding for the safety of Bridgetown: God knows how many more poor black devils consigned to the sugar and tobacco plantations of São Paulo—not to speak of the red faces at the Admiralty Board when that confounded interfering old woman William Wilberforce and his Anti-Slavery Society got to hear of it.

Another glance at a flag on his wall-map of the eastern Caribbean reminded Harvey how a pair of his cruisers had come upon the famous schooner when the latter, having delivered her convoy to Brazil, was heading to pick up yet another group of slavers off Puerto Rico. Instead of showing flight, as might have been expected—for the navy ships would have had not the slightest chance of catching her—the slavers' escort shortened her blue sails as if challenging her opponents to try their luck. There then followed a game of chase-me-Charlie among the tangle of islands and shoals to the east of Puerto Rico, in which the quarry showed an almost uncanny knowledge of those highly dangerous waters. It spoke well for the captains of the navy ships that they gallantly persisted in the chase until—as the senior of them stated in his report— "We were in waters uncharted and trusting in Divine Providence to bring us out, while taking constant soundings and keeping all-round masthead lookout."

Six hours after the beginning of the chase, when the schooner had lured her pursuers into the very heart of the perilous archipelago, she upped all sail and sped like a bird for the far horizon, leaving the navy to find their way out as best they could. No sooner was their quarry out of sight than the leading ship's constant soundings recorded fifteen fathoms, then seven, swiftly followed by three. She struck rock immediately after. Divine Providence did not, however, desert the navy men, for the damaged ship was floated off by the expedient of jettisoning the guns, and an inter-island trading boat came upon them and guided them into the nearest harbor with the bilge-pumps losing against the sea, so that no sooner had she touched the side of the dock than she settled safely upon the muddy bottom.

Or in the dark hours of the night, Commodore Harvey, having solaced himself with his third bottle and with his resignation already written out (to be sent off in the event of a refusal of his request for yet more, and better, cruisers), could turn his rheumy eyes upon evidence of yet another disaster to his arms. This was a record of an encounter between the frigate H.M.S. *Gladly* and the mysterious schooner, penned by the *Gladly*'s first lieutenant, a gentleman of literary ambition who was also skilled with pencil, brush and water color, and who had accompanied his report with the first graphic representation of the phantom vessel, showing her under full press of blue sail, with white water creaming half her length yet scarcely a sign of a list to leeward. The artist had added a singularly perceptive comment, penciled beneath the line-and-wash sketch, as follows: "Suggest she must have an extraordinarily large and deep keel."

Harvey entirely disregarded this explanation for the schooner's astonishing stability under such a spread of canvas, on the grounds that to write to the Admiralty Board and suggest that the pursuit and capture of the slavers' escort would call for a complete revolution in ship design would only bring down obloquy on his long-suffering head. Instead, he forwarded to London a copy of First Lieutenant J.F.R. Jackson's report, in the pious hope that its stark revelation of the disparity in performance between the phantom schooner and the sort of cruisers they were sending out to him from England might stand him in good stead at his possible future court-martial for dereliction of duty.

Having opened his fourth bottle, the Commodore would frequently, in that most ruinous time of his career, with *Argo* making her second and protracted foray into the Caribbean, add to his misery by reading and re-reading Lieutenant Jackson's report, saying to himself over and over again: "What's to be done? What are we going to do about that feller, whoever he is?"

Report of engagement between H.M.S. Gladly, 28-guns, and an unnamed schooner. A first-hand account of same by an eye-witness. Writ by Richard Jackson, R.N., First Lieutenant of H.M.S. Gladly.

I was awakened at four bells in the morning watch by the call to General Quarters, and repairing on deck was informed by the officer of the watch, Lt. Golightly, that a blue sail had been sighted on the starboard beam. We were at that time approximately 60 miles N.N.E. of

Cape Engano, Hispaniola, on a westerly course, with the wind on the larboard quarter. Immediately afterward, Captain Jacob arrived on deck and ordered that we close with the schooner.

I cannot express the excitement I felt to be about to encounter the vessel (if it was indeed she—but who else?) that has set all the Station by its ears since the engagement off Anguilla. We went about and rapidly closed the other, till four other sail were sighted to leeward of her and on the same course, which was southerly. It was clear that the convoy—for convoy it was—had intended to pass between Hispaniola and Puerto Rico and on into the Caribbean, but upon our approach and clearly upon a pre-arranged plan, the slavers broke company with their escort and scattered downwind. The schooner held her course toward us.

Captain Jacob then gave orders to load with roundshot and be ready to open fire on the schooner at extreme range. This we did, turning so as to bring the starboard guns to bear. From my station I observed our broadside strike water 1-2 cables short and reported as much to the captain, who nevertheless gave orders to reload and fire again, which maneuver was brought to naught by the fact that the schooner, almost before our gunsmoke was cleared, could be seen to have turned sharply downwind after her consorts. The chase was on.

Gladly, being swifter than the slavers (all four of them old merchantmen, and, though running with studding sails, so heavily barnacled that they were making scarce six knots), was rapidly overhauling them and would have been among them within the hour. I then observed (and reported as much to the captain) that the schooner appeared to have taken in her flying jib and was luffing so as to take the way off her, so that *Gladly* was rapidly overhauling her also. I took this opportunity to leave my station for'ard and, repairing to the quarterdeck, gave it as my opinion to Captain Jacob that, mindful of the action off Anguilla, we must expect the schooner to attempt to confound us with some trick of swift maneuver. Capt. Jacob would have none of this, but ordered me back to my station, which order I obeyed without question (see statement of witness Mr. Midshipman Charles, attached).

At about 8 o'clock in the forenoon, the chase having gone on for two hours, the relative positions of the ships were as follows:

Gladly: rapidly closing with the schooner.

The schooner: ahead and fine off our starboard bow about 2 cables distant, running with the wind on her larboard side. Occasionally luffing.

The convoy: ahead by a mile and coming up fast.

It was then that I perceived Capt. Jacob's tactic, which was simply to overhaul the schooner, and, when she came abreast to starboard, to rake her at close quarters with round-shot fired at point-blank range, relying upon our superior weight of metal to offset her return fire. (It will be remembered that *Gladly* reloaded her starboard battery after the first broadside and the guns were still not discharged. The guns on the larboard side were never loaded throughout the entire encounter—see statement of witness Lt. Hawkes, Gunnery Officer, attached.)

In fairness, it has to be said that, positioned as she was almost abreast of us, there seemed no point in loading the guns on our opposite side; in a few moments' time *Gladly* would blow the small schooner out of the water.

It was not to be.

I was the best witness of her maneuver. Only a ship's length ahead of us, and still on our starboard bow, the schooner turned sharply to larboard. At first I thought that her tactic was to ram us in the bow; indeed, I gave the order to the fo'c'sle party to throw themselves flat. The Captain of Marines did likewise to his men who were there, so that not a single musket-ball was fired at the schooner. Next instant, her bowsprit passed ours with no distance to spare, her entire length and taffrail to follow. The discharge of ordnance, with 12-pounders of her larboard side firing chain-shot and other into our sails and rigging at spitting range not to mention divers swivel-guns similarly loaded, was a clatter never to be forgotten. She was gone and away before we could return so much as a pistol-shot. And *Gladly* was under bare poles and helpless.

I have to report that Capt. Jacob is missing. Last night I was summoned to the poop just after change of watch at midnight. A shot had been heard. The captain's pistol was found there, newly discharged. There was a pool of blood and a wide smear of same on the taffrail capping, which the ship's surgeon Mr. Thomas Thackeray opines to have been arterial and of fatal quantity . . .

The day after her encounter with H.M.S. *Gladly,* the *Argo* guided her charges along the southern coast of Hispaniola, en route for Cuba. And Jason Cambronne discovered that his traps had been opened up, riffled through, searched in a hurry.

He woke Blackadder, who was sleeping through the first watch ready to take the middle, and showed him how an unknown hand had forced his chest and delved in through everything, even to ripping open the bottom—presumably in search of a secret compartment.

"Wait a minute!" exclaimed Blackadder. "Let's see if I've been similarly blessed!" And he ran back into his cabin, to emerge moments later with his own sea-chest. "I never lock the damned thing as you do, Captain," he explained, laying the bulky chest on the deck and throwing open the lid. "Oh, my God!"

"You've been turned over too!" said Cambronne.

The inside of Blackadder's chest—even allowing for the owner's inherent untidiness, of which Cambronne had by that time been witness to many examples—was a shambles of upturned linen, bric-a-brac and screwed-up papers, all inextricably tangled.

"Who in the hell . . . ?"

"Who's been down aft here since the dog watches?" demanded Cambronne.

"Only Swede," replied the other. "He came down to deliver a plug of tobacco that he's cured and rolled for me. But—no, Captain, not Swede! Hell, I'd trust him with my life!"

"Trumper?"

They gauged each other's glances in silence for a moment.

"She's been aft all day, like always," said Blackadder. "Made up our bunks, cleaned our cabins, served food. It could have been her."

"Or she could be party to it, know who the fellow is," mused Cambronne. "We'll see her. Fetch her, if you will, Master."

"Right." Blackadder made for the screen door. Paused on the way. Turned. "Permission to make a request, Captain?"

"Go ahead," responded Cambronne.

"That you'll let me interrogate her," said Blackadder. "Mebbe a certain—*harshness*—will be called for if we're to get the truth of the matter."

Cambronne shrugged. "As you will, Master," he replied. So Blackadder had almost certainly divined that his captain had taken the cabin-girl to his bed on one occasion. The Jerseyman was not sure, and certainly did not care.

The passing months had wrought wonders with Meg Trumper. Her blue-black hair had grown out considerably—almost to shoulder length—and she had disposed of the headscarf. Her lips, innocent of paint, seemed to have softened, and her figure, no doubt because of the improvement in her diet since her days of hardship in Boston, had rounded and grown more womanly. She came at Blackadder's call.

"Fetch Swede," ordered Blackadder. "Tell him to lay aft here."

"Yes, sir." She went.

Silence. And then Blackadder pointed to his sea-chest.

"What's odd to me, Captain, is that whoever did that made no attempt to conceal what he—or she—was about."

"Or perhaps he—or she—was disturbed in the act," said Cambronne. "And didn't have time to tidy up afterward."

Further speculations were prevented by the return of Meg Trumper with Swede in tow. The grinning giant ducked his head in a curious little bow to see his captain, and the cowlike eyes turned affectionately to his mentor Blackadder.

"Stand right there, Swede," said Blackadder, pointing. "And you'll sit down there, Trumper."

The girl, suddenly alarmed, did as she was bidden and took her place at one of the seats set around the table, folding her hands demurely on her lap.

"What brought you aboard this ship, Trumper?" demanded Blackadder.

The girl gave a start. "I—I don't know what you mean, sir."

"It's simple enough, Trumper. When you decided to go to sea as a boy, why did you pick on the *Argo?*"

"Well, I heard on the waterfront that an English skipper was looking for crew." She stole a shy, sidelong glance at Cambronne, adding, unsmilingly: "They didn't place him for a Jerseyman, you see."

"Where did you get this information, Trumper?" demanded Blackadder. "Who told you?"

"I—I had it from someone who had it from Jack the Cat," faltered the girl. "He said Jack the Cat had been asked by this Englishman to keep a weather eye open for crew. So I went to see Jack the Cat."

"With your hair cut short and dressed up as a boy."

"Yes, sir."

"And he didn't recognize you as the young whore who'd bested Chelsea Nye's champion a few nights before—which was the talk of the waterfront by then?"

She flushed, dropped her gaze. "No."

"You took a lot of trouble to get aboard the *Argo*, didn't you, Trumper?" demanded Blackadder. "And a considerable risk. I mean, Jack the Cat might have recognized you. Captain Cambronne might have recognized you. Yet of all the ships in Boston looking for crew—and there were plenty— you chose theirs. Why? Why did you want to get aboard the *Argo* so badly, Trumper?" His voice rose in a shout.

"I—I don't know."

Very quietly, Blackadder asked her: "Have you heard of the Anti-Slavery Society?"

"Yes."

"Know anything about its activities?"

"No."

"You surprise me, Trumper," said Blackadder. "Surely it's common knowledge. I would've thought that even a little dockland whore would know that the society has agents— spies—in every seaport and in many ships. Their job is to collect information. News. Rumor. Most of all—evidence— Evidence that would bring the likes of Captain Cambronne and me to the Execution Dock!"

Meg Trumper shook her head, and the ends of her blue-black hair lashed her cheeks. "I don't know why you're saying these things to me, sir."

"Apart from the captain and me, Trumper, who's been aft today since, say, the first dog watch? Answer up smartly!"

A moment's thought. "Swede," she said. "He came to deliver your plug of tobacco."

"And he put it—where?"

"Laid it in your cabin, sir."

"Laid it in my cabin—ha! How long did that take him, in my cabin?"

"He just went in and out."

"Just went in and out—ha!" Blackadder reached and took the girl by the shoulder. She flinched away. "When did you search my traps, Trumper?" he shouted.

"I—I didn't . . ."

"That would be in the dog watches, wouldn't it?" demanded *Argo*'s master. "While the captain and I were on deck. But you were interrupted when I came below to get my head down in the first, so you weren't able to tidy up the mess you'd made."

"No! Please, I . . ."

"So while I was asleep you tackled the captain's traps," continued Blackadder. "And again you were interrupted by the sound of the captain coming down the companionway, so again you had to leave the job unfinished." He shook her roughly by the shoulder, and ended in a note of furious contempt. "I don't know what sort of a whore you made, Trumper, but you make an uncommonly bad spy!"

"I—I'm *not* a spy!" she cried.

"Admit it!"

"*No!*"

Blackadder stepped back, drew a deep breath, folded his arms. Cambronne was put in mind of the first encounter he had had with the man: the same calm resolve, the same quirkish, lopsided smile.

"What do you think of her, Swede?" he asked. "Not your sort of whore, I reckon. You like a wench with a bit of meat on her bones, eh?"

The giant's look of incomprehension melted into a grin.

"Big wench—is gut! Gut!" And he accompanied the declaration by sketching a rotund shape with his massive hands.

"Still, you've been at sea for three months, Swede," said Blackadder, "and hard times make strange bedfellows. Now,

Trumper here—you've had a view of her charms, along with practically everyone in the ship. How would you like to tup her, Swede?"

"No!" breathed the girl. *"No-o-o-o . . ."*

"Don't mind the captain and me, Swede. Go right ahead. Take her and welcome. Now."

The giant's grin wavered in puzzlement, then burned brightly in comprehension. He took a pace forward toward the shrinking figure in the chair, reached out a hand for the neck of her shirt.

"Enough of that! Have done!"

All eyes turned to Cambronne. Swede's in slow dismay, Meg Trumper's with stunned gratitude, Blackadder's with anger.

"Captain, sir, I protest!" cried the master of the *Argo*.

"Your protest is noted, Mr. Blackadder," said Cambronne. "Send that man for'ard and the girl to her duties. We'll speak then."

A curt order from Blackadder and, with one last, wistful look at Meg, the giant shuffled out of the cabin. She followed after, as soon as his footsteps had retreated up the companionway.

Alone together, captain and master faced each other.

"I had her then!" cried Blackadder. "That stupid big bastard had only to lay his hand on her and she would have admitted everything!"

"And she a whore?" queried Cambronne. "Is a dockland strumpet so discriminating?"

"She's no whore!" said Blackadder. "I've known whores, and I tell you, Captain, she doesn't have the stomach for that game. But she's a spy, and a bungler to boot." He spread his hands. "I ask you, Captain. Who else could have done it?"

"Ask me, rather," said Cambronne, "why should she, or anyone, search my traps? Or yours?"

Blackadder frowned in puzzlement. "Why, sir, for the reason I gave," he said. "To obtain evidence that could hang us all. Names, times, places, addresses. That kind of thing."

"Do you carry such evidence among your belongings, Tom?" asked Cambronne, smiling. It was the first time he had addressed Blackadder by his given name since appointing him his subordinate.

"Sir, I do not," declared the other.

"And neither do I," said Cambronne. "No, Tom, we shall have to look further for our culprit than little Trumper, who I am convinced is innocent. And I think we shall have to look for different reasons, different motives, for the searching of our traps."

Eight bells rang out from the deck.

"Well, I have to go on watch," said Blackadder. "Your reasoning is too subtle for me, sir, and that's a fact. I still think that five minutes of that brute's gruesome attentions would have loosened her tongue."

"Your experiment worked," said Cambronne. "I saw her face from where I was standing, more clearly than you. And the look in her eyes when he came at her."

"And what did you see there?"

"A woman afraid."

"Of course."

"More than that. A woman afraid, who had nothing to tell, nothing in the world she could confess, that would save her."

At nine o'clock, as two bells sounded, Meg Trumper brought his supper and he ate it alone. The girl had been crying again. Her face was a mess, her nose red and swollen, her eyes puffy. Not for the first time, Cambronne speculated on the idea that women—women of any pretensions to good looks—should never permit themselves to cry, or, if so constrained, they should hide their faces behind heavy veiling of the oriental sort until nature had restored the damage. This line of philosophy kept him occupied during the lonely meal of salt tack, ship's biscuits and cheese. He had the morning watch, so he turned in early. Scarcely had he stripped, washed and climbed into his bunk than there came a tap on his cabin door.

"Come in."

The door opened.

Cambronne closed his eyes. "Oh, Trumper—Trumper," he said. "Was that *really* necessary?"

She had darkened her swollen eyelids with kohl, lightened her nose with rice powder, painted her lips more subtly than a whore will paint. Her sable hair she had gathered into a chignon secured with a wisp of silk, and she had tucked an artificial flower over her right ear. She wore nothing but an ankle-length nightshift that was unbuttoned all the way down.

On second glance he saw that her nipples were tinted the same color as her lips. And the nether lip was trembling.

"I listened at the door, when you and Mr. Blackadder were talking about me," she said.

"One shouldn't eavesdrop," admonished Cambronne. "It's a temptation brought about by the pious belief that one will hear something greatly to one's merit. Alas, one almost always hears things one could very well do without."

"You both said nice things of me," she replied. "Even Mr. Blackadder, he said he didn't think I was a whore. And I don't believe even he would have let Swede rape me. As for you, sir"—again the lower lip trembled. She really does have the most expressive nether lip, thought Cambronne—"you didn't believe anything bad about me at all."

"And so?" asked Cambronne.

She lowered her eyes, met the sight of her body exposed to his gaze. Instinctively, her fingers plucked at the edges of the nightshift, drew them together.

"I came to thank you, sir," she whispered. "It's the only—way I have."

"Oh, Trumper, you silly little goose."

"I'm not a silly goose!" she flared, making an eloquent gesture with her hands, so that the edges of her garment sprang apart again, all unregarded. "I am a woman in love! That's the part you didn't hear, the part I didn't tell Mr. Blackadder, though I might have come around to telling you that night we were together."

"Tell me—what, Trumper?" he asked. "What are you trying to say?"

"Why do you think I sought out Jack the Cat, when I heard you had set him to look for crew?" she demanded. "I, who had forsworn being a woman and was all set to become a lad. I had but to look at you, Captain Jason Cambronne, in that tavern that night, sitting beside a painted trollop like myself, a pistol in your hand, a cigar sticking out of your handsome, silly face, and I was finished. An end to wanting to be a lad. I would have been your whore for nothing. But what else could I do to be with you but dress myself as a lad the way I'd planned? Oh, Captain Cambronne, Captain Cambronne! The night you blessedly revealed me for what I was, the night you ripped open my shirt, my insides turned over from the sheer wanting of you."

He shook his head. "Trumper, Trumper, what am I going to do with you?" he said, holding out his arms to her.

She ran to his side, perched herself upon the edge of the narrow bunk, pressed herself to him.

"Do anything with me that you will, sir," she breathed against his chest. "Anything. *Anything!*"

CHAPTER 10

She rose, renewed, from the fire that had entirely consumed her; lay in the imprisoning circle of his arms, tasted the salt sweat on his shoulders, breast, belly. "You are the kindest, gentlest man I've ever known," she whispered.

He tousled her hair in the dark. What began as a rough gesture of comradeship ended almost as a caress.

"Trumper, you talk too damn much," he said.

"There was one other gentleman," she said. "The only other one who treated me as if I were someone and not just another thing to be undressed and mauled. It's strange, but he never laid a hand on me and it never occurred to me to give him any encouragement. He wanted to marry me, the only man who ever asked me. I wouldn't have him because it didn't seem honest, because I felt for him the way I used to feel for my father. He knew that, too. Said all he wanted was to give me a home and look after me. He kept a tobacco store in town and his name was Arthur. He was twenty years older than me. I've never forgotten him. Not a very exciting romance. Have you ever been in love?"

She felt the whole length of him stiffen against her, and the hand that was wrapped around her waist drove fingers so deeply into the soft flesh of her side that she whimpered with the pain of it.

"Damn you, Trumper," he murmured.

"Why did you hurt me then?" she asked. "Was it because she hurt you, too?"

"Do you know, I think I'm inclined to tell you about her," he said. "If only to still your damned wagging tongue for a while. Or perhaps because I don't give a fig for your opinion of me, or is it because there's nothing I could do or say that would rid you of the notion that I'm the kindest, gentlest man you've ever known? So that confessing to you would be like going to the priest of an entirely beneficient god, who would see nothing but good in one's actions, however vile. Do you want to hear?"

"Yes I do," she said. "I want to know everything about you."

"Then you shall, Trumper, you shall. As you correctly divined, there was a woman for whom I felt the nearest thing to what you are pleased to call 'love.' That's to say, I bedded her frequently, found a not inconsiderable pleasure in her company out of bed, felt my heart quicken at the sound of her voice, her footstep on the stair, suffered unexpected jolts of pleasure when I passed someone in the street who looked remotely like her."

"You were in love with her," said Meg Trumper. "For those are the ways I feel about you, more's the pity."

"Don't interrupt me with trivia," he said. "Where was I? Yes, this woman, who shall be nameless, was a wife to me in all but name. Part of my body. Sharing all my confidences. And I am not one to share my confidences, so it's beyond all belief that I should be telling you this.

"I told her, perhaps, too much. The burden I laid upon her must have been very considerable. There was, you see, a price on my head. I was a hunted outlaw. Because of this, I made the most elaborate contrivances to stay alive and free, constantly altering my appearance, changing my aliases, never staying two nights consecutively in the same place. Only she—my woman—knew me for myself all the time, remained with me all the time when I was ashore, was able to say with certainty that I was who I was and how much I was worth alive or dead."

Meg Trumper gave a sharp intake of breath, turned her head away and buried her face in the pillow they both shared. Her voice was muffled.

"I think I know what's coming, and I don't want to hear it," she said.

"You have opened this Pandora's box, Trumper, and will face the evils you've unleashed," replied Cambronne.

"No—please . . ."

"Did I tell you she was very young? I call her a woman, but she was no more than a child. Willful. A little selfish, the way beautiful children are selfish and narcissistic. And, though I didn't appreciate it at the time, she was inordinately fond of money. Not for what money will provide, but for its own sake. All this I remembered later, piecing together the small occurrences of our life when I was ashore.

"The night when it happened (it was winter and the English Channel was torn by gales, so I was harbor-bound with the rest) we met, she and I, in a tavern on the edge of Romney Marsh that was one of our favorite rendezvous. I remember now, looking back (and God, the days and the nights I have relived it in every particular detail!), how she seemed more animated, more breathlessly talkative, than usual. Eating little at the supper table, drinking more than was her custom. Nor was she too ready to go to bed, but made every pretext to put off the time when she must lie in my arms. It was at midnight precisely, and the steeple bell was striking the hour, and she had not yet undressed, when the Revenue men broke in through the door."

"Oh, no!" breathed Meg Trumper.

"Three of them," continued Cambronne. "All armed. One of them with a bell-mouthed blunderbuss as would have cut a man in half at five paces, notwithstanding which I called to her to throw me my coat, in the pocket of which I carried my under-and-over pistol. And she would do no such thing, but handed the coat, pistol and all, to the Revenue officer. I knew then who had betrayed me."

"She did that—to *you*—for money?"

"She did. I have heard her likened to Delilah, and me to Samson," said Cambronne. "That was the way she would have had it. But this Samson was not to be taken so easily. While the officer was delving into the pocket of my coat and bringing out my pistol, I leaped upon him, thrust him between me and the fellow with the blunderbuss, and backed toward the window. He broke from me, but not before I had retrieved the pistol. The way lay clear but for the fellow with the blunderbuss, who was bringing his weapon on aim. I shot him dead. Next, cursing she who had betrayed me, I burst out of the window, glass, shutters and all."

"But what about her?" breathed Meg Trumper. "Was she paid for her wickedness, even though you escaped them?"

"She was paid," replied Cambronne shortly. "And in very hard coin."

"What do you mean?"

"When I killed that man," said Cambronne, "I had as lief

put the bullet through her breast. Nay, I would have performed a kindness by so doing."

"Why—why?"

"They were none too pleased with the outcome of the night's business," said Cambronne. "One man dead and an important prisoner slipped through their fingers. The law looked around for vengeance, and the law found its victim. By a cruel stroke of irony, such as frequently informs the affairs of mere mortals when they try to play God and dispose of the lives of others, she was caught up in the trap of her own devising. The law declared her to be an accessory to murder, and she was so indicted, tried, found guilty by twelve good men and true, and sentenced to be hanged by the neck till she was dead. I was present at her execution outside Canterbury jail."

"My God—no-o-o-o!"

"The customary span of life had been allowed her betwixt sentencing and execution," said Cambronne. "In those few short weeks, the willful girl of nineteen was translated into a crone. The condemned cell had turned her hair as white as bone and driven her out of her mind. They say—I had it from the criminal fraternity on whose fringes I existed—that she repeatedly offered herself to her jailers if they would aid her to escape, and they took what was offered and laughed at her. She was dragged screaming to the scaffold, and how the crowd loved it. They roared with delight when she lifted her skirts to the hangman in a last desperate plea for him to spare her. It is to the fellow's eternal credit that he eased her suffering as well as he was able by swinging on her legs when she was suspended and breaking her neck. I watched it all, dry-eyed. It was I who killed her."

"No! No—you did not!" cried Meg.

"And now I know why I have made my confession to you, Trumper," he said. "It was just as I declared from the first. You have listened, you have considered, and you have found me guiltless."

"It wasn't your fault," she pleaded. "She brought it upon herself. You said that yourself."

"I was a mature man," said Cambronne. "An outlaw, furthermore. She was eighteen when first I met her, and it could be said that I seduced this willful, wayward child, and that, if she had not met me, she might have married some decent fellow and raised a family, instead of which she was buried in quicklime behind the high walls of Canterbury jail. How can you say that I did not kill her?"

Meg Trumper touched the pendant that hung about his neck.

"And this is a memento of her?" she asked. "I have been meaning to ask you, from the time I first saw it, if you wore this thing in token of some woman."

"You've asked too much already, Trumper," replied Cambronne. "I hear seven bells going, and it's me for the morning watch, so I'll thank you to vacate my bunk. And a very good night to you, Trumper."

Obediently, she climbed out of the narrow bunk and wrapped the nightshift about her, buttoning it from neck to hem. Outside, in the main cabin, she busied herself by clearing away a glass and a tantalus of spirits that Cambronne had left. The sound of his gentle snoring reached her as she went out of the screen door.

Having safely delivered the four slavers to Havana (the largest consignment of slaves transported from Africa since the official abolition of the trade), the *Argo* made a swift passage back to her "fox's earth" off Manatee estate, where Cambronne was delivered a note from Lord Basil, informing him that the sum of ten thousand pounds sterling had been deposited in his name at a Spanish Town banking house: the proceeds of his voyages so far, and more than the Jerseyman could have earned in a lifetime of honest sailoring. He celebrated his new fortune by buying himself a new suit, ready-made at an Indian tailor's emporium in Kingston, and a marmoset monkey on a leash. On the first evening of his arrival in Kingston, he went to see Alissa at her Gothic retreat. Marmoset and all.

She received him in her drawing-room. Constantly surprising in her assaults upon the eye, the lovely mulattress (who could not possibly have predicted his arrival) was dressed in the manner of the Pacific islands women, in a gaily patterned skirt wrapped about her voluptuous hips and tied there. The ensemble was completed by a thick necklace of hibiscus flowers that covered most of her bosom some of the time. She was reclining on a day-bed, with a male slave fanning her in the heat of the tropical dusk.

"Cambronne! You've returned! Embrace me, *mon brave!*"
She dismissed the slave with a peremptory wave and, wrapping her lithe arms about the Jerseyman's neck, dragged his head down to meet her ready lips.

Presently Cambronne, disentangling himself with some difficulty, showed her what was on the end of the leash that emerged from his pocket.

"A present for you, Alissa," he said.

"But he is adorable!" she cried. "Already I love him. Come to *Maman*, my baby!" She hugged the little creature to her bosom, and the marmoset gave Cambronne a self-satisfied, sidelong glance.

"How are life and times on the island?" asked Cambronne.

"You mean—are Basil and the little Yankee married yet?" she said. "Set your mind at ease, Cambronne. He has not tied the knot and bedded her yet, nor, would I wager, has he simply bedded her *tout court*. Indeed, mamselle is being, in my opinion, somewhat coy. She continues to extend, week by week, the duration of the mourning for her mother. Tell me, Cambronne, was the child greatly attached to her *Maman*? And what manner of woman *was* Mrs. Holt, pray?"

"As to the former question, I cannot answer," said Cambronne. "As to the character of the late Mrs. Holt, I can only say that she struck me as being a lady capable of great affection. Yes, I would say that Miss Virginia might well mourn her, and continue to mourn her for quite a while yet."

Alissa eyed him sidelong, tightly smiling. "Don't preen yourself, Cambronne," she said. "As I have told you, as I have warned you before, there is nothing there for you. Basil Lasalle will have her or all heaven must fall. He has never let go of a woman yet, not of his own accord. And it would be a shame to rile him, particularly since you stand so high in his regard."

"I'm well paid for that," said Cambronne. "So far as his regard is concerned, I don't give a damn."

"I'm not speaking of your exploits afloat, Cambronne," said Alissa, "but of his regard—and gratitude—in matters personal."

"As for instance?"

"As for instance, being conveniently at hand to assume the mantle of protector to the supplanted companion," said Alissa. "I refer, of course, to myself. Without you, dear Basil might have found me something of an embarrassment. As it is, you have stepped neatly into the breach and removed the only obstacle to his wedding and bedding the nubile Miss Virginia. But, my dear, if he only knew the truth of it: that you nurse a secret passion for the little Yankee, and, I shouldn't wonder, she for you in return."

Cambronne was pondering upon this when a sensation of warmth in his lower limb caused him to glance and see that the marmoset, perched upon the edge of his new mistress's day-bed, was gravely urinating down his leg. Alissa dissolved into a paroxysm of mirth. When she had recovered, she found Cambronne still stern-faced.

"Come, my dear," she said. "Where is your sense of humor gone? The little darling was simply making a display of his affection for you. It's the way of marmosets, didn't you know?"

"Alissa, there's something I must tell you," said Cambronne.

"Oh—I see. And, from your expression, it's something I'm not going to like, I think. Correct?"

"Well . . ."

"Supposing you sit down to tell me." She patted the suavely upholstered day-bed, and the movement caused one perfect breast to appear from behind the hibiscus.

"I think I had better remain standing," said Cambronne.

"As you choose. Do continue."

"Alissa," said the Jerseyman. "As you know, I hold you in considerable esteem."

"That is the most depressing declaration I have heard in a long time," she commented.

"We have enjoyed together a very considerable intimacy."

"Not to be mealy-mouthed about it," said Alissa, "we have romped and frolicked in every manner known to man, and with innumerable variations of our own devising. That gives you a considerable latitude as regards myself, but it does not extend to you the privilege of boring me, and you are being very boring at the moment. Come to the point, I beg you."

"Alissa, I've had plenty of time to think things over during the last three months at sea, and I've come to the conclusion that we should perhaps see rather less of each other than formerly."

"I see," said Alissa. "Well, there it is."

Cambronne looked greatly relieved. "It's very understanding of you to take my point so neatly, Alissa, but then you are a very understanding and very intelligent person. I've always said so."

The lovely mulattress settled herself more comfortably on the day-bed, arranged the hibiscus necklace more discreetly, picked up the marmoset and held the little creature to her cheek, and all the time her eyes never lit upon the man standing at her side.

"There are just one or two points upon which my understanding is deficient, Cambronne," she purred. "Perhaps you will enlighten me."

"Of course," he replied.

"This villa," she said, "you understand that it is mine entirely, even though I am no longer Basil Lasalle's companion and châtelaine. Your little Yankee friend may have supplanted me, but I am not by any means thrown out on to the rubbish heap."

"Er, quite," said Cambronne, puzzled. "Very glad to hear it, Alissa, but I don't see how it . . ."

"I had thought," said Alissa, "after your sojourn here before you went to sea again and did a lot of thinking things over, that you were going to move in here and regard the place as your home. Indeed, though you did not say so in as many words, you clearly gave that impression, on the strength of which I have had a room next to mine redecorated as your dressing-room, and have bought a quite expensive slave to act as your valet."

Cambronne shifted his feet uncomfortably. The blandness of her tone, coupled with her almost indefinable air of something very like—was it menace?—left him with the feeling of having lost his way.

"I'm sorry if I gave you that impression, Alissa," he said.

"Oh, please—apologies are so tedious," said Alissa.

"We shall meet very often," he said.

"How can we not? Jamaica is a very small community."

"At Lord Basil's for instance. I've been invited to dinner tomorrow, and I would suppose that you'll be there also."

"Oh, yes. You would scarcely believe it, but your little Yankee and I have struck up quite a friendship. Common interests, you know."

The marmoset yawned. Outside the window, a swan reared

itself up in the still waters of the lake, flapped its wings vigorously, and went on its way.

"I must go," said Cambronne.

"Ah, the call of duty."

"Yes."

The Jerseyman's retirement posed something of a problem. Alissa did not offer her hand, nor her cheek, let alone her lips. Cambronne made the clumsy compromise of implanting a kiss upon her bare shoulder, which valediction the mulattress accepted unflinchingly.

She sat perfectly still, listening for the sounds of his departure: the rattle of hooves and grinding of iron tires on the gravel outside her front door; a call from the hired coachman to his horses; the moving-off, accompanied by a whipcrack.

She got to her feet, crossed to the French windows that led out on to a wrought-iron balcony of the sort that is called a Trafalgar balcony, which commanded an excellent view of her ornamental lake and the drive that snaked alongside it. In the distance, the open landau, with Cambronne's gold-banded cap. She watched till it was out of sight.

Alissa looked down at the little monkey in her hand. The marmoset looked back up at her and yawned.

"This morning, I thought I had a lover," she said, addressing it. "Now I only have *you!*" So saying, she drew back her arms and threw the little creature far out across the lake; tumbling over and over, it fell with a splash into the glassy water. A swan, hearing the sound, turned and sped to the spot, hopeful of finding a tidbit. By the time it got there, the marmoset's tiny struggles for life were over and it had gone.

That was the beginning. Next, Alissa indulged her pent-up fury in an orgy of destruction. First she rent her vestigial garments, rendering herself nude. Her hair she tore in several places. Then, screaming, she smashed everything that was breakable in her elegant drawing-room: mirrors, glassware, the delicately turned furnishings, bibelots, a French clock in an alabaster case, a bowl of tropical fish.

Her servants and house-slaves gathered in the corridor outside the drawing-room door, listening to the screams, the crashings, and too scared to interfere—the servants for fear of dismissal, the slaves for fear of the whip.

Not till everything that could be broken had been broken,

not till she had spent herself into a panting, sweat-streaked
nude fury, did the tormented creature sink to her hunkers
amidst the ruination of her elegant drawing-room.

"Damn you in hell, Cambronne!" she panted. "No man
casts Alissa aside cheaply. And least of all for the sake of a
whey-faced chit of a girl who can never—will never—be
yours. Wait and see, Cambronne. Just you wait and see . . ."

Lord Basil Lasalle was well pleased with himself. Taking
stock of his circumstances, he acknowledged that he was
singularly blessed by good fortune: he enjoyed excellent
health, was of good appearance, rich, successful in his
commercial ventures, possessed a fiancée fifteen years younger than himself and of breathtaking loveliness, whose refusal
to be bedded without first being wedded only served to make
her the more desirable in his eyes. Of course the past months,
when the child had been mourning her mother and the
nuptials had been repeatedly postponed, had been tedious to
a degree, especially since he had had to push Alissa into the
background for prudence's sake. Naturally, one did not live
like a monk, for there were the female house-slaves as
stop-gap. One was with him that afternoon, sharing his cool
bath in the conservatory: a high yellow chit especially bred
for the bed, trained by one of the most proficient madams in
Spanish Town and bought by him for a cool five hundred
guineas.

It was a pity about Alissa, for there was no one to match
her in the arts of pleasuring a man. Happily, she was glad to
remain in the Petit Trianon, which he had willed over to her
for life, together with a handsome annuity. At some future
date, when his little wife was a little less straitlaced about her
husband's carryings-on, he might take up Alissa again. Meanwhile she was, happily, content with that fellow Cambronne,
who fancied himself as a stud, and good luck to him.

And now it was time to dress for dinner. There would be
thirty guests at table, including poor old Harvey, who was on
his last legs as far as career was concerned. The Governor had
let drop that the Admiralty were almost certainly going to
recall him following the besting of H.M.S. *Gladly* and her
captain's suicide. It would be ironic, as always, to see Harvey
and Cambronne *vis-à-vis* at table, to speculate what the
Commodore would not give to hang the captain of the

phantom schooner from the highest yardarm of his flagship in Kingston Harbor. Alissa would be present, also, as well as darling Virginia. There was a certain irony, a touch of the piquant about that too: the propinquity of the pair of them.

He good-humoredly slapped the high yellow girl on the rump and sent her scurrying to pick up her clothes and be gone. He himself departed from the conservatory in a more leisurely manner, followed by his deaf-mute.

He was dressed by his valet. White, as always. White frock coat and knee breeches, white neckcloth. Even his pumps were of softest white kid leather. His hairdresser sleeked back the master's blond locks and tied the end in a satin bow at the nape, after the manner of the previous century. A faint dusting of rice powder at the cheeks and nose, the application of a discreet black patch to mask a pimple at the corner of the mouth—and he was ready to receive his guests.

First came Alissa. He received her in the annex to the Chinese dining-room. She came straight to the point, informing him that Cambronne and Virginia were lovers, or seeking to be lovers.

"I don't believe a word of it!" That was Lasalle's reaction.

"There's the pendant. He wears it around his neck day and night. If you don't believe me, Basil, have your men overpower him and rip it off him. Show it to the little Yankee and ask her if she recognizes it."

Lasalle strode over to a side-table and poured himself a bumper measure of brandy, which he tossed back in one swallow.

"My God!" he exclaimed. "If I thought that that fellow had had his way with Virginia before I have so much as laid a hand on her, I'd kill him! But no—she's a virgin if I ever saw one in all my life. A self-inflicted nun."

"Nunlike she may be to you, Basil," retorted Alissa. "But it may simply be that she doesn't fancy you in that way."

Lasalle covered the half-dozen steps that separated them in a single bound. His free hand was raised to strike her across the mouth. She met his gaze unflinchingly.

"If you were a man, Alissa, I'd have the flesh flogged from your back for that remark!" he grated.

"If I were not Alissa," she retorted, "you would have the flesh off my back for that remark, woman or no." And she kissed him full on the lips with passionate vehemence.

Their subsequent dalliance was somewhat protracted. Alissa straightened her gown and patted her sleek hair into place again before a pier-glass, watching him meantime as he paced the room behind her.

"What the devil am I going to do, Alissa?" he demanded. "Advise me, I beg you. You're a woman and know the ways of women. How can I find out if there's anything—or ever *has been* anything—between them, without coming out in the open about it and making myself the laughingstock of every drawing-room in Jamaica? I tell you, I'm not marrying any other man's cast-off, nor any woman who lusts for another man. It may be that in the past—when they took passage together from Boston, perhaps—she conceived a girlish attachment to him. After all, he's a dashing, personable bastard. If that were all, I'd go ahead and marry her as planned."

"Give me a cigar, Basil," she demanded.

He obeyed her, lit the cigar from a candelabrum and watched as she drew in deeply and expelled the aromatic smoke.

"Well, what do you think?" he asked.

"It may be as you suppose," she replied. "But this I know: she may or may not be lusting after him, but Cambronne is lusting after her. And he'll take her if he has half a chance."

"If I had proof of that, he'd never leave this house alive!" said the master of Manatee.

"What—you'd challenge him to a duel and kill him in front of all your guests?" asked Alissa. "That would brand you as a cuckold *manqué* and make you—as you say—the laughingstock of every drawing-room in Jamaica. There are surely more, shall we say, *oblique* ways of disposing of your rival."

"You're right, as usual," said Lasalle. "I am over-hasty. I'll consider how he's to be got rid of if and when you have proved your case against him. How's that to be done, pray?"

Alissa examined the glowing tip of her cigar. "Cambronne is newly in from sea," she said. "While he has been away he has had plenty of idle hours and the opportunity for contemplation. I fancy—it was my distinct impression when I saw him yesterday—that he is a man who has come to a decision. And that decision, I am sure, concerns Virginia Holt."

"You think that he . . . ?"

"I don't know what he will do," said Alissa. "But, Basil, if you want to get at the truth of the matter, I think you must provide him with an opportunity. Remember, since their arrival here he has met her only in company. I think their first meeting, following upon his three months' parting from her, must be contrived so that they are alone."

"Alone together—you mean tonight?"

"It can surely be arranged, Basil. All things can be contrived."

Virginia, who was still residing at Government House and had been invited to remain there till her marriage, would greatly have preferred to move in with her "Uncle" Jeff Carradine, who, upon arrival on the island, had secured for himself an elegant lodging in Spanish Town. But, oddly, the languid *flâneur*, despite his oft-professed affection for his "niece," had not made the offer. She arrived at Manatee that evening with His Excellency and Lady D'Eath. Their carriage, instead of entering the main gates, was directed by a mounted groom to another, smaller entrance to the grounds and came to rest by a noble staircase leading to the south wing of the mansion. By this contrivance the Government House party—and Virginia in particular—was not brought into immediate contact with fellow guests who had already arrived. Furthermore, who should be awaiting them at the foot of the steps but Uriah Needham, who, having succeeded to the unfortunate Percy Hetherington's position, had greatly improved in dress and appearance, and had taken on an air of quiet assurance that was quite out of character with the nervous, hesitant young man of Boston days.

"Good evening, Your Excellency, ladies. Sir, if I may intrude upon your patience for a few minutes only, Lady D'Eath and yourself may be interested to see a rather intriguing report that has just come from London concerning the death of Lord Castlereagh. I have it in Lord Basil's study, if you would kindly step this way . . ."

Virginia yawned. She found the D'Eaths and the Government House *ménage* incredibly overpowering, top-heavy with protocol, and a hotbed of boring political scandal. She had never heard of Lord Castlereagh, nor of that dubious politician's suicide the previous summer. The D'Eaths, on the other hand, were all agog to see what new dirt had been dredged up concerning the affair. She trailed after them, looking about her, wondering what lay in store for her that evening. Basil, as usual, would be attentive and charming to a degree. And would almost certainly return to the question of their wedding day. Yes, she had mourned poor dear Mama long enough, and the living must be served. She had heard that Jason Cambronne was back in Jamaica. Would he be present tonight . . . ?

"Miss Virginia." Uriah Needham broke into her reverie, opening a door for her enter. "Perhaps you would like to join the other guests? I believe one or two have already arrived."

"We will be with you presently, my dear," said Lady D'Eath with an arch smile.

The door closed behind her, and she knew where she was. The "small ballroom" was so designated because, though as big as the nave of a fair-sized church, it was dwarfed by the great salon where the larger Manatee functions were held. It possessed a wide sweep of floor, numerous sofas set around its perimeter, and a minstrel gallery set on high at one end, with an enormous pipe organ. Down one side was a long row of tall windows that commanded a splendid view of the water gardens.

A tall man in grey was standing by the center window, looking out. He turned at the sound of her footfall, and her heart gave a treacherous lurch to see that it was Cambronne.

"Miss Virginia, how nice to see you. How are you?"

Surely he must notice her sudden breathlessness, and was her face flushed? He must be remembering that scandalous night on the schooner, when she had made play with asking him to fasten the bracelet, and she showing everything she had out of the top of her dress. Strange, he was taller than she remembered, and his eyes were the most unusual grey. He was holding her hand much longer than custom demanded and she would not, could not, have drawn it away for all the world. And she had said nothing in reply to his greeting, but was looking at him, willing the moment of existence to extend into an infinity of time. Then he was taking a half-step nearer to her, still holding her hand. She closed her eyes.

His hand upon her waist was so light that she might never have noticed it. His lips, when they met hers, were cool and dry. They lingered there, and he spoke one word—whispered against her mouth:

"Virginia . . ."

The vision crazed like a broken glass, shattered and fell apart. Eyes still closed, she saw him as he had been that morning, looking out of the window at the stern of the *Argo*, in his shirtsleeves, with that shameless blackie-white woman lolling at his side, scarcely troubling to conceal her nudity . . .

She turned aside her head, snatched his hand from her waist, would have struck him across the face, but stepped back instead.

"Sir, how dare you take such a vile liberty with me?"

His expression told her nothing. He was quite unshaken.

"My deepest apologies, Miss Virginia, for offering you the offense."

"It was more than an offense, sir," she flared. And how cheap he must think her. Remembering, perhaps, the incident with the bracelet. Her fury rose. "It was a deliberate insult to me and to my fiancé, whose guest you are this evening!"

"You are quite right, Miss Virginia," he said. "I will immediately withdraw. I beg you to convey my respects to Lord Basil and make my excuses for having to return to the ship."

No—don't go. Not like this . . .

"Good night, Miss Virginia."

She did not reply. Silently, she called to him to stay, but she dared not meet his gaze, so he did not see the entreaty written there. He bowed, turned on his heel and strode to the door. And in her heart she followed him all the way.

The door closed behind him.

Behind her, high in the organ loft, a screened wicker door was silently closed, and the two conspirators within the loft were able to speak unheard by the girl in the ballroom below.

"Well, now do you believe me?" demanded Alissa. "If she hadn't protested, he'd have had the clothes half off her by now. I know Cambronne's little ways. None better."

"The coarse-grained bastard!" hissed Lasalle. "Laying his filthy hands and lips on my property." Then he smiled his thin, joyless smile. "But did you mark, Alissa, how she sprang away from him? And how she spoke up for her honor. And mine, also. 'A deliberate insult to me and my fiancé'— her very words, hey? Bully for her."

"She was in no great hurry to spring away," replied Alissa dryly. "There's no doubt but that she's had an infatuation for him at some time. And that she's got over it. Or thinks she has. Basil, you'd be well advised—since you've asked my advice—to remove temptation from her way."

"That I'll do," said Lasalle. "No man, in my philosophy, is indispensable. And friend Cambronne, for all his expertise as a sea captain, has made himself eminently dispensable."

"But you'll not kill him, Basil!" cried Alissa. "To do that would be to lay yourself open to scandal. And if it were thought that you'd done it out of jealousy—why, you'd never live it down in the West Indies."

"Don't fear for me, Alissa dear," replied Lasalle. "It's truly said that there are more ways than one of belling a cat, and Captain Cambronne is singularly vulnerable in many respects. And now I think I will go down and collect my delicious little fiancée, who has demonstrated her chastity with all the fervor and conviction of a latter-day Lucrece."

The dinner party passed off uneventfully. Lord Basil Lasalle was so entranced with his bride-to-be that he scarcely had time for his guests, but allowed them to pursue their individual conversations without his usual dictatorship. Commodore Harvey ate little and drank a lot, and gazed often at the empty place opposite him, where, as he understood, Captain Cambronne would have sat but for the exigencies of duty. It would have been, thought Harvey, a vastly comforting thing to have spread his great load of cares before a fellow officer who had no axe of rank and preferment to grind. And he poured himself another bumper of claret, belched, and wiped his rheumy eye.

In her place of relative honor at table, Alissa also ate little, and drank less. At the back of her mind was the uncomfortable thought that she might have been a little over-zealous in her pursuit of vengeance upon Cambronne. She had certainly deflected Basil Lasalle from any thought of killing him in a duel. And even the master of Manatee would shrink from having the man quietly murdered by bully-boys.

Or would he?

One outcome of the otherwise uneventful dinner party at Manatee that night was that, as a result of Lord Basil Lasalle's impassioned lobbying of his bemused fiancée, he was able to announce in the island broadsheet the next morning that a marriage had been arranged and would take place in the private chapel attached to the mansion on the following Tuesday, the banns having already been read.

* * *

Cambronne saw the announcement on his way to Kingston, having bought the broadsheet from a vendor on the edge of town. He cursed, balled up the offending paper and tossed it over the side of his carriage and into an irrigation ditch.

Someone whistled to him from the sidewalk. It was Jack the Cat. The Jerseyman called to his coachman to stop.

"Want a ride into town?"

"It'll be welcome in this heat, Captain." The other climbed in.

"We'll have a drink. Stop at the next tavern, boy."

"Yes suh."

Jack the Cat eyed his captain sidelong. "Forgive my remarking on same, sir, but are you not deviating from your accustomed practice of not drinking till the sun is over the yardarm?"

"I've got something to drink about, damn you," growled Cambronne.

The other shrugged. "The state you describe, sir, is very familiar to me. I call it 'life.'"

"If this is life, you may keep it," said Cambronne.

"I shall keep it for as long as I am able to endure it," replied the other. "Happily, one needs greater virtues to bear good fortune than bad, so I am better equipped than most, being light on virtue and heavy on bad fortune."

"What happened, then, to your new-found contentment, Jack?" demanded Cambronne. "What happened to the little black girl here in Kingston who pleasured you so unstintingly?"

"I am afraid," said Jack the Cat, "that she has gone the way of all successful whores. That's to say, she saved her money, bought herself a strapping young fellow to look after her and is now settled down to a life of quiet domesticity. *Sic transit gloria mundi.* But why should it always pass away from me?"

"I think we both need a drink, Jack," declared Cambronne.

It was market day in Kingston. They clattered through a stone archway into the market place, to be greeted by an assault of sound, color and movement. Indian merchants vending cheap cottons, brassware and rugs; manumitted slaves from the hills with their baskets of scrawny chickens and turkeys; hard-eyed white traders of fruit and vegetables, meats and fish; and all were shouting their wares. There was even a solitary cattle-pen, in which a very large black bull eyed the passing scene with mild, ruminative eyes.

"That place will do, coachman," called Cambronne, pointing.

The caravanserai of his choice was a tavern set up from the level of the market place, with a shaded verandah that commanded a view of the square and the bustling throng. Paying off the driver, they settled themselves at a table on the verandah and ordered a bottle of rum and a jug of chilled lime juice.

"We will drink," said Cambronne, when they had been provided, "to the future happiness of Miss Virginia Holt, who is to marry your former schoolmate at eleven o' the clock next Tuesday morning."

"Lasalle?" exclaimed Jack the Cat. "My God, Captain, can you not prevent it?"

"What do you mean? Abduct her? Kill him?" Cambronne drained his rummer to the dregs and refilled it to the brim. "Neither very palatable options, but I don't see any other. Do you?"

"I'll speak frankly with you, Captain," said the other. "And speak my mind, which is this: I would have thought that Captain Jason Cambronne would have presented a better option for the young lady in question than that hellish swine Lasalle."

"And I will speak frankly in return, Jack," said Cambronne. "I had hoped so too. But I am afraid that I have irrevocably blotted my copybook with Miss Virginia by tumbling another lady."

"You refer to the blackie-white girl?"

"The very same."

"Tch, tch! I never should have allowed her aboard that night when I was standing as officer of the watch," said Jack the Cat, "but should have shoved her off with a boathook. I thought I was doing you a good turn, Captain, to turn a blind eye to boarders."

"Mmmm."

They both looked despondently into their drinks. Breathed heavily. Swallowed them up. Poured more.

"Shall you be invited to the wedding, Captain?" asked Jack the Cat.

"Shut your mouth," responded the other.

"Aye, aye sir."

"Call for another bottle."

"Aye, aye, sir! Boy, *encore de la putridité!* More rum!"

Both drank deeply again. And again. A bottle and a half of rum between them (they had eschewed the lime juice) rendered neither of them drunk and incapable, for both were well-practiced at the art and craft of imbibing strong liquor. Indeed, it seemed to each that his imagination was sharpened, his perceptions polished to a bright finish.

"I give you a toast, Captain," said Jack the Cat, raising his rummer to one of his slit eyes and peering at Cambronne through the dense glass, fishlike, unearthly. "I give you a toast of 'Love and Death.'"

"'Love and Death'?" repeated Cambronne. "That's a damned odd toast, Jack. What does the conjuncture of those two states mean to you, might one ask?"

"A very great deal, I assure you, sir," said the other.

"And to me," said Cambronne. "Indeed, you may say that the tragic combination of Love and Death, which has inspired the poets down the ages, has wrought great upheavals in my life. Moreover, I am inclined to tell you a tale that I have so far told only to one other person. And this I do in return for an occasion when you diverted me during a long night watch with a tale of your own life."

"I remember it very well, Captain," said Jack the Cat.

"Pour us both another measure, and I will tell you of my brush with Love and Death," said Cambronne. Whereupon he proceeded to recount the story of his betrayal by the girl whom he had loved and trusted, and of her hideous end—just as he had told it to Meg Trumper.

Jack the Cat listened in silence, sipping at his drink, nodding sometimes, closing his eyes in agony at the most harrowing portions of the account. And when Cambronne had finished, he said:

"Captain, there shall be no more secrets between us after that. My own tale, when I recounted it to you, was all tail and no head, in a manner of speaking. I will now put the record to rights and tell you what it was that set my foot upon the course of self-destruction which brought me to my present pass."

"And the theme is Love and Death?" ventured Cambronne.

Jack the Cat nodded. "That is so. I will transport you first,

Captain, to a summer's afternoon many years ago. There are two boys, one a year or so younger than the other. The elder, by reason of the absurd laws of primogeniture which ordain that the first-born shall succeed to all while the others who come after shall have nothing, is heir to an ancient title and broad acres."

"And which brother were you, Jack?" interposed Cambronne.

The hideous grin split the other's face. "Peace, Captain. All will be made known to you at the end."

"I'll not interrupt again. Please continue."

"Picture a remote stretch of open moorland," said the storyteller. "The brothers are fishing, barefoot, among the rocks and shallows of a stream. Suddenly there is a shouted warning from the elder to the younger. The latter does not comprehend his danger and makes to move. His brother, barefoot as he is, kicks out at a full-grown adder lying coiled and asleep on the warm rock where the younger boy must certainly place his next step. The snake wakes. Strikes—twice —at the unprotected ankle of the elder. It is high summer. The adder is in the full pride of his venom. A four-mile walk over rough ground must certainly cause the poison to circulate more rapidly, possibly with fatal results. It is resolved, therefore, that the wounded lad shall lie in the shade while his young brother runs to fetch help. And this he does: runs four miles to the nearest farm. In due course he returns with men, a pony to carry the injured lad. And then a physician, who, upon examining the patient, opines that in all his long practice on the adder-infested moorland, he has never seen a worse bite, nor one that might more likely have killed if the lad had attempted to move. Now, what is your summation of my story so far, Captain?"

"I would say," replied Cambronne, "that the elder brother, by taking the snake bite upon himself, put his own life in hazard for the other."

"But the younger, by his action in fetching help, may well have prevented a tragic outcome, don't you think?"

Cambronne shrugged. "That was the least he could do," he replied.

"But there is a matter of self-interest," said Jack the Cat. "If he had tarried on the way, if his brother had died as a result, he, and not the other, would have succeeded to title and fortune by the laws of primogeniture."

"In that case, a monster would have succeeded!" growled the Jerseyman.

Jack the Cat nodded. "To continue," he said. "In the fullness of time, their father having passed away, the elder brother takes all and the younger—nothing. The latter lives by grace and favor in the home where they have both been born and raised. Any money he must beg for from the other, cap in hand. As a proud man, he will more often than not go without."

"It is not a circumstance," commented Cambronne, "that is likely to stoke the fires of brotherly love that the younger brother should rightly feel for his sibling."

"Nor does it!" declared Jack the Cat. "There are quarrels between them. Petty rivalries. Jealousies. The younger is particularly jealous of his brother's mastery of horsemanship, of which the latter is extremely proud. Proud to the point of arrogance. One night (and they have been drinking heavily together, Captain, as we have been drinking heavily this morn), the talk between them turns to a famous steeplechase course in the district: a matter of a ten-mile gallop over moorland and bog, with fifteen five-barred gates to jump, which had taken a score of riders' lives since the course was established by a group of local bucks soon after the Civil Wars. The elder, who has completed the course many times, opines that he can repeat his feat blindfold—then, under pressure from his brother, avers that he can at least do it at night. This night. And they will have a wager on it. Says he: "I'll lay you five thousand guineas that I can do it, which, if I lose, will set you up for years to come. As to if I win (which I intend to do), I will demand the price you must pay. And it will not be in money, for you have none. Agreed?"

"The wager is agreed before witnesses. Five thousand guineas against an unspecified prize. Accordingly, at midnight, the elder brother sets off on his favorite hunter: across moorland and bog, over towering five-barred gates in the moonlight, where a misplaced hoof might bring man and beast tumbling amongst the granite outcrops, or a miscalculation of a jump by horse or rider might spell disaster in the night. And meanwhile the younger brother and their friends kept watch on the terrace, drinking hot negus against the chill air, watching and waiting for signs of the steeplechaser's return. Time passes. Ever and anon, the witnesses mutter among themselves, glancing sidelong at the younger brother, recalling that it was he who inspired the wager, and how, if his sibling is killed (as many have been killed on the course), he will stand to gain not five thousand, but everything!"

A long silence followed. Jason Cambronne drained his glass, waited a while with commendable patience, and then asked:

"And what was the outcome?"

"The outcome?" Jack the Cat gave a mirthless laugh. "Well, long after comes the sound of a tired, lame horse returning. The elder brother has completed the course and won his wager, though by the state of his clothing it is obvious that he had taken a tumble at least once—and he the finest horseman in the county.

" 'Now, brother, I will collect my prize,' says he.

" 'And what's it to be, brother?' demands the other.

" *'You, yourself, will also complete the course tonight! Now!'* "

The sound of fifes and drums silenced the hubbub in the market place below where the two men were sitting, and a party of redcoats marched stiffly through the throng, bayonets gleaming, pipeclayed bandoliers stark white against the scarlet. They advanced in swift time to the opposite end of the square, where their sergeant called upon them to halt.

Cambronne returned his gaze to the hideous face opposite.

"And so?" he prompted gently.

"And so, you must know that the younger brother is no horseman to speak of," replied Jack the Cat. "Oh, he can hack around on a horse with more looks than style. But to attempt such a course, and at night—for him it is suicide. For him who demands it as the price for winning his wager it is —*murder!*

"It is gone three o'clock in the morning when the younger brother sets off," continued Jack the Cat. "At daybreak, hunt servants and grooms go out to find him. In a drizzle of light rain I am standing at the end of the drive, and I see them carrying him toward me on a hurdle. His neck is broken! Dead! I killed him!"

To the tune of fife and drum, another detachment of soldiers was crossing the market place, this time from the archway through which Cambronne and his companion had been driven earlier. Leaving behind three men with fixed bayonets to stand sentry at the archway, they took up station at the corner of a street that entered the square opposite.

Cambronne glanced from one party of redcoats to another and swore quietly under his breath.

"What is it?" demanded Jack the Cat.

"Something's afoot!" murmured Cambronne. "Do you not see that they have completely sealed off the market place?"

"You don't think that . . . ?"

"We are in business to think, Jack. And to stay alive. Drink up your drink, and we will calmly stroll to the rear part of the tavern, where, with luck, there will be a back exit. Too late . . . !"

As he spoke, a young ensign trotted swiftly up the steps leading to the verandah. At his heels came a red-faced sergeant bearing a partisan, followed by a pair of redcoats armed with bayoneted muskets which they carried at the high port, ready for use.

Cambronne got to his feet. Jack the Cat did likewise. It was then they noticed that the officer carried a pistol in his hand.

"Captain Cambronne—Captain Jason Cambronne?" piped the ensign, who was no more than a boy.

"I am he, sir," responded the Jerseyman.

"Sir, you are under arrest, by order of His Excellency the Governor."

"Upon what charge?"

"You will be conveyed to Spanish Town jail," replied the other, "where you will be confronted by witnesses and a charge will be laid. Who is your companion?"

"I'm . . ." began Jack the Cat.

"I never saw him before in my life!" interposed Cambronne.

"Secure them both!" snapped the ensign. "Carry on, Sarn't!"

"*Sah!*" The N.C.O. presented the point of his partisan to Cambronne's breast, swiftly shifting it to Jack the Cat's, thus demonstrating his speed of attack with that most ancient and effective of close-range weapons. "Prisoners fall in between the escort!" he barked.

Cambronne and Jack the Cat looked at each other. The former nodded briefly. They took their places between the two bayoneteers.

"Prisoners and escort, quick—*march!*" screamed the sergeant.

The market place of Kingston, Jamaica, had all at once ceased to trade. Every eye was on the tall, naval-looking fellow and the hideous creature at his side as they descended into the square among the redcoats, and many were the speculations about them. At a whistle-blast from the ensign, the soldiers who had been guarding the exits from the enclave began to move forward to join up with the prisoners and escort, leaving the exits clear—a fact that did not escape Cambronne.

"I'll make a diversion. Race for that archway and get free!" he muttered to his companion as an aside.

"But—what about you?" replied Jack the Cat.

"Silence between the prisoners!" shouted the sergeant.

And then—a voice like something from the Old Testament:

" 'GOD HIMSELF IS WITH US FOR OUR CAPTAIN! AND HIS PRIESTS WITH SOUNDING TRUMPETS TO CRY ALARM!' SECOND BOOK OF CHRÓNICLES, CHAPTER 13, PART OF VERSE 12."

"My God—it's Bosun Angel!" exclaimed Cambronne.

"And, by the look of him, drunk as a fiddler's bitch!" said Jack the Cat. "If anything else were needed to make sure that we end up on the gallows, it's him—in *that* state!"

The zealot bosun was clearly far gone in drink, though without any impairment of his general faculties, insofar as he could stand, walk, rant and shout. He was hatless, and his hair stood on end. He had lost one shoe and had by some means contrived to get his shirt half ripped from his back, so that the rib cage of his cadaverous frame stood out like a ladder. Foursquare and defiant, he blocked the path of the advancing detachment of redcoats and their prisoners—and ranted!

" 'AS THE LORD SENT MOSES TO BE A DELIVERER, SO WILL I DELIVER MY CAPTAIN FROM THE HORDES OF THE UNRIGHTEOUS!' "

"Seize him, Sarn't!" cried the young ensign. "I want him alive!"

"*Sah!*" said the sergeant, regarding the zealot's form—which though cadaverous, was massively boned—with some trepidation. "You, you and you, get 'old of 'im!"

The three soldiers designated for the task of subduing the apparition before them laid aside their muskets and gingerly approached him. No sooner had the nearest put a restraining hand on Tobias Angel's arm than the bosun of the *Argo,* roaring like a lion, struck out with both bony fists. By a means which, because it all happened so quickly, was not quite clear to the observer, all three soldiers fell back together in a tangled heap of scarlet with white crossbelts. The boy ensign piped another order, and the sergeant sent forward three more aspirants. They fared no better. It was then deemed prudent to clear the way ahead by the simple means of shooting down the offending obstacle. And then Jason Cambronne decided that the time had come to intervene.

"At 'em, Jack!" he cried, felling the soldier on his left with a sledge-hammer blow to the side of the head, then turning upon the man behind him, side-stepping a vicious bayonet thrust and kicking the soldier in the lower gut.

All was pandemonium. Jack the Cat had managed by some means to lay hands on the sergeant's partisan and was flailing about him with the heavy shaft, using it as a quarter-staff. Cambronne was fighting at odds of three to one, using fists and feet. Tobias Angel was performing unbelievable feats merely by the exercise of his skeletal arms and fists. And ranting all the while:

"'THUS DID JEHU DESTROY BAAL OUT OF ISRAEL!'"

The crowd cheered wildly to see the soldiers being bested, for the military were not popular on the island. Some of the onlookers, indeed, while not openly joining with the prisoners in revolt, gave occasional, surreptitious aid, as when the sergeant, falling back into the crowd from a blow of his own partisan, was in no way improved by having a bottle broken over his head.

It was Jack the Cat who freed the big black bull from the cattle-pen. The huge creature stood docilely enough, turning its great horned head this way and the other, undecided as to what use to make of its unsolicited freedom. If one of the soldiers had not panicked and accidently fired his musket in the air, the bull's presence might have made no difference at all to the immediate outcome. As it was the report, deafening in the enclosed space of the market place, made it charge the nearest group of redcoats.

Three men fell to its trampling hooves and one was tossed headlong onto a fruit stall, bringing it down in an avalanche of capering oranges, limes and lemons. The bull rested for a few moments to regard the havoc it had wrought, the rent sleeve of a British army tunic hanging from one long horn. Then it espied another group of soldiers who, upon a panic-stricken order from their officer to slaughter the animal, were shaping to fire a volley. The bull charged them. The thin red line wavered, broke and ran, leaving the

bull—and to a lesser extent the three seafarers—the victors of
the field.

It was a victory that could not last. Cambronne and his
companions were about to make a bolt for the freedom of the
maze of narrow streets beyond the square when a fresh
company of soldiers came doubling onto the scene, led by a
mature officer of very different calibre to the boy ensign. He
gave an instant order to his men to form line and present.

The unwavering aim of a score of leveled muskets settled
the matter. Cambronne had no option but to surrender.

As he and the others were marched out of the square,
hands pinioned behind their backs, the owner of the bull was
leading the huge animal—docile, now, as any shorn lamb—
back into its pen.

They were marched to Spanish Town. Along the dusty road
bordering the winding River Cobra. Eight miles, and all in
the tropical noontime sun. The soldiers marched at a smart
pace, to the rat-a-tat-tat of a kettledrum, red-necked and
uncomplaining. Bosun Tobias Angel, having fought and
sweated out most of the liquor, and his fighting fury having
given way to religion, was moved to sing the 107th Psalm in its
entirety, all forty-three verses; nor did the officer's curt order
for him to desist produce any result, even when reinforced by
a cut from his riding-whip. And so they came to Spanish Town
jail.

The cadaver of the executed slaver still hung on high,
though the head had finally become detached from the
carcass and lay in the bottom of the cage. The sentries at the
great, iron-studded door stamped to attention and presented
arms as prisoners and escort marched into the yard. The door
slammed behind them and the heavy bolts were drawn.

They were brought to the office of the prison governor, a
man of advanced years with a pronounced squint, a bag wig
that must have been the height of fashion during his youth,
and breath of villainous stink.

Again Cambronne's name was demanded, and then the
names of his companions. Jack the Cat announced himself as
Jack Smith. Next, the witness was brought in.

At the first sight of him, Cambronne seemed to feel the
noose being put about his neck. He was tall, sparely built,
with too much nose and too little chin. He had the anxious air

of a man who knows he is up to no good and wants to dispatch the business with all haste in the pious hope that all traces of it will go away. He was in the uniform of a British naval officer.

"You are Captain Amos Hellbore, Royal Navy?" demanded the governor.

"That is so."

"Formerly commanding the frigate *Archer?*"

"Yes."

"Do you recognize any person here present?"

Hellbore looked confused; he glanced from one to another of the three pinioned men who stood before him and finally settled for Cambronne. He pointed.

"That man."

"In what circumstances did you meet that man, Captain Hellbore?" asked the governor, taking from a fancifully fashioned tortoiseshell box a copious fistful of perfumed snuff.

"Why, sir, off Anguilla," replied Hellbore. "He was captain of the schooner—I may say *the* notorious schooner—that escorted three slavers on the occasion."

The governor of Spanish Town jail was clearly stretching himself fore and aft and athwartships to be fair, for all that he must have known the evidence was addled. He said:

"You saw him plain, Captain?"

"That I did, sir."

"What, then, was his composure? I mean, where was he, and how standing? How did you know he was captain?"

"Why, sir, he was on his quarter-deck, where as captain he should have been at such an occurrence. Moreover, he carried a speaking-trumpet and was pointing this way and that and issuing orders."

"Undoubtedly the captain, then?"

"Oh, indubitably, sir."

"Thank you, Captain Hellbore. You may stand down and retire. You will not be required to attend again till the trial of the accused, which, as I see, is not, cannot be"—the governor riffled through a sheaf of papers, prising them this way and that, losing some of them and finding no answer—"much before the end of Michaelmas Term, as I see it."

"Thank you, sir."

"Thank you, Captain Hellbore."

The naval officer bowed to the governor and, without so much as a glance at the man against whom he had given evidence, scurried out of the room. A sentry closed the door behind him. The governor of Spanish Town jail cleared his throat.

"Do you have anything to say, Cambronne?"

What to say, Cambronne? Tell this creature, perhaps, that when the frigate sailed close past the *Argo* it was nevertheless not close enough for Hellbore to see enough of her captain to recognize him again? Add also, as corroborative detail, that you never have need to use a speaking-trumpet? That was only to condemn yourself out of your own mouth.

"I've nothing to say."

"Take them away. Lock them up."

Thank God, thought Cambronne, that one has powerful allies in Jamaica. That fellow Hellbore is drawing his bow at a venture, surely? Presumably there's a reward offered for the capture of *Argo*'s captain. But why should he point the finger at me?

Yes, thank God for Lord Basil Lasalle and his puissance. As soon as Lasalle gets to hear this he'll have us out in a trice, even if he has to bribe His Excellency the Governor of Jamaica himself—and I wouldn't put it past him.

"This way, you three!" growled a turnkey.

CHAPTER 11

Alissa told herself, always, that she was not a bad woman. Her favorite phrase to describe herself—privately—was "an honest whore." Concerning Cambronne, she told herself that it had never been her intention to do him any serious harm, merely to direct Lasalle, through his jealousy, to teach the Jerseyman a sharp lesson. In other words, like so many of us, she was self-deceived.

Nevertheless, conscience—or something of the kind— brought her to Manatee that afternoon, through the worst heat of the day, when she would ordinarily have been lying naked in her salon with a Negro slave fanning her glorious body. She found Lasalle in the conservatory, immersed in his favorite iced water. He smiled his paper-thin smile:

"A delightful surprise, Alissa. What brings you visiting at this hour?"

"I was—passing," she said. "May I have some tea?"

Lasalle pointed to a bell-rope, and the little deaf-mute rose from his hunkers and pulled it.

"Come, come, my dear," said the master of Manatee, gently taunting. "You didn't come for tea, nor were you just passing. You have heard the news about Cambronne, I guess."

"What about Cambronne?" she asked.

"Ah, then you haven't heard. He was arrested in Kingston at midday, along with two of his crewmen. The crewmen are irrelevant."

"Arrested?" cried Alissa. "But—how? Why?"

"I arranged it," said Lasalle.

The mulattress's great almond-shaped eyes widened.

"Surely, isn't that a very dangerous thing to do, Basil?"

"You mean, the good captain will implicate me? I think not. He won't know, you see, that I was concerned in his arrest. Indeed, he will think that I shall bend every effort to

248

secure his release; and indeed I shall appear to do that very thing. But, unfortunately, I shall be unable to save him."

"You'll let him hang?" cried Alissa.

"Not on the public gallows," said Lasalle. "That would be—imprudent. Indeed, it would be imprudent to allow him to come to trial. No, in a few days' time, when he learns that I have been unable to secure his release, he will take his own life in a fit of despair by hanging himself from the bars of his cell. His companions will be similarly disposed of. It is truly said that dead men tell no tales, and if by chance Cambronne did find out that he has me to thank for his plight, he would shout my business from the rooftops. Ah, here comes the tea. Will you pour, my dear? I like it with cream and no sugar. But of course no one knows better than yourself about my small eccentricities. What was I saying . . . ?"

Tea at the Residence of His Excellency the Governor of Jamaica was as unlike the *ad hoc* affair in the conservatory bath-house at Manatee as could possibly be. Her ladyship, for instance, always changed into a hostess gown for the occasion, and herself dispensed the fragrant brew from a dumb-waiter, asking each one present if he preferred Indian or Chinese, with or without lemon or cream, with or without sugar. The daily ceremony lasted from half past three to half past four every afternoon, winter and summer, and anyone who had been formally received at Government House was entitled to attend without invitation. The rules were few and simple: one did not attend more than once a month; one stayed for half an hour, no more, no less; one had two cups of tea only. House-guests—like Virginia Holt—were exempt from the rules.

How she hated that interminable hour every day! Balancing a cup and saucer on one's knee, listening to the boring and eternal small-talk of upper-crust Jamaica, dying for it all to end, for the blessed moment when, the chimes of the clock on the chimneypiece thinly tinkling the half-hour, in would come the butler and his four acolytes to clear away.

"More tea, Virginia dear?" Lady D'Eath showed a row of gravestone teeth when she smiled. Her ladyship had become quite attached to the young Bostonian, whom she regarded as a triumph of sensibility over the unfortunate drawback of coming from Colonial stock. And now she was to marry Basil Lasalle, and who would have believed that she—an untried gel—would land such a prize from under the noses of every eligible woman in Jamaica?

"No thank you, ma'am," said Virginia, stealing a glance towards the chimneypiece. Nearly four o'clock. The last of the tea-time guests were due to arrive. She could hear them now. The booming voice belonged to Commodore Harvey. He entered.

"Good afternoon, Lady D'Eath, ma'am."

"Good afternoon, Commodore. And how are you?"

"Mighty pleased, ma'am," replied the officer. "As mighty pleased as I've been for many a long day, I may tell you."

"And why so, Commodore?" asked Lady D'Eath—but cautiously and feeling that she was walking on eggs. One knew, of course, that poor, bumbling Harvey was likely to be recalled to England, stripped of his command, perhaps even court-martialed for dereliction of duty over the so-called "phantom schooner affair."

"Why, ma'am," replied the sea-dog, "we have caught him, ma'am. We have laid the scoundrel by the heels."

"Who, sir, who?" inquired her ladyship.

"The captain of the blue-sailed schooner, ma'am!" replied Harvey.

Those tea-time guests who had not the slightest interest in the commodore and his affairs—and they were many—ceased their chattering as the import of his declaration was borne upon them. In the silence—the, for Harvey, extraordinarily gratifying silence—that followed this realization, he allowed a little time to elapse before enlarging upon his sensational news.

"And furthermore, ma'am," he said, "your ladyship and others here present have met the rogue socially. Indeed, he has been well received by none other than Lord Basil himself, and what do you think of that, hey?"

"Who is he, Commodore?" demanded Lady D'Eath.

But, like every harbinger of news that bodes ill for someone else, Harvey was not for letting the cat out of the bag so readily; instead, he embroidered the edges of his tale.

"The rogue was recognized by Captain Hellbore, formerly of the *Archer*," he said. "Hellbore, who saw him plain when they encountered off Anguilla, came upon the fellow again in Kingston market only this morning and straightway sought a warrant for his arrest, which was effected within the hour while the rogue sat drinking with one of his pestilential crew."

"That was uncommonly astute of Captain Hellbore, sir," observed Lady D'Eath. "And considering how he suffered loss of command and severe reprimand at his court-martial, one hopes that his latest action will not go unrewarded."

It would have taken a very perceptive eye to have noticed the slight shiftiness in the good commodore's expression as he shaped his reply.

"I—we have every reason to hope that Hellbore's action will cause the court-martial result to be set aside, ma'am," he said.

"But the name—the name of this demon, whom, you say, we have met?"

"The accused, who will shortly be tried for piracy in company with his two fellows, and who must certainly be found guilty and hanged—is that fellow Cambronne!"

A disturbance at the other side of the room: a choked cry, a tinkle of fallen teacup and saucer.

" 'Pon my word, what ails the lass?"

Slowly, with considerable dignity and the rustle of silks, Virginia Holt slipped to the floor in a dead swoon.

They were locked in together. The cell, which stood on the corner of a corridor on the second floor of the building, was airy and commodious, being intended for white inmates. One entire wall of the cell was filled with a lattice of iron bars as thick as a man's hand, breast high. This looked out across the corridor to a window that gave a view over the distant heights in the hinterland of the island. The furnishings of the cell were vestigial: three wooden cots with straw mattresses and a commode. The stone floor was strewn with straw, and verminous; but Jack the Cat, who had spent nights in cells uncounted, opined that it was one of the best he had ever seen.

"We shall all hang, the three of us, of course," he added.

"Not if Lasalle can prevent it," said Cambronne.

"Lasalle!" Jack the Cat flashed his hideous, mirthless grin. "As lief look for help from Old Nick as from that hell-hound. It would not surprise me in the least if, far from getting us out of here, it was he who put us in. Or you in, at any rate, Captain."

"Your prejudices are showing," responded Cambronne. "Why should he do that, pray?"

"I can think of one good reason," said the other. "And she is blond of hair, blue-eyed and lately resident in Boston."

"Virginia Holt?" cried Cambronne. "Now for why would he pursue me so on her account? He has won her, hasn't he? The wedding-date is fixed, isn't it? What was that you just muttered?"

"Nothing, nothing." Jack the Cat turned his back on his captain and commenced to stroll up and down the cell, six paces one way, six the other. He had been doing it most of the afternoon.

Bosun Tobias Angel, worn out with drink, fighting, marching and psalm-singing, was fast asleep on his cot, two bony hands clasped together and serving as a pillow for his wasted cheek—like a babe.

A tramp of feet, a jangle of keys. It was the turnkey, and a visitor: Virginia Holt.

"As long as you like, Miss," said the turnkey, simpering like a man whose pocket has been well lined—as indeed it had. "No need to hurry. Call me when you're ready to go. I'll be within earshot." He leered at Cambronne, who was looking fixedly at Virginia, as she at him. "Not *too* near, though," he added.

Jack the Cat ceased his pacing up and down and threw himself upon his cot, which was at the far end of the cell, turning his back upon the couple over by the iron grille.

Cambronne went close to the bars, taking hold of them with both hands. He could have reached out and touched her. She was wearing black, as she had for the period of mourning for her mother. She had clearly been crying and looked near to tears again.

"Why have you come here—*why?*" he whispered.

"How could I do other?" she replied, also whispering.

"Lord Basil sent you?"

"No, I haven't seen him today. I heard about your arrest at Lady D'Eath's. And I came straight away. Lady D'Eath arranged it through the Governor. But even then I've had to bribe everybody from the duty sergeant to the man who brought me up here. You wouldn't believe the corruption in this place. And they say the're going to hang you! *Hang* you!"

"Will that concern you very greatly, Miss Virginia?" he asked.

Her hands were on his, fingers twined about his. Their faces were very close.

"You know it will, Jason Cambronne," she whispered. "You know that I've doted on you from the very first, from the night of my birthday ball, to the time that I offered myself to you like any cheap little whore, to the other day when you kissed me and I rejected you for the same reason that I accepted Basil's offer of marriage—because you slept with that blackie-white bitch."

"I see," he murmured.

"I doubt if you really see," she said. "I think you regard me as a spoiled minx whose eyes lit on you as a new plaything, something I had to own or I would have screaming tantrums. And I think you despised me for it, perhaps still despise me. But it doesn't matter to me anymore, and it doesn't matter that you've made love to Alissa. All that matters is that they say they're going to hang you. And if they do, I shan't want to live either."

He reached out and touched her cheek, felt the dampness of a tear.

"Little Virginia," he whispered.

"Why didn't you take me when I was yours for the asking?" she said. "Now it's too late—too late!"

"Not for you it isn't, Virginia," he said. "You've a whole lifetime ahead of you. Don't throw it away on my account. What am I when all's said and done? A pirate. A jackal of the filthiest trade on earth."

"You are part of the slave trade, then?" she asked. "Just as they say."

He nodded.

"And my father—he's your employer?"

"Yes."

"And Basil—he's connected with it also?"

"Don't ask any more questions, Virginia," he said. "It could be dangerous—for you."

"I'll get you out of here!" she cried. "My father owes it to you. He put you here. I shall write to him immediately. Tell him that he's got to save you. That he must lobby his powerful friends in the government. Offer bribes. Do anything—anything—to get you out of here for my sake. He can't refuse me that."

"No need, Virginia," said Cambronne. "No need. Lord Basil will do anything that needs to be done. If he can't secure our freedom, no man on earth can."

She squeezed his hands more tightly. "Yes, you're right,"

she said. "Basil can do it. I shall go to him on bended knees. Beg him to save you. Only . . ."

"Only what, Virginia?"

"It's going to be difficult, because I have really forfeited the right to ask favors of Basil. You see, I must also confess to him that it's you I've loved all this time, and that I can never marry him."

Uriah Needham was extraordinarily pleased with his own progress. Had he not advanced in every respect since leaving Boston? By overthrowing that too greedy fool Hetherington, he had succeeded to a splendid company house, not to mention the manifest delights of Pushpam and Issy. Nor was that the end of it; in addition to taking over the late Hetherington's place as principal agent of the Augusta Line in the Caribbean, he had, thanks to his good standing with Lord Basil Lasalle, also become unofficial contact between Lord Basil and His Excellency the Governor. In the snob-ridden-corruption of island society, a man such as he was highly suitable, since he—unlike Hetherington—knew how to walk circumspectly, while also being capable of—not to put too fine a point on it—handling other men's filth without unduly soiling his own fingers.

Lord Basil had sent for him today, and it might well be in connection with this Cambronne affair. News of the latter's arrest had put him—Needham—in a highly privileged position, since he was one of the very few outsiders who could piece together the connection between Cambronne and the *Argo,* the *Argo* and the slave trade, the slave trade and Cyrus J. Holt's Augusta Line. (And what, he wondered, did the appetizing Miss Virginia think about her daddy being a slaver?)

Waiting in the antechamber of Lord Basil's study at Manatee, Needham's mind went back to a conversation he had had with Cambronne back in Boston: how he had put it to the Jerseyman that there must be more to the Augusta Line than met the eye. Well, now he knew what it was all about, and Lord Basil, who was obviously in the business up to his neck, knew that he knew. It was quite likely, thought Needham, that he would be offered even further advancement. He had performed well while not a party to the secret; now he was to be given the opportunity of extending his talents. He rubbed his hands with deep satisfaction.

He looked about the room, which was used as an office by Lasalle's various secretaries. A pile of letters lay open on a leather-topped table. Needham, who never overlooked an opportunity for extending his knowledge, riffled through them. An invitation to Government House, several acknowledgments of the invitation to the wedding on Tuesday (what wouldn't he give to take Lasalle's place that night!), an account from Lord Basil's Indian tailor, tradesmen's handbills. Nothing of interest.

He glanced at the clock: half past six. Lasalle's message, delivered by a mounted groom, had required him to come immediately. Well, he was not a man to be tired by waiting, for he had done plenty of that in his time. With luck, if his guess was correct, the time of Uriah Needham's waiting might soon be over. Tonight, if all went as he anticipated, he would celebrate. Habitually abstemious, he would have champagne with his dinner. And afterward there would be Pushpam. Or Issy. Or both . . .

It was then that he heard a door open and shut in the next room, which was Lasalle's study. And then voices: Lasalle's and a woman's voice—Virginia's.

Soft-footed on the rich Persian carpet, Needham tiptoed over to the communicating door and placed his ear against it. The first words that he overheard made him draw breath sharply . . .

"Basil, I've a confession to make."

"You, my dear? Surely not." The voice was indulgent. Honeyed. "What sort of transgression could a sweet child like yourself commit that could possibly call for a confession?"

"I—I visited Jason Cambronne in jail this afternoon."

"Did you, by God?" Gone the honeyed tones.

"That is not my confession, Basil, though I understand that you have a right to be angry with your fiancée for visiting another man in prison."

"I think it was—indiscreet, Virginia."

"Oh, Basil, my indiscretion went further than merely visiting. Oh, I don't know how to tell you this, for I've made such a bad beginning, and now I can see that you're angry with me. Let me start again. Basil, you are doing everything in your power, are you not, to secure Jason Cambronne's release?"

With only the slightest hint of a hesitation, Lasalle replied: "Of course! It's an outrageous charge, brought on the slenderest of evidence. The fellow who claims to have seen him . . ."

"No—Basil! Please, please don't tell me any white lies. He confessed to me, you see. Jason Cambronne admitted everything."

"Did he so?" The eavesdropper could picture the expression that went with the remark: teeth bared in a thin-lipped snarl, green eyes narrowed to points of fury. "That was mighty accommodating of him!"

"Basil, listen to me. I don't want to know any of your business. Nothing about the *Argo*—where she goes, what she does—nothing! I just want your promise, as a dear and loving friend . . ."

"I had thought that we were somewhat more than that, ma'am!"

"You see?—I've made you angry with me, Basil, and that's the last thing I wanted to do. Oh, I'm doing this so badly. *How* can I?—*What* can I . . .?"

"Might I suggest, Virginia, that you revert to your original beginning and make your confession? About the—in your felicitous phrase—'indiscretion that went further than merely visiting.'"

"Very well." There was a pause, in which the eavesdropper could visualize the speaker gathering up her courage, perhaps wiping a tear from her cheek with a fingertip, raising her chin, taking a deep breath. "I visited Jason Cambronne in jail to tell him that I loved him and that I have always loved him!"

"Aaah!"

"Basil . . ."

"Yes, Virginia."

"I—I can't marry you, you see." It was almost a whisper. The listener almost missed it.

"You won't reconsider?"

"It wouldn't be fair—to you."

"Perhaps you will grant that I am the best judge of that, Virginia."

"Basil, I will speak plainly. I don't think that Jason Cambronne loves me in return. I think he looks upon me as a capricious, spoiled child, a flirtatious flibbertigibbet. He may not love me, I may be all those things and more, but one thing I know . . ."

"You want him to live," supplied Lasalle. "And you want me to save him."

"Will you do that for me, Basil? Despite everything—despite the fact that I can't marry you on Tuesday after all?"

"I will do—everything in my power, and that is considerable, to bring a happy outcome to this affair, Virginia."

"Oh, Basil, I knew in my innermost heart that I could depend upon you . . ."

The eavesdropper pictured—correctly—how Virginia leaned forward and deposited a kiss—a chaste, sisterly sort of kiss, a not-to-be-repeated sort of kiss—on Lord Basil Lasalle's forehead.

"And now I must go, Basil."

"So much to do?"

"I am also going to enlist Lady D'Eath's support. You'd scarcely believe it, but Lady D'Eath, whom I never liked very much, has turned out to be a true friend. When I heard the news about Jason, I fainted outright at her tea-party. Of course, she asked me what it was all about, and I confided in her. Do you know? She has become almost like a mother to me; insisted that the Governor arrange for me to see him. I know she'll use her influence to set him free."

"Then how can we fail, Virginia?"

"Oh, you're so understanding, Basil. Goodbye, dear, dear Basil. So sorry about Tuesday."

"Goodbye, Virginia."

Needham heard a door being opened, then heard it close. He took some paces back into the center of the room, expecting to be confronted by the master of Manatee. Instead —silence.

And then—a deafening crash. Something like the discharge of a pistol. He was at the communicating door and wrenching it open before the last reverberations had died away.

"What the devil do you mean—bursting in here, you scribbling louse?"

Lord Basil Lasalle was slumped in an armchair opposite him. At his—Needham's—feet lay the bust of a Roman emperor, who by the crown of laurel and distinct lack of hair could have been Julius Caesar. It had been hurled from its plinth across the room and was broken in half.

"Sir—Lord Basil—you asked me to call upon you," said Needham.

"So I did," replied the other. "But it will wait. Get your stinking, low-bred hide out of here."

"Lord Basil . . ."

"*Out!*"

"I overheard your conversation with Miss Virginia. And I think I can help you."

"The devil you do!"

"Captain Cambronne," said Needham, moistening his lips, "knew Miss Virginia's mother, Mrs. Augusta Holt, late wife of my employer."

"Knew? What d'you mean—*knew?*"

"Carnally."

"The devil he did!"

"Yes, Lord Basil."

"Where and when did this—knowledge—take place?"

"In Boston, sir. Shortly after Cambronne was appointed captain of the schooner."

"Can you prove this?"

Uriah Needham smiled. "No, sir. But I know Cambronne. He will not deny it if the question is put to him—*by a certain interested party.*"

Lord Basil Lasalle matched smile for smile. A prescient onlooker might have observed that the two men complemented each other perfectly.

"By God, you're a cunning devil, Needham," declared the master of Manatee. "I'd thought to make further and better use of your talents, but I had no idea that you would serve me so good a turn as you've done today!"

After Virgina's departure from the jail, not a word of reference to her passed between Cambronne and Jack the Cat. The latter remarked to himself how his captain seemed greatly lightened in spirits, and formed his own opinion of the cause—not without some unease.

A supper of boiled pork, black-eyed peas and rice was served to the three prisoners at sundown, the meat of such poor quality as even the most parsimonious ship's purser would not have purchased for his crew. Tobias Angel ate his readily enough, saying grace before and after. The others ate slowly, without appetite, conversing in the desultory fashion of those who deliberately avoid the topic uppermost in their minds.

Presently, after protracted prayers, Tobias Angel fell upon his cot and slipped instantly to sleep. Cambronne and Jack the Cat sat on the floor of the cell, their backs to the wall, looking out across the corridor beyond the iron grille to the barred window that led out onto the tropical night of stars and the myriad of winking lights sprinkling the distant hillsides. From somewhere down in the town there came the thrumming of a guitar. And a dog barked.

"I was taught to play the guitar by my brother," said Jack the Cat from out of the darkness beside Cambronne. "No horseman he, but his musicianship was of a very high order, and he was in great demand as an amateur entertainer at the country houses of our friends and acquaintances. If he had lived, I confide that he would have gained some considerable repute in a wider field."

A long silence.

Cambronne said: "Do you imply that you deliberately engineered his death?"

"If I could answer that question, even to myself, I think I would not be what I am now, Captain," replied the other. "And it is not for want of asking, for I have done it a million times in the years since."

"Where's the impediment to the truth, Jack?" asked Cambronne.

"The impediment is in myself," replied Jack the Cat. "You see, all those years before, while I lay with the snakebite, waiting for help, I had the fevered notion that George would tarry on the way to effect my death so that he would succeed to the inheritance."

"Did you have cause to believe that he would do such a thing?" demanded Cambronne. "Your own and only brother?"

"We were opposites in every way," said the other. "On my side, at least, there was no understanding of his nature, though I think he knew me very well. For instance, he knew, when he returned with the helpers, that I had mistrusted him. He knew from my looks. From the feeling of guilt that I could not hide. It destroyed what bond there had been between us, for I never felt at ease in my brother's company again for as long as he lived."

"And so?"

"And so I concealed my feelings of guilt towards him with bombast. Because my nature would not allow me to go to him and say, 'I misjudged you, please forgive me,' I went the other way. I flaunted my horsemanship, my skill at shooting and fencing—all the things he was able to do only badly, if at all. Later, when I succeeded to the inheritance, I took delight

in making him come cap in hand for every penny—the better
to humilate the man, you see, who had laid this intolerable
burden of guilt upon me."

"And then came the wager," prompted Cambronne.

"And then, as you say, Captain, came the wager. You must
remember that we had both been drinking, together with
other young bucks of our age. And I, bombastic as I was, had
drunk more than most. I must have been intolerable for
George to have thrown that challenge at me, but, do you
know, it came as a blessed release to receive it. I was able
to say to myself: 'You have been right all this time. He
was tempted to kill you then. And this time he will
do it if he can.' I lived. Thanks to me, he died. *C'est
tout.*"

"But not quite all, I fancy, Jack," said Cambronne.

"Not quite all. After the funeral, when we had laid him to
rest in the family mausoleum, I went through my dead
brother's effects and found a diary. It was all there: the record
of my suspicion that he was the sort who might have left me to
die for the sake of the inheritance. He had seen that suspicion
clearly in my eyes and his life had never been the same after
that. That I, who had placed my own life in jeopardy on his
account, could think that he would repay me in such filthy
coin destroyed something within my brother. It also destroyed
the fraternal love that he had borne for me, the hero-
worshipping adoration that a younger sibling often feels for
the older, so that in the end he grew to detest me for what I
had become, and was able to say in effect: 'All right, you
boasting drunken fool—if you want to go and break your
damned neck, go with my blessing.'"

Out in the night, the sound of the guitar died away in a
muffled chord. Many of the lights on the far hillside had been
extinguished. The world was going to sleep.

Cambronne said: "How easily we are destroyed when we
lend a hand to our own destruction."

"Indeed, yes, Captain," replied Jack the Cat, "when you
consider that with one look, one misplaced suspicion, I set in
motion a chain of circumstances that killed my brother, killed
the love between us and brought me to my present state. Do
you wonder that I have sought death?"

"Thanks to meeting me, Jack, you may soon find what you
have been seeking," said Cambronne.

"A melancholy thought, and quite unlike you, if I may say so, Captain," said the other. "This afternoon you were full of Lasalle and how he would save our necks at all costs."

"My view has not changed," said Cambronne. "It is greatly to Lasalle's advantage to free us. The *Argo*'s record since she came out here is such that our employers simply could not afford to let us hang."

"I expect you are right, Captain," said Jack the Cat, "for you usually are. All the same, while reposing a certain reluctant trust in that bastard Lasalle, I will hedge my bet tomorrow by getting to work on those bars over there. I notice that the mortar is quite rotten and may succumb to the tender ministrations of this spoon which I filched from our supper platter. Good night to you, Captain."

"Good night, Jack."

Jack the Cat lowered himself to his cot. Cambronne remained where he was for some time, looking out to the flickering lights on the far hillside, lost in thought.

Lasalle would certainly not stand by and let them hang. The faceless creature who employed them both had pledged that he would not permit it to happen if he could prevent it. He had powerful allies.

And yet, and yet . . .

He remembered the chill declaration that Lasalle had so recently thrown at him: "No man is indispensable." And what if, despite his denial, the master of Manatee was The Man after all?

Cambronne stood up and went over to his cot. The straw mattress was hard as a sack of nails and crawling with bugs. He closed his eyes and let his mind roam to the sweeter pastures that it had occupied for most of the time since Virginia had left him with one last squeeze of the hand, one final, adoring glance.

"*I am loved*"—the phrase had the power to move him. "*I love*"—what of that? It sounded oddly disturbing, and when he said it in his mind, Virginia's face was somehow overlaid with the image of another face, one equally lovely, not unlike in features and coloring and equally capable of moving him. And it was a face that mouthed a soundless scream of mortal terror, with a hangman's halter about the slender neck.

* * *

"Virginia, for the sake of the love that you bore for your mother, I would have given anything to have kept this from you."

"I know that, Basil, You are the kindest, dearest friend I have."

Morning and blinding sun; the dust of the crowded streets of Spanish Town. Lasalle had thought it best not to let Virginia sleep on the appalling secret of her dead mother's adultery with the Jerseyman, but rather to delay giving her the news and then force her hand. Accordingly he had called at Government House shortly after ten o'clock, with Needham in tow. And there, in Lady D'Eath's drawing-room, with the master of Manatee as witness, Virginia had been obliged to listen, white-faced and trembling with horror, while her father's former secretary gave a bald account of her mother's guilt and Cambronne's admission of same, at the end of which Lasalle had silently signaled to Needham to make himself scarce.

And now they were driving through Spanish Town to confront Cambronne in jail: Virginia and Lord Basil Lasalle, in his open landau drawn by two spanking, high-stepping greys, with coachman and postillions, with the chief overseer of Manatee—a handsome brute in his master's rifle-green livery—as outrider.

And Virginia was already having second thoughts . . .

"Basil, I can't face it—I can't! Take me back, please. Let me just think it over for a while."

He took her hand in his. "Be strong, my dear," he advised. "If you fail yourself now, the rest of your life will be a question mark."

"It can't be true—it *can't!*"

"I personally have no doubt," said Lasalle, "that the whole thing is a complete fabrication concocted by Needham to serve his own ends. Though for what reason I cannot guess. But that, my dear, is beside the point. For your dead mother's sake, for your own peace of mind, even—it has to be said—out of regard for Cambronne's honor as an officer and a gentleman, you must nail this canard."

"But what shall I say—how shall I frame the words?" she asked.

"When the moment comes, you will find the strength," he

assured her. "You will put the question to him direct—'Is this thing true or false?'—and he will answer you with honesty. Am I not right, Virginia?"

"Yes, I'm sure you are, Basil. Only . . ."

He squeezed her hand. "Put aside all doubts, my dear. You have the strength to go through with it."

And the master of Manatee turned his head to regard the passing scene and allowed himself the luxury of a thin smile of triumph.

It was a short drive from Government House to the jail. They clattered into the open square before the eyeless facade of flaking white paint, with its great door and scarlet sentries. As on her previous visit, Virginia averted her gaze from the horror on high, while Lasalle presented to the sergeant of the guard a letter from His Excellency which invested the bearer with sweeping and specific privileges concerning the prisoner Jason Cambronne, Captain. A glance at this caused the sergeant hastily to summon his officer, who conducted the distinguished visitors to the prison governor. The latter, his distaste for whom Lasalle, holding a scented handkerchief to his fastidious nostrils, made no pretense of concealing, read the letter and unctuously requested to know Lord Basil's desires regarding the prisoner. When he was told that the lady must interview the said prisoner alone, he expressed only surprise and raised no impediments save that, for the lady's own safety, the prisoner would have to be manacled—a condition that brought a sob of horror from Virginia and a shrug and a nod from Lasalle.

The master of Manatee stayed with her till the last moment, till shuffling footfalls and the clank of heavy chains indicated that the object of the their visit had been brought down from his cell.

A touch of hands. A chaste kiss on her cheek. "Remember to be strong, my dear," said Lasalle. "Bear in mind that you have loved this man, and love him still. For his sake and for yours, you have come to nail this calumny."

"Yes, yes," she breathed. "I feel strong now. Thank you for sustaining me, dearest Basil."

He left her. Virginia remained standing in the center of the dingy, sparsely appointed office, with its desk and high stool, its shelves of dusty dossiers recording the lives and frequently violent deaths of inmates long gone, its all-pervading jail stink, and the hum of countless flies that strayed in and out of the single, narrow window.

The door opened. She tensed her fingers together and held her breath.

"Get inside!"

A scowling turnkey gave the manacled man a shove and sent him staggering into the room, clumsy-footed from the heavy chain that secured ankle to ankle, ill-balanced from having the wrists similarly pinioned behind his back. The prisoner gave a low curse at his tormentor, narrowed his eyes against the sudden glare of the window, saw the slender figure standing in the middle of the room, recognized her.

"Virginia!"

He carried two days' stubble on his dark-complexioned jaws, and there were traces of straw in the short curls of his gleaming black hair. One sleeve of his shirt was ripped clean away, revealing an ugly bruise on the upper arm, while the right cheekbone bore a bayonet slash that would mark him for life. He was barefoot. Twenty-four hours, only, had rendered him stinking and lousy in that hell-hole of a jail, but Virginia felt a pulse treacherously quicken in her temple and seemed to see him again as she had first seen him from her bedroom window in Boston: a man with unforgettable looks and presence, the wild sea-rover who had strolled carelessly into her life and taken possession of her dreams and waking hours.

He grinned: the same heartening grin that softened the deep lines of austerity on his cheeks, and which had both affronted and won her at first sight.

"I passed Lord Basil in the corridor," he said. "He gave me a very agreeable nod and a smile. Dear little mouse, I suppose that you have been nibbling away to break through my prison walls and get me out. No—don't come near me, for I'm unwashed and hopping with fleas. The standard of valeting in this establishment leaves much to be desired." Again that breath-robbing grin.

Virginia closed her eyes, the better to assemble her disordered thoughts.

"Captain Cambronne . . ." she began.

"Ah, this is a formal visit," he replied with gentle mockery. "I am at your service, Miss Virginia. Pray continue."

"There is something that I must ask you," said Virginia. "And I beg you—please—to hear me out in silence. When I have said what has to be said, I shall wish you to give me an answer—yes or no. And that will be the end of it."

"Very well, Virginia," he responded, all the mockery departed. "Please go on."

She found it easier to be on the move, so she walked to and fro with slow and deliberate steps, swinging her slender hips and shoulders and—did she but know it—displaying her freshly budded womanliness to such advantage that the manacled watcher was aroused with desire for her. And, as she paced up and down before him, she spoke what was in her mind, the words tumbling out almost unbidden.

"I had visitors this morning," she said. "At Government House, where I am staying. Straight after breakfast they came. I knew that it was a matter of some seriousness. Indeed, I thought from their demeanor that they were going to tell me that you had been executed overnight. No—please —don't say anything!

"Basil Lasalle, it was. And Needham. Basil told me that—that Needham had some disturbing news to impart. Those were his very words. Now I have to explain that, though I have from time to time amused myself by lightly flirting with Uriah Needham, I heartily dislike the creature. I think he's—grubby, and that a look inside his mind would disgust me. Picture my distaste, my utter humiliation, when, in front of Lord Basil Lasalle of Manatee, whose good opinion I have always sought (for snobbish reasons, you may think—and I don't deny it), I was obliged to listen to an appalling calumny concerning my dear, dead mother and— yourself!"

"My God!" exclaimed Cambronne.

She cut him short. "Listen to me!" she cried. "Listen to all I have to say, listen to the humiliating filth I had poured over me from Uriah Needham's hesitant, hypocritical mouth (and how he enjoyed it, every moment!).

"He told how, with some time to spare before attending upon you near your lodgings in Boston, he chanced to see a veiled woman quitting those lodgings in some guilty haste. He did not see her face, but was able to describe to me, in some particular, how she was wearing a silk day-gown that was striped in blue and gold and cut low at the bosom. Such a gown had my dead mother—as he knew well. That is no proof, but . . ."

"Virginia," said Cambronne. "Listen to me I beg . . ."

"Be silent, damn you!" She screamed the words in his face. "Hear me out, for there is not much more. Direct proof, he did not have. But he claims to have questioned you later, in the carriage on the way to Noggs Wharf, so he said. He told you that he had seen his employer's wife leaving your lodgings. Not sparing my feelings, he told me how he had asked you what she was like in bed!

"Well how was my mother in bed, Captain Cambronne?"

His eyes—those eyes that had looked upon storm, fire and disaster with equanimity—fell before her fury.

"What can I say?" he whispered.

"Comment would be superfluous!" she retorted. "Oh, I have seen it written all over your face, Cambronne, since first I began my tale; I have seen the guilt gathering there. I, who came here in great fear of defaming my innocent mother and forfeiting your regard, who but for the good offices of a dear and sincere friend would never have known of this . . ." She broke off, choked by the bitter words that rose in her gorge.

The manacled man took two paces toward her.

"Virginia," he said. "I deny nothing. But please, I beg you, let me say something in defense of that lady who . . ."

Her eyes flared like those of a mad woman. "You seduced her!" she screamed. "Lured her to your lodgings on some pretext, and then beguiled her to your will." She searched his face, turning her head this way and that, wild-eyed. He met her stare evenly and said:

"Your mother, Virginia, was a good woman. A true and sincere lady who, as I believe, had not known the happiness that was due to her. She came to see me at my lodgings with honest intent, and I . . ."

Virginia drew a hissing intake of breath. "You raped her!" she screamed. "Of *course* Mama would not have fallen for your blandishments. She was like a frightened fawn before men. All frills and furbelows, tuck and laces, yet she could not even abide her own husband to share her bed. You took her by force, Cabronne! You enticed my poor, bemused mother into your lodgings and ravished her!

"Deny it, then—*deny it, you animal!*"

He bowed his head upon his breast and bore it all: bore it when she screamed into his face, splattering him with her spittle, suffered the small fists that ineptly belabored him, the sharp fingernails that scored his exposed neck, the clumsy, fumbling kicks that her daintily shod feet directed at his stalwart legs. And said nothing.

Finally, breathless, choking, crazed, she reeled away from him and, encountering the far wall, leaned there. Her thumb stole into her mouth and gave her some comfort. The Jerseyman watched, silent, manacled and helpless, as she hung by her fingertips over the abyss where madness waits, knowing in his wisdom by harsh experience that one ill-timed move, one maladroit word on his part, might send her toppling into insanity.

An age passed. She lifted her golden-maned head, and her eyes were wide and childlike as she looked across at him. The thumb stole—guiltily—from her mouth, and she wiped it surreptitiously on her skirt. The hands joined, each clasping the other to quench the trembling.

"No, it wasn't like that," she said. "I beg you to tell me that it wasn't like that, Jason."

He answered: "Virginia, I deny nothing."

She came to him then; wheedlingly, insinuatingly, putting the soft words into his mouth:

"She threw herself at you. I lied about my father, he never sought her bed after I was born. She was mad for a man, and oh, how she must have craved for you to have risked so much and entered a common tavern in search of you! Even I, Jason, wanting you as I did, could only toy and daydream with the notion. Tell me this is how it was, Jason. She came to you, uninvited and unexpected. She wantonly offered herself to you, and you pandered to her lust, without love or affection. As a stallion will serve a mare in season. Or a dog a bitch. A boar a sow. Mare, bitch, sow—she was all three!"

"No, Virginia. You do not describe your mother in any particular."

"Then tell me how it was—*tell me!*"

Cambronne thought for a few moments, and then he said: "I will tell you plainly how it was. In the first place, your mother came to see me in all innocence that day . . ."

"In all innocence!" she scoffed, and the lovely shape of her mouth was ruined by bitterness. "Since when does a married woman visit a bachelor in his private apartment in all innocence? Did she perhaps come to take tea and chat about the price of fish? Come, come, Cambronne! If from some twisted sense of chivalry you are trying to salvage my dead mother's reputation at this late hour, you are wasting your time. I was not born yesterday." She paused. "For all that I'm an untried virgin whom you yourself once repulsed with contempt."

"She came," said Cambronne doggedly, "to solicit a subscription from me toward her favorite charity, the Anti-Slavery Society run by your father."

"The Anti-Slavery Society!" Virginia laughed, and the sound of it jarred in his ears. "Oh, the sweet irony of it! Mama goes to collect a subscription for a charity that does not exist, from a self-confessed jackal of the slave trade which that society is supposed to oppose—and gets herself bedded for her pains. I find that very amusing." The tears were coursing down her smooth cheeks.

He said: "She came in innocence. And in innocence she allowed me to probe her defenses. I learned that she had not been pleasured by a man in all those years. And so—I took the greatest delight in making good the deficiency."

He closed his eyes when she hit him across the mouth.

"I would add," he said, "that your mother had little choice in the matter. I am a very strong man. I suppose some would call it rape. When I had had my way with her, I left her weeping." His eyes clouded with the bitterness of true recollection. "I believe your mother must have hated me—and herself, too, as the receptacle of my lust—for the rest of her short life."

Virginia drew breath harshly. "You took my mother against her will!" she cried. "I—who offered myself freely—you scorned!" Her trembling fingers sought the fastenings of her high-collared bodice. "Well, that chance is gone forever, Cambronne. I do not know or care whether you found my mother to your liking, but before I go you will catch a brief glimpse of what you missed. And I hope, if they hang you (and I don't care now whether they hang you or no), you will carry the sight to hell!" And with those words she unfastened her bodice to the waist, opening it out to reveal bare breasts that rose in twin triumphant peaks above the limit of her tight-laced corset. She flaunted their glory before the pinioned man, secure in the knowledge of his sudden arousal.

"They are not for your hands and lips, Cambronne," she said. "And I am not for you. On Tuesday, as arranged, I shall wed Basil Lasalle. And you will not be among the guests!"

She refastened her bodice without another word and strode to the door, head high, dry-cheeked, leaving him there.

Lasalle was waiting at the end of the corridor. With him was his chief overseer and the prison governor. One look at her face, at the wildness of her eyes and the prancing manner of her bearing, and he knew that his stratagem had succeeded.

"My dear," he said, taking her gently by the elbow, "make yourself comfortable in the carriage and I will join you in a few moments, after I have had a quick word with the governor." And, to the chief overseer: "Escort Miss Virginia to the carriage, Jago."

"Yes, m'lud," responded the other. "This way, ma'am."

Lasalle waited till Virginia and the man Jago were beyond earshot, watching their progress with his head cocked sidelong, green eyes narrowed. He then turned to the governor.

"Concerning the prisoners," he said. "Cambronne and his two companions."

"I await your orders, Lord Basil," responded the other, "as to the manner of disposal."

Lasalle sniffed peevishly, raising his scented handkerchief to his nostrils. "It is to take place before Tuesday next," he said. "As to the manner of disposal, I will give some thought to it and send Jago with your final orders. And mark, man, you will not receive the second part of the payment till all three are dead and buried!"

"As you say, Lord Basil," fawned the other sibilantly, grinning to display blackened fangs. "'Tis ever a great pleasure to do business with you, Lord Basil."

Lord Basil of Manatee, like so many predators and creatures of the night, slept only in penny packets of a few hours at a time when the feeling took him, and mostly during the day in his exotic bath in the fabled conservatory, in company with one or more of his trained odalisques.

On the night following his visit to the gaol with Virginia, he took a short nap after supper, drank a considerable amount of brandy and champagne mixed, then stalked the empty chambers, halls and corridors of his huge mansion, hands clasped behind back, neck thrust forward and eyes fixed upon unimaginable evils of his own devising, with the tails of his long, brocaded dressing-gown swirling about him like the wings of some great colored bat.

Through darkened rooms hung with priceless tapestries, soft-footed on rugs that had been old in the time of Tamburlaine, up and down gilded staircases where sprawling gods, goddesses and putti stared from painted ceilings he went, till he came at last to his own study—scene of his late, searing interview with his affianced and the highly profitable encounter with Needham. It was there, in the dark antechamber, that he thought he discerned a thin loom of light seeping from under the closed study door. And that was curious, surely, for had he not himself extinguished the candle upon quitting the room for supper? A servant, anticipating his master's return, must have relit it. But, then, why had he not lit the candles in the antechamber . . . ?

Lasalle paused, his hand hesitating above the latch, then bore down on it, opening the door.

He saw, beyond the glimmer of candle flame set upon his desk, three figures. Two were standing, caped and hatted. Both carried short-barreled carbines of the kind used by dragoons. Their faces were in deep shadow. Seated between them—at his desk—was The Man.

"You will pardon the unorthodoxy of the intrusion, Lord Basil," came the muffled voice, "but these rendezvous are sometimes best contrived in this manner. Pray be seated."

Lasalle, when he sat down upon the chair facing the masked and shrouded figure, found that his hand trembled upon the chair-arm. Suddenly, he craved a drink. He licked his dry lips.

"Well, sir?" he essayed.

"Well, sir," responded the other. "I'm told you are to be wed."

"On Tuesday, in the private chapel here."

"You must regard the acquisition of little Miss Virginia of prime importance, to have gone to the lengths you have." There was an edge of contempt in the unclear voice.

"Indeed?" commented Lasalle, and shifted uneasily in his seat.

"I refer, of course, to the removal of your rival, Cambronne. Was that—*wise?*"

The question having been posed, his judgment having been sought, Lord Basil felt on surer ground.

"You have heard me expound my philosophy many times, sir," he said. "Cambronne is as expendable as the next man."

"And who will captain the *Argo* now?"

"Blackadder—and he will serve as well as Cambronne— perhaps better. He is more—pliable."

"And Cambronne's immediate future?"

Lasalle laughed shortly. "Cambronne's future is of the most immediate sort possible. He and his companions will be disposed of in the gaol. Before Tuesday."

The Man leaned forward in his seat, and for a brief moment Lasalle caught the glitter of eyes behind the narrow slits in the executioner's mask.

"They had better, Lasalle!" hissed the other. "Bungle that, and you are finished. I have perused the evidence you have trumped up against Cambronne, and it may well hang him from the highest yardarm in Kingston dockyard; but he must never be brought to trial. One word, one iota of suspicion, that you have brought this upon him—and he will tell all! In open court!"

"I'm aware of that," said Lasalle. "And for that reason . . ."

"See that it's done, and done well!" hissed the muffled voice. "Dispose of your rival. Settle your personal affairs. Wed the little Miss Virginia, and I wish you well of her. Appoint Blackadder captain of the *Argo*. But see to it that 'tis done—*unslovenly!*"

Lasalle relaxed in his seat, breathed more easily. "That I will, sir," he said. "And I am grateful for your considerateness in this personal matter, and for the trust that you repose . . ."

The other silenced him with a brusque gesture of a gloved hand.

"Have done!" said the shrouded figure. "The matter is at an end, and we move to more pressing business. I must shortly return to Boston, where the activities of the Anti-Slavery people are making further incursions into our organization . . ."

Lasalle, the fumes of brandy and champagne still upon him, sank deeper into his chair, assumed an incisive and attentive expression and let the muffled, droning voice sweep over and past him. This was routine business. The worst part was over. He had feared this encounter, and how The Man would react to his own undoubtedly high-handed approach; but The Man had given him *carte blanche*. He was trusted. Indispensable. Inviolable . . .

The brief cancellation of the nuptials never having been made public, no one in Jamaican high society was one whit surprised to see, or learn, that Lord Basil and his intended occupied themselves the whole of the next day with a shopping expedition among the most expensive and exclusive of Spanish Town's emporia. At Madame Lavallière's _boutique_ in Main Street, the master of Manatee sat and puffed at a cigar while indulgently inspecting a whole wardrobe of small clothes and accessories that Virginia put on and displayed before him for his delectation and approval. Madame Lavallière remarked afterwards to her principal _vendeuse_ that it was "Milord" who did all the choosing, and that the pretty little _yanqui_ accepted her fiancé's dicta unquestionably, indeed with seeming indifference; though Madame was quick to add that it scarcely mattered because Milord's taste was impeccable, just as his choice was lavish as to quantity, and his settlement (when received, for _les aristocrates Anglais_ regarded it as a mark of the _bourgeois_ to stump up on time) gratifying.

It was this information—a confirmation that the wedding was still going ahead despite the protracted shilly-shallying of the bride-to-be—that may have added the fatal penny-weight to the delicate balance of Alissa's mind, where elements of _sangfroid_, passion and wild savagery were constantly at war.

She had abandoned her drawing-room, which was still in exactly the same state of chaos as she had put it into after Cambronne's fateful visit (her butler, when he had made tentative suggestions about getting the painters and decorators in, had had a vase thrown at his head), and spent most of her days in a medieval-style solarium at the shady side of the house: a pretty conceit of glass and curlie-wurlies terminating in a gothic spire set with knobs of multicolored stones. It was there, in her tiny crystal cathedral overlooking the lake, that the beautiful mulattress daily gave herself into the hands of Thomas, her favorite house-slave: a huge Negro of unsurpassed gentleness, whose pink-palmed hands were capable of drawing from his mistress's satin skin the worst of strains and stiffnesses and soothing her spirit in turn.

On this particular day, however, Thomas appeared to be laboring in vain. For over an hour the gentle giant had massaged every smooth inch of Alissa's perfect body, but without making any inroads against the peevishness of her movements as she turned this way and that to assist his manipulations. The poor fellow, puzzled and uneasy at the failure of his performance (as a star actor, sublimely confident of the groundlings' appreciation over the years, will think the world turned upside down when he sees a row of nodding heads), redoubled his efforts. His naked body, black as darkest ebony, shone with sweat as hers did with suave rubbing oils, and his movements became, through nervousness, ever less skilled. Finally Alissa, in a gesture of exasperation, seized hold of his wrists and pulled him down upon her. They coupled. Briefly. On her part, joylessly. When he had spent himself, she thrust him from her with a curse and ordered him to go away.

Alone, the mulattress turned over onto her belly and, staring out through the sweetly tinted glass of her tiny profane cathedral, soliloquized:

"God in heaven—why did it have to happen to me? A few short months ago, I was the acknowledged mistress (no more mealy-mouthed talk of 'companion and châtelaine,' Alissa, we are alone!) of the most desirable man in Jamaica, indeed in all the Caribbean.

"Look at me now! I have everything that the most self-pampered and extravagant woman could wish for. (Thank God, though he's cast me off, Basil has not thrown me into the streets to earn my living as a casual plaything for sailors!)

"And what do I do all day? I lie around reading cheap novels. Can't get any pleasure anymore from Thomas's wonderful hands. Haven't enjoyed a cigar for weeks. Never go out, save on the few occasions when Basil has invited me up to Manatee. And I think I'm losing my looks and my figure"—here she reached for a looking-glass.

"That's right. That's it. Those tiny lines at the corners of my eyes: they weren't there before all this began. And I've got grey hairs sprouting everywhere. And I'm sure my lips are thickening. God—and my breasts are sagging! What was it that woman said, that Madame Rita the *corsetière*? 'Once you can hold a pencil underneath one of your breasts, your figure's finished.'

"A pencil! Where is there a pencil? Never anything to be found in this damned place! Servants rob me blind, and I'm losing my looks. I remember my mother. She must once have looked very like me, but—oh!—the way she looked in her coffin: a little old wizened nigger woman. We all end up like that! I shall end up like Mama, like some crone in a mud hut in Africa: all wizened, with dugs like chamois-leather bags half filled with water!

"Why, oh why, did this thing have to happen to me?

"I was perfectly happy before it happened—and look at me now!"

Jack the Cat and Tobias Angel never commented on their captain being taken away in manacles, for the expression he wore when he was hurled back into the cell precluded anything of the sort. In the days that followed, the hideously mutilated English aristocrat-turned-seaman busied himself with working on the rotting mortar that inadequately held in place the lower ends of the thick bars which spanned one wall of their cell at breast level. It was on the third day of their incarceration, after hours of scraping with the sharpened tip of the pewter spoon he had filched from under the eye of the turnkey, that he let out an exclamation of guarded triumph:

"By Jove! These damned bars are only inserted one inch—less!—into the confounded mortar!" he cried. "And the mortar—why, it must have been here since Drake's time. I tell you, we have only to scrape away the lower line of mortar and we can pull out as many bars as we need to climb out."

"And what then?" demanded Cambronne.

Affecting not to notice his captain's sour tone, Jack the Cat grinned his hideous grin. "Then we lurk behind the door at the far end of the corridor," he said. "When the turnkey unlocks it and comes through—*thung!*" He suited the word to the action by miming a blow to the side of the man's head.

"Humph!" was Cambronne's only comment.

"You may be right at that, Jack lad," said Tobias Angel, who was scratching at the crumbling mortar with his ragged thumbnail. "If 'tis the will of the Almighty that we be set free, then it runs not contrary to Divine Will if we do but anticipate Him somewhat. Jack, I will do a turn with your spoon so that you can rest."

"Well said, Tobias," responded Jack the Cat. "And I'll wager you can turn a quotation from the Good Book to cover the situation."

" 'Bring out the prisoners from the prison, and them that sit in darkness out of the prison house,' " responded the zealot. "Isaiah, Chapter 42, Verse seven."

Cambronne watched as the bosun of the *Argo* ground away at the ancient mortar with the tongue of the spoon. His expression softened.

"We can disperse the powder around the floor, mixing it in with the straw," he said. "The problem lies with the holes. We should plug them up with something."

"Food, perhaps?" ventured Jack the Cat.

"Mashed up into a paste with water," said Cambronne. "That damned salt pork's fit for nothing else."

He and Jack the Cat exchanged a grin.

"One thing, Captain," said the latter. "We have plenty of time, since we're not likely to be tried, or so we were told, much before the end of Michaelmas Term, so we'll not be dancing on ropes' ends much before the New Year." He looked quizzically at Cambronne. "Always supposing that my old schoolmate doesn't get us out first—as you never cease to promise us."

Cambronne did not respond to the intended taunt, but threw himself down on his bunk, pillowed his arms behind his head and stared up at the mildewed ceiling.

The effort bent towards the lure of escape, the battered old pewter spoon which was the tool, the contrivance by which they concealed the work from the turnkey on his twice-daily visits with their rough victuals, all served to fill the void of night and day. In fact they worked right round the clock, timing themselves by the bells of a nearby steeple clock in naval watches of four hours with two dog watches of two hours, each man waking his relief and turning over the precious spoon.

Within a couple of days they had cleared away a channel of mortar from around two of the bars, and reckoned that three would suffice. The space they filled with mashed-up salt pork mixed into a malleable paste with water. To their dismay, it had turned out to be not only the wrong color, but also very obviously the wrong color, so that a passing glance would have identified it as not being mortar. All seemed lost till Tobias Angel conceived the notion of saving a small amount of the pulverized mortar dust and sprinkling it on top of the food paste. It served perfectly.

The disaster occurred on the "morning watch" of their third day, with very little left to clear away before they would be able to prise loose three bars and make the first part of their escape bid. Jack the Cat, who had just "come on watch" allowed his attention momentarily to wander away from the work under his fingers. The end of the spoon slipped against the edge of hard stonework, causing him to bark his knuckles against an iron bar and lose his hold on his tool. The spoon sailed through the bars and landed in the corridor outside. Out of reach.

He called the others. There was no word of recrimination, no hard looks. With the turnkey due at midday with their victuals, there was the urgent need either to retrieve the spoon or at least conceal it from the man's eyes. They discussed removing the two bars already loosened, reaching through and down, one-handed, recovering the spoon and attempting to have the third bar removed before the man put in an appearance, but decided they could neither reach their precious tool by that means nor clear away the last of the mortar before midday.

"We could say we had a quarrel and one of us threw the spoon," said Jack the Cat.

"We're not supposed to have a spoon in our possession," said Cambronne. "It's a tool. Once it's found, they'll look to find what use we've made of it. It's no good, we'll just have to wait and trust to luck."

Their luck nearly held. By noonday the spoon, which had been lying tantalizingly in a patch of bright sunlight, had become obscured by shadow. When the turnkey opened the door at the end of the corridor and came shuffling down with a bucket of skilly, he walked right over the spoon without seeing it. Three mugs he dipped into the skilly and slid through the bars of the door. Then he stooped to pick up the bucket. And spotted the spoon.

Cambronne licked his dry lips. Tobias Angel's prominent Adam's apple bobbed up and down like a markerbuoy in a tideway. Jack the Cat gave his horrible, wide-mouthed grin. Not a word passed between them, gaoler or prisoners. The man at the other side of the bars picked up the spoon and turned it over and over, thumbing the tip of the bowl, where constant grinding against a hard substance had worn it almost razor-thin. He looked up from under beetle brows at the three men watching him, then directed his gaze to the row of iron bars set breast-high. He reached for one of them, shook it. It yielded slightly. A moment later he was digging out pulverized spoon.

He left them—again without a word. And was back within five minutes.

This time he was not alone. Three scowling redcoats aimed

their muskets through the bars and directed the prisoners to line up facing the wall with their hands behind their backs. They had no choice but to obey. Then the turnkey and his two henchmen—big, grinning brutes—entered the cell and proceeded to manacle the prisoners' wrists behind them. They were ordered to turn round.

"Let 'em have it, lads!" said the turnkey.

His bully-boys went for the helpless men, starting with Jack the Cat. With fists and boots, they beat him to unconsciousness and still kept on. Next, Tobias Angel. Finally, Cambronne.

He was floating up through the sea-wrack with the slow fingers of the tide pulling at his tattered clothing and the wail of mermen loud in his head. He choked on his own vomit, causing his ribs to ache intolerably; he tried to open his eyes, but they seemed to be glued together. Another paroxysm of choking brought him to the edge of unconsciousness again and he sank back to the sea-bed.

Next time, an age later, he rose swiftly, opening his eyes as he went, directing them to the life-giving patch of light that was the world above. When he was fully conscious—or near enough—he found himself lying in another cell from the one they had occupied. Jack the Cat and Tobias Angel were two dark, sprawled figures in a corner. There was one small, barred window up on high. No furnishings of any kind, not even straw on the pitted stone floor.

He racked his brain to remember . . .

Something had happened. At some time during the preliminaries of the savage beating he had suffered—the part where one of them supported him upright against the wall while his companion kicked him repeatedly in the groin—he had felt something being slipped almost tenderly into his hand. It had been so unexpected, so at variance with what they were doing to him, that he had retained his grip on the object—it felt like a folded piece of paper—till blessed unconsciousness rid him of his agonies.

It was still in his hand. He opened his palm, unrolled the slip of paper lying there, strained his eyes against the thin light from the high window to read what was written there upon it:

You will be rescued tomorrow night.

CHAPTER 12

Manatee was in a riot of preparations for the master's nuptials. Lord Basil had ordained that, following the ceremony in the chapel (which was a copy of the royal chapel at Versailles), the reception would take place in the water-garden for coolness' sake. Further to pamper the seven hundred guests, a huge marquee roof was to be erected over the entire garden to keep off the blinding rays of the tropical sun. All day long the sound of carpenters' hammers accompanied the raising of the thirty great flagpoles from which the blue and white striped awning was to be suspended; mingled with this came the barked orders of overseers commanding the small army of slaves who were laying a scarlet carpet (it had last been used on the occasion of Lord Basil's parents' silver wedding) the entire length of the garden, up the double curve of steps and into the front portals of the Grange. And the whole medley of sound was punctuated by the crack of the overseers' whips as they descended upon black backs.

Lord of all he surveyed in the vast kitchens that occupied the entire basements of the west wing, the great chef Lablanche, formerly cook to the Grand Ducal household of Hesse-Darmstadt, who wore the silver cross of merit of the Order of Philip the Magnanimous on his shocking white frock-coat, sat in his high chair in the center of the main *cuisine*, from which vantage point he was able to supervise the ordering of affairs in much the same way as a general commands a battle. The *sous-chefs* were his staff officers; they were summoned to his side at the raising of a finger, a brief instruction was given, the recipient raced away to see it carried out.

The wedding feast was to center on an enormous cold buffet erected at the base of the Neptune fountain in the water-garden. Lablanche, who was also an artist-draftsman of some repute and who had exhibited at the Paris *salon*, had himself composed the brilliant *mise en scène:* from a great semi-circular table there rose a towering pyramid of luscious pinks: lobster pinks, salmon pinks, the subtle pink of the giant prawn, all overtopped with a leaping dolphin carved out of pink-tinted ice. The eye was, by the artist's simple device, carried up and continued in its flight to the sea-god Neptune himself, his family and his retainers, perched on high and behind the buffet in the seagoing quadriga.

Naturally, it being only the penultimate day before the nuptials, most of the thousands of sea creatures destined to make up the gastronomic pyramid were as yet unslaughtered; at that stage the great chef was concerned with the preparation of the classic sauces, *espagnoles, blondes, garnitures*, and so on. Many of these called for long and complicated processes, for it was the dictum of Lablanche that a sauce should possess a distinctive character—whether it be sharp or sweet, savory or plain—yet that one should not fall into the error of so flavoring the sauce as to render it too blatant on the one hand or too insipid on the other. On the afternoon of the penultimate day, and after no less than sixteen attempts on the part of the sauce chefs, Lablanche conceded that the simple *bechamel maigre* was of a quality that could be presented under his august name; but he directed that they must continue their efforts with *sauce aux anchois* and be not so fiercely predictable with the lemon. At about that same time, the master of Manatee did a tour of inspection of the arrangements. He was accompanied on the tour by Uriah Needham, who had played a not inconsiderable part in those arrangements.

"I am pleased with you, Needham," said Lasalle. "Quite apart from providing me with the means to trump Cambronne's ace, you have proved yourself useful in a score of unexpected ways. Now that you are privy to the secret of our activities, I am going to extend you even further. His Excellency has intimated that he would be happy to have the services of a Counsellor for Trade, a post which is not allowed for in the Governor's establishment. The job's yours, Needham—and that's in addition to all the perquisites you picked up from the death of Hetherington, the Honorary Consulship and so forth."

"Lord Basil, I am most deeply grateful," replied Needham,

his unhealthy pallor taking on a flush of pride and pleasure. "Your patronage has been most . . ."

"Mark you, there'll not be a penny piece in it for you," said Lasalle, "for, as I said, you will be extra to establishment and unpaid." He smiled thinly. "In fact, you will be in my employ and *I* will pay you. In our trade, it is most felicitous to have the ear of the Governor. You will be my ear, and my mouthpiece, at Government House."

"I am honored, sir," breathed Needham. "Honored."

They progressed through the water-garden and entered the chapel, which abutted on the east wing of the mansion. In the green gloom from the tinted windows, the elaborate plaster-work of the ceiling took on an unearthly hue. There was a sweet stench of arum lilies, and someone up in the organ loft was sketching out the theme of a Bach fugue. Lasalle sat down in one of the elaborately carved pews and Needham—after waiting to be invited—took the place beside him. Close by the altar rail, a Negro craftsman was delicately applying fresh gold leaf to the eagle lectern; he never saw nor heard the two men entering the chapel, nor raised his eyes from his work.

"Touching upon the matter of Cambronne," said Lasalle.

"Sir?" responded Needham.

"I am hopeful that the schooner's master, one Blackadder, will replace Cambronne as captain. In the meantime, Black-adder is in nominal command and has been informed that every effort is being made to free the three men from Spanish Town jail, whether by legal means, by bribery and corruption or by force. It goes without saying that by none of these means will Cambronne and his companions ever see the outside of the jail walls again."

"When is their trial, Lord Basil?" asked Needham.

"There will be no trial," replied the other. "Captain Hellbore, having come forward with *prima facie* evidence which secured Cambronne's committal, will have his court-martial sentence discreetly quashed; likewise Commodore Harvey will retain his command. I have therefore in a sense killed two birds with one stone: I have rid myself of Cam-bronne for personal reasons and also insured that one incompetent naval captain and his fleet commander remain upon the station in active service."

"And Cambronne's fate, Lord Basil?"

"Cambronne's fate is settled. He will be disposed of

tomorrow night, along with his companions. And now, my dear Needham, let us go along and inspect the kitchens."

Preparations at Government House were scarcely less hectic. To transport the bride-to-be to her nuptials, His Excellency had caused the Governor's state coach to be taken out of a stable in the corner of the mews, where it had rested since last being used at the victory parade for Waterloo, and completely renovated: the worm-eaten panels replaced, new tires put on the great wheels, and the whole re-painted and re-gilded.

Lady D'Eath fussed around her charge like a mother hen, anxious for the girl's well-being, puzzled by her melancholy and her silences. A childless woman and, despite her forbidding looks and manner, a kindly soul, her ladyship had conceived a genuine fondness for her "little Colonial gel", would have done anything in her power to secure Jason Cambronne's release on bail pending trial, but had immediately come up against an impenetrable wall of silence and evasion whenever she raised the matter with her husband's legal aides. And His Excellency flatly refused to speak of the case.

So now, despite her confiding in the Governor's lady that she loved Cambronne and had always loved him, Virginia was going to wed Sir Basil after all. Taking all in all, Lady D'Eath believed the "gel" was doing the best thing. And said as much to Virginia in her habitual forthright manner:

"To marry for love and position, my dear, that is one thing," she declared. "But unfortunately rare outside the pages of popular fiction. To marry for love alone is dangerous, for it permits young persons of disparate rank, birth and upbringing to form conjugal unions to the detriment of the proper ordering of Good Society, which is bound together by the ties that I have mentioned already, but also by ancillary bonds such as school, regiment, the pack with which one rides to hounds, whether one is Tory or Whig by persuasion, and so on and so forth. I speak only of *English* Society of course, and I am given to understand that matters are ordered differently in your own—er—country." Her ladyship closed her eyes as if in pain. "But of that I cannot speak. However, to return to my argument, it is in marriage for *position* that the proper ordering of Good Society finds its strongest prop. For that is a proceeding in which, unblinded by the toils of passion, one may consider the opportunities for one's proper advancement. As to advancement, it is entirely in order for a man to marry a gel who is several degrees below him in rank or station. That is proper. The reverse is not true. For a man to marry above his station is to bring down obloquy upon his head, and the suspicion that he is attempting to upset the proper order of things, since the proper order of things demands that a man must rule in his house and in his family—and how can he do this if he is untitled, distantly connected with trade, and his wife the daughter of a duke?

"Which brings me, my dear, to your own case, which is that of marriage to Lord Basil. I have it from your own lips that blind passion has not dictated your choice, nor his. Lord Basil has considered your attributes in tranquillity, and in tranquillity he has chosen you. The disparity between your stations in life is of less importance than might have been the case by reason of your Colonial origins, and the same applies to the fact that your papa is engaged in trade. The colonies were built on trade.

"I confide, my dear, that you will make Sir Basil a good wife of whom he will be proud. And I consider that it speaks well of your soundness of character that you have put behind you the hopeless passion for this other man who, if I am correctly informed, will presently find himself upon a capital charge."

Throughout the entire monologue—delivered by Lady D'Eath at the end of tea, when the last of the half-hour guests had departed, along with the trolley, and the two females were alone together in her ladyship's drawing-room— Virginia had sat, and apparently listened, without interrupting. The Governor's lady, who could not see very well even with the assistance of her lorgnette, was extremely gratified and quietly congratulated herself that Virginia's modest and respectful manner served to confirm her own assessment of the child.

If her ladyship's eyesight had been equal to the task, if she could have focused clearly upon the pretty face opposite, she would have seen a creature bereft of spirit and of will, drained of passion, dry-eyed, expressionless.

A human puppet, responsive only to the jerk of the strings.

"We don't know how it's to be done," said Cambronne. "And we must be prepared for anything. I wish to God I had with me a certain blackthorn cudgel that I used to carry on boarding parties."

"It's possible that we shall just be quietly shown the door," said Jack the Cat.

"Alleluia!" intoned Tobias Angel.

They were sprawled on the filthy floor of their new cell, with the thin daylight dying slowly up the streaked wall. Cambronne had shown his companions the cryptic note as soon as each had recovered consciousness—and that was not quickly in either case.

All three bore the marks of their punishment in half-closed eyes and puffed-up lips. Jack the Cat had lost his front teeth, which by a happy accident had the effect of softening the horror of his grin. All three felt as if they had been beaten from head to foot with sledgehammers—as indeed was almost the case. Of the three of them, only Tobias Angel had suffered a grave disability: his right arm had been stamped on and broken underfoot.

"If it comes to a fight," said Cambronne, "If we're to be snatched out of here by force, then you stay close to me, Bosun."

"Aye, aye, sir," responded Tobias Angel.

The band of sunlight rose higher up the wall. Grew more rosy by the minute.

"Nearly night," said Jack the Cat. "And the last night, I hope, that we'll be spending in this stinking hellhole."

"Mayhap the lads from the ship are going to carry the jail by force," said Tobias Angel. "As by faith the walls of Jericho were caused to fall down."

"It's possible," said Cambronne. "We'll just have to bide ourselves in peace and wait to see."

"Amen to that, sir!"

Silence. Only the drip-drip of moisture from the ceiling: their own sweat, risen in steam to the cold stonework above, condensed there—and returned to them.

The last of the daylight went.

"It must be close on midnight."

"Hush! Listen!"

Dragging footfalls in the corridor outside. At first it seemed that they must pass by the door; but then they paused. A key was inserted—none too steadily and not at the first attempt—into the ancient lock, was gratingly turned. The heavy door groaned open.

"Out, all of yuh!"

The newcomer carried a lantern, revealing himself to be a stranger to the three prisoners. A regular turnkey, undoubtedly: he had the heavy leather waist-belt dripping with rings of keys—the badge of his office. And he was staggering drunk.

"Foller me—an' don't get up to any tricks."

"Such company one is obliged to keep," murmured Jack the Cat, "once one strays from felicity."

They followed their guide's unsteady progress down corridors and along gantries, up and down echoing stone steps set into sheer-sided circular keeps all unknown to them, since all three had been carried that way unconscious. And presently they came to the ground floor of the gaol, and to a part that was familiar to Cambronne at least, since it was there that he had been brought in manacles for his last, searing interview with Virginia Holt. And it was outside the self-same office of the prison governor that their drunken guide swayed to a halt and, jerking a thumb at the door, addressed the Jerseyman:

"Someone to see yuh in there, Mister! Alone."

They looked from one to the other.

"What then, Captain?" asked Jack the Cat. "Do we part company, or do we stay together?"

"Alone!" growled the turnkey. "She sez as he was to see her alone!"

"I'll go," said Cambronne. "Any tricks—if you're set upon—mark that you sing out loud and clear, and I'll be with you."

"Aye, aye, Captain."

"Good luck, Captain."

Cambronne entered the dingy room of such bitter memories. It was lit by a single lantern, and a cloaked figure stood with its back to him in the middle of the floor—in the same spot where Virginia had stood . . .

The figure turned.

"Alissa!" exclaimed the Jerseyman.

Under the somber dark gray cloak, she was all Alissa: dressed in some barbaric finery of silks and feathers. Her hair was drawn back with some severity under a black silk scarf. Her long, almond-shaped eyes were heavily limned with kohl and stood out in dramatic contrast against her olive-skinned face, as did her thickly painted lips.

"Surprised, Cambronne?" she murmured.

"Considerably," he replied. "I suppose you are an emissary from Lord Basil?"

She laughed. "My dear Cambronne, do you still continue to believe that Basil Lasalle is going to raise a finger to save you from the gallows?—Considering it was he who put you here in the first place. He has you where he wants you, and tomorrow he will marry Virginia Holt."

Whereupon, in brief and uncompromising terms, Alissa recounted to him the means by which the master of Manatee had engineered the removal of his rival. Omitting nothing, save how Uriah Needham had revealed poor dead Augusta Holt's pathetic adultery to her daughter—an incident of which she was not aware. Nor did she jib at confessing to Cambronne how it was she who had betrayed him in the first instance by telling Lasalle about the garnet pendant and arranging for the Jerseyman to trap himself and be overheard doing so.

"More than anyone, I had a part in trying to put your head into a noose, Cambronne," she said. "Now, by way of making amends, I have outbid Basil Lasalle, who had arranged for you to be quietly disposed of tonight, the eve of his wedding. The doors are open for you. A boat awaits you down by the river, and you can be back aboard your ship and away on the next tide. Why do you stare at me like that, Cambronne?"

"Is this a trick, Alissa?" he replied.

"A trick! Merciful God!" The mulattress threw back her head and raised her magnificently shaped arms on high. She rent at the black headscarf, freeing the sable cascade of her hair; ripped her clothing and bared her heaving breasts. She was all Latin, now. All Africa. "Do you know, Cambronne, what it has cost me to outbid Basil Lasalle?" she demanded. "I will tell you. That walking corpse who calls himself governor of this cess-pit informed me that he had already received five hundred guineas from Lasalle to have your necks wrung before morning. The swine invited me to enter into an auction and better Lasalle's bribe. And this I did: this day, I gave him jewels that should have seen me comfortable in my old age. This I did for you, Cambronne. But that was not all. When my jewels were locked away in his safe, this governor, this stinking, walking corpse, by insinuating his filthy hands beneath my skirts and gusting his charnel-house breath against my lips, implied that he required an additional bonus to seal the compact. Well, a bonus he had, Jason Cambronne. For your sake that suppurating old goat enjoyed the favors of the most envied courtesan in the Caribbean. You see, I am being honest tonight, Cambronne. I am holding a mirror up to myself and telling you what I see."

"But why, Alissa?" demanded Cambronne, taking her by the shoulders. "Why are you doing all this for me?"

A knock on the door. A tipsy shout.

"You must go!" cried Alissa. "Everything hangs on a few minutes when the main gate will be opened for you. Go! Don't tarry for explanations. Oh, my God! No—stay to kiss me! Touch me, I beg you—here! Aaaah—that was divine! And here! And here . . . !"

"Oh, why did this have to happen to poor Alissa?"

The door burst open. The drunken turnkey swayed on the threshold, and they could see Jack the Cat and the bosun behind him, just beyond the loom of the lantern.

"You'd best come straight away," said the turnkey, with the truculence of the inebriated. "Come five minutes and I'm raising the alarm, and you may all go to the devil."

"You have been well paid, pig!" cried Alissa.

"Aye, and it's been drunk—every penny," sniggered the turnkey. "Come, all—your last chance!"

Alissa clung to the Jerseyman as they went out into the night. The yard was empty. No—a solitary redcoat stood over by the far wall, urinating there. He affected not to notice the small party as they crossed the yard towards the iron-studded door, which was wide open. They went through it and into the square beyond, past the guardhouse, unchallenged. The sentry-box outside the gate was empty. No one to see them steal across the wide square; only the cadaver up on high in the night sky, whose eyeless head lay in the bottom of the gibbet-cage.

Alissa released Cambronne's arm at the far side of the square, where a high-walled street ran due eastward through Spanish Town.

"That's your own way," she whispered. "Beyond the town there is a bridge over the river. On the far side, downstream of the bridge, a boat is tied up to a fishing wharf. It's yours. Go now—don't tarry an instant. They'll be raising the alarm in the jail."

"Alissa . . ."

"Go, Cambronne—go!" she cried. "And a whore's blessing go with you. No more—go!" She turned and ran away from them, across to where her carriage was waiting for her by the shadowed wall of the jail, directly under the scaffold. Her coachman alighted and gave her his arm to mount the step.

"Where to, ma'am?"

"Home."

"Yas'm."

They were gone, the three dark figures, when her carriage circled the square and passed the end of the road down which they had departed. With the eye of faith, she thought she could see them racing in and out of the shadows, and imagined that she picked out the tallest and straightest.

"Go with Alissa's blessing, Cambronne," she whispered, half aloud. "For you are the only man that she ever loved. And was never loved in return. And—oh!—that you had never come to Jamaica!"

Cambronne, who had studied the charts of Jamaica, knew that the river—that same River Cobra whose snakish convolutions they had followed on their march after capture—presented the best means of escape from Spanish Town, and that the down-river navigation to its mouth in Hunt's Bay just west of Kingston would put them within a night's hard rowing (or maybe the boat carried sail) of the *Argo*'s secret moorings. This thought burned high in the Jerseyman's brain as he and his companions moved at a steady, light-footed trot, pausing at every road intersection and peering round corners, avoiding patches of bright moonlight, cursing whenever their passing aroused some dog to bark.

Tobias Angel ran awkwardly, nursing his broken arm, but never joined in the cursing. He moved like some big, awkward, wingless bird, the rags of his garments fluttering behind him. Once he tripped on a cobblestone and fell, which must have caused considerable agony to his arm. As his companions picked him up he uttered no word of complaint at their roughness, but meekly thanked them.

The last tall block of stone buildings ended in a straggling line of farmsteads, no better than smallholdings. A cockerel, mistaking them and the bright moonlight for dawn, let forth his challenge to the new day, realized what a damned fool he had been and fluffed up his feathers, returning to sleep. The bright line of the River Cobra appeared ahead of them.

"One more bell of the watch and we're there, Bosun," said Cambronne. By now, he and Jack the Cat were supporting Tobias Angel, one each side. A jagged end of bone had appeared out of the blackened skin of the zealot's forearm and was dripping blood.

"Praise be, Cap'n!" responded Tobias Angel. "Praise be. Sinner that I am, I confess I do greatly crave a tot o'rum."

"We'll splice the main-brace as soon as we're aboard the *Argo,* Bosun," promised Cambronne. "Best foot forward, now. There lies the bridge."

The bridge over the Cobra was a rickety, wood-built affair that looked as if one more hurricane might bring it down in a pile of splinters. A copse of dark palm trees at the far side part-shielded a white-painted farm building. Cambronne had the fervent hope that they would not rouse another dog.

Still supporting Tobias Angel, they crossed over the bridge and peered out into the gloom on the downsteam side, where the thin finger of a landing stage jutted out from the bank.

"There's our boat!" said Jack the Cat, pointing. "Just like the lady said. All ready and waiting to go!"

A dozen worn steps led down to a fishing wharf and the rich stink of offal. There were several craft hauled up on the jetty, all much too large and unwieldy for two men and a disabled comrade to launch into the tideway; but tied alongside the jetty, with two pairs of oars provided, with rudder and tiller already in place, was a robustly built ship's dinghy of about twelve foot. They helped Tobias aboard and settled him in the stern-sheets with the tiller.

"Let go!" whispered Cambronne, shipping his oars.

"All gone for'ard!" responded Jack the Cat, as the head-rope slapped into the water.

The small craft nosed out into midstream, propelled by a couple of sharp pulls from Cambronne the bow-man, and turned neatly to point down-river to the sea. Nothing now separated them from the holystoned decks of the *Argo* but a long night's row.

And then—it happened.

An order was shouted from out of the night. There came the clatter of hobnailed boots on the wooden planking above them, as a line of dark figures emerged at the double-march from the palm-tree copse and strung themselves along the entire length of the bridge. Cambronne's gorge rose with a tight spasm of alarm to see their white crossbelts in the moonlight.

"It's a trap!" he cried. "Give way handsomely, Jack! Let's get the hell out of here, or we're all dead men. Steady as you go, cox'n—don't lose an inch of headway!"

The dinghy leaped forward as they put their backs into a fast, deep-cutting stroke in perfect unison. The water hissed about the transom.

From the bridge: *"Present!"*

"Here it comes!" muttered Cambronne. "Keep your heads low!"

"Front rank, prepare to give fire!"

Tobias Angel muttered a prayer.

"Front rank, give fire!"

A dozen frizzen-pans sparked skywards on the bridge: no more than a line of children's fireworks set up on a wall, all sound and color but no fury. Then came the discharge of a dozen Brown Bess muskets that had ripped the heart out of the French cavalry at Waterloo.

Balls kicked up the water astern. Two or three slammed into the transom and right through. Cambronne both heard and felt one zip past his right ear. Tobias Angel slumped forward into Cambronne's lap without a moan, and the Jerseyman felt his drenching hot blood. The back of the zealot's head had been carried away.

"Rear rank, prepare to give fire!"

"We're a sitting target!" cried Cambronne. "Abandon ship, Jack—and good luck to you!"

As he plunged over the gunwale his last sight was of the redcoat's muskets discharging out of the gloom, and his last thought was that he had come a very long way, and survived a lot of hazard, and it seemed oddly unfair to be shot like a dog in some turgid tropical river.

They were waiting for Alissa when she arrived back at her bijou confection of a house: three hard-eyed men who had gained admittance to her home, frightening her servants and house-slaves half out of their wits in the process so that they had all fled.

She faced up to them with all the dignity she could muster: stood on the sitting-room threshold and tried to shame them with her glance. They were not the sort to be easily shamed.

With slow, easy grins, they uncoiled themselves from her armchairs, first taking their feet off convenient pieces of furniture upon which they had been resting. One of them stubbed out the butt of his cigar on a marquetry-topped table, hawked and spat.

She demanded to know what they meant by the intrusion, thinking all the time that she already knew only too well.

The man to whom she had addressed the question was Lasalle's chief overseer, the handsome brute Jago. He was dressed, like his companions, in a none-too-clean white linen suit, with a broad-brimmed straw hat tipped forward over his brow. A pistol was stuck in his belt. His whip—the rawhide whip that was the badge of his calling—was coiled in his hand.

He laughed at the question. Addressing her with heavy irony as *"Madame* Alissa," the style by which she had always been known at Manatee, but no longer. He asked her if she had enjoyed a-visiting the gaol at that late hour. And Alissa knew that she was done for.

Jago played words with her for a while, earning the sniggering admiration of his loutish assistants, who did not have his ready turn of wit. Asked her: did Captain Cambronne and his lads get away safely? For Lord Basil was most particular to know, since he'd made such careful arrangements for them to be met at the bridge and be seen on their merry way—this last sally had his men in stitches. For a while, Alissa declined to join the game, answered only in monosyllables and non-committally; so Jago led her on by more pointed questions: was it true, as that old goat boasted to them, that in addition to taking her jewels he had had his way with her? And had she planned to join Cambronne aboard the schooner and sail away from Jamaica? If so she was going to be sadly disappointed.

In the end she screamed at him to tell her the truth of it, and even then they played with her: making a statement, contradicting it in the next breath. It was some time before they tired of the sport and she had the truth unvarnished . . .

No sooner had she made an approach to the governor of Spanish Town gaol than he had immediately betrayed her to Lasalle, who had instructed him on how to act. The manner and the timing of the prisoner's escape, the boat that was waiting at the bridge—all were ingredients of the murder plot devised by the master of Manatee. And then, in answer to her frenzied entreaties, they told her that all three had been shot by the redcoats, who had been alerted to the attempt. "Killed while attempting to escape"—the cynical euphemism beloved by tyrants and oligarchs the world over—was to be the hypocritical epitaph to the three men of the *Argo*.

And now, the game over, as to why they had come to visit her . . .

Alissa, a woman of her time and of her station, might have sought to buy them off with anything she had; she was never given the opportunity. What they wanted of her, they took: each in turn and repeatedly. And when they had slaked their lusts, they carried her out into the night, to a pretty bridge constructed in the chinoiserie manner that spanned the narrowest, yet deepest, part of her ornamental lake. And there they tied a heavy piece of her own sitting-room furnishing—a plinth of veined green marble that had supported the bronze head of a nymph—to her ankles and threw her, alive and screaming, into the water, to the depths of which she immediately sank. And then they went back to Manatee, to report to their master that the task was done.

Nightjars calling, and a restless pheasant in the landscaped wood. Silence in the little Gothic mansion, whose doors and windows hung open, whose lights still burned. In the early hours of the morning, slaves and house-servants found courage to creep back, fearfully, in twos and threes. In the sitting-room they found signs of their mistress's last struggles, but though they looked for her and called for her she was not to be found.

Thirty feet down, the drowned Alissa moved to every fitful undercurrent: nude, upright and with arms extended like a dancer on the stage; hair streaming in a phantom wind; turning, swaying, bending, pirouetting in an eternal ballet of Death.

An unheralded and quite unseasonable downpour of fine rain in the early dawn provided an added benison to the occasion of the nuptials at Manatee Grange, washing away the thin tilth of dust that had accumulated during the long, dry summer, brightening the gesticulating marble statuary, cleaning out Father Neptune's grubby ears, accenting the sparkle of the brand new gilding, freshening each waxen leaf of flame-headed exotic.

Chef Lablanche, a general before a battle, had retired to

his makeshift bed in an alcove off the main *cuisine* at three in the morning with stern instructions to be called at six. At half past six, he was regarding the erection of his gastronomic pyramid in front of the Neptune fountain. And Lord Basil Lasalle was enjoying his last hours' sleep as a bachelor.

They called the Master of Manatee at nine, when he breakfasted *à l'Anglais* on grilled ham and eggs, deviled kidneys, kedgeree, while listening to the latest report from his chief overseer, who had acted as his creature (a familiar role for the brute Jago) in the matter of disposing of his rival and his adherents. Yes, the military had recovered the dinghy with the corpse of the seaman Angel lying in it. Search was still continuing for the bodies of Cambronne and the Seaman Smith—the one with the face like a creature from a nightmare. No, they had not yet been found, but the officer in charge of the—execution party—had reported several hits on the two men and a lot of blood. Oh yes, Lord Basil was assured, there was quite enough moonlight to see blood streaming in the water. Lord Basil nodded, called for his dressing-gown and took a tepid bath.

First to arrive at the Manatee chapel was a choir of little boys from the English grammar school at Kingston, together with their choirmaster. In addition to carrying the burden of the choral part of the ceremony, they were to sing Handel's setting of *Te Deum Laudamus* by way of an anthem. Soon after came the Rev. Dr. Scopes, incumbent of the parish church of St. Barnabus in Spanish Town. Dr. Scopes held his living through the patronage of the Lasalle family and knew which side his bread was buttered. A three-bottle man and rider to hounds, he was a good preacher of the old sort and very sound on hellfire.

At eleven o'clock the first of the guests began to file into the chapel, picking up hymn-books and the Book of Common Prayer from the liveried house-slaves attendant at the portals. The punctuality of the guests' arrivals was in reverse ratio to their social standing: last to arrive were the Governor and Lady D'Eath, who took their places of honor in the richly carved and gilded family pew of the Lasalles.

At a quarter past eleven (and it was by then stiflingly hot in the packed building, with fans fluttering and feathers wilting) Lord Basil strode purposefully up the aisle and took his place at the altar rail. Dressed, as ever, in white from head to foot, with his air of pale, aristocratic composure, he had every female heart in the place—eligible and ineligible—reaching out to touch his coattails. With him for best man was Commodore Harvey.

The tropical noontime crawled languorously to its apogee. The pipe organ played fragments of Bach and Handel. Repeatedly. A stout lady, overcome by the heat and airlessness, slipped slowly to the parquet and had to be carried out by no less than four stalwart gentlemen. They passed the bride coming in.

At a signal from a small black boy who was crouched by the organ loft with bright eyes fixed upon the chapel door, the organist struck up a lively march. The congregation rose, all faces turning to regard the astonishing little creature who had landed the biggest fish in the Caribbean. The fluttering of fans took on a wilder beat. Many were the sharp intakes of breath. Comments were loud and unguarded, mostly from the menfolk:

"By heaven—what a filly!"

"Lasalle's a lucky bounder!"

"Look at the figure on her, begad!"

Virginia came in on the arm of Jeff Carradine, who was to give her away, and who was looking as handsome and distinguished as ever in dove-grey frockcoat. Her bridal gown was of white lace, with a train borne by six little boys from the best families in Jamaica. She was veiled, but subtly, so that the delicate buttermilk and wild rose complexion (and how had she retained *that* in Jamaica? asked all the ladies) showed clearly through the flimsy silk gauze. Her golden mane was piled on high and topped with a tiny gold crown of medieval style. She carried for a bouquet a posy of white roses. But it was the beauty of her figure, suavely announced by the drifting lace that so lovingly clung to her youthful roundnesses that brought the watching womenfolk to despair and their squires to wild flights of lustful imagery.

Lord Basil Lasalle turned at the altar rail to regard the vision that approached him, and was well satisfied that she had been worth all the trouble he had been put to in hunting her down and bringing her to heel. And, by God, there'd be as little time wasted as possible at the post-nuptial junketings, for he'd have her bedded before the afternoon was out!

Commodore Harvey brightened considerably, for he appreciated a pretty face and figure, and the sight of the lass coming up the aisle under full sail was enough to gladden a heavy heart and a heavier conscience. But, after all, matters had turned out uncommonly well, had they not? The means to the end were perhaps not what Nelson would have approved of (Harvey had served under the Little Admiral in H.M.S. *Elephant*), for at his court-martial Hellbore had attested that he had not been close enough to the phantom schooner to be able to describe her captain's appearance, and he had now changed his tune. But that fellow Cambronne was undoubtedly guilty. And had now been done for, if the news was correct. Well, one's conscience was clean, was it not? And appointed best man to a nabob like Sir Basil, that was something, was it not? A fine connection for a serving officer. And this little bride of his—a splendid morsel . . .

Lasalle reached out and took Virginia's hand. Ignoring the Rev. Dr. Scopes's introductory intonation, he drew her to him and, having done so, lifted her veil with both hands, slowly, as if deliberately to tantalize himself.

He exhaled a sigh of relief. Yes, he had done right. Here was undoubtedly the jewel of all his possessions, and worth all the conniving. Was there ever such perfection? And the little darling, she was weeping.

Weeping tears of joy on her wedding day.

The ceremony over, Handel's Utrecht *Te Deum* sung, vows exchanged and blessings given. Lady Basil Lasalle, her delicate finger bearing a thick gold band that looked far too weighty for it, went out into the sunlight and the flung rice on the arm of her handsome groom.

From the chapel porch the newlyweds proceeded, by way of a balustraded balcony that entirely surrounded the mansion, to the terrace overlooking the water-garden, there to see and to be seen without having to rub shoulders with all and sundry of the seven hundred guests assembled there. Lord Basil's English butler and his acolytes were there to keep back the throng and insure that the couple had the terrace to themselves.

"Well, my dear Virginia, we are wed," observed Lasalle, smiling his tight, cool smile down upon her. "Did you find it greatly affecting. I notice that you wept, indeed your eyes are still brimming. What a tender-hearted little thing you are, to be sure."

"I—there are so many people," she faltered. "In the chapel I felt—overawed."

"We must give them their show," he replied. *"Noblesse oblige.* A brief appearance. A few words with the really important people. And then, my dear"—he squeezed her hand—"we'll retire to our bridal suite. I am sure that a brief —rest—will set you up admirably."

Her suddenly frightened eyes avoided his. "Yes, Basil," she whispered.

The appearance of the newlyweds on the terrace above the water-garden drew forth a spontaneous burst of applause from the massed guests. Below where the brilliant pair were standing, the Neptune fountain sent its hundred jets of bright water hissing as high as the lofty canopy of blue and white canvas that entirely covered the garden, and beyond that rose chef Lablanche's monstrous confection of pink on pink, into which the more gastronomically inclined of the guests had already made considerable inroads.

"You must throw your bouquet, Virginia," said Lasalle.

This she did. The posy of white roses sailed out over the balustrade, and a score of eager young hands were raised to snatch it out of the air. Alas, it evaded every grasp and fell into the bowl of the Neptune fountain, where it was immediately deluged in the downpour of diamond droplets and strewn into a forlorn carpet of white petals bobbing in the maelstrom.

"I'm so sorry, Basil," whispered Virginia. "That's so—so unlucky!"

"Oh, for heaven's sake don't apologize," he snapped. "I don't hold with damned omens and portents. Come, let's leave the hogs to their swill and take a glass of champagne in our bridal suite." Really, he thought, I mustn't be so short-tempered with the poor little thing, for she's as frightened as a kitten. And very right and proper too. Who would want an eager virgin?

Inclining his blond head in a graceful bow to the guests below, Lasalle took Virginia by the hand and led her toward the line of French windows that gave admittance to the mansion. Together they stepped into the cool gloom of the room beyond, and after the glaring sunlight were not immediately able to discern the two men who watched their entry.

"Hello, Lasalle! Enjoying married life?"

The master of Manatee peered across the room. "Who's that? Who the devil are you?"

"Cambronne!" cried Virginia Lasalle.

* * *

By the time Lasalle's eyes had become accustomed to the gloom, Jack the Cat had circled the bridal pair. Reaching out one bare foot, he gently pushed the French window closed.

"We don't want to be disturbed, do we—*Lucifer?*" he said.

The green eyes flashed puzzlement. "Where did you learn to call me that?" hissed Lasalle.

Jack the Cat grinned hideously, but made no reply. Lasalle whirled round to face Jason Cambronne.

"What are you doing here?" he demanded. "I was told that you . . ."

"The soldiers were a little over-exuberant," said Cambronne. "And their shooting rather wild. By what you imply, their report also erred on the side of optimism. I assure you we are very much alive. As to why we are here—we have come to settle the score."

"I've only to raise my voice," said Lasalle, "and a dozen men will burst in here and take you where you stand!"

Cambronne shook his head. "Not on your wedding day, I fancy," he said. "I don't think you will wish so thoroughly to foul your nest in front of the entire Jamaican high society. And I promise you we shall not be taken with—discretion."

Virginia found her voice. "Have you—escaped?" she faltered.

"Yes, Lady Basil." The Jerseyman gave a heavy edge of irony to her newly acquired title. "Between them, your husband and Alissa engineered our release. I don't know where the blame mainly lies—though I'd swear that Alissa was sincere—but we were pointed straight into a murder trap!"

She looked helplessly towards the man with whom she had so recently exchanged the most sacred and specific vows.

"Basil, I don't understand!" she cried. "What is he *saying?*"

"I am saying, Lady Basil," interposed Cambronne, "that your new husband is a two-faced, murderous swine! A few hours since, one of my crew—a true, God-fearing man and a staunch comrade—was shot like a mad dog. And I have come here to avenge Tobias Angel!"

"*We* have come to avenge him!" corrected Jack the Cat.

"The privilege is mine, Jack," said Cambronne. "You are out-ranked!"

Two spots of anger burned on the pale cheeks of the aristocrat. He had been watching Virginia to gauge what effect Cambronne's accusation was having upon her. What he saw there made him turn his furious gaze to the Jerseyman.

"I will have your life for that, Cambronne!" he breathed.

"Name your weapon!" responded the other.

"Captain!" wailed Jack the Cat.

Lasalle's thin lips twisted in his particular travesty of a smile. "Need I say that my weapon is the sword?" he purred.

"So be it," replied Cambronne.

Jack the Cat intervened again. "Captain, you are a fool!" he declared. "If I had known that you were going to throw your life away like this, I never would have agreed to come here with you. You know this swine's reputation with the sword. He'll skewer you at the first pass!"

Lasalle smirked. "Oh, but I will give the gallant captain every consideration . . ." he began.

"Like the consideration you gave to poor Oliver Graveley when you strung him up and castrated him—*Lucifer?*"

Virginia cried out in horror, eyes fixed upon the man she had married, who was staring at Jack the Cat as if he were an apparition.

"Again you call me by that name!" breathed the master of Manatee. "How do you, how *could* you—a common seaman —know that I was once so called? And how could you possibly know about . . . ?"

"About little Oliver Graveley?" demanded Jack the Cat. "I should know, for it was I who cut him down after you had robbed him of his manhood—and his life. Oh yes, Lucifer, we went to the same immortal school, shared the same kind of aristocratic birth, though, I hasten to add, *not* the same vile proclivities."

Lasalle stared at the other for a breathless moment. Then, snapping his fingers, he pointed.

"The hair!" he exclaimed. "I remember it well, now—the red hair. It's *you*—mealy-mouthed prig that you were!" He turned to his wife of a quarter of an hour, heedless of the fact—so great was his exultation, his imagined moral triumph over his tormentor—that she was staring at him with unconcealed horror. "My dear, we have been mistaken all this time, you and I. This common seaman you see before you, this ragged, barefoot, stinking . . ."

"Not stinking!" interposed Jack the Cat. "The captain and

I have been washed clean by the waters of the River Cobra. Insofar as the River Cobra does not stink all that badly, we do not stink that badly anymore."

Lasalle made a dismissive gesture. "As I was saying, my dear, he is not what he seems. My dear Virginia, may I present the Most Right Honorable, the Marquess Slatterdale! An old school chum."

"Your servant, Lady Basil," said Jack the Cat, bowing with gravity.

"And that is not all, my dear." Lasalle's eyes were wild, his manner uncaring. "My Lord Marquess, who was so priggish and mealy-mouthed about a silly boyhood prank of mine that went awry (the other boy stupidly upped and died, would you believe?), then went and killed his own brother over a mere wager, or so the story goes. Now, what do you think of that?"

Virginia continued to stare at him, her lips moving soundlessly.

"If you lose to him, Captain," said Jack the Cat, "I shall have second go at the bastard and kill him!"

"That will be *your* privilege, Jack," said Cambronne.

Lasalle pointed. "There are a pair of rapiers on the wall yonder."

"I'll get them," said Jack the Cat.

Virginia Lasalle, *née* Holt, fell back against the nearest wall for support, and there she remained huddled through all that came after, hand pressed to her mouth, eyes staring, frightened and trembling. From somewhere very far off she could hear the junketing and merrymaking of her own wedding; but the participants in the grim tragedy being played out before her could as well have been on the moon, for not a soul among all those seven hundred guests would have presumed to mount up to the terrace and enter the mansion in the wake of the Lord of Manatee and his new bride. There was not one among them who was not aware—at first hand, or by repute—of Lord Basil's insatiable appetite for womanflesh; and as they gorged their way through chef Lablanche's pink pyramid, his classic sauces, *espagnoles, blondes, garnitures,* many were the prurient speculations about what must be happening in the newly furnished bridal suite, where, so it was rumored, Lasalle's unique collection of eighteenth-century erotic prints was on display for the little Yankee's instruction. As for chief overseer Jago and his bully-boys, far from intruding into the mansion, their brief was to keep everyone else out while the master was busy tupping his newest—and most expensive—acquisition.

Cambronne and the master of Manatee were armed. The latter was now in his shirtsleeves and had kicked off his pumps. The Jerseyman was stripped to the waist and barefoot.

"En garde!"

The blades met with a slithering sound. And again. It became clear from the first that Cambronne was not permitting himself to be overawed by Lasalle's acknowledged superiority in the arm, but had determined to exploit that most deterring of situations for a really expert swordsman who knows all the rules and plays by the rules: which is to be confronted by an opponent who neither knows and plays, nor cares a damn, for them.

Using the fine-bladed dueling rapier for all the world like a naval boarding-cutlass, Cambronne made heavy and extremely telling slashes at his opponent's head and neck. Lasalle, poised like a dancing-master, with his practiced skill trembling between brain and fingertips, was reduced to making similarly clumsy moves to prevent himself being quite seriously injured by the whip of flying steel, giving ground all the time and being set thoroughly off-balance both as to physical presentation and in moral superiority. In short, he was put completely out of countenance and made to feel at a loss.

It was a circumstance that could not last—unless Cambronne was able to make a quick kill. And even Lasalle was not so completely put out of countenance as to permit that. Accepting the unexpected circumstances, he devised his strategem to deal with the problem presented to him. Instead of seeking desperately to parry his opponent's wild cuts and thrusts, he gave ground and awaited an opening, meanwhile remaining perfectly in balance. It was a stratagem that, barring accidents (and swordsmen of Lasalle's class do not allow themselves the luxury of accident), spelled death for Cambronne.

And yet, through sheer daring, the Jerseyman stayed alive longer than Lasalle would have wished. He left his breast unguarded to a straight thrust—and was immediately aware of it. Not possessing sufficient skill to make the correct, effective parry, he simply slashed. And Lasalle was reduced to a retreat.

But the end was inevitable. In the fence, balance is all. Lasalle saw his opponent wildly off-balance after a brutal cut, which, if it had been a cutlass he was wielding, and if Lasalle had not been the fencer he was, would have secured a clean decapitation. Perceiving his opening, the master of Manatee brought his weapon up in a disarming movement—that same movement which had brought about the downfall of Ensign Hatchwell—at the same time continuing his advance, exerting sufficient power with his sword-arm to over-topple his opponent. Cambronne fell heavily to the floor and his rapier skittered and clattered across the polished parquet to land at the feet of Jack the Cat. And the Jerseyman's bare chest lay open to Lasalle's gleaming point.

Virginia screamed.

Lasalle was in no great hurry. Thin-lipped, eyes narrowed, he poised himself for a deep, killing thrust . . .

Silently, barefoot, Jack the Cat raced forward, gathering up Cambronne's fallen weapon *en passant*. Six paces separated him from Lasalle and Lasalle's undefended back, and it may have been the consideration of stabbing a man in the back that moved him to shout:

"Take this, Lucifer, in memory of Oliver Graveley!"

For Jack the Cat it was a fatal consideration . . .

Lasalle's movement was like falling quicksilver. His point, in one instant directed to Cambronne's chest, was on the next re-directed to parry a clumsy thrust from the rear. Parry and thrust! He pierced Jack the Cat in the left breast an inch below the heart, and drove home as far as the rapier's quillons so that a clear two feet of bloodied steel protruded from the back of the stricken man. And then withdrew. Slowly, choking on his life's blood, Jack the Cat folded to the floor.

With a cry of fury and anguish, Jason Cambronne uncoiled himself from his prostrate position and, without regaining his feet, threw himself full-tilt at the master of Manatee, one hand groping for the other's sword-wrist but not finding it—for Lasalle was already drawing back his arm to make a close-quarters stab to the Jerseyman's guts. They were *vis-à-vis*, eyeball to eyeball, panted breaths mingling. Cambronne, aware of the menacing rapier's point, drove his forehead against Lasalle's aristocratic nose and felt the bone shatter, the other's hot blood pour over his face. Lasalle screamed, broke his grip and fell away, dropping his rapier.

Like mummers in a tragical mystery play, they acted out the final scene before Virginia's fixed and unblinking stare. She saw Lasalle gather himself and race for the French window and Cambronne start after him. The quarry had the door open and was rushing out into the sudden sunlight of the terrace, screaming for Jago and his men, with the hunter at his heels. The scream silenced the hubbub in the water-garden below the terrace the way a wheeling hawk above will silence the chattering of jays.

Lasalle reached the balustrade and looked down. Seven hundred pairs of eyes turned up to regard him, yet not a hand to lend assistance. He turned back to face his enemy, slack-lipped, drained.

"You may have anything you wish for," he babbled. "Anything. Take what you like. Money. Gold—I'll give you enough gold to keep you for life!"

Cambronne came on. Slowly. Inexorably.

"Take the woman!" cried Lasalle. "She's nothing to me—only a plaything. I only wed her out of a caprice, and would have tired of her long since but for her interest in you . . .

"No! Don't hurt me! Take the ship—you love that ship, don't you? I'll see to it. I'll see that The Man is squared!"

Only that halted Cambronne from his immediate intent.

"The Man!" he cried. "Where is he—where in Jamaica?"

Lasalle shook his head wildly. "You're too late!" he cried. "I had a note from him last night. He sailed on the tide—for Boston. In a fast brig."

Another question sprang to Cambronne's mind: "Was it in collusion with you that Alissa had us freed from the jail?"

"No! The bitch did it herself, but the Governor sent me news."

"And what did you do to her?"

Lasalle licked his dry lips and looked sidelong.

"I had her . . ."

"You had her—*what?*"

There were running footfalls on the red-carpeted steps. Jago and his men were coming to their master's aid. Alone of the assembled multitude, they were ready to brave the wild, unshaven and half-naked creature who was menacing the master of Manatee.

"I had her—killed! Aaaaaah!"

He screamed when Cambronne took him up: picked him from his feet and held him aloft like a rag doll. He was still screaming when he plunged down, cartwheeling over and over, to the shallow basin of the great Neptune fountain far below, where he struck surface and sank from sight. Cambronne did not stop to see the end of his enemy, but darted across the terrace and through the French window, which he firmly bolted behind him.

Virginia was on her knees beside Jack the Cat. She turned her agonized eyes to regard the Jerseyman.

"He's going fast," she whispered.

Cambronne bent over his shipmate. The clever, cynical eyes opened and met his. The hideous lips parted in a curiously gentle grin.

"You're a fool, Captain," he murmured. "It could have been you lying here."

"But for you, Jack, it would have been," replied Cambronne.

"Tant pis. I have sought Death, and now he has caught me. Goodbye, Captain. Like poor Tom Bowling, I have been broached to, but 'tis gratifying to be dying in—affluent surroundings . . ."

He was gone.

They were thundering on the French window as Cambronne gently closed the dead eyes.

"Sleep soundly, my Lord Marquess," he whispered. "No noble ancestor of yours who rests beneath a marble monument could ever have died—or indeed lived—so well."

A crash of glass. One of the men was attacking the door with a pistol butt.

Cambronne glanced at Virginia.

"What about you?" he asked.

"Take me away from this place!" she pleaded.

"Come on!"

He snatched at her hand and dragged her after him, flung wide a door at the far end of the chamber and bounded through it. Their passing went unimpeded, for all of Manatee was congregated in the water-garden. Pausing only to snatch a pistol from a display of arms on a wall, Cambronne brought his charge at last to a rear exit of the mansion that led out into a mews. Standing there in the shade was a row of six carriages and horses with patient coachmen nodding in sleep on their boxes.

The man at the head of the line opened his eyes wide to see

the unkempt face and the dark muzzle of the unloaded pistol that was presented to his forehead.

"Drive off!" rasped Cambronne. "And drive like the wind!"

Someone found someone who knew how to turn off the fountain. Forlorn and silent in their quadriga, the sea-god Neptune and his companions gazed stonily ahead while Negro footmen rolled up their buckskin breeches and waded into the wide basin to bring out the humped form that floated, face downwards, at the base of Neptune's craft.

"De master's dead! Neck's a-broken!"

"Ooooh! I think I'm going to swoon!" Lady D'Eath stole the honors by collapsing into the arms of her husband, who, looking desperately about him for assistance, was gratified to see Uriah Needham elbowing his way through the packed throng.

"Permit, me, Your Excellency. Your ladyship, give me your arm. I have a bottle of sal volatile that I carry always for this very emergency." Needham's pale countenance was a study in concern and compassion as he ministered to the needs of the stricken wife of Jamaica's Governor; nor did he look around from his task of gently wafting the bottle of sal volatile under her august nostrils when the dead Lasalle was carried past them, dripping water, the head lolling hideously at the end of the broken neck.

Presently, her ladyship recovered her equilibrium and beamed upon her savior.

"Thank you *so* much, Mr.—er . . ."

"Needham, ma'am," supplied he. "Lately attached to His Excellency's establishment as Counselor for Trade." He looked wistful. "Though only in an honorary capacity."

"So kind, so kind," opined Lady D'Eath.

"Dunno how I'm ever goin' to repay you, young feller," observed His Excellency.

Uriah Needham made no comment. In his small, mean, but ever-surviving heart, he thought he knew the coin of His Excellency's repayment, and that he—Needham—had, in his own phrase, "fallen on his feet again."

They rattled swiftly, by way of the long lanes through high walls of sugarcane, toward the jetty overlooking the *Argo*'s moorings; nor did the terrified coachman, hideously aware that the wild-looking white man might blow off the back of his head with his pistol, draw rein for an instant.

Virginia had said nothing since they had mounted the carriage. It seemed to the Jerseyman that she was struggling with an indecision, and that when she abruptly turned to face him she had settled the matter in her mind.

"Captain Cambronne," she said. "Are you in the mood to give me some straight answers to straight questions?"

"I will answer to the best of my knowledge, ma'am," he replied.

"Concerning the—the man I married this morning (God! It could only be an hour since!), was he everything that you and Jack the Cat accused him of being? Was he indeed monster, torturer, murderer, and worse? Tell me straight, I beg you. What I saw and what I heard from his own lips have left me with no feelings towards that man save repugnance, even, of his memory."

"To speak ill of the dead, Lasalle was all those things," said Cambronne.

"Ah! And it was he who contrived your arrest, thinking that you were his rival for my—affections? And he would have had you killed for the same reason?"

"He gave the order. My own killing was bungled through no fault of his."

She looked away, across the passing walls of sugarcane.

"And when he brought Uriah Needham to me with—with the story of my mother's adultery," she whispered, "It was not out of regard for me, to save me from giving myself to a man who had bedded my own mother in adultery, nor did he have any regard for the hurt I suffered on hearing of it, for his sole intent was to turn me against you. He did not even care that I might loathe my poor mother's memory for the rest of my life. Do I tell it how it was?"

He nodded. "That was how it was, how he intended it."

She drew a shuddering breath. "What I have to say now, Captain Cambronne, comes very hard to me. With reluctance, I have to thank you . . ."

"For what?" asked the Jerseyman.

"For telling the truth about my mother," she said, "and clearing her name, so that I shall not hate her for the rest of my life. And I remember that I gave you every opportunity to lie, to brand her as wanton, shameless. But you told it to me plain—how you had taken advantage of her and ravished her against her will. It cost you my love, Jason Cambronne, but you saved my mother's honor and, in a sense, your own."

Cambronne made no reply to that.

One turn in the rutted lane and the jetty came in sight, and beyond that the *Argo*'s moorings, where the schooner lay in the shadow of the great rock that guarded her. The watch on deck espied the approach of the carriage, and a squint through a telescope brought recognition of their captain in a trice. A bosun's pipe shrilled out across the water, followed by a voice calling away the jolly-boat.

"What shall you do when you reach Boston?" asked Virginia. "Will it be safe for you? Surely not—not when news of what happened in Jamaica reaches there."

"I shall be safe once I reach Boston," he assured her. "And on the way, I hope to settle some unfinished business."

"Would it be prudent for me to ask after this unfinished business? And does it concern my father?"

"It would be most imprudent—and yes, it concerns your father very nearly."

"I see."

The jolly-boat was putting out from *Argo*'s gangway.

"Are you returning with us?" he asked. "To Boston?"

She shook her head. "Return to Boston and my father's house?" she cried. "Never! That—hypocrite! To think that my poor dead mother worked her fingers to the bone for his so-called Anti-Slavery Society and never ceased telling people what a kind and dedicated lover of humanity he is. Lover of humanity! No, I shall never enter his house or speak to him again."

"Then where shall you go?"

"To my uncle Jeff Carradine, who is the dearest, sweetest man in the world. A lifelong bachelor and the soul of truest kindness. I shall go to him, and he'll advise me and look after me till I have the courage to stand on my feet again. One thing I shall certainly *not* do . . ."

"And what's that, ma'am?"

"I shall never make claim upon the Lasalle estate, though I have every right to do so." So saying, she glanced down at her right hand, and gave a start of revulsion to see the thick gold band that Lord Basil had placed there that morning. With a cry, she tugged it from her finger and threw it out into the dark sea as the carriage drew to a halt at the water's edge.

"So ends my marriage and widowhood!" she declared. "I am back where I was when I woke this morning, and thank God a virgin still!"

"Since this is a day for disposing of tokens," said Cambronne, "I had best square my account with you." And he took from the pocket of his ragged breeches the garnet pendant and chain. "I have carried this since Boston," he told her. "But now I must give it back, for the hope of which it was a symbol is lost to me forever."

There were tears in her eyes as she took the pendant from him and placed the chain around her neck.

"I have loved you, Jason Cambronne," she declared. "And I believe that you have loved me—perhaps still love me—in a way that a man is able to love, but which is impossible for a woman. There stands between us the ghost of my dead mother, whom you ravished. For me—a woman—that specter will stand between us for the rest of our lives. I think that if you were to touch me in passion, my flesh would burn and scar as if from a hot iron."

The jolly-boat's crew were tossing their oars, preparatory to coming alongside the jetty. Blackadder was at the tiller.

Cambronne said to the coachman: "Boy, take this lady wherever she wants to go, or it'll be the worse for you when we meet again!"

The coachman rolled his eyes in terror, nodding vigorously.

Blackadder leaped ashore with a glad cry, and the two men embraced like long-lost brothers.

"We heard nothing of you, Captain," said the master of the *Argo*. "Nothing but promises—promises, that you would be freed. And now you are!"

"Not freed, Tom," said Cambronne. "Only escaped."

The other stared hard at him. "And what of Jack the Cat, sir, and the bosun?"

"Dead, both of them, Tom. Killed."

"Oh, my God!"

The coachman whipped up his horses and the carriage drew away from the jetty. Virginia Lasalle, *née* Holt, did not look back.

"What's the state of the tide, Master?" demanded Cambronne, harshly.

"As you see, sir," said the other, pointing. "On the last of the ebb."

"Then we catch the last of the ebb."

"Where bound, Captain?"

"We head for Boston, Massachusetts," replied Cambronne. "And, with luck, there'll be a little unfinished business along the way."

If we can only overtake that brig, he thought. Unless Lasalle was lying, after all, and The Man has never left Jamaica . . .

CHAPTER 13

They crowded the upper deck to welcome their captain's return: Ebenezer Harker and the men from Nogg's Wharf, shocked silent to hear of Tobias Angel's end, seeking solace in Cambronne's living hand-clasp; Master Gunner Stokes, Black Dick, Turnip, Angus Dunbar and the rest. Swede towering above them all. And Meg Trumper.

The fo'c'sle party prepared to cast off from the for'ard mooring-buoy; the schooner was already freed aft. The hands on watch were raising sail. Cambronne and Blackadder went to the poop.

"I don't like the look of the weather, Captain," said the latter. "There's been a heavy swell out beyond the bay since yesterday afternoon early, and the barometer's been dropping all night. And see the clouds up yonder to the southeast? They weren't there an hour since." He pointed toward the horizon, where high clouds with irregularly curved white threads covered the entire sky from south to east.

"A hurricane on its way?" mused Cambronne.

"The signs are all here," said Blackadder. "Did you see last night's sunset?"

"Last night, I was otherwise engaged than watching sunsets," said Cambronne dryly. "I merely watched a patch of daylight climbing up the wall of a prison cell."

"It was brilliant red," said Blackadder. "And the wind was veering and backing in all directions."

"Well, if there's to be a hurricane, we must hope and pray that it passes us by," said Cambronne. "For, hurricane or no hurricane, we are on our way. Ready to make sail and cast off, Mr. Blackadder?" He strode to the taffrail and looked down to make sure they were well clear of the after buoy.

"Aye, aye, sir," replied the master.

"Then make it so," responded the captain of the *Argo*.

A party of horsemen—armed overseers of the Manatee

estate—arrived at the jetty in time to see the *Argo's* blue sails blossom in the breeze, and the slender grace of the schooner slip gently away from the mooring and, rounding the guardian rock, head out to meet the oily swell beyond. The men of Manatee fired off a few random pistol shots that struck water well clear of the receding vessel, and called out abuse, which was lost in the rapidly widening distance between them. They watched till the *Argo* was out of sight around the arm of the small bay and then rode back the way they had come.

Once under way, Cambronne called for a bucket of water, clean clothes and food—in that order. Washed, dressed and ravenous, he sat down to a meal in the cabin, with a chart of the approaches to the Windward Passage on the table beside him. Meg Trumper appeared in a skirt which she had made up, patchwork-fashion and with commendable skill, out of old flag bunting. In addition, she had made some considerable inroads on taming her hair, which was growing out quite sturdily. With a paper flower over one ear, a brave scarf around her waist, and a decent clean shirt, she might have expected some comment from Cambronne. He never raised his eyes from the chart. Not till she came to clear away his empty dishes did he look up and give her a second glance.

"Good God, you're dressed like a woman, Trumper!"

"Yessir!" she said, piling the dishes with a trifle more noise and vigor than was necessary.

He looked at her, head on one side, appraisingly. She flushed before his scrutiny.

"Y'know, Trumper, you don't look half bad with the muck washed off your face and dressed like a decent, respectable woman. You'll find some honest fellow to marry you one day, I shouldn't wonder."

"Oh, do you think so, sir?" she said. "Surely not."

"A tradesman of some sort, nothing grand."

"Nothing grand."

"And not a sailor, Trumper. Avoid sailors at all costs."

"Oh, I will, sir, I will! You may have my word on that!"

She swept out and slammed down the dishes on the pantry table.

Jeff Carradine was staying at a superior boarding house in Spanish Town. On the last afternoon of his freedom, he sat and contemplated his godchild and surrogate niece over the rim of his crystal champagne glass. The horror associated with Virginia's marriage and sudden bereavement was—it seemed to him—sitting uncommonly lightly upon her slender shoulders. He loved her dearly, he told himself; but there was in darling Virginia that same *capable* quality that had characterized her dear mama, God rest her soul; a soft, oblique sort of capability, but none the less effective for all that. One remembered how one was called upon to repair a broken doll's leg just when one was departing for the club. No real *pressure* had been applied, merely a wide-eyed glance . . .

"I don't know what I would do without you, Uncle Jeff," she said. "I arrive on your doorstep. You ask no questions. You don't probe my wounds. You just accept me. Oh, my dear!" She leaned forward and kissed him on the brow, just below the line of his fine, leonine mane.

"I am very fond of you, Virginia," responded Carradine, "as I was very fond of your mama. Whatever demands you may make upon me, I accede to unquestioningly."

Virginia sat back in her chair, reassured. "Then there is something I must tell you in particular detail, Uncle Jeff." she said. "It is of more concern to me than *anything* which happened today—*that* I can put behind me!" She shuddered.

"Tell on, my dear," he said.

"Back in Boston," began Virginia, "—it was only a very short time before I came to the West Indies, and you were there to comfort me on the night that it happened—I formed the beginning of what was to be a deep and disturbing attachment for—someone."

"The night of your birthday ball," he supplied. "The gentlemen you confessed you had been rude to. You and I valsed together. I remember it so well."

"Jason Cambronne," said Virginia with a sigh.

"*Cambronne?*" cried Carradine, sitting up with a start and spilling most of his champagne. "But—I had no idea . . ."

"There's no reason why you should have known," replied Virginia. "I confided it to Lady D'Eath—no one else . . ."

"Oh, my God!" cried Carradine.

"Uncle Jeff, what's the matter?" she demanded with alarm. "What are you trying to tell me?"

"What am I trying . . . ?" The other took from his breast-pocket a red silk handkerchief and mopped his brow. "Virginia, I beg you not to ask me, not to probe me."

She looked levelly at him, seemingly composed. "Very

well," she said. "But I have to tell you that this man to whom I gave my heart, my first real love"—her fortitude deserted her and she dropped her gaze—"he—he raped my mother."

"That he did not!" declared Jeff Carradine stoutly. "What's more, I had it from your mama's own lips that he did not!"

"From my mama?" cried Virginia. "But how could you?—How could she *possibly* have told you . . . ?"

Carradine rose to his feet, took down from the chimney-piece a long churchwarden pipe which he proceeded to fill with tobacco.

"Virginia," he said, "your mother sent for me on her death-bed to confess what she considered—though not a lady of any strong religious persuasion—to be a mortal sin. I am happy to say that, having heard the tale, I was able to convince her that her little adventure had been well conceived and thoroughly well deserved. And she died without it on her conscience."

"Are you telling me, Uncle Jeff, that she—my mother—sought out this, this—*adventure*—deliberately?" cried Virginia."

"She went to Cambronne of her own free will," said Carradine. "And for what she received she was truly grateful." His fine brows furrowed slightly. "Though she did say there was some slight *tristesse* between them at the end," he added.

"Then why did Jason Cambronne tell me that he had . . . Oh!"

Carradine spread his elegant, long-fingered hands. "Don't you see, my dear? He told you that to shield your poor dead mama's reputation, and your regard for her. He is obviously what I have always found those of the sea-going persuasion to be: a thorough-going gentleman. I would advise you to marry him."

Virginia's blue eyes blazed.

"She seduced him!" she cried. "That woman! That over-heated bitch! How many other men did she take to her bed, I wonder? How many . . . ?"

Jeff Carradine slapped her—none too lightly—across the face. She stared at him, unbelievingly.

"No other man save one, my girl," said he. "Not even her husband. Cyrus Holt is the unfortunate sufferer from a physical deformity that renders him incapable of congress.

One's natural compassion for the fellow is somewhat mitigated, however, by the fact that he did not see fit to inform his prospective bride before the wedding night!"

"How can that be so?" she cried. "If, as you say, my father is—what you say he is—how could I have been born?"

"*I* am your father, Virginia," said Jeff Carradine.

Virginia had graduated to a footstool by the side of his armchair, and thence to curling herself up on the floor by his feet, laying her unbelievably golden head in his lap for him to stroke.

"I'm going to devote my life to you, Daddy," she said.

"There's Cambronne," said Carradine.

"Jason Cambronne I have forgiven," said Virginia. "But I must have time, plenty of time, to think about him and get used to the idea that he was my mother's lover." She squeezed his hand. "I don't think of *you* as merely my mother's lover, darling, but as my own dear daddy. Jason Cambronne—yes, all I have to do is snap my fingers and he'll come running."

"Cambronne or no," said Carradine, "there'll be other suitors. Here and in Boston. There's Henry Davenport for a start. Oh no, I quite forgot—he's to marry the Duveen gel next month."

"None of them are for me," said Virginia dreamily.

"But, dear Virginia . . ."

"We'll go away for a holiday together," she said. "Europe. To Menton, Biarritz, Bath."

"I don't like Menton and Biarritz. And Bath I can only barely abide."

"And when we return from Europe," said Virginia, "we must shift house to somewhere more suitable for a father and daughter to live together. Oh, you poor darling, lonely old bachelor who never had a woman's loving care! How happy I am going to make you! No more brooding alone in some stuffy club. We'll go to parties, balls. We'll dance the nights away . . ."

Jeff Carradine met his own reflection in the pier-glass opposite. It seemed to him (though it might have been a trick of the light, he told himself) that the fairy godmother who had been present at his birth, who had granted him the blessing of seemingly eternal youth, had unaccountably abandoned him and taken her gift with her.

Surely that was a suddenly frightened old man watching him uneasily from the glass . . . ?

With the wind southeasterly (from which direction the hurricane must come, if come it did), the *Argo* had been obliged to tack away from the southern coastline of the island till she could turn and take the channel between Jamaica and Haiti. During this proceeding, Cambronne noted with some concern that Blackadder was right: there was a distinct ocean swell out in open water, with a frequency two or three times that of normal waves; moreover, the barometer continued its steady fall.

Of more immediate concern was the fact that no sooner had the *Argo* cleared the headland that masked their view of Kingston than they sighted three navy ships—a 64-gunner flying a commodore's broad pennant and a pair of large 28-gun frigates—tacking in line out of the harbor; and, despite the *Argo*'s vastly superior turn of speed, the enemy had at least five miles of the weather gage, with all the attendant advantages.

"It's my friend, Commodore Harvey," said Cambronne, snapping shut his telescope. "And, if I'm not mistaken, the second in line is H.M.S. *Archer,* whom we last encountered off Anguilla. I wonder if Captain Hellbore, having laid more or less false evidence against me, has already been restored to his command? I sincerely hope so, for if Hellbore does not acquit himself better than last time, we can discount the *Archer.*"

"We can indeed, sir," agreed Blackadder. "I suggest we go about again."

"Carry on, Master," said Cambronne.

Throughout the afternoon, the schooner gradually nudged her way to the southeast and the navy ships dropped ever more to her lee. Presently Blackadder looked up from the chart-table, upon which he had made the latest fix on Jamaica's easternmost edge of land.

"We can weather Morant Point handsomely now, sir," he said. "And the navy will be too far away to touch us."

"Very good, Mr. Blackadder. Go about and steer due north."

"Due north it is, sir."

Neatly, the *Argo* turned in her own length and presented

her tapered starboard quarter to the wind. Running before the southeasterly, Cambronne reckoned on no trouble from any quarter—certainly not from the navy ships, who were a mile on the larboard bow and still tacking to clear Morant Point. It was possible that the *Argo* might pass them just close enough for Harvey to relieve his feelings by loosing off a ranging shot or two, but a hit from that quarter would come within the category of damned bad luck.

No, thought Cambronne, looking back into the eye of the wind, his greatest concern was for that hurricane—if hurricane it was. And with that sky building up, with the wind increasing its gusting and the threat of squally showers, a hurricane it certainly might be.

He walked over to the wheel and checked the ship's head from the compass. Gunner Angus Dunbar was doing the trick as helmsman. Cambronne felt a wayward pang of deprivation when he remembered Jack the Cat and Bosun Tobias Angel at the wheel.

"Word with you, sir?" It was Blackadder again.

"Certainly. Have a cigar."

"Thanks, Captain."

The two men lit up from the tallow dip that was kept forever burning at the bottom of the companionway. Cambronne drew a luxurious mouthful of the aromatic smoke and nodded to the other to speak what was on his mind.

"Concerning this voyage, sir," he began. "To Boston, as I understand . . ."

"To Boston, yes. What of it?" asked Cambronne.

"Captain, there was something you said on the beach back there just before you came aboard. And it's been puzzling me a little. I won't say it's not been worrying me a little." His searching eyes probed at Cambronne's face.

"And what was that I said, Tom?"

"You said we head for Boston and that there's a little unfinished business along the way. Now, you've told us what happened up at Manatee, how you settled your score with that bastard Lasalle. I'm worried for your sake, Captain. What score is it you have to settle on the way to Boston?"

Cambronne studied the end of his cigar, noting how the fitful, gusting wind from the starboard quarter made the smoldering leaf sparkle to rosy life.

"Tom, have I ever lied to you?" he asked.

"That you have not, sir," said the other, with his quirkish, lopsided grin. "Leastways, I've never caught you out at it."

"Then I'm not beginning now," declared the Jerseyman. "I could tell you the soft lie, and you'd be satisfied. The truth I can't tell you, and that's the end of it."

"I see," said the other, and looked thoughtful.

"No, you do not, Tom," said Cambronne. "But it doesn't matter."

There the conversation ended, and their cigars were put out—a heavy rain squall descended upon the schooner. One moment they were in blustery, dry wind, the next, it was impossible to see a cable's length ahead, and everything on deck was immediately saturated by the driving rain. The squall ended as abruptly as it had begun; they saw the end of it—a receding line of mist and kicked-up water—moving rapidly ahead of them and out of sight on the horizon. Scarcely had it vanished before another was upon them. When that had gone away and the view was clear astern, Blackadder pointed upwind.

"Look, Captain! There it is for you!"

Rising straight out of the sea behind them, its anvil-shaped upper portion depressed as if by the open palm of some giant hand, was a massive thunderhead, the first of many that were coming up over the horizon.

"The main wall of the hurricane," said Cambronne, unable to keep the note of awe from his voice. "Men call it the 'bar of the storm'!"

"And we're right in its path," said Blackadder. He did not sound unduly alarmed.

"But racing ahead of it," said Cambronne. "I doubt if it's moving more than ten miles an hour, even though the winds within its vortex might be gusting at anything up to two hundred miles an hour. At the pace we're going we can keep ahead of the hurricane, which, from its direction, will probably spend itself against the mountains of southern Cuba tomorrow or the next day. By which time we shall be out into the Atlantic. How's the navy faring?"

He lifted his telescope and peered into a bank of squally mist to larboard, from out of which there presently emerged the topsails of Harvey's sixty-four.

"Poor Harvey still hasn't made enough ground to weather the Point," said the Jerseyman. "All he's doing is effectively barring our passage back to Kingston. And for why should we want to go *there*?"

Tom Blackadder made no reply—on the grounds, perhaps, that it had been only a rhetorical question.

The sixty-four was now clear of her own personal rain squall, and could be seen in plain view something short of a mile on the *Argo's* larboard beam, with the frigates strung out behind her; all three vessels were sailing close-hauled on the larboard tack, still clawing their way up-wind and making none too good a job of it. Poor Harvey, thought Cambronne. A better squadron commander would have sent his frigates, with their superior sailing qualities, up ahead to make what shift they could to close with the *Argo;* instead of which they must wallow along in line after a slow old two-decker. Perhaps Harvey had the wild fancy that he was fighting Trafalgar all over again . . .

"She's firing! The sixty-four's firing!"

Sure enough, a billow of white gunsmoke fanned out from amidships of the two-decker.

"But his guns aren't bearing on us! What the devil's he about?"

The *Argo* was moving so quickly with wind and wave under her tail that the navy squadron was well past her beam. Morant Point was clear ahead, and the wide stretch of sea beyond, all the way to Cuba.

"Perhaps Harvey's according us the honor of a farewell salute," quipped Cambronne. "Do you think we should make reply? I quite forget how many guns constitutes a salute for a squadron commander—is it three or five?"

Blackadder made no reply to his pleasantry, but continued to stare sullenly in the direction of the British ships. And what in the hell's he sulking *about*? wondered Cambronne.

Then, from the *Argo's* masthead lookout:

"Sail on the starboard bow!"

"Where—where?"

Cambronne lifted his telescope. All hands on deck rushed to the starboard rail and strained to look ahead.

"And another sail, further on the starboard beam!"

"I can't see a damned thing," said Cambronne, giving his glass to Blackadder. "Maintain your present course. I'm going aloft."

Blackadder made no reply as his captain went to the starboard chains of the mainmast and swung himself up. A fore-and-aft schooner does not afford the advantages of a ship-rigged vessel as regards masthead lookouts; the *Argo*'s unfortunate sat uncomfortably on a small cross-tree a bare two thirds of the way up the tall pole, and was constrained to hang on with both hands most of the time. Notwithstanding which, the present incumbent pointed away from bow to beam and shouted to his captain:

"There they are, sir. Navy ships, I reckon!"

"My God, I think you're right," said Cambronne.

They looked like frigates. Two of them. Sailing from right to left in such a way as to block his passage past Morant Point. And widely strung out, the two of them, so as to preclude any chance of the *Argo* attempting the passage further to the east, nearer to Haiti. Well, perhaps with the *Argo*'s vastly superior sailing qualities one just might get upwind of that second frigate and duck past her stern . . .

"There's another one, Cap'n!"

"Yes—you're right!"

The third sail—it was another frigate, or a sloop—slammed the door on any hope of cutting through to the east. She was positioned with an unassailable command of the weather gage. Oh, one might jink and juggle around till sunset and then slip past her, but . . .

He looked back over his shoulder, at the great white and black thunderheads massing from the southeast: the "bar of the storm." *The hurricane will be here long before sunset!*

Think, Captain Cambronne. The way ahead is barred. To larboard is Kingston, with Harvey and his squadron, and even Harvey and Hellbore and friend, sailing as if to cut the line of the Combined Fleets off Cape Trafalgar, could scarcely bungle this one. One broadside of that sixty-four would settle for the *Argo* if he so much as ventured a couple of cables in that direction.

The way blocked ahead and down-wind. Nemesis breathing down the back of his neck in the shape of an oncoming hurricane. Which way, Captain Cambronne?

He swung himself down.

"Keep a good watch!" he shouted to the lookout. "Report any further sail. And abandon your post when the ship goes about, or you might regret it!"

"Aye, aye, Cap'n." The lookout was young, scared, but not without a sense of humor. He grinned, showing broken teeth.

Cambronne reached the deck. Blackadder was standing by the wheel, and by his looks had not improved in temper.

"This is the way it is," said the Jerseyman. "Harvey was firing to signal three of his frigates who are effectively blocking our way through the channel ahead. From the topmast of that sixty-four they sighted them long before we did, of course. Of course, Harvey didn't contrive this trap. Couldn't have. It was pure luck. Lucky for him. Damnably unlucky for us."

"And what are you going to do—surrender?"

The Jerseyman stared at his companion. "Are you *drunk?* he demanded.

The other looked away. "It might be the prudent course," he said lamely.

"Any course that lands us all on the gallows could scarcely be described as prudent," said Cambronne. "Here's what we are going to do, Mr. Blackadder. We are going to run for it!"

"Run?" Blackadder stared at him uncomprehendingly. "Run—where to?"

Cambronne pointed astern.

"Into the eye of the hurricane!"

There was a little time left, time to make reasonable arguments, time to swing Blackadder to his point of view. Blackadder, after all, was master of the *Argo,* his opinion was worth something, his counsel should be listened to. Curiously enough, the man's opinion, his counsel, seemed to be addled . . .

"It's too much of a risk!" That was the stand he was taking.

Cambronne stared at him with incredulity. "Is this the man," he asked, "who brought the *James R. Stover* to St. Vincent under jury rig after three and a half days at sea-anchor, with everything carried away and the captain brained? Are you telling me at this late date, Blackadder, that you are—*scared?*"

"I think you should put into Kingston and take the chance," was the reply.

"Then you have been drinking after all," declared Cambronne. "The only chance in Kingston is the gallows. You are relieved of duty, Blackadder. Get below."

Their exchange had been carried out in moderate tones of voice, but the men on deck, aware of the peril in which they stood and looking to their officers for decision, could not but have been aware of the argument taking place between the captain and the master: the latter's reluctance to meet the former's steady gaze, the vehement whispering, the pregnant silences between. From the corner of his eye, Cambronne was aware of Swede staring at him from over by the foremast, bovine-faced, chewing on a plug of tobacco.

"I am turning the ship about and we will tack down-wind into the hurricane," said Cambronne. "Where I confide that Harvey will not follow. And you will get below, Mr. Blackadder. Now!"

Blackadder's hands were stuffed into the pockets of his jerkin. When they emerged, there was a pistol in his left. The muzzle was pointing straight at Cambronne's heart. He had the look of a man who has thought things through and has come to a decision. He had almost recovered his habitual jaunty self.

"No, Captain," he said. "We are putting into Kingston."

"Why?" asked Cambronne, unshaken.

"I will tell you the way it is, Captain. We have nothing to fear from the navy, nothing from the law. Our employers, the cabal, will square the navy and the law. Lasalle may have gone, and good riddance, but the cabal still has plenty of power in Jamaica, and the cabal will look after its own."

"You appear to know one hell of a lot about the power of our employers in Jamaica," said Cambronne. "And you put a name to it—'cabal.' That's a name and a half and no mistake. It means a secret clique. Where do you stand in that secret clique, Blackadder?"

"You ask a lot of questions, Captain."

"I am lacking a lot of answers—Master."

The lopsided grin came out. "Put it this way, I stand higher than you, Captain. You were merely appointed as a hired help, mostly on your record and also on your own cognizances. Someone had to keep a weather eye on you on the principle of *'Quis custodiet ipsos custodes?'* 'Who is to guard the guards?' I was chosen."

"I see," said Cambronne. "And while we're parading our schoolboy Latin, I am reminded of the phrase, *'Latet anguis in herba.'* You are the snake lurking in the grass. You are well named—Blackadder!"

The other looked hurt. The grin faded and became almost a pout.

"Provided always that you fulfilled your contract to the cabal," he said, "my liking for you as a man did not in any way clash with my own duty. The business you had with Lasalle over the woman—that was your business, private business. But when you refuse to tell me what this score is that you have to settle on the way to Boston, then my—custodian's—suspicions overtake my liking for you."

"It *was* you, was it not, who searched my traps that night?" demanded Cambronne.

"Yes."

"And found nothing."

"Nothing."

"So what, then, do you think of me now?"

"I think," said Blackadder, "that you are a spy!"

"Why so?"

"Well, from the start, you have never struck me as a slaver."

"And you *are* a slaver?" asked Cambronne. "Your nine years in the deep-water trade—that was all lies?"

"I went straight into slaving from the navy," said the other. "And I was captain of the *Jeremy T. Fawcett* when we killed that limey skipper and raised the brouhaha that led to your being appointed to the *Argo.*"

"And the cabal—they saved you from the gallows?" said Cambronne. "But not the poor devil who hangs on high in the gibbet above Spanish Town jail."

Blackadder shrugged. "He was my bosun," he said. "No, the rest of the crew were hanged, every one. But the cabal got me out, and will again." He pointed the pistol against Cambronne's chest. "And now I am going to give the order to turn about for Kingston."

"And I shall countermand that order," said Cambronne. "And then we'll see who commands aboard this ship."

"I *am* right—you *are* a spy, Cambronne?" There was a note or urgency—even of anxiety—in Blackadder's voice.

"I have never lied to you, Blackadder," said the Jerseyman. "And I'll not begin at this late stage in our acquaintance."

"We are going about," said Blackadder. "Don't let me have to kill you."

"You have the pistol," said Cambronne. "I have the authority. Let us see who wins."

The force of the wind was by then intense and continuous. Wavetops were being whipped into white frenzy. The ships of the Royal Navy had not much changed their positions relative to the schooner. The *Argo* was still caught like a rat in a trap—with only one way out.

Blackadder thumbed back the hammer of the pistol to full cock.

"To Kingston," he said. "And you go, dead or alive, Cambronne!"

They were standing on the lee side abreast the mainmast. Cambronne saw Swede begin to shamble towards them from the foremast where he had been gathered with the rest of the hands of his watch, and from where they could scarcely have missed the fact something was badly amiss between captain and master—even if they had not espied the pistol in the latter's hand. The shaven-headed giant came padding on bare feet the size of wardroom serving-dishes, clinging to pieces of rigging as the quite violent motion of the vessel upset his balance. Blackadder became aware of Swede's presence when the giant was a few paces away; he turned, regarded him for an instant, and faced Cambronne again.

"I am counting to three, Cambronne," he said. "Either you give the order to turn for Kingston, or . . ."

Swede's hamlike hand took Blackadder's pistol wrist as if it had been the stem of a daisy. Blackadder screamed as the bones snapped loudly and the weapon clattered to the deck. Next, he was gathered up—screaming still—in two massive hands, raised above the bald, domed head, and hurled over the side. He floated for the few moments it takes for heavy leather seaboots to fill up, then sank in full view of all.

Cambronne glanced up into the pale blue, unrevealing eyes of the giant. Gingerly.

"Why?" he whispered. *"Why? He was your friend!"*

The giant was puzzled to explain. He pulled at the stump of ear that had been chewed away by the Chinese whore in Cochin. And then, by some obscure feat of reasoning, he lit upon a formula that satisfied his needs. He grinned.

"Tom—friend, ja!" he said. "But captain is—CAPTAIN!"

They were sailing close-hauled and directly away from Harvey and his two consorts. Any doubts that the Commodore may have had about his quarry's intention must have been laid to rest when the *Argo* tacked again: her advance was to the southwest, toward the oncoming hurricane. It amused Cambronne to speculate on the dismay, disbelief and consternation on the flagship's quarterdeck, the busy exchange of signals with the frigates, and, inevitably, the surrender to circumstances. No naval commander would dare to hazard an entire squadron in a hurricane—not with a safe harbor under his lee. Nevertheless, Cambronne decided that Harvey would stay at sea till the last minute, reckoning on the possibility of his quarry turning about and making a dash for the channel—and in this assessment Cambronne was right.

The wind by that time was near to gale force and the rain heavy and continuous. The blue sails were reefed down, despite which the schooner was making good between eight and ten knots against the turbulent seas. And the "bar of the storm"—the massive wall of black cloud where all hell was being let loose—was about ten miles ahead.

Cambronne sent for Meg Trumper. She came on deck wearing an old cloak of his. Her dark eyes widened with fear to see the state of the seas and the uncanny darkness ahead.

He greeted her at the top of the companionway. "Come no further, Trumper," he said. "And hold on tightly while I talk to you. Can you hear me, or must I shout louder?"

"I—I can hear you, sir," she replied.

"Well then, see here, Trumper, we are presently sailing into some considerable hazard, since the *Argo,* being only a small vessel, is likely to take a bad hammering. Things will happen—things that you would scarcely believe. You may be tempted to despair, but you must *not* despair, Trumper. You must remember this: no matter how bad things may look—or feel—the *Argo* will win through. Do you understand me?"

"Yessir." Her face was pinched with fear, but her gaze was steady.

"Very good. Now, listen—secure everything breakable or valuable below and tie down everything that's loose. Then there's my sextant, with which I shall navigate this vessel to safe harbor when the storm is past us. You know my sextant, Trumper? It's in my cabin, shut away in a fine mahogany box with brass fittings."

"I—I know it, sir."

"I charge you to guard that sextant with your life, Trumper," he said. "Get you below. When you have made everything else fast, tie the sextant securely to your own body and yourself to one of the big upright stanchions in the main cabin. And then pray. Understood?"

The girl nodded, turned and went back down the steps.

"Oh, Trumper . . ."

She turned. "Sir?"

"And see you guard that sextant well, mind. And yourself, too."

No reply. She was gone.

Cambronne made his dispositions. He reckoned that, once within the "bar of the storm," there would be no hope of making any changes in sail, since it would be impossible for anyone to remain on the upper deck unless securely lashed. It followed, then, that his plan must be formed with the aim of keeping the *Argo* sailing as near as possible under control in all circumstances. Accordingly, he had the foresail taken down completely, and also the great flying jib. With only one headsail and with the mainsail reefed right down, the schooner, being perfectly balanced fore and aft, handled perfectly well; no great strain was placed upon mast and rigging and the vessel remained reasonably upright—even in the conditions that obtained on the fringe of the hurricane. Cambronne accepted, however, that once beyond the "bar" his careful dispositions might be hopelessly awry.

Three men only, he decided, would remain on deck: the helmsman, someone who could be trusted in dire emergency to cut away broken spars and cordage—and he himself. For helmsman he chose Master Gunner Stokes, who was acting bosun. Swede was the obvious choice for "trouble man." The bovine giant had showed not the slightest emotion about having saved his captain at the cost of killing his friend. According to his simple, black and white logic, Blackadder had broken the compact that a seaman makes with his captain and was guilty of mutiny. And the penalty for mutiny is death.

With the wall of black cloud almost upon them, with the wind changing direction almost constantly, the Jerseyman gave the order to clear the upper deck and all hands went below, tied themselves to stanchions and waited for whatever fate had ordained for them. Swede tied himself by a long length of stout hemp to the foremast, whence he had scope to attempt any task that might be demanded of him from fore to aft. Stokes attached himself to his wheel, Cambronne to the compass binnacle.

And so they crossed the "bar of the storm" and entered the hell that lay beyond.

A hurricane is like a whirlpool, in which the wind is drawn

in circles towards the center. The earth's rotation plays a considerable part in the formation of the circular vortex; in the northern hemisphere, in the Caribbean, the rotation determines that this aerial whirlpool turns in an anti-clockwise direction.

The *Argo* was sailing in predominantly south-easterly wind when she entered the hurricane. She immediately hit the outer ring of the vortex, which was blowing from a northerly direction in that segment of the sprawling, fifty-mile-wide circle of death. The effect was like a giant fist hammered against the weather side of the schooner; she was instantly laid over on her beam ends. Then began the incessant pounding of the white-capped waves, towering mast-high, that passed beneath her.

The sails held, though strained to within an ace of ripping point, and the vessel made some headway into the vortex, although it took the combined strengths of Stokes and Cambronne to hold the kicking wheel and keep her steady.

And so they progressed through the first circle of hell.

Two hours on, and their slight forward movement coupled with the advance of the hurricane had brought them further into the vortex, where the wind doubled in its fury. No longer able to distinguish between air and water, they existed in a world of whiteness and constant clamoring sound. The schooner, permanently at her beam ends (which meant that the two men at the wheel were working in a lying-down posture), was from time to time subjected to an extra large comber that turned the angle of her decks to the vertical—and beyond. It was during one of these nightmare plunges that the ship's boats were carried away, together with the bower and sheet anchors (their snubbed hawsers were snapped like cotton), and everything else on the upper deck that was not screwed down, plugged, tied, wedged or otherwise attached. And much else besides, including the elegant stern lantern. Cambronne and the master gunner were totally immersed, in the particular inundation, for fully half a minute, when it seemed that the *Argo* needed only one more slight shove to capsize completely. They returned to comparative light and air, choking, bruised and enfeebled—and addressed themselves again to their task of edging the schooner further and further toward the center of the vortex.

Cambronne had sailed through hurricanes on two other occasions, both times in large and well-found ships-of-the-line, and knew what to expect. As they penetrated each succeeding band of the vortex, the force of the winds would be likely to increase by at least half as much again, till they finally reached the periphery of the so-called "eye," where all known and acknowledged methods of reckoning the forces of nature fell by the wayside and one simply endured in stupefied disbelief and clung to the crumbling edges of one's sanity. The *Argo* had at least one more circle of hell to pass through before she came to her ultimate trial.

It was then that one of the twelve-pounder brass cannons, straining against its securing blocks and tackles, jerked so violently that it pulled one of the retaining ring-bolts straight out of the bulkhead. Now held by only one tackle, the heavy barrel and its carriage slewed sideways on the stubby wheels and began a methodical clouting at the base of the mainmast.

THUM!

THUM!

From where he half-crouched, half-lay by the wheel, Cambronne could see that the iron-bound carriage and the protruding cannon barrel were knocking splinters of wood from the shaft of the mast with every massive smite. What was not apparent—but infinitely more sinister—was the grave damage the pounding must be causing to the inner structure of the mast, the splitting and rending that must so weaken it that the pressure of the wind upon the vestigial sail area must surely carry it away. And to be dismasted in the heart of the hurricane, to have no steering way, was to be carried before the wind and broken at its mindless whim.

"There goes Swede!" cried Master Gunner Stokes above the howl of the tempest. "He's going to try and secure it!"

The bald-pated giant on the end of his line—a great shambling monkey on a leash—ran a few paces towards the mainmast while the deck was poised on the end of a monstrous roll, then clung to the bulwarks while the *Argo* was driven even further on her beam ends and the wave that had done it broke over her mast-high. Swede vanished from sight in white water. When the deck had emptied, he was still there and creeping forward on hands and knees.

THUM!

The destructive pendulum smashed against the mast just as Swede reached the other side and clasped hold of it. The heavy iron-bound carriage left a splintered groove in the mast close by the giant's scrabbling fingers.

Immersed as they were in their own task, Cambronne and Stokes were only able to spare an occasional hasty glance toward the drama unfolding in the waist of the vessel. As ever, Swede's brute instinct served him where a man of intelligence would have told himself that the task of taming the juggernaut was a physical impossibility. The giant first secured hold of the block and tackle that had become disconnected from the bulkhead. This in itself was a daunting task, for the block was a brass-bound mass of teak the size of a man's head, with a formidable hook attached to one end of it and a tangled gallimaufry of ropes trailing from the other. Swede captured it during a quiet period between its poundings and threshings, seizing hold of the tail-end of the rope and, taking a turn around the mast, commencing to haul in the slack.

THUM!

Deprived of a foot or so of its scope, the deadly pendulum did not strike, next time, with such brutal force. And as the carriage wheels ceased to turn, and the whole mass was poised for another movement, he hauled in on the line. The mechanical advantage of the block and tackle was denied to him because it had no purchase. It was by his own brute strength that, inch by inch, giving a little and taking a little, the way a fisherman plays a salmon, he brought the cannon to a stop, till it was secured between the bulkhead on one side and the mainmast on the other, till he was able to take the end of the rope and wrap it around and around cannon and mast the way a spider entraps a fly. And then he had only to haul taut on the tackle connected to the bulkhead and the cannon was no longer a living force of destruction, but a dead-weight amidships.

He had only just time to claw his way back to the comparative shelter and safety of the foremast before the *Argo* broke out into the last, innermost circle of that watery hell.

The winds were gusting at between a hundred and two hundred miles an hour, which meant that, for some distance into the sky, air and water were as one. The schooner ceased all movement of her own accord and lay upon her side with the lee rail submerged and the boom of the mainsail trailing. The first gust of the new, madder wind had ripped the headsail to rags. In any event, the *Argo* no longer had steering way; the hurricane was simply passing underneath her. She lay like a hulk, though with masts and spars intact—a tribute to the genius who conceived her and the master craftsmen who built her.

Sightless, deafened, helpless to do anything but breathe—some of the time—and hope, Cambronne and his companion hitched their safety-ropes even tighter, clung to the wheel, and waited.

Compounding their agonies, but a source of comfort and encouragement to Cambronne who knew that the phenomenon meant that they were nearing the eye of the hurricane, was a continuous and torrential downfall of heavy rain. Rain that cascaded, that filled ears and nostrils. Rain that might drown a man if he unwarily opened his mouth. Rain that descended nearly horizontally, borne on the wind's insane breath, that thrummed upon their bruised bodies and numbed their aching fingers as they clung for life.

And suddenly, all was still . . .

"Gawd be praised, Cap'n—we're in the eye o' the hurricane!"

They moved, in the space it takes to slam a door, from the inner circle of the vortex to the core that it tightly enclosed: from darkness to light, from agony to easement, from death to life.

In a roughly oval shape, no more than fifteen miles at its greatest width, was an area of complete calm at the heart of the hurricane. Above was pure blue sky, where evening stars were beginning to shimmer. Light airs occasionally ruffled the surface of the sea; one almost expected to see swallows swooping down to touch the water, or swans going about their arcane business. The only disquieting thing was the dark wall of cloud that entirely surrounded the enclave of calm, and the roar of thunder and the moan of phantom winds beyond that wall.

The *Argo* became alive again. Men came up on deck and looked about them in awe. Some were limping, others had arms and heads in rough bandages—tokens of the havoc that the wild seas had caused down below. Unable to leave his post, Cambronne sent a messenger aft to inquire how Meg Trumper had fared. The lad returned with a curt message from the cabin-girl that the captain's precious sextant was undamaged.

"What now, Cap'n?" asked Stokes, whose hair was drying

out and standing in a fringe about his bald dome, giving him his habitual ecclesiastical appearance again. "Do we go on through t'other side o' the hurricane?"

Cambronne had been studying the chart. By dead reckoning (and star sights would be out of the question because there was no horizon from which to measure altitudes), he estimated that they were about fifty miles southeast of Kingston.

"No, Stokes, we will remain as close as possible to the center of the eye," he replied. "Make all sail. The *Argo* will go like a bird, even in the lightest airs. We will go where the hurricane takes us—within reason. From what I can see, it will pass between Jamaica and Haiti, which is exactly where we were originally heading. I want the best helmsmen to take tricks on the wheel from now onwards, Stokes. I shall remain on deck till we're out of the hurricane. See to it."

"Aye, aye, sir." The concept of sailing inside a hurricane was one that strained the master gunner's credulity; but, like every other member of the crew, he had unquestioning faith in Cambronne's professionalism and—excepting the incident with the navy earlier—in his good luck.

In fact, given the *Argo*'s excellent handling qualities, the Jerseyman's plan was quickly found to be perfectly feasible. The wind inside the eye, such as it was, could only be described as fickle. The *Argo* made good use of it: tacking, going about, gybing, as the occasion demanded, and making good about nine knots to the northwest. It was a manner of advance that put a tremendous burden upon the helmsmen, and the watch on deck were constantly trimming sails (the ruined blue headsail had been replaced by one from the suit of white), while Cambronne was hard put to it to keep a dead reckoning of their movements on the chart. But, yes, he told himself, as night closed in, and the eerie, fitful glow of far-off lightning illuminated the dark walls of the cloud banks surrounding them, they were going in the right direction, and no vessel in the long history of man's engagement with his beloved enemy—the sea—had ever been so well-protected from its foes.

A hurricane will never die over the tropical seas that nurture it, cosset it with warmth and moisture, and over which it rampages like a blinded, murderous giant. It will either shift to higher latitudes and be sucked into the prevailing winds of those regions, or it will dissipate itself over dry land, even over small islands, particularly of the mountainous sort.

In the event, the demise of the hurricane that had accepted the *Argo* into its maw was near at hand.

By dead reckoning Cambronne estimated—accurately, as it turned out—that the eye of the storm would carry them in a north-easterly direction and through the self-same channel between Jamaica and Haiti as he had originally intended to use: a stretch of water about a hundred miles in width, with several small islets, and notorious banks and rocks, both dry and submerged, that render the passage far from easy even in favorable conditions. And with nothing but dead reckoning to go on, with all-round visibility limited to the "eye" (which was forever shifting its shape), the safe navigation of his vessel strained the Jerseyman's professionalism to its limit. As soon as he reckoned them to be in the latitude of the south coast of Jamaica, he had the leadsmen in the chains constantly sounding the depths. All that day the call continued to be *"No bottom, sir!"*, and Cambronne knew that all was well, for most of the channel lay at depths of a thousand fathoms and more. Then came the startled cry: "By the mark, seven!"—and a shocked leadsman was standing in the chains and staring down at the piece of red bunting marking the line, which showed that the *Argo* no longer had profound depths beneath her iron keel, but had moved into rapidly shoaling waters.

Cambronne immediately lowered sail and allowed the *Argo* to nose stealthily forward on a single headsail, with lookouts for'ard and aloft, and continuous soundings.

"By the mark, seven . . . A deep six . . . By the mark, five . . ."

Thirty feet only! And that meant there were only ten feet beneath the keel. And still shoaling!

At that moment, a lookout from the foremasthead reported an object in the water on the starboard bow, on the edge of the cloud bank, and as they drew closer and the clouds moved on, the object was revealed as a fang of rock jutting out of the water. Far from being alarmed, Cambronne rejoiced, for here was his first naviagtional fix since losing sight of Jamaica the previous day. And with the aid of his splendid chart he was able to check that his dead reckoning had not been far out. The rock was part of the notorious Formigas Bank, forty-five miles northeast of Morant Point, and no hazards lay beyond it. The chart did not lie: they gave the rock a wide berth and by the time it was abreast the bottom shelved away rapidly, so that soon the leadsmen were again calling out: *"No bottom, sir!"*

They were through the channel!

The "eye" which guarded the *Argo* was still surrounded by high winds, though, as Cambronne had predicted, the hurricane was doomed to spend itself the following day on the rugged southern coastline of Cuba—from Cabo de la Cruz to Santiago, from Santiago to Cabo Maysi, causing untold loss of life and property in the towns and villages and destroying the fishing fleets taking refuge in the wide stretch of Guantanamo Bay. Satisfied that the worst of the crisis was over, Cambronne was about to go below for a quick bite to eat and a tot of rum, when there came a hail from the foremasthead lookout:

"Sail ahead! No—she's dismasted! And sinking by the look of her!"

Cambronne climbed to the foremast chains, an indefinable excitement biting at his brain, a rumbling certainty of menace eating at his innards.

He had no need of a telescope. A dark form had just emerged from the wall of cloud ahead, the receding edge of the vortex. The strange vessel—a dismasted brig—was still rolling from the buffeting received in the periphery of the "eye"; but, even when she passed into the light airs and glassy swell of the hurricane's calm center, the long-drawn-out and sickening roll of the hull persisted; token of a vessel doomed, waterlogged, holed, with sprung planks, and—by the look of her—abandoned.

"Steer straight for her, helmsman!" cried Cambronne.

"Aye, aye, sir!"

A slight creak of rigging, a small shifting of sail, and the *Argo* moved the couple of points to starboard, which would bring her close by the hulk; and, as they drew swiftly nearer, it was clear that hulk she indeed was, with no lights visible and no one on the upper deck, which, tilted as it was by reason of her wild list in the *Argo*'s direction, showed holystoned planking whitely in the moonlight—and nothing that moved.

Cambronne kicked off his seaboots.

"Bring me as near alongside as possible," he called out.

"Cap'n sir,—you ain't swimming over to that hulk?" This from Stokes.

"All the boats having been carried away, I have no alternative," responded Cambronne.

"But, sir . . ." The man's honest, ecclesiastical face was a battleground of indecision: how to point out that it is the height of eccentricity for a ship's captain to board a passing wreck—and *swim* there? And for why? There was no question of taking the dismasted brig for a prize; she would be at the bottom before you could get a rope secured aboard her.

"Keep as close as you're able," said Cambronne, seemingly unaware of the soundless questions surrounding him. "Don't attempt to secure alongside in case she takes a sudden plunge. I will be back before the tail-end of the hurricane is here."

"Aye, aye, sir," said Stokes, defeated.

The *Argo* came within a cable's length of the brig, close enough to see the tangle of sails, spars and cordage piled about the stumps of her masts and trailing over the side. In her day, thought Cambronne—and her day was yesterday—she must have been a fast sailer. But for the hurricane, we might have waited days to catch up with her; perhaps she might have given us the slip somewhere beyond the Windward Passage, among the tangle of outer islands and reefs. Man proposes and God disposes!

Here goes . . .

He threw his legs over the side and let himself fall. It was an easy swim through the oily calm, and an easy climb up onto the brig's deck, by way of a rope ladder of tangled ratlines trailing down into the water. Reaching the deck, Cambronne was markedly aware of a sensation that he had experienced only once before, and that aboard another sinking ship: the sluggish, hesitant roll, the tired antics of a thing already delivering its death rattle.

He went aft along the sloping planks. The ship was—had been—well found and well appointed. There was gold leaf in plenty at the quarter-deck screen as he passed through and continued on toward the stern cabin, whose door hung open and creaked gently to and fro with every small movement of the dying vessel; and everything was of the best: choice woods and metals—soon to be rotting in two thousand fathoms.

The moonlight flooded through the sloping windows of the stern cabin. It shone upon upturned chairs, scattered rugs, a pile of crockery broken in a corner, some books. And a table set against the long window, at which, with his back to the full moon, casting him all in silhouette, was the seated figure of a man whom—even before he spoke—Cambronne knew to be the object of his quest aboard the doomed brig . . .

"Cambronne! How did *you* get here?"

(Of course, his—Cambronne's—face was presented to the other in full moonlight. Odd that the voice was no longer muffled. That would be because he was no longer masked, perhaps.)

"Lasalle told me you had left for Boston in a brig," replied Cambronne. "He told me before he died."

"Died? But I thought that it was the Court of Hymen to which he was bound yesterday, not the Bosom of Abraham!"

"He was wed. I killed him by way of a wedding present."

A thin, mirthless laugh was interrupted by a racking cough. When it was done, the man by the window said: "You amuse me, Cambronne. I take it that you forestalled your rival at the killing match. Did you also take the prize—the lady?"

Before Cambronne could reply, another fit of coughing assaulted the man. The sound of it—agonized, liquescent— was familiar to the Jerseyman from the aftermaths of a score of close-quarter battles on blood-slippery decks during the late wars.

When the other was done, Cambronne said: "I think you are wounded, yes? Your lung is pierced and you are bleeding badly?"

"I tried to prevent the cowardly captain from abandoning his ship when the hurricane overtook us," said The Man. "While he was making up his mind, his damned bosun stabbed me in the back. They've all gone. Took all the boats. At least I had the consolation of watching them all drown within screaming distance of these decks. Is the hurricane past, Cambronne?"

"Half of it," replied the Jerseyman.

"And the rest?"

"Will be here within half an hour. Perhaps a little more, for some of the force of the storm has abated."

"But this brig won't survive another blow?"

"Even supposing this brig lasts another half-hour, a Portsmouth bumboat, rowed by a single old bum-woman, would fare better."

Silence . . .

"I always had certain—reservations—about you, Cambronne," said The Man. "Your credentials—excellent. The way you came to the attention of my agents in England—impeccable. But you were always just a little too good to be true. Blackadder never quite trusted you, you know. On that account, I set him to watch over you. Where is he now, by the way?"

"Dead," said Cambronne.

"All of them dead! You really are a most valiant and expert gentlemen, Cambronne. And what is there in it for you? I take it that we are being frank with each other at last. You are a spy, of course?"

The Jerseyman shrugged. "Call me what you like," he said. "I made a secret compact with Mr. William Wilberforce of the Anti-Slavery Society and the British Cabinet. I was to insinuate myself into the cabal and uncover the principals both here and in Jamaica. That I have done."

A sneering voice answered him: "That you have, Cambronne. You have quenched a blaze. The blaze will start up again. Fool! We are everywhere: in the West Indies, in London, in Boston. Politicans, great men of business, even heads of state. That's why Commodore Harvey never got the ships he asked for. That's why the West Indies got Harvey! Mark my words, Cambronne, no one alive today will see the end of the slave trade!

"Mark you, Cambronne," he continued, "this is not to denigrate your effort. You have played a dangerous game, with dangerous men, and mostly outside the law. If you had been condemned to the gallows, I doubt if your friend, Wilberforce, or the British Cabinet would have lifted a finger to save you—correct?"

"What you say is perfectly true," admitted Cambronne. "But thank God, I've won my freedom. I'm no longer an outlaw. And they also promised to make me a Companion of the Order of the Bath if I won through—though they made it plain the decoration wouldn't be gazetted, but quite unofficial and never to be worn in public; kept in a locked drawer and looked at occasionally—birthdays and Christmases and so on. *'Trio Juncta in Uno.'* "

"What?"

" *'Tria Juncta in Uno'*—the motto of the Order of the Bath. It means 'Three joined in One'. Very nice sentiment, if a trifle obscure. Who *are* you?"

The hulk gave a lurch, a creak. The steep list increased.

Again the figure seated behind the table was stricken with a paroxysm of coughing. Cambronne waited, three paces distant, feet apart, legs braced against the perilous heel of the deck.

Having recovered, the other said: "Approach me, Cambronne. No further! I have a pistol trained to your heart. Regard me. Look into my face. Do you remember me?"

Cambronne, who had closed to within a pace of the table, but was still out of reach of the other, craned his neck to regard the profile that was presented to him, and then the three-quarter profile—as the head was turned slowly toward the moonlight streaming through the wide stern windows.

It was a face that he did not immediately place, though something of the recognition was immediate. Where had he—and only briefly—seen that countenance . . . ?

Perfectly formed, it was, although marred with the deep pits of smallpox and approaching death from a newer ill. Eyes of a snake: quick, cunning, unknowing of mercy, a stranger to compassion. Only vanity—vanity to be recognized even in the portals of death and at the verge of disaster—gave that face the weakness of a certain humanity; the rest was all animal. Monster.

"Well?" said the man.

Cambronne snapped his finger and thumb, directed a pointing forefinger at the other.

"I remember!" he cried. "Virginia Holt's party! After I was given the job of captain of the *Argo*. Holt it was who introduced us. But—no—that can't be right. Holt whispered to me that you'd walked out of the meeting after a disagreement with The Man, and that isn't possible. Your name—wait a minute—I've got it—Winterfield. No—Waterfield . . ."

"Winterburn," supplied the other, and a smirk touched the cruel lips. "Josh Winterburn."

"But you're supposed to be dead—I remember that! They said you'd hanged yourself, but I had the notion that Holt thought you'd been disposed of for disagreeing with The Man. You were buried—I heard tell of the big society funeral!"

Winterburn settled back in his seat and turned his vile face away from the moonlight, mercifully shrouding it from Cambronne's sight. He had not been lying about the pistol; it lay in the thin, white hand which was steadied upon the table-top, and it was aimed at the Jerseyman.

"I am The Man," he said. "And I have always been The Man. As a precaution of concealment, I employed an actor to play my role during occasional meetings of the inner council of the cabal in Boston and elsewhere. His name was Noel Chatterton, once one of the finest Shakespearian actors in America. Brilliant Lear. Superb Othello. Drink was his problem—that and hashish. I provided him with hashish—easy with my slaving connections in the East—and coached him in the part. In the end, I suppose Chatterton knew as much about the business as I did myself; but the constant supply of the drug kept him loyal to the end. The night of your appointment was his last appearance on that or any other stage. He died of a heart attack. There had been prior warnings. I was prepared to lose him, and had made plans. The incursions of the Anti-Slavery Society had already decided me that Josh Winterburn must cease to exist before the crash came and all the members of the cabal were exposed. The fortuitous arrival, that evening, of a genuine corpse to be palmed off as Josh Winterburn and to be buried in his family mausoleum provided the perfect answer."

"Corpse—what corpse was that?" demanded Cambronne.

"An agent of the Anti-Slavery Society," said the other. "He was found in the grounds of Holt's house on the night of the meeting—by *my* men, I hasten to add, and not by Holt's."

"But—why . . . ?"

Again that mocking laugh in reply, followed by the choking cough, long in subsiding. "You ask why the poor devil's life was risked when you yourself were also there, listening to everything that was going on? My dear Cambronne, for one so astute in many ways, you are also very naïve."

The irony of it seeped into Cambronne's brain. And he remembered another occasion, and the same argument . . .

"You refer," he said, "to the principle of '*Quis custodiet ipsos custodes*'?"

"Of course. You do not suppose that Mr. William Wilberforce, the British Cabinet and all would repose entire trust in a disgraced naval officer and proven smuggler with a price on his head—with or without the incentive of the Order of the Bath?"

From near at hand there came the double beat of a ship's

bell, thrice repeated. Winterburn gave a start, turned and looked out of the stern window, presenting once again his hideous profile to the Jerseyman. "What was that?" he hissed.

"The _Argo_'s ship's bell," said Cambronne. "And since it isn't yet six bells of the First Watch, the peal must be a warning to me that the tail-end of the hurricane is nearly upon us. I must return to my ship."

A choking cough, a throaty rattle. The pistol slipped from the white hand and fell upon the table-top. It was a while before Winterburn recovered himself. When he did so, he addressed the Jerseyman in a voice that was half aggressive, half self-pitying:

"You will not take me with you, eh?"

"I have to swim back," said Cambronne, "for we have no ship's boat left. Anyhow, to move you would only be to hasten your end, which, hurricane or no, can't be far distant. I commend you to pray to your Maker for a merciful end that has certainly not been accorded to many of your victims. And I bid you farewell."

He turned to go.

"_Cambronne!_"

The pistol was in hand again, the hand certainly wavering, but the range was short and the moonlight shining full upon the intended target.

"Yes?" replied the Jerseyman, turning to face the other again.

"Can you give me one good reason why I should not kill you?"

"You have just the single shot—none other?"

"One shot—yes."

"Then I would advise you not to waste it on me, Winterburn," said the Jerseyman. "Speaking as one who has half-drowned on no less than three occasions, I have to tell you that it is a most unpleasant way to go. Save your bullet. When the time comes, I think you will be grateful for its swift benison."

"I thank you," said he who had been known as 'The Man,' "for your most expert and valued counsel.

"Pray think nothing of it," responded the other. And left.

Out on deck, he could see the approaching wall of cloud and the clear sky of winking stars abruptly ending five cables distant. The first whispers of final disaster were already quickening the wave-tops around the doomed brig, and she rolled sickeningly with every touch. Her larboard rail was already under water; it was a miracle she still floated. Cambronne had only to step over the side and strike out for the *Argo*, which was flirting with light airs close at hand.

He reached her with a dozen powerful strokes, and there was no shortage of hands to haul him aboard.

"I thought as how I should warn you the time was running short, sir," said Stokes.

"You did well," said Cambronne. "Make for the center of the "eye" and stay there."

"Aye, aye, sir."

The *Argo* responded like a racehorse to the touch of the wheel, turning on the arm of the fickle winds within the "eye" and slicing away to safety. Cambronne, and as many others as were not usefully employed, watched in awful fascination at the fate of the sinking brig as she was inexorably taken in by the maw of the hurricane. First, as the seas about her grew angrier, the waterlogged hulk's uneasy rolling increased. Next, some shifting of the water within the hull caused her to settle by the bows, so that the wide windows of the stern cabin pointed skywards, reflecting the moonlight and the stars in the leaded glass.

"Watch it, now! There she goes!" cried someone.

The end was quick. Almost as soon as the brig was overtaken by the wall of cloud, a mighty wave, sluicing out of the "eye's" periphery, took the upturned stern and raised it on high, where it remained poised in the trough of the comber. The next great wave entirely swamped what was left of the brig. When it passed by, she had gone.

"Damn me if I didn't catch the sound of a pistol-shot just afore she took her plunge," opined someone.

Signs of the hurricane's collapse were everywhere by the middle watch. No longer was the wall of cloud constantly being illuminated by lightning, and the roar of the winds had lessened below screaming pitch. Cambronne reckoned—correctly as it turned out—that with dawn's light it would not be imprudent to break out of the "eye" and head for the Windward Passage.

He turned in an hour after midnight and ordered Meg Trumper to have him called at six. He half-absently registered the impression that she was sulking about something.

He slept badly. There was a nightmare—a half-waking, half-sleeping image of dawn outside Canterbury jail, with a nineteen-year-old girl turned white-haired crone: abject, abused, screaming. He sat up in his bunk and wiped sweat from his eyes. Was it for that he had pursued Virginia? he asked himself. Another spoiled, wilful child? And in the wayward hope that it might all have come right?

He got up, pulled on his boat cloak and stepped into his seaboots; he went up on deck.

The moon had gone in. Only the sweep of the Milky Way illuminated the glassy stillness of the "eye." There was a small figure humped over the taffrail: it could only be Meg Trumper. She turned at the sound of his approach.

"What—can't you sleep either, Trumper?"

"I can't stop my mind thinking," she said.

She looked very small and vulnerable, white-faced in the moonlight, with the high collar of a seaman's jerkin framing her wide-eyed stare.

"Thinking? About what?" he asked.

"About the end of the voyage," she said. "About what I'll do then."

"What shall you do then, Trumper?"

She looked away, toward the wall of cloud briefly lit up by a lightning flash that was followed by a drum roll of thunder.

"I shall seek out, Arthur," she said. "He's the gentleman who keeps a tobacco store in Boston. I told you about him the second time we—came together."

"I remember," said Cambronne. "And what is the attraction of this Arthur fellow, pray?"

She rounded on him, furiously.

"Need you ask?" she blazed. "I've been whore, and hated it. I've been ship's boy and abused roundly. You took me to your bed and treat me worse than you treat the lowest seaman when you're not after my body. What's Arthur's attraction? I'll tell you what—he wants to make me happy, to care for me, to cherish and warm me. He wants to marry me. That's the difference, Captain Cambronne!"

Cambronne tapped the capping of the taffrail and thought it through. Suddenly illuminated, it seemed so easy, like fixing one's position by the declination of a heavenly body, something that had been there all the time.

"Marry me, Trumper," he said.